SLEEPING DOGS

GORDON CARROLL

1

ITALY

March

Anthony Carlino patted the soil around the newly planted vine with loving hands.

Hands that had once been responsible for shedding rivers of blood.

The soil, heavily laden with water, clumped around the base of the plant. The combination felt exactly right to him. Cool and firm —*strong*—filled with the promise of life.

Like spring itself.

He smiled. The gentle heat of the Italian sun rained lightly on his hair and the nape of his neck.

Some days he wore his favorite broad-brimmed, floppy cloth hat, but summer was still a way off, and this fine March day was not overly hot. The breeze flowing in from the ocean felt cool, tinged with a hint of salt that felt good to the touch and tasteful to the tongue.

Grapes from these very vineyards had produced the wine he

drank in celebration of his wedding to his beautiful wife, dead and buried five years now, God rest her soul.

Anthony Carlino did not overly imbibe, as did many of his compatriots. He'd only been drunk three times in his entire life.

Once, while still a young lad, when he had first been inducted as a runner for the Cosa Nostra.

The second, after having been stabbed. An old woman from the village worked to save him from the deep wound in the upper thigh that nicked his femoral artery, nearly ending his life. The only sedative the old woman had was wine ... and so.

The third, and last, after making his first kill.

Anthony Carlino did not get drunk the night of his marriage.

He did not get drunk the day his son, Nickolas, was born.

He did not get drunk the day his daughter Carla was born or even when he was made the Capofamiglia by the Cupola.

No, Anthony Carlino had learned early on that losing control of one's senses was an efficient way of getting killed ... *or worse* ... losing face. Some of his friends and many of his enemies had made the mistake of thinking him out of control because of his occasional outbursts of anger. But these were part of a carefully constructed facade. He did get angry at times; this much was true, but he never lost control. Not ever. His mind always stayed calm and detached— thinking, calculating, planning. And that was why he was still alive when so many of his contemporaries were not.

Kneeling, he spied an errant string sticking out from a knot tied around a guiding stake. He snapped open his lighter, a golden work of art—a gift from his Bella on their twentieth anniversary.

He rarely cried at the thought of her passing. Not anymore. Mostly now, he was just thankful for the many years they enjoyed together.

Giving the soil a final caress, breathing in the rich earthy smell, Anthony Carlino stood. A cold ache in his knees and lower back was becoming a near-constant companion. He winced and rubbed the spot as a burst of gunfire erupted from close by. The sounds were suppressed—or at least as suppressed as automatic gunfire *could* be with expensive baffling devices attached.

Most people would not even know what the muffled pops were, but Anthony Carlino had been too long in the business not to recognize the distinct sound signature of automatic weaponry. Just as he had been too long in life not to know they had come for him.

No matter that he had retired five years ago. No matter that he was now just a simple vinedresser. An old man with no power or worth.

No, none of this mattered.

There were always grudges, generational feuds, secret hatreds, unrequited revenge.

Those rivers of blood for which he was responsible.

The biblical notion, "He who lives by the sword dies by the sword," was never more evident than in the Mafia. And so he knew, without doubt, that the sounds were intended for him.

Anthony Carlino moved toward the little shed, just thirty impossible yards away. Inside was a double-barreled shotgun that his grandpa had given him when he was nine. The weapon, still in perfect condition and always loaded with slugs as thick and heavy as a large man's thumb, rested to the side of the door.

When he was halfway there, a small war exploded behind him. The last of his bodyguards staggered backward from the courtyard and into the vineyard, blood pouring from his scalp and several holes in his pressed suit. He fired twice at his attackers and then shook and fell as bullets obliterated his chest.

A small army appeared, spreading out in line formation. All were armed. Anthony Carlino continued to run for the shed, but his old legs were no longer capable of the speed of youth. He could never hope to make it before they killed him, but Anthony Carlino's mind had already calculated that he had no chance against them with just his hands. Making it to the gun was his only hope.

Two of the men ran after him, shotguns pointed at his back. Twin booms of the big guns sounded in unison, and he felt the double impacts, *like Chuck Norris kicks* strike him in the center of his spine and just above his right kidney. The pain was minimal for an instant, and then lightning shot down from Heaven, and he almost shamed himself by screaming. His muscles locked, dropping him face-first into the moist dirt. Agony engulfed him as the Tasers ran their five-second cycles. When they finished, he lay there, eyes closed, chest still, not breathing.

The closest of the men reached him and, sliding a gloss-shined shoe under his stomach, turned him onto his back. Anthony Carlino reached up and grabbed hold of the shotgun, wrenched it from the surprised man's grasp, spun it expertly around and shot him in the face.

Instead of blood and brain exploding, as Anthony Carlino expected, an electric arc snapped and crackled from the probes lodged in the man's cheek, a dangling base hanging by wires attached to the probes. He racked another round into the chamber and turned it toward the second hitman, but he was a hair too slow. He felt his body lock tight as another Taser round caught him in the chest before he could pull the trigger. An overwhelming sensation of lightning from God engulfed Anthony Carlino's every thought. And then the heavy stock of carbon-fiber from the butt of the man's gun connected with his forehead, sending him to the land of dreams, where rivers of scarlet washed over him, filling his soul with memories of a red, brighter than wine and thicker than blood.

The sun crested the horizon to the east, casting a beautiful purple blaze over the snow-capped mountain peaks that stood proud and seemingly impassible to the west. Trotting up the side of the hogback at an easy pace-eating gait, Max searched for something to kill, his mood foul—ugly. The night's hunt had been unfruitful and frustrating. Twice he'd caught the scent of predators, once on the rocks by the brook and another near the copse of trees in the valley. But both times, his prey eluded him.

Behind him was the reason.

He waited for Pilgrim to catch up.

Usually, Pilgrim was sound asleep when Max left for the hunt. *Max preferred to hunt alone.* It was safer that way.

Safer for Pilgrim.

But his feelings for the big animal had subtly changed since Pilgrim survived the battle that Max had thought would surely kill him.

Max had smelled the scent of death on him.

The big dog was slower than Max, but he'd healed well, and although he was old, he didn't fall too far behind.

But he was noisy.

A fat, gray rabbit hopped out from beneath a sparse bush five yards to his right. Max's lightning-fast reflexes almost cost the animal its life, but he checked himself and took note of Pilgrim finally making it to his side.

Max thought he should have probably left the old dog at home. He wasn't going to catch much at this rate.

The breeze, slight as it was, came from down the mountain, bringing the sounds and smells from below up to him. He heard the cars and detected the rolling dust they produced long before he saw them.

Pilgrim didn't catch it at all.

But Max let it go.

He recognized two of the scents from months ago. *Two men.* Max had almost killed one of them. *And he would have killed the other,* but the Alpha stopped him.

The cars wound their way up the road heading for the house. Max looked to Pilgrim, but still, he hadn't caught their scent. Max nudged him and stuck his own nose in the air. Pilgrim copied Max's behavior, scenting in quick little head bobs and jerks. It took him a few seconds, but then he got it.

Max ran to cut the men off.

Pilgrim followed as best he could.

Max didn't wait for Pilgrim this time. He smelled something other than the men. Something other than the cars, weapons, guns, oil, or gunpowder.

He accelerated his pace, leaving Pilgrim far behind. Max would beat the men to the Alpha ... and he would be waiting.

T he small caravan reminded me of when Senator Alvin Marsh and his entourage arrived on my mountain not so long ago. The senator had hired me to find a little girl named Keisha who had been kidnapped by a man named Jerome. Jerome was buried next to an old snitch of mine from my police days about fifty yards from where I stood.

This time, instead of government black SUVs, the group was made up of three custom-built, black limousines decked out with chrome wheels and high gloss waxed paint jobs.

I had just sunk an ax head into a thick stump I use as a type of anvil after finishing up a cord of wood and was about to head inside for a flaxseed shake when I saw the cars rounding the bend toward my house. I was beginning to see why Batman had his Bat Cave and Superman his Fortress of Solitude. After all, *I do have an office.* I pay big bucks for it in downtown Denver, just down the street from the baseball stadium. With a secretary and everything. Where clients are welcome to call and make an appointment. This barging in on my off time at my home was beginning to get old.

Glancing at my watch, I saw it was only 0730—that's early morning for those who don't know military time. I spent some years in the Marine Corps and then some more years as a cop at the Sher-iff's Office before getting canned for going after the guy who murdered my wife and daughter, events which led me to become the glamorous private investigator I am today.

I still needed a shower and a change of clothes, seeing as how I was still dressed in running shorts and a blue tee-shirt with the logo "The Just shall live by Faith" splayed across the front. The neck was wet with sweat, as was my forehead. I bet I *smelled* nice too. Not exactly ideal for meeting new clients, who I assumed were riding in the cars that were pulling up. Either that or they were real classy killers come to get me.

Turned out both were sort of the truth.

The trio of vehicles stopped, and Nick Carlino stepped out of the back of the middle car. Big Sal, his bodyguard, unfolded his giant frame from the front passenger seat and squinted at me. The driver of each vehicle stayed inside their respective cars, while three big, tough-looking Mafia types piled out of each of the other two cars and formed a protective circle around Nick as though they thought I was going to attack him.

A younger guy got out of the car with Nick and stood beside him. I recognized him as Nick's nephew. He was a muscular kid with some nasty scars on his throat, courtesy of Max, from an unexpected visit Sal and the kid paid to me a few months ago.

The whole thing had been a misunderstanding, but still, it didn't turn out well for them.

The kid looked at me, his eyes hard.

Nick walked up to me, his circle of protection moving like water, facing away from him, watching everywhere else. I noticed all of them were sporting fully automatic SMGs (small machine guns). *It's the kind of thing one tends to notice.*

The guards flowed past me, allowing me access to the circle. It was a well-executed, precision movement worthy of a crack military drill team.

Color me impressed.

Nick held out his hand. I shook it.

"Nice place you have here," said Nick.

Nick's a good-looking guy, slim but not skinny, jet-black hair, no beard or stash, very expensive gray suit. Italian gangster all the way.

"Thank you," I said.

I waved my hand at the circle. "Do you always travel like this?"

Nick didn't smile. "Dangerous times call for dangerous measures."

I was pretty sure that wasn't the way the saying went, but correcting Mafia godfathers could be tricky, so I let it go. "Dangerous times?"

"We have much to discuss," said Nick.

"Want to come inside?" I asked.

Before he could answer, Pilgrim came trotting over the berm from the west and approached. Two men pointed guns at him, but Sal waved them down. Pilgrim came through the circle and sidled up beside me, his tongue lolling and tail wagging. He was breathing hard and limping a bit ... but not too bad. I scrunched his ears and rubbed his head, so happy he was alive. Pilgrim had a run-in with an old friend of mine turned enemy, and I almost lost him. Instead, I lost the old friend turned enemy—*and I'd kill him again right now rather than lose Pilgrim.* I saw Nick's nephew take a step back, his hand inside his suit coat, the unmistakable sign of reaching for a gun.,

I shook my head, looking him in the eye. "He's not the one you need to worry about," I said. I shifted my eyes behind him, and he jerked around. Max was sitting, not three feet away, still as death. He'd somehow breached the circle without anyone seeing him.

I saw the kid's face go pale, and he started to shake a little.

Couldn't blame him. Not after what Max did to him last time.

"Go lay down, Max," I said.

Max looked past the kid to me as if considering. Then he turned and casually walked out of the circle and out of sight around the front of the house.

I knew he wasn't far ... and ... *that he was watching.*

Nick's gaze followed Max till he was gone, then turned back to me. He nodded. "That's actually scary," he said. "And I don't scare easily."

I nodded. "You don't know the half of it."

"This one, though," said Nick, pointing at Pilgrim, "this one's cute. Mind if I pet him?"

"He loves attention," I said.

Nick knelt down and played with Pilgrim's giant head, his face up close and personal to inch-and-a-half-long canines. If he'd seen the damage those tusks had caused just a few months earlier, he might have thought twice.

Nick stood up. "Yes," he said, "inside would be good."

The circle flowed around us as we made it to the front door.

"You need your men to search it first?" I asked, remembering the senator's guards.

"No," said Nick. "We are friends, you and I."

I opened the door, and Nick, Sal, Nick's nephew, and I went inside, Pilgrim following. Nick's nephew kept his eyes from mine as he brushed past and entered my home. Pilgrim went to his water bowl and lapped noisily. Nick laughed at the sound. When Pilgrim finished, he went to his bed and thumped down. He was asleep almost instantly.

"Want something to drink?" I asked, looking around at the three of them.

"Whatcha got?" asked Sal.

"Water, coffee, tea, orange juice, pop ... milk?" The first time I saw Sal, he was drinking a glass of milk. That was before he punched me.

Sal stuck out a lip. "Whiskey?"

"It's like seven-thirty in the morning, Sal," I said.

Sal stuck out his lip again.

"Whiskey it is," I said.

"Nick?"

"Some orange juice would be good, thank you."

I gestured to the kitchen table. "Here or in the living room?"

"You and I in here," said Nick, pulling out a chair at the table. "Them in there."

The kid hadn't responded about a drink, so I let it go. *Why push it?* I gave Nick a full glass of orange juice and pulled out a bottle of

Pappy's Fifteen-Year Reserve from the upper cabinet and poured about a third of a glass for Sal. He took it, grinning.

"The good stuff, thanks. You're all right, Mason."

I rubbed my forehead. "I respect a good punch." Sal had knocked me out cold with that punch. And I don't get knocked out easily.

"If it's any consolation," said Sal, sniffing the whiskey, "my mitt hurt for a week. You got a hard head."

"I've been told that before," I said, grinning. "And, yes, it is some consolation."

He winked at me and took a sip—two warriors showing respect.

Sal and Nick's nephew went into the living room and sat on the couch. I sat across the table from Nick.

"I hate to be abrupt," said Nick. "But time is somewhat of the essence here, so I'm going to get right to it."

"Of course," I said. "Please do."

"We are friends," he said, and it wasn't a question. "And as a friend, I have a favor to ask of you."

My mind went instantly to The Godfather movies, and I saw Marlon Brando with his cotton-stuffed cheeks saying how he was making an offer that couldn't be refused.

This felt like that.

I bobbed my head once, not sure how to proceed. "Who do I have to kill?" I asked, hoping to release the tension I was suddenly sensing.

"It's possible some killing will have to be done," he said.

I looked to see if he was joking ... *I certainly had been* ... he wasn't.

"Would I be killing good guys or bad guys?" I asked, thinking of Arnold in *True Lies.*

He smiled a closed-lipped smile, as though I had passed a test I didn't know I was taking, and reached into his coat pocket. He took out a rectangular gift box, set it on the table, and pushed it toward me, motioning for me to open it.

Inside was a severed finger ... with a gold wedding ring still attached. The finger lay on a bed of white cotton.

"Someone you know?" I asked.

Nick stared at the table. "My father," he said. "It's his finger. His wedding ring." His voice was low, controlled, but then he looked up at me from under dark brows, and I saw the rage. "My sainted mother died five years ago. My father never took that ring off in all the years they were married. *Not once*. And now, even though she has passed, he refuses to remove it."

"I'm sorry, Nick," I said. "Do you know who kidnapped him?"

"I have not yet received a demand, but I expect one soon."

"And what is it they are going to want? Money? Or is this a turf war?"

His lips turned up at the corners, appreciating that I understood the game, at least on a limited level.

"Not money," he said. "No one would be so foolish as to take my father for mere money."

Nick reached across the table and put the lid back on the box. He moved to take the box back, but I stopped him with a raised hand.

"I'll need that," I said. "I have a ... friend ... that may be able to get some information from it."

"It must not be lost," he said, "or damaged."

"No ... no, of course." I took it up and put the box in a plastic zip-lock baggie and stuck it in my freezer before returning to my seat at the table. "I assume you do not intend to involve the police or FBI?"

"No," he said. "You and I will handle this."

"What exactly does that mean?"

"You, and certain select men I will send with you, will find my father and free him."

I thought it out. "And the possible killing I might have to do?"

"Once you have liberated my father, you will stay with him until we arrive. You will protect him. You will protect him no matter what. You understand? My father is not to be further harmed."

"I understand."

"You will free him—protect him. Like you did for the little girl."

I nodded. "Yes, Nick. I will protect him."

His jaw clenched and worked, holding in the passion.

"I have a few questions still," I said.

Nick ran a hand through his dark, slicked-back hair. He gestured with his hand, granting me permission.

"Where was he kidnapped?"

"His vineyard in Italy."

"Italy?" I echoed. "As in Italy the country?"

"He retired to our ancestral estate after my mother died."

Nick reached back into his pocket and set a thumb drive on the table. "My father's information, as well as details about the vineyard, is on this, along with any other information I thought might be useful."

I took the drive and set it over on the counter. "When was he kidnapped?"

"Two days ago," said Nick. "There is video of his capture on that device. I received the box last night by bonded courier. The courier had nothing to do with the incident and has no knowledge of it. He was hired from an internet contact, and money was wired to him. The courier picked up the sealed and packaged box at a bus station and then delivered it to the address that was given to him in the email." Nick pointed to the drive on the counter. "All of that is also included."

"Do you have the packaging material the box was delivered in?" I asked.

"Sal has it secured in the car. I took great care with it once I understood its contents." He held up a hand. "However, it is unlikely you will find useful evidence on it. These men, whoever they are, are extremely efficient."

"I'll need it just the same," I said. "Anyone can make a mistake. I'd also like to talk with the courier."

Nick gave me blank.

That scared me.

"Nick, you didn't kill the courier?"

"No," said Nick, "but I had to be sure he told me everything. He will be of no use to you for a few weeks, and that will be too long."

I felt bad for the guy. I remembered being tied to a chair in the basement of Nick's casino with Big Sal getting ready to work me over. But couriers like that aren't paid what they're paid for delivering ordinary items. They make big bucks for the big risk, and sometimes their number comes up. It's similar to being a mercenary.

"So," I said, "you think he's still in Italy?"

"Yes," said Nick. "I have people looking. We will find him, but it might be too late. I trust you. That's why I'm here."

"Best guess on who took him?" I asked.

"There are several possibilities," said Nick. "None more or less likely than the others. We are not at war with the other families at this time. Which really means nothing. I have them all listed on the thumb drive."

"Of the ... *families* ... who has the most control in Italy?"

Nick smiled, but it was a cold smile. "I do."

"You're sure?" I asked.

"Absolutely."

I looked at Nick and tapped the table three times with my index finger. I pursed my lips, thinking of the least harsh way for this to come out. "Nick, you know that the most likely scenario is that your father is already dead."

"No," said Nick. "I understand why you think that, but that is not the way these things work with us."

"Okay," I said. "I'll accept that. I pray you are right."

"One last thing," said Nick. "My father is old, and he has been maimed, but if you come in contact with him, you must understand this one truth. My father is the most dangerous ... the most cunning ... the most ruthless man you will ever encounter in your life. If he thinks you a threat in any way, or if you disrespect him, he will kill you. But worse, before he ends you, he will hurt you in ways you never imagined possible."

4

Max beat the cars to the house. He hid in the tall grass next to the road as they drove past and stopped. The men got out, even the two he had almost killed. Max smelled the fear on the man he had bloodied. *The fear smell was rich and deep and dark*. The human was a fool to return. Max could hardly restrain himself from breaking cover and ripping his throat out. He had been warned ... *been allowed to live* ... and he had now ignored the warning and returned. He would not survive Max's second attack. The pack the man had brought with him would not save him. The man was alive now only because of the Alpha's authority, and it was that authority alone that kept Max in check.

But it was hard.

And then Max spotted *their* Alpha. The man exuded confidence and power. This man was not afraid. If Max had to attack, he would kill whoever crossed his path ... but this man would be his target.

The two Alphas met. They did not attack.

After having finally caught up, Pilgrim went toward the group. He was not quiet. He did not approach low and hidden. He bounded right into the circle, open and defenseless. Max watched closely. If any of the men attacked Pilgrim, Max would kill them. Two men trained weapons on the old dog, and Max prepared to launch, but the men quickly stood down and allowed Pilgrim to go to the Alpha. Only the man Pilgrim had once attacked continued aggressive movement by stepping back and reaching for something.

Max used the diversion to sneak past the men and into their circle. The men were weak, undisciplined, blind. He slid up behind the man whose life he had held between his jaws and sat.

Waiting. *Watching.*

The man was afraid of Pilgrim. Adrenaline rushed through his system, changing his scent profile. The difference affected Max physically, and once again, he found it difficult not to attack. But the Alpha caught Max's eye, so he remained still.

The Alpha alerted the man to Max's presence, and the man moved away ... *fear replaced by terror* ... as it should be.

The Alpha ordered Max away.

It was hard to understand the Alpha sometimes ... *often*. If this other pack attacked, Pilgrim would be of little use. But the Alpha had proven himself. And the Alpha was the Alpha. So, Max complied. He left the circle, went around the house, and entered through the pet door.

If things went wrong and the Alpha needed him, he would be close.

5

Nick and his army drove away, but he left something behind. His nephew, Billy Carlino.

We stood next to each other, watching the cars wind their way down the mountain, neither of us knowing what to say. Finally, he turned to me. He was a head taller than my five-ten — young and big.

"Where's my gun?" he said. "I want it back."

"Your gun?"

"Yeah, the KRISS."

A KRISS is a high-end, very expensive, small machine gun. Billy had lost his on the night Max grabbed him by the throat.

"Oh, that gun," I said. "The one you left the night you were trespassing on my property. I'm keeping that."

"You're what?"

"Finders keepers," I said.

"Do you know how much that gun cost me?"

"Don't care," I said. "Consider it the cost of doing business."

"Your dog attacked me!"

"You were going to attack *me*. Max was just doing his job. Besides, I'm the one that saved your life and bandaged you up. Not to mention, you got blood all over my kitchen and living room that I had to clean up. I'd say we were about even."

I could see he didn't like it.

I opened the door and went inside without holding the door. Billy followed. I walked to the kitchen and took out a cutting board, a crockpot, and a coffee cup.

"Want some coffee?" I asked.

He gave me contempt. Guess he still wasn't happy.

I shrugged my shoulders and poured a cup for myself. It was hot and black and strong and tasted like heaven.

Billy sat at the table while I took a small roast and some vegetables from the refrigerator. I added a couple cups of water to the crockpot and plopped the roast in. I got it heating and then started chopping carrots on the cutting board.

"What are you doing?" asked Billy.

"What does it look like? I'm preparing dinner."

"You're supposed to be finding my grandfather."

"Soon as I get this going. Takes about nine hours in the pot."

"Did you hear my uncle? He said time is of the essence."

I smiled. "So is food, and if I don't get this cooking, we don't eat tonight."

"I'll order us pizza," he said.

I started peeling potatoes. "You do that."

Contempt changed to disgust.

"I'm gonna kill your dog," he said. "Not now—not if he doesn't bother me. But after the job, I'm going to kill him."

"Max?" I felt my lips twitch up at the corners. "You think you can kill Max?"

"Yeah, the mean one. The one that did this." He pointed to the scars that ran from just under his jaw to below his collar and tie.

"I wouldn't try."

"I'm not going to try. I'm going to do it. And you'd better not get in the way."

I'd have knocked him out right then, but Nick gave strict orders that he was to tag along. Hmm ... me, taking orders from a Mafia godfather. Who'da thunk?

"You're not going to kill my dog," I said. "And if you try ... I'll kill *you* ... that is, if Max doesn't do it first ... which he probably would. So don't say it again."

"You ... kill *me*? Not a chance," he said. "You're what ... like fifty?"

That hurt.

Kids.

"And I'm still going to kill your dog, and if you try and stop me, I'll wad you up into a ball and ..."

He shut up pretty quick when the knife I had been using to cut the veggies was vibrating in the wall next to his ear.

"Oops," I said, "Sorry, slipped. It's the arthritis."

"That's not funny, old man," he said, jumping to his feet, his hands balling into tight fists. "I'm a cage fighter. I've won seven fights, all knockouts. I could rip your lungs from your chest..."

I interrupted him.

"You know the problem with MMA?" I asked, turning my back on him and tipping the thick butcher block cutting board over the top of the crockpot, allowing the potatoes, onions, and carrots to plop gently into the water, "Just that ... it's a *sport*. It's not real."

"*Not real*?"

"Yeah, cage fighting has too many rules," I said.

"Rules?" He was still fighting mad, ready to attack. "What rules?"

"Oh, you know," I said, my back still to him, "like ..." I turned fast, swinging the cutting board in a tight arc, catching him on the temple with the corner. It sounded like a gunshot. Billy's head snapped halfway around. He crumpled like someone had removed all his bones ... straight down without a sound.

"... no cutting boards." I looked at him lying there, all unconscious. "I told you not to say you were going to kill Max."

I let him lie there as I seasoned the roast with some salt, pepper, and a little garlic. Once I finished with that, I did a quick pat-down on Billy and took a few weapons off him. I set them on the table, noticing the goose egg that was swelling and already beginning to purple at his temple. I took a bag of frozen corn from the freezer and broke it up inside the bag before laying it across his head.

After that, I reheated my coffee in the microwave and sat down at the table. *Still tasted like heaven.*

I called Kenny, my friend who could find out anything.

"Hey, Mal," he said, answering before the phone even rang. *How does he do that?* Kenny's a geek on all things Sci-Fi and, most of all, the movie *Serenity* (TV series *Firefly*). He fancies himself after the character Mr. Universe, a purveyor of information who sits at the center of the galaxy collecting data from the *Verse* via the *Wave*. Kenny calls me Mal, the protagonist of both the series and the movie, both of which are great.

"Hi, Kenny," I said. "Got time for a couple of questions?"

"Anything for you, Mal."

"Hear anything about a kidnapping in Italy?"

"Little bits and little bytes, here and there. Ones and zeros, sequentially linked, telling their story to the Verse."

"Is that a yes?"

"Nothing can hide or stop the Wave, Mal. Anthony Carlino's estate was attacked, his bodyguards killed. And, unlike most such actions, this wasn't the doing of a government psyop. Just Mafia stuff. Or so the story goes." There was a brief pause. "Are you getting involved?"

I ignored the question.

"Any info on which family is responsible or where they are holding him?"

"I'll have to dig a bit, link some chains, string some algorithms."

"How long?"

"Not long."

"I appreciate it."

"The food smells good."

I looked at the crockpot, then at my phone.

"You're just guessing," I said. "You can't see me ... and you certainly can't smell anything here ... not through a phone."

"You keep telling yourself that, Mal. Nothing can hide from the Wave. Someone is always watching ... listening ... even smelling."

He hung up before I could respond.

I looked at my phone suspiciously. Then at my watch.

Creepy.

I called Sarah Gallagher, my friend at CBI (Colorado Bureau of Investigation). She's one of the top forensic criminal specialists in the world.

"Gil Mason," she said, her words flowing like liquid music. "How's Pilgrim?"

"Sleeping," I said. "And doing good. It's amazing. I think he's better than before he got shot." Sarah loves Pilgrim; he helped save her from a rapist once.

"I miss him. I'll have to come to see him, and maybe you too."

Sarah is like the most beautiful girl in the world's prettier sister, but behind that sleek exterior lies a mind to rival a Cray computer.

"Could you?" I asked.

"Could I what?"

"Come see me ... *us.*"

Pause.

"You mean now?"

"I do," I said.

I could hear her thinking.

"I want coffee and a danish," she said. "I didn't get breakfast."

"Deal," I said. "One more thing, though."

"Yes?"

"Could you stop and pick up some danish?"

6

I took a quick shower and changed my clothes. I wasn't worried about Billy. I'd checked his pulse ... *he was still alive* ... and I made sure his eyes weren't too wonky when I lifted his lids. Thick skull—in more ways than one. I'd spotted Max lying between the sofa and loveseat, down low and almost hidden, watching him. *I hadn't even known Max was in the house.* I wasn't worried about Billy waking up and causing trouble.

When I came back to the kitchen, Billy was still out, and Max was still watching him. I checked on the roast and then pulled the knife from the wall where I'd thrown it to make a point. A point that Billy apparently didn't get. It left a slit in the drywall that I'd have to spackle and paint. I took the knife and the cutting board to the sink, checking to make sure Billy's head hadn't damaged the corner of the board. It hadn't. I guess his head wasn't *that* hard.

I received an early education on knife play from a Brazilian on an Alaskan crabber boat that I'd run away to when I was barely in my teens. Like Napoleon Dynamite, I learned secret ninja skills that not only saved my life that season but several times since. I could just as easily have put the knife through his eye, but he *is* Nick's nephew ... and so ... *the spackle*. Still, I did warn him about saying he was going to kill Max again, so the knot on his head was on him. *Literally*.

I heard a moan and then a groan, and Billy opened his eyes. He blinked several times, touched his temple, winced, and scrunched his face in pain. He shook his head, which, from his reaction, I guessed hurt about as bad as touching his temple had, and he went through the whole wincing process again. He looked up at me from the floor.

"What did you hit me with?"

"Cutting board," I said. "I told you, the cage has rules ... like ... no hitting the other guy in the head with a block of wood. Real life ... no rules. See the difference?"

He stretched his jaw and rubbed his forehead, careful not to touch the lump.

"I *feel* the difference," he said. When he sat up, he looked at the bag of corn lying next to him where it fell. He hefted it in his hand, scrunching it between his fingers. It was no longer frozen. "For the swelling?"

"Best thing," I said.

He nodded. "Thanks. For the corn ... and the lesson." He looked at me. "I won't forget."

"That's good. Could save your life."

"Yeah. That's the first time that I've been knocked unconscious. And I've been in some fights."

"What do you think?"

"I don't like it."

"You planning on going another round?"

Billy grunted, pushing himself up so that he sat straight. "No. And I'm sorry for calling you old. I guess I should have said *experienced*. I'm thinking maybe you can teach me some stuff."

"I could," I said. "And how about my dog? He's lying behind you, over by the couches."

Billy's face went a little paler, and he turned so he could see him. Max didn't move ... just watched.

"Yeah," said Billy. "I guess I could maybe learn from him too."

"Fair enough," I said. "We'll start over."

I offered him a hand and helped him to his feet. He swayed a little but quickly settled. He looked in the sink.

"Cutting board, huh?"

My lips twitched at the corners.

"Cutting board."

BY THE TIME SARAH ARRIVED, I'd finished my second cup of coffee. Billy had taken some aspirin, eaten three eggs, four pieces of bacon, two pieces of toast, and five pancakes that I'd cooked up for him. *I guess time isn't as much in essence when one is hungry.*

Sarah didn't knock; she never does. She just walked in and went to Pilgrim lying in his bed. She knelt down in the way that women in short, tight dresses do and stroked his head.

I thought the forkful of pancake was going to drop out of Billy's mouth. *Sarah has that effect on men.* He looked at her, then at me, then back at her.

"A lot to learn," I said, patting him on the shoulder as I walked by.

"Has Daddy been treating you good?" she said to Pilgrim, scratching his ears and under his chin. She looked up at me, a smile playing at her lips and in her eyes. "Well, Daddy, have you been good to him?"

I went to the freezer and took out the box.

"I'm always good to him," I said. "I have a present for you."

She gave Pilgrim a final kiss on his snout and stood, smoothing her dress and brushing off some fur that had gathered.

"I hope it's a ring," she said.

My eyebrows raised. "Actually ... it is," I said, handing her the box with the ring ... and attachment.

She opened it, then looked back, giving me exasperated. "Not exactly what I meant," she said, then looked more closely. "On the other hand, it certainly raises questions." She turned the box this way and that, examining the finger from every angle, without touching.

"Notice the slight pinching at the side edges where it was severed ... indicates a clipping action. Probably wire or bolt cutters coming down from the top would be my guess. Do you know who it belongs to?"

"Anthony Carlino," I said. "*We think*. I'll get you some DNA to match it with so you can run a comparison."

"Carlino ... Carlino ... that case you had a while back with the guy at the Casinos?"

"His father," I said.

"Kidnapping?"

"Yes," I said.

"Demands?"

"Not yet."

"Looks to be two, maybe three days old," she said. She held it close to her nose. "Tomato, basil, maybe a touch of fish, and cheese ... parmesan or asiago. Where was he kidnapped?"

Wow, and I thought Max had a good nose.

"Italy."

"That fits," she said. "I need to get this to the lab right away before it deteriorates further." She looked at Billy. "Who's he?"

"The finger's grandson," I said.

Her eyebrows went down. "Gil," she said.

"What?"

Sarah walked over to Billy, who stood at her approach.

"Ma'am," he said.

She hugged him, and I thought he was going to melt into the floor.

Couldn't blame him.

"I'm so sorry," she said. "But trust me when I say that Gil is the best man to have on this, despite his uncouth behavior. If your grandfather can be saved, Gil will save him and bring him home to you." She kissed his cheek and stepped away. Billy's face and ears turned fiery red. Sarah hooked her arm in mine and walked out the front door with me in tow.

Once outside, she closed the door and pointed a beautifully

shaped and lacquered fingernail at me. "You be nice to him. He's grieving."

"He's a gangster," I said in my defense.

"Did you do that to his temple?"

"Not just any gang," I said. "He's Cosa Nostra ... as in Mafia."

"I know what the Cosa Nostra is, Gil. He's still human and just a boy. And his poor old grandfather has been kidnapped and had his finger cut off." She touched my chest with her fingernail. "So, you ... be ... nice."

She turned without kissing *my* cheek and walked to her car.

"Oh," she said as she floated into the car and behind the wheel, "and thanks for the ring." She grinned and drove away.

I wanted to tell her how Billy had threatened Max, *see what she thought of pretty boy then,* but she was already gone. I shook my head and walked back inside.

She didn't even bring danish.

Jonas pushed back from the table and took his plate to the sink. Irmgard, his eight-year-old daughter, played with her vegetables, moving them around her plate, shaping them into a variety of creatures. First a cat, then a rooster, then a snake. Jonas smiled, shaking his head and remembering back when he was a small boy. He had done the same thing, stalling from having to eat the foods he hated. Foolish when one thought about it. Sooner or later, you had to hold your nose and shovel it in. No matter how bad it tasted. Wiser always to get it over with and move along.

Children.

"Finish your food," he said as he walked out of the room.

Irmgard gave him *the look*, just as his wife used to do, God rest her soul, but it was such a funny look on her small face that he let it go and continued past the hallway and out the front door.

It had been almost a year since cancer had taken his wife, and times had been hard. The farm was not doing well, and to be truthful, his heart just wasn't in it anymore.

Jonas lit a cigarette and watched the smoke swirl away with the German mountain breeze, much as his dreams had when she died.

She was only twenty-eight. Thankfully, it had been relatively fast, *painful,* but fast.

He looked past the screen door and saw Irmgard still fussing with her greens. She was the reason he went on. It was for her that he had done what he had done. Or at least that's what he told himself.

It started with gambling. Just a little, here and there. Cockfights. Having raised animals on farms most of his life, he had a good eye and bet well. The money kept the farm from going under. But then he had a run of bad luck, and just like that, he *owed* money. And the man he owed the money to was not a man you *should* owe money to.

The cigarette tasted good, so did the night. He breathed both in, holding them in his lungs for as long as he could before releasing what was left of their essence.

He'd delivered the packages. Jonas never looked inside them. He just did as he was told. They could have been sugar or flour or toys, for all he knew. The first time he had hesitated, looking at the strange boxes with their plain brown wrappings, tied so carefully. They all weighed the same in his hand. Jonas was good at judging weight. He had sat looking at a stack of the packages on his kitchen table, just as Irmgard sat there now. And like her, he had moved them around, like arranging nasty-tasting vegetables on a plate, adjusting their position, putting off what he had known he had to do. There was no choice, not then and not now. He had taken the man's money, and he belonged to him.

He smiled sadly. Perhaps children and adults were not so different after all, each trying to postpone the inevitability of that *bad taste.*

The sheep rustled in their pen, and Jonas, ever so slowly, turned his head. The moon was partially covered in mountain clouds, giving off only enough illumination for Jonas to see a *darker* shadow among the shadows of the night, gliding along silently, as if the creature were somehow absorbing the darkness into itself, moving with the stealth of a great cat. Only this was no lynx or cougar or even a panther.

Twice now, in as many months, Jonas had lost sheep to this monster. Jonas had caught only the briefest of glimpses as it vanished into the trees, the hills, and the dark, carrying a fifty-pound ewe in its giant jaws. It ran as fast as a fast man could run, the weight seemingly insignificant.

Slowly, quietly, Jonas opened the screen door and reached inside, his callused palms finding the rifle that rested against the doorjamb. Jonas pulled it to him, fitting it firmly into his shoulder. He pointed it at the shadow within shadows, and all movement stopped.

Jonas didn't know if his eyes were playing tricks on him, but he saw nothing there, save the edge of the sheep pen and the wall of the barn. He blinked twice, fast, feeling a supernatural dread he didn't even know he possessed. He looked to the right and to the left, wondering if perhaps he had just imagined it. But no, he was sure he had seen—*something*. He considered taking a shot into the darkness, hoping for a hit, but he remembered the size of the thing he had seen on the other occasions as it ran away with the ewe. Its speed, its musculature, its grace—its *power*. If he missed, what then? Most animals, even a wolf—and that's what he was sure this thing was, would flee at the sound of gunfire. But something told him this animal was not like others. If he missed—*it would not*.

As cool as it was this high in the mountains, sweat popped out on his forehead and ran down into his eyes. His heart was a thudding drum in his chest. Gritting his teeth, he closed one eye, took aim into what he imagined to be the center of the darkness, then took up the slack on the trigger.

Headlights flashed through the trees, blinding Jonas and splashing the front of the house with light. He lowered the gun, trying to block the light to look for the darkness, but it was gone.

Two cars pulled up and stopped, the lights still blazing. A door opened and closed. Jonas saw a vague outline from behind the light.

"Are you going to shoot me, Jonas?"

Jonas recognized the man's voice, and his blood ran cold—even colder than it had with the monster a moment before.

Because this man, too, was a monster.

Two Fingers sat in the front passenger seat as the car took the winding turns. His dog, *Odin*, sat in the back watching. At nearly forty-six kilograms, the creature was big for a Malinois. Two Fingers thought there must be another breed mixed in the bloodline somewhere several generations back, but he didn't care. He only cared that Odin was the champion of the fighting ring. He'd killed nineteen dogs. On second thought, *killed* was too light a word. Slaughtered was more accurate.

Of course, the man's name wasn't *Two Fingers*, but he'd developed quite a reputation since losing the rest to that *other* Malinois. And the moniker added to his stature—as though he were a supervillain with a supervillain's name. It scared people. *And he liked scaring people.*

The trees rushed past as he watched out the window. The countryside made him think of when he'd lost his fingers. He was very close to where it happened—where the American had shown up and stolen his prize. Two Fingers had searched far and wide for the pair, but he'd come up empty. That's why he'd obtained Odin. The dog was nearly a mirror image of the dog that had maimed him but bigger, stronger, tougher. No animal could defeat him.

As they approached the farm, Two Fingers saw a man standing in front of the house. *Jonas*. And he was holding a gun. Jonas couldn't know that Two Fingers was coming, so why the weapon? Two Fingers had his driver pull up where his lights would illuminate the man. He told him to wait and, as he got out, motioned for the occupants of the second car to stay inside.

"Are you going to shoot me, Jonas?" he said from behind the cover of the light.

"No," said Jonas, lowering the rifle immediately. "No, of course not, sir. There was a—wolf—or something."

Two Fingers walked over.

"Where?"

Jonas pointed in the direction he had seen the shadow and heard the noise. "Over there."

Two Fingers squinted into the dark but saw nothing.

"Odin," he said, and instantly the giant dog was at his side. Two Fingers pointed at the darkness. "Kill."

The dog was an arrow as he disappeared into the dark, coming back a few seconds later and heeling at Two Finger's side.

"Nothing," said Two Fingers.

"It was there, though, as you drove up."

"Gone now, forget it. Do you have my money?"

Jonas took a step back.

"I have until Friday...."

"You have until I say," said Two Fingers, and his tone brooked no objection.

Jonas shook his head, too frightened to speak.

Two Fingers smiled.

"It's okay," he said, putting an arm around Jonas' shoulders. "Instead, you will do me a favor."

"A favor?"

"You and your daughter will stay in town for a few nights, maybe a week. I have need of your farm."

"My—my farm?"

"Just for a little while."

"I—we—have nowhere to stay."

Two Fingers removed his arm and took a wad of money from his wallet. "You will find a hotel," he said as he shuffled through the bills. "A *nice* hotel." He put the money into Jonas' hands. "My treat. You and your daughter ... Irmgard? will be on holiday."

"But—the farm—the animals?"

"I will take good care of everything," said Two Fingers. "No more talk. Get Irmgard. No packing. Buy what you need. Just take her and go. Now!" At the change in his tone, Jonas nodded quickly and started for the house.

That was when the sound came from the trunk of the other car— banging and muffled screams. Jonas stopped and looked toward the sound.

Two Fingers looked at the car, then back at Jonas. He held up his hands and shook his head.

"Too bad," said Two Fingers. He took out a pistol and shot Jonas in the forehead. Odin didn't even flinch.

The men from the second car got out and pulled the old man from the trunk. He was struggling, and he'd managed to get the gag out of his mouth, but his hands and feet were still secured. There was no threat of him escaping.

Two Fingers motioned for one of his men.

"Get the girl."

"Kill her?" asked the man.

Two fingers thought it over. He pursed his lips.

"No, just bring her. She'll fetch a good price in Amsterdam."

The man headed for the house and for Irmgard.

IRMGARD PLAYED with the peas on her plate, although she wasn't really playing. She hated them. They made her gag, and no matter how hard she tried, even when she held her nose and her breath, she still couldn't get them to go down. Her mother used to play a game with her that helped, but even then, it was hard.

The sound of the car made her forget the peas; they didn't often get visitors these days. She scooted off the chair, went into the living room, and peeked out the screen door, keeping her body off to the side so no one could see her.

Irmgard took after her mother. Her father called her shy, but she didn't like it when he said that. She liked how her mother said it better. Her mother used to say she *didn't like attention*.

But that didn't mean she wasn't curious. She peeked around the doorframe and watched as the man put his arm around her father. They must be friends, she thought, because no one but her mother, or Irmgard herself, ever hugged her father.

A commotion near the cars caught her attention, and then the man she had thought was her father's friend took out a gun and shot him. Growing up on the farm, Irmgard was well acquainted with the concept of death. That, and what had happened to her mother. But this—seeing her father murdered right before her eyes was beyond her scope of understanding.

Irmgard watched, horrified, as other men dragged an old man out of the trunk of a car. His hands and feet were tied.

And then another man started walking toward the house. The house and *her*.

Irmgard ran through the kitchen and out the back door. She ran as fast as she could. Out past the sheep pen, past the barn, and into the night. Irmgard was a good runner for an eight-year-old. She had long legs and a thin, sleek torso, and she played in these hills every day. She ran and ran, even when she heard the men yelling down below her. She knew they were looking for her. Fear pushed her past the point that would usually tire her and force her to stop. She cried as she ran. She cried because she was afraid and because her mother and father were dead, and now she was all alone. But even though she cried, she kept running until her lungs ached and her legs screamed. She ran and ran.

And the men did not find her.

Not then.

But there was another hunter in the mountains and woods that night. A hunter even more deadly than the men.

9

Anthony felt the car lurch to a stop. It was cold, and he was still dressed in his gardening clothes from when they had kidnapped him. His finger ached ... well ... the stub anyway. It was a very strange experience. It didn't feel like a stub to Anthony. It felt as though the finger were still there, but *not really*. There was a stabbing pain, all the way to the fingernail, yet there was no finger—no nail. It was a weird sensation. *He didn't like it.* He would make them pay. He would make them pay in ways their puny minds could not hope to comprehend.

They should have left him alone.

Anthony had fallen into a sort of waking sleep after his Bella died. The color in life had dulled. Not to black and white like the first television they'd owned, where he would sit and laugh as he watched Jackie Gleason in *The Honeymooners*. Not like that.

Worse.

Life had drained from the colors, making them obscene in some macabre way, a mockery of their former brilliance. And in the same way, taste and smell, sounds and touch, were all—*less*. He couldn't explain it any better. Not to the useless shrink he once visited, not to his family, and certainly not to himself. Money, power, respect, responsibility—none of them mattered to Anthony anymore.

He turned the empire he'd built through *literal* blood, sweat, and tears over to his most capable son, Nicky.

And he felt nothing.

No loss.

He'd gone into seclusion, to his family's vineyard in Italy, and did nothing for nearly a year. Slowly, a small bit of the color came back. Not much, certainly not all. But a little.

He'd always wanted to grow grapes, make wine, and so he started. The vineyard was there, well cared for. All there was to do was put the work in, and Anthony had always been a hard worker. So he'd put on his work clothes and started getting his hands dirty again—*literally*. Anthony had a lifetime of dirty hands, but this was different. It was clean dirt, free of blood and pain and suffering.

Life was no longer what it had been with Bella, but it was becoming something *different* from the nonliving experience he had been hiding under since her passing. Not good, *not yet*, but less bad.

There was light at the end of the tunnel—just a spark. Of promise, of *hope*. Something he thought he would never again experience or feel.

And then *they* had come.

They'd invaded his home. Killed his men.

They'd zapped him with electricity and bound and gagged him. They'd cut off his finger. The finger itself meant less to him than the ring that circled it. He might well forgive an enemy for maiming him, but this—this he would never forgive. For this, he would take vengeance.

They'd moved him. He didn't know where at first, but he'd been taken, first on a small plane, then on a boat.

When the new men took control of him at the port, he understood that he must be in Germany. Anthony spoke German well. He wondered if the men knew this about him. If not, he would not make them aware of it.

And now he was here, in the trunk of a car, still bound and gagged. They had been driving for hours. When the car stopped and the men began to talk, he scraped the tape off from over his mouth on the edge of metal by the right taillight. He started yelling in Italian that he was in the trunk and that he had been kidnapped. He heard a gunshot but didn't feel any pain, or see any holes near him, so he continued to yell.

It didn't take long for the men to open the trunk and drag him out. His legs and arms were numb from the long ride, but he swung forward and smashed one of the men in the nose with his forehead. Anthony was punched and kicked and knocked to the ground. When they finally picked him up, he saw the man he had smashed in the face rolling around holding his nose, blood dripping through his fingers.

There was a dead man lying crumpled at the feet of another man. The dead man sported a bullet hole in his forehead. The other man held a pistol and had only two fingers on his left hand.

Join the club, pal, Anthony thought, feeling the ache in his own hand.

Anthony smiled a tight-lipped smile. He had upset their plans in at least some minor detail. He looked back at the man rolling on the ground. His blood was not the dull gray that all colors had taken on since the death of his Bella. No. The blood was bright and vibrant, filled with life—and the promise of death.

They should have let him sleep.

K enny called me around noon. I'd just finished reserving flights to Italy for Billy and me.

"Hi, Mal," said Kenny. "I see you're by your computer. That's good."

I looked around to make sure he wasn't magically standing behind me. He wasn't. And that was maybe even scarier than if he had been.

"I'm going to send you some vids," said Kenny. "Surveillance of the kidnapping. Some from Carlino's security feed, some from satellites, some from—another source."

Satellites? Another source?

I looked behind me again, a little chill tickling my spine.

"I also canceled your flights to Italy," said Kenny. "They already snuck Carlino out of the country. I booked you and Billy an international flight to Germany that leaves DIA at 2100 hours. Remember to be there at least two hours early to make it through security. I also took the liberty to alert them about your carrying guns and that you'd be traveling with your service dog."

My jaw dropped.

"Germany? How do you know that?"

"It's complicated," he said. "At least it would be complicated explaining it to you. But basically—*very basically*—nearly all the mobs are tapped. Wiretapped. Actually, there are no wires. I guess you could call it *digitally tapped*. But then everyone is. Cell phones, security systems, tablets, home smart devices, watches. Virtually every word you speak and most of your visible actions are recorded and held in vast storage facilities that contain servers and data collection devices more advanced than you could possibly believe. It's the Verse, Mal. And the Wave moves through the Verse freely. Ones and zeros, like I said before."

That did nothing to ease my apprehension. Big brother scares me more than regular bad guys any day.

"Anyway," continued Kenny, "looks like they got him out of the country in a Cessna, landed on a private airstrip in Germany, loaded him on a boat that ferried him across to a dock, where they tossed him in the trunk of a car. My guess is the Carlino family is too well established for them to hole up in Italy for very long. That's why they shipped him out." Kenny tapped a few keys. "I just sent you the info on where they reached port in Germany. Two cars were waiting for them. I have a video feed that shows them loading him in the trunk of one of the cars, then driving off. License plates on both vehicles are clearly visible. *Rentals*, of course—routed through false names and addresses. Unfortunately, the feed loses them a short distance down the road, and I haven't been able to reacquire them ... *yet.*"

"Any idea who took him?" I asked.

"Three possibilities. I'll narrow it down. It's all in the numerics I sent. I don't have the German faction that's helping yet but give me time."

"Numerics?"

I could almost hear him smiling over the phone.

"Ones and zeros, Mal."

"Nice work, Kenny," I said. "You never cease to amaze me."

"The Verse sees all—even the kid there next to you. Carlino's grandson. That's why I booked him the flight with you."

"You're creeping me out, Kenny," I said.

"The Verse sees all, hears all, knows all," he clicked off.

I saw Billy watching me.

"You got some weird friends," he said.

Doing my best David Carradine from *Kill Bill*, I said, "Baby, you ain't kiddin'."

He gave me confused and said, "Is that from a song?"

Kids.

11
___

Irmgard didn't know how long she'd slept, but she thought it hadn't been long. The dream woke her. It was a bad dream. A scary dream. A *terrible* dream. In the dream, her father was— but then she remembered—it wasn't a dream. Her father *was* dead. She started crying again.

The big boulder she crouched beneath shielded her from the night's breeze, but still, she was getting cold. She hadn't had the time or the sense of mind to grab her coat before running out of the house. At least she was wearing long sleeves, jeans, and hiking shoes. If she'd been in her nightgown, it would be worse.

The crunching of snow stopped her tears. She stared, wide-eyed, in the direction of the sound. *They were still looking for her.* She turned her head slowly, scanning the darkness. She wasn't certain, but she thought she saw something coming up the mountain from below. She strained her eyes as hard as she could, and *yes,* she was sure now. Two faces—at least two. Not close, but not far either. Irmgard stood and made her way around the boulder. She knew these mountains better than anyone. She tried to think of the best place to hide, but there were no caves this way, and she didn't think she could make it around the men to where there were.

She decided on the trees.

But even they held a problem. The ones that would hide her, the pines, were hard to get into and climb. The others had no leaves, offering little concealment except for their height.

Finally, she decided and crawled under a wreath of green needles until she reached a trunk, thick and rough. The heavily decorated branches blocked out the scant light the night provided, and she found herself in near-total blackness. Irmgard felt out and up, her fingers finding the bare wood of the branches, and she started climbing. It was difficult. The bark, *sharp and sticky,* cut at her hands. Small twigs kept jabbing at her eyes and catching in her hair, but she kept on and up until she was a good way off the ground.

She was unaware of the creature that marked her progress from a short distance away.

～

THE WOLF HAD PICKED up her scent from near the barn and had tracked her to the boulder. He was about to attack when the sound of the men stopped him. He watched as she made her way around the boulder and to the tree. He could have taken her easily, but he was not the apex predator of these mountains for no reason. He was patient, careful, wise. Besides, the men were almost to him.

"This way," said Karl.

"Do you really know what you are about?" asked Heinrich. He was not as fit as Karl and was struggling to catch his breath. "Or are you just trying to be the big man?"

"She came this way," he said. "You saw the rock where she rested. I think she's close."

Both men carried rifles.

The rifles would not help them.

The wolf struck with such speed and power that he knocked them both to the ground. He ripped out Karl's throat with one massive gesture and turned to Heinrich, who was trying to scrabble for his weapon. The monster dove forward, crushing the man's groin

in jaws of steel, ignoring the screams and hapless flailing. The wolf
moved up to the man's stomach, tearing through the coat and past the
flesh to the fragile intestines. And still, the man screamed—but not
for long. Soon there was only the sound of Karl choking to death on
his own blood and the crunching and snapping of the wolf's feeding.

The girl watched it all from the tree.

The wolf knew she watched. He *let* her watch. He *wanted* her to
watch.

12

S arah had gotten right to work on the finger when she made it back to her lab, pushing her other projects to the side. Gil never failed to keep things interesting.

She started with photographs and videos, of course. Then she dabbed and swabbed and scraped before fingerprinting the loops and whorls. Strangely, it was almost always easier on a severed finger —no convincing the human mind to go limp and let her do the work. People couldn't help but to try and *help,* which inevitably messed up a good print.

Next, Sarah removed the ring, a plain gold band. She noted the deep imprint and paleness of the skin. It had been in place for a long time. She took new photographs and searched the inside of the ring. *No inscription.* She noted the three-dimensional aspects of the finger: height, width, and length. Then she measured the severed end from top to bottom and side to side. She scraped the edges of the wound, collecting skin, dried blood, and hopefully, microscopic metal fragments from the instrument used to clip the finger from its host hand. Sarah dug under the fingernail and again collected the contents. She X-rayed the finger, checking for an old fracture or pins. Later she would run the ring through a series of advanced spectrographs. It was possible there had once been an inscription that time and wear had worn away. If so, different wavelengths of light could bring them to the surface for photographing. But for now, she concentrated on the flesh. Metal took a long time to deteriorate—meat, not so long. Of course, she would be using chemicals to preserve it, but first, she wanted to get what she could in its purest state.

Sarah's mind drifted to Gil. He'd looked tired to her. She wondered how he'd been sleeping. She knew about the nightmares. Sarah had personal knowledge of the horrors of the dreamscape. Memories of her rape had plagued her nights in twisted versions, chasing her through her dreams. And what had happened to Gil, and to his wife and daughter, was even worse.

And if that wasn't bad enough for him, he now had the memories of *Gail*, the woman who had played with Gil's heart and mind, only to betray him in the end.

Sarah loved Gil; it was as simple as that. She'd loved him even before the Double Tap Rapist had visited her for the *first* time. Reflecting on the rapist filled her with terror, halting her breath and her heart, even after so long. The terror and the repulsion—*his hands—his mouth—his weight—his smell. The things he said to her, the things he did.* She forced her mind to leave it, to go back to Gil. How good he was. So strong. In will and strength and character. She knew he'd killed people in the war and after—*he killed the Double Tap Rapist.* But the people he killed deserved it.

Sarah had seen far too much in her line of work not to know that some people needed to die. If the man who had raped her stood before her, here and now, she would gladly slice his throat from ear to ear ... watch him bleed out. She would scream in his face as he died. Even now, she hoped he burned in Hell. Sarah wasn't much of a religious person, not like Gil, but she wanted to believe in a hell where he would suffer. That's how much she hated him.

With Gil, she felt safe. But it wasn't just that. She didn't just love him for that. She loved him for everything he was. And he had suffered so much. She wanted to comfort him, the way he had comforted her. She wanted to hold him, to kiss him, to love him. She wanted to take all the bad dreams away. She didn't know if she could do it. *How do you fight a ghost? How could she hope to compete with his memories of Joleen and Marla?*

In the mind, the dead are always perfect. Forgotten are the arguments, the hard times, the dissatisfaction. The dead remain eternally the way you *need* to remember them in your heart. The living are just what they are—imperfect—moody—with bad hair days and stress. *What chance did she have of competing?* And yet, Gail Davis had accomplished it. At least on some level. Sarah didn't know how far things had gone between them, but she knew Gil well enough to understand *something* had happened. That he had had *feelings* for Gail.

How did Gail do it? Sarah had seen her. Gail had been an assistant district attorney, and Sarah had testified on cases with her. She was pretty. But lots of pretty girls had come on to Gil Mason with no results. What was it about Gail Davis that had broken through his defenses?

Sarah decided she needed more data.

A smile touched her lips as she worked. Gil was always referencing movies and using their lines. One from *Dumb and Dumber* came to her mind, and she saw Lloyd saying to Mary, *"So you're telling me there's a chance."*

Before Gil, she had never felt like this for a man. It had always been the men who chased her. She thought she should feel embarrassed, but she wasn't. She loved Gil with her all, and she would do anything to get him to love her in return.

For the next hour, Sarah went over the finger with an electron microscope, zooming in and out, using the miracle piece of equipment as though it was everything from a high-priced magnifying glass to a machine capable of piercing the secrets of the atom.

When she finished, Sarah started the DNA growth and sequencing process. Then she went to work on the ring.

And all the while, her mind contemplated just how she would go about obtaining the data she needed to win Gil over.

13

"So, what do you have against MMA?" asked Billy as he forked in another mouthful of roast and potatoes. The swelling at his temple was almost gone, but it had been replaced by a nasty purple and yellow bruise that faded out about halfway down his face.

"Nothing," I said. "I love mixed martial arts as a *sport*. It's just that it's advertised as no holds barred, but it's not. It can't be because, in the end, it's a sport and not the real world. Always remember ... right tool for the right job."

Billy shook his head.

"No, it's the ultimate. That's why it used to be called The Ultimate Fighter. Nothing can beat it."

"You're forgetting," I pointed at his face, "cutting board."

He snorted and took another bite.

"Cheating," he said.

"No such thing in a fight," I said. "Not in a real fight in the real world—outside of a cage or a ring. Everything is situational. And that's how you need to approach it. Sometimes fists work. In that case, MMA is a good start. Krav Maga brings it even closer to the streets. Sometimes you might need a knife, or a handgun, or a scoped rifle. Then there are fully automatic rifles, twenty-millimeter cannons, missiles, and finally, the *big* bomb. Situational."

"What do you mean Krav brings it closer to the streets? That's all it's for."

"Krav leaves out cutting boards," I said. "When I was just a kid, a little Brazilian guy taught me the truth about fighting. One punch, one kick, one bad fall in a fight could end your life instantly. Intentionally or unintentionally. Either way, *you* are just as dead. So take every fight as a life-or-death situation because it could be."

I looked around the kitchen. "Everything in this room is a weapon if utilized properly. The saltshaker, the pepper, the plate, the table, the wall. *All potential weapons.* And every part of your body is vulnerable to something if I can get through your defenses to reach it. The salt or the pepper thrown into your eyes or breathed in could incapacitate you for a few seconds, giving me the opportunity to break the plate and jab a sharp edge into your throat. Then I could smash your nose into the table and crush your skull against the wall. *Dirty*? Okay, but why are we fighting? What is it you are wanting to do to me?"

He swallowed another bite.

"I'm wanting to get my gun back," he said.

"The KRISS Vector Gen II Sub Machine Gun with the Defiance HPS 4GSK suppressor you left behind?"

"So, you do have it."

"Never said I didn't. And you want it back?"

He nodded, grinning. "Yes, I do."

"Not gonna happen," I said. "Wouldn't be prudent." I dropped the Carvey. "Consider it another lesson."

"Expensive."

My turn to smile.

"Good lessons often are."

"You know I'm Mafia, right?" he said.

"About that," I said. "Why?"

"Why what?" He asked as if he hadn't a clue.

"Why are you going the goon criminal route?"

He lost the smile as though I'd insulted him or something.

"You trying to be funny?"

"No, Billy, I'm being serious. You have so much going for you. Why this?"

He shrugged, took another bite, swallowed. "Cause I can't sing or dance."

I sat back, impressed. "Did you just make a *Rocky* joke?"

"You got it," he said, grinning. "I love fighting movies." He wiped his mouth with a napkin. "It's a family thing. I don't really have a choice. I mean, I do—but I don't."

"Is it what you want?"

"Most of the time," he said. "I mean, I like the respect, from most people that is, present company excluded. I like the excitement, the cars, the guns, the women—stuff like that. Some things I don't like so much."

"You could stop... you could quit."

He shook his head.

"Nah. I've—I've done some things."

"We've all done things," I said.

He looked me in the eyes. I saw the pain. He saw mine. Two men who had ... done things.

He broke eye contact.

"Yeah, well, like I said, it's a family thing. The things our family has done go back a long way."

"God says you can quit," I said.

That made him look at me. He held up his hands, gave a half-grin, and shook his head again.

"God? What's God got to do with it?"

"God says if a son has a wicked father—in this case, we could say a wicked family— and he sees it and decides not to do what they do, then God won't hold the son accountable for the father's actions. He'll judge the son on what the son does, not on what the father does. We are each responsible for our own choices. Not our fathers' or our families'. So, you could quit."

He wagged a finger at me.

"I know my Bible," he said. "Years of catechism at St. Mary's.

Confirmation, the whole deal. And you aren't telling the whole story there. What about Canaan? God cursed *him* for his father seeing his granddad naked, and he wasn't even born yet."

"That's good," I said. "You do know your Bible. But let's look a little deeper at what it really says. First off, do you know what an idiom is?"

"Do I know what an idio ... yeah ... *yes*, I know what an idiom is. I may be a thug, but I'm not stupid. It's when you use a saying where the words don't really mean what the words are, but everyone knows what you mean because, well, because we all just know."

"Exactly," I said. "Like if I were to say, *let's hit the road*. Now, I don't mean to go out and punch the road, which is *literally* what the words say. What I mean is, *let's get going*. And since the culture understands that's what I mean, it works. The Bible is full of metaphors, parables, and idioms. Take, for instance, the one you just misquoted. *Ham saw his father's nakedness*. Now, most people these days think that means God threw out a curse because Noah's adult son saw his father naked. But that's not what happened."

"It's not?"

"No. What really happened, when you read the whole Bible and understand the Jewish idiom of *uncovering nakedness*, is spelled out quite clearly in Leviticus 20, verse 11 to be exact. It means to *lie with* ... and by *lie*, the Bible doesn't mean *sleep*. The verse says, *'The man who lies with his father's wife has uncovered his father's nakedness.'* So, when the Bible says that Noah got drunk and his son, Ham, saw the nakedness of his father, it's really saying ..."

Billy broke in. *"That Ham slept with his dad's wife?"*

"That's right," I said. "Noah got drunk, and Ham raped his own mother."

"Whoa! That is sick!"

"It gets worse, though," I said. "Noah later proclaims a curse on Canaan for what his father, Ham, did. Now it wasn't God that put the curse on Canaan; in fact, it wasn't even Noah. Noah just stated the fact that there was a curse on Canaan. So, why? And what was the curse? The *why* is that Canaan was the *product* of Ham raping his mother. In other words, Ham got his mother *pregnant* with Canaan. *That's the why.* Now, what was the curse? It wasn't a curse from God but rather the natural consequences of his father's crime. Imagine, back then, how other people would treat the product, the *child*, of such a crime. I mean, today, if a woman gets raped by a *stranger*, not even her own son, society screams that she should murder the baby. So how do you think that child, back then, would fare among his relatives? It would be a *harsh* life. Even though his father committed the crime and the child was completely innocent, that child would be cursed by the way everyone would treat him. That's what God means when, in other verses, He talks about visiting the iniquity of the fathers upon the sons to the third and fourth generations. That's how long it can sometimes take to get out from under the shadow of a father's sins. People have long memories. They don't forget. And they gossip. That's just part of the sinful, human condition."

"Wow," said Billy. "I've never heard it like that before. I always thought it was weird that he got in trouble for seeing his dad naked. I mean, it wasn't like they lived in mansions. People had to see each other taking whizzes and stuff like that. This sheds a whole new light on it. A gross light—but still."

"So, you see," I said, "you really do have a choice. You don't have to stay in the family. You can go your own way. You *should* go your own way."

"Obviously, you aren't Italian. And even more obvious is that you aren't part of the *family*. Gangs are a whole different animal than regular life. I was born into this one. It's just how it is."

"I've been in the two biggest gangs in the world," I said. "The United States Military and law enforcement. Green and blue, no other gang comes close. When the time was right, I got out of both."

Billy shook his head. "That's different."

"Maybe," I said. "Only maybe not as different as you think. Mull it over; give it some time. We're all capable of change. The sins of your family don't have to be visited on you. You are your own man."

Billy pointed a finger at me.

"You know, you're a dangerous guy. I feel kind of like you hit me in the head with a cutting board again. You bring up dangerous ideas. Ideas that could get someone hurt. Maybe get someone killed."

"I think you can take care of yourself," I said. I looked at my watch. "We'd better start getting ready. Our plane leaves in a few hours. And I've got a call to make."

14

The wolf ate what it wanted of the two dead men, then turned its attention back to the girl. Most animals do not care for the taste of human flesh, but the wolf did not care about taste. He was not like most animals. He was the ultimate predator, and he cared only for survival and domination. The men were good for food; how they tasted meant nothing to him. The little girl was a matter of domination.

For months, since widening his area of control, he'd smelled her. She played on the hills and rocks and trees as if she owned them. The wolf had marked the area numerous times, but she had ignored his warning. He had let it go for a time because she and her father herded the sheep he was able to steal whenever he wanted. But there were limits, and tonight she had breached them.

Tonight, she would die.

He circled the tree and locked on her eyes high above.

The pine boughs could not hide her from him, but they did pose a problem. He didn't like to climb. He'd had mishaps in the past and had fallen, striking limbs on the way down.

Fighting in trees was dangerous.

A broken leg would mean death.

The wolf did not think in these terms, but experience and instinct had merged, making him tactically wise.

And so, he stalked, circling the tree, watching her. She would tire. She was young, weak. The wolf was strong, and he never tired.

But again, he heard men *searching*. They came from below, noisy and clumsy. This time, there were more than just two. Men carried weapons his animal brain could not fathom, nor did he try. He knew danger, and that was enough. But still, they could be defeated—killed, if handled properly. The two partially eaten dead men at his feet were proof of that.

The wolf looked up at the girl, not wanting to leave her. She was his. He had claimed her, and he would not allow her to escape.

But first—the men.

IRMGARD WATCHED from high in the tree as the wolf eviscerated and partially ate the two men. It was a horrible sight, but it was moderated by the fact that she knew these men were with the one who had murdered her father. *And they were hunting her.* She thought herself safe; *she'd never seen a dog that could climb trees,* and she doubted a wolf could either. *But men—men could climb trees.* She didn't know what the man had meant when he said she would *fetch a good price in Amsterdam,* but by the way he said it, she knew it wasn't good.

Suddenly the wolf looked away from its meal, turning its attention down the mountain toward her home. His head cocked this way and that. He stared, motionless, *hearing something that she could not.* She knew dogs could hear better than people—her father had taught her that. The thought of her father brought tears, but she fought to hold them in.

The wolf suddenly disappeared into the dark, and Irmgard was alone with the night and the remains of the two dead men. Somehow that was scarier than having the wolf waiting for her below.

She held fast to the tree and listened. And then she heard a scream—and a gunshot—and another scream. It was far away, but the sounds echoed through the woods and the rocks. Irmgard started to tremble. She cried, and this time she couldn't stop. Her teeth chattered, and it wasn't just from the cold. She wanted her mother—her father. She wished she'd eaten her peas as her father had wanted.

"I'm sorry," she whispered through her tears. *"I'm so sorry, Daddy. I need you! Please don't leave me here. I'll eat the peas. I'll do whatever you want. Daddy! Don't leave me alone."*

But her father didn't answer. There were only the hollow echoes from the far away shots and screams. After a while, she made herself stop crying. The tears ended, but the trembling only got worse. This time it *was* the cold. The wind gusted through the trees and the branches, offering little protection.

Irmgard made her decision.

She climbed down the tree, went to the two dead men, and took a hooded jacket and gloves. It would be a long trek to her house.

~

THE WOLF SAT BEHIND A TREE, the dark completely hiding him. He watched the men spread out in a wide, ragged line as they made their way up his mountain. There were five of them, their lights swinging carelessly across the landscape. He waited until they passed him, one of them close enough to touch.

But the wolf did not attack them.

Not yet.

He let them get above him, then moved to the far left edge of the line. He chose this side because the man there lagged a little behind the others. He was huffing and puffing and used the low limbs of trees for support.

From the rear, the wolf caught the man on the inside of his left thigh. He moved fast, silent, biting in and snapping the man's femur, severing the femoral artery. The wolf did not let go as the man toppled, falling partially onto the wolf's head and back. Instead, he kept moving forward and away from the other men, deep into the trees. The man was so shocked he didn't scream, but as the wolf carried him through the woods, his head smacked against the trunk of a tree. Bright sparks exploded behind his eyes, bringing blood that ran down his face and into his eyes and mouth.

And then he did scream.

Flashlights swung in their direction, but already the woods hid them. The sound of the screams was dwindling as men ran to try to find what had happened. Someone shot in their direction, but it was out of panic with no target in sight.

The wolf dropped the screaming man and lunged into his throat, where he crushed down and held on until the man was still.

The line of soldiers had become a group of disorganized beams of flashing lights that flew about in useless patterns.

The wolf returned to the hunt.

He circled and attacked from the right, again from behind. This time, the man screamed instantly. He was big, with strong muscles that did nothing to save him. The wolf carried him away as easily as he had the first man. The big man tried to fight—punching, grabbing, and kicking as he was dragged through the dirt and leaves and rocks. Bullets pelted through the trees in their direction, but, like last time, none of them came close. The wolf disengaged behind a large rock, letting the man fall to the ground, and then slashed in, tearing into the man's face. The man had dropped his flashlight and gun some distance back, and one of his gloves had come off. He tried to reach for the wolf's muzzle with his bare fingers, but the monster slipped past his arms and caught him under the chin. Again, the man punched, hitting the big animal about the skull and neck. Soon his attempts grew weak, and he died, just like the other man.

But now, a small group of three gathered under a leader who took charge. Lights flashed in the wolf's direction, and rifles started putting bullets much closer to him, chipping wood from tree bark and sending up tiny geysers of dirt. One of the slugs struck the dead man in the head, and the wolf decided it was time to leave. He dropped the dead weight and began circling to get at the men from behind.

The soldiers did not scatter this time. They huddled together in a tight group, all sides covered with their lights and their guns. The wolf waited as the group began to move forward, and again, they drew near. Lunging, he caught a man mid-forearm, but before he could drag him into the trees, the soldier next to him swung and fired. The bullet missed, but it was close. It singed the fur near the wolf's tail, forcing him to release and slip back into the safety of the forest before a lucky shot could take him.

The wolf wanted to kill the men. But he wanted to live more.

He also wanted the girl, but the only safe path made getting to her a long journey. The men still gave chase, but slowly. The wolf disappeared into the trees and the dark.

15

We didn't make the flight that Kenny, *Mr. Universe,* had scheduled for us. Unbeknownst to me, Billy made a call to his Uncle Nick, and before it was time to leave, a limousine pulled up in front of my house. Billy grinned and told me to get in. The driver tossed our luggage into the trunk, and Max hopped inside. Max made Billy apprehensive, but because Max entirely ignored him, Billy had pretty much relaxed before we made Centennial Airport.

The jet was *unbelievable,* and I don't say that lightly. It was a Gulfstream G700, nineteen-passenger business jet, powered by two Rolls Royce Pearl 700 Turbofan engines with a top speed of seven hundred and nine knots (that's over eight hundred miles per hour). The maximum range is seven thousand five hundred nautical miles (almost the same as regular miles, only over water), and it can fly at an altitude of fifty-one thousand feet. The inside was pure opulence.

Other than the flight crew, we were the only occupants.

There was no x-raying of luggage, no handsy pat-downs, no checking for weapons or even passports. We just boarded and took off.

A guy could get used to this.

"What does one of these things cost?" I asked Billy.

Billy grinned and took a sip of his Jack on the rocks. "If you have to ask, you can't afford it."

"No, really," I said.

"This one?" he motioned around the ginormous cabin. "I think my uncle paid about seventy-five for it—*new*."

"Seventy-five," I said. "You mean, like seven million five hundred thousand?"

He took another sip and shook his head. "No. Like seventy-five million."

I almost spit my Dr Pepper across the cabin, but I held it in.

I couldn't afford the cleaning bill.

It was the greatest flight of my life. Definitely better than being loaded up with ninety grunts in the back of a C130.

The flight took about ten hours, so, with the eight-hour time difference, we got in around one in the afternoon, German time. Max slept most of the way. One of the flight attendants, a sweet girl that looked like she was about nineteen, asked if she could pet him. I told her he wasn't the petting kind of dog.

Billy snorted and said, "You got that right."

Five of Nick's men met us at a gas station outside the airport.

It was cold now, not freezing, but maybe on its way.

Marco Brambilla, boss man of the security detail, came over and shook my hand. He had the look, short and stocky, packed with lean, cut muscle. He reminded me of bodybuilder Franco Columbo, Arnold's old friend, who took the Mr. Universe title back in '76. Next to him was Piero Romano (no relation to Ray Romano or the cheese, as far as I know). Then there was Enzo Bianchi and Leonardo Esposito. All very competent looking men.

And such cool names.

The last guy, Vincenzo Mancini, was in charge of them all. He wore a three-piece suit, while the rest were decked out in digitized gray and white camo gear, thick coats with hoodies, gloves, boots, and sun-activated goggles riding high on their heads. Vincenzo looked old country all the way. Classy, with fine streaks of gray at his temples.

He shook my hand without saying anything, then started talking to Billy in Italian.

Max watched all of them.

Piero gave Max a wink and a half-smile.

Max started licking himself.

Rude.

Piero's half-grin disappeared, and he moved his gaze to me.

I shrugged my shoulders and said, "Kids."

His expression didn't change, neither did his stare. Maybe he didn't understand English.

I looked down at Max. "Thanks a lot."

Max stopped his licking, looked up at me, burped, went back to licking.

I shook my head and glanced back at Piero. He was grinning again.

Vincenzo finished talking with Billy and took two large backpacks out of the trunk of one of the cars and handed them to him.

Billy came over and gave me one.

"There's gear inside like theirs. A few other things too. Let's go change."

We both crowded into the single-seat restroom, and when we came out, we looked like a matched set with the others—hunters going on an outing (which was actually accurate) except the prey we were hunting walked on two legs and cut off old men's fingers.

Vincenzo spoke with Billy for a few more minutes while I checked over my equipment, including a fancy Swiss-made compass watch that probably cost about as much as Nick Carlino's jet. When they were done, Vincenzo shook my hand, again without speaking. He started to leave, but I stopped him.

"Did you recruit these men?" I asked.

Vincenzo stopped, and turning back to me, said, "Si."

"You speak English," I said.

He smiled.

"Yes, of course."

"Where?"

He looked puzzled. "Where?"

"Where did you recruit them from?"

Vincenzo looked to Billy as if for understanding—or perhaps for permission.

"Maybe I have it wrong," I said. "Is Billy actually in charge, or are you?" I looked at Billy.

"It's sort of both," said Billy, holding out his hands. Vincenzo is in charge of this area for the family. My father gives him complete control and has absolute confidence in his abilities."

I nodded. "But you ... what ... outrank him?"

"Yeah," said Billy. "I guess you could say that. Vincenzo here is a *made man*. Sort of like he was adopted into the family. But I'm blood. I was *born* into the family. There's a cultural difference. Vincenzo knows the area and the contacts, so he's in charge of operations. Me, I follow his orders because he knows more than me when we're here."

"But if push came to shove, you could disregard his orders and make him do what you want, right? Because you're Carlino blood, and he's not?"

Billy looked a little embarrassed.

"Yeah, sure, that could happen. But it won't. Vincenzo's a good man. He knows what he's doing."

I looked at Vincenzo again. "So, where did you get them?"

Vincenzo stepped back to me, measuring. Finally, he nodded as if coming to a decision about me.

"These men are part of a special unit that Don Nickolas keeps at the ready."

"For occasions like this?" I asked, smiling.

"For occasions like this," he said, smiling a little himself.

"And what if we need more?" I asked.

"More men like this?" He looked over at his soldiers. "They are the best in the world at what they do. You will not need more."

"But what if we do? Can you get more? Fast?"

Vincenzo looked back at Billy, questioning. Billy shrugged, not knowing where I was going with this.

"I can get others," he said.

"Like these?" I asked.

"No. These are the best, but others."

"From where?"

I could tell he was starting to get exasperated.

"We have men scattered about. Some in the German army, some in the American armed forces, others, civilians in different occupations. If I need them, I can get them."

I let the smile go.

"Fast?"

He looked into me, recognizing my seriousness.

"Yes, fast."

"And how about equipment? Can you get that fast too?"

"I told you already," he said. "I have contacts."

"Then start getting them ready," I said. "Whoever organized all this, on the other side, is smart, efficient, and has access to a lot of resources. They kidnapped a former Mafia boss, which, I would think, takes a lot of courage and confidence. They murdered his security guards and cut off his finger to show their commitment. Then they smuggled him out of a country that he supposedly owns to a country that he doesn't. And you guys still don't even know who did it."

I was being hard, but I felt it necessary to let them know exactly where we stood. It was time to organize, to set the rules. Because once the fighting started, there would be no time. I've seen enough combat and led enough men to know that anything with more than one head is a monster, and monsters cost people their lives.

In combat, there must be one clear voice that everyone answers to.

I bore down on Vincenzo.

"I figure you for the real-life gangster version of *Pulp Fiction's* Winston Wolfe, *the Fixer*, played beautifully by Harvey Keitel, by the way, so I figure you gotta be good at what you do, but just how good I don't know."

I tossed a thumb back at the guys he brought me. "Now, you bring me a handful of, *supposedly*, the world's finest soldiers, *no offense*," I said, holding up a hand toward the guys, "to search an entire country. Again, no offense meant, but we have no idea just who or how many we might be going up against. So, yes. I want you to get your contacts ready and waiting at a moment's notice. Because when the caca hits the fan, things will be moving fast. And if *you* aren't ready, all of us, and Anthony Carlino too, could end up dead. That's why you need to understand that it's really *me* that is in charge. I'm not blood, or Mafia or a fixer, or one of you, but from this moment on, everyone will take their orders from me. Do we all have that straight?"

Vincenzo started to look at Billy again.

"No," I said, and there was steel in my voice, "don't look at him. He's not in charge. Don't make me tell you again. Look at me. I'm the man you answer to. Do you understand?"

He didn't like it, being spoken to like this, I could tell. Truth is, I didn't like *having* to talk to him this way. But they had to take me seriously, and there was no time to play games.

"I understand," he said, his voice monotone.

"I want you to think outside the box on this. We're working on the turf that *they* picked. That gives them an advantage right off the bat. I don't like that, so it's up to you to shift the advantage to our side. I don't want to just *level* the playing field—I want *everything* tilted in our favor. Hit the *military bases* you were talking about. Get men and equipment set up for us. Think Neo in *The Matrix* when all the guns come sliding up magically to him in the training room. If I call for reinforcements, I want them *stat*."

"Guns," said Vincenzo. "You want me to have extra guns on standby." He laughed. "I already have plenty of guns in the trunks of your cars."

"Good," I said, "nice start. Whatever you got ... *I want more*. And like I said before, I want you to think outside the box. Guns, rockets, planes, whatever it might take. Get it ready."

Vincenzo shook his head, looked at me, then nodded, holding up his hands. "Okay, you're the boss." He actually grinned.

I stuck out my hand, and we shook. He walked away without talking to Billy and got into his car.

Progress.

"Is he as good as you say?" I asked Billy.

"Better. Trust me; he'll be there if we need him."

Billy took me to the trunk of the car and opened a big duffel bag. Inside was Neo's training room.

"Wow," I said. Maybe I was too hard on him."

Billy laughed. "I told you he was good." He took out three small electronic devices and handed me one.

"Transponders," he said. "One for me, one for you, and one for my grandfather. If we get separated or need to split up, we can activate it and find each other."

"Good," I said. "See? Thinking outside the box. I like it."

Forty minutes later, we were settling into our hotel when my phone rang.

"Nice digs," said Kenny. "And that jet! High class, baby."

I looked over my shoulder and around the room to make sure he hadn't somehow followed us here.

"You have something for me, or are you just showing off?" I asked.

He laughed. "Oh Mal, don't be like that. I called to warn you that the bad guys are everywhere and to keep a close watch."

"Have you found him for me?"

"Carlino? No, but I'm sending you what I've got on the cars and all the possible routes from their last location. I think they went off-grid."

"Off-grid? What does that mean?"

"They haven't shown up on any camera feeds since I lost sight of them. So, I think they may have taken the rural route, going into small communities or maybe up into the mountains. I worked out an algorithm to search cell phones in those areas. You never know; a tourist, or even a local, may have caught a glimpse while recording something else. You'd be amazed at what gets caught in the periphery of your phone's picture range."

"You can do that?" I asked, getting that creepy feeling again.

"I can do anything, Mal. I'm Mr. Universe. The tricky part is going through all the data and separating the useful stuff from the dross.

But that's the genius part of my algorithm. It's a lot of data, but I'll pick them up somewhere. Like I said before, nothing can ..."

"I know ...," I broke in, "... hide from the Wave."

I heard him smile over the phone. "You are learning little padawan. I'll be in touch."

I called Sarah Gallagher. She was staying at my place taking care of Pilgrim for me. I'd called before I left for the airport.

"Ah, Gil," she purred into the phone. "There you are in exotic Germany while you leave me here to pine."

"As if," I said. "Sorry to leave you there alone."

"Oh, I'm not alone," she said. "I have my love buddy here, lying in my lap as we speak. I'm feeding him string cheese while I sip on wine and enjoy the fireplace with him."

"Always goofing off," I said. "Did you get any work done on the finger?"

"Well, I checked the DNA samples against the ones your Mafia friend supplied, and they were a hundred percent match. I ran the fingerprint through AFIS, and it came back to one Anthony Carlino, same age, DOB, and physical description you gave me. The wound, condition of the tissue, and blood coagulation suggest he was alive at the time of amputation. There were metal fragments and pressure marks at the site of the wound, indicating a snipping tool—pruning scissors, or maybe wire cutters. I found dirt— *fine* dirt—*planting soil,* to be exact, under the nail that traces back to Italy. I'm doing some more advanced tests to see what region, but they won't be ready until tomorrow afternoon. I'm guessing it's going to be to a vineyard or something equally Italian. The ring is standard gold, with an inscription that I was finally able to raise. It says, *Eternal love, Bella,* which checks out as being his deceased wife's name. I also located two other DNA signatures. Not much, but I'm growing the cell numbers so I can get a good sequencing. That also should be ready sometime tomorrow; then, I'll run them through CODIS and see if we get a match. Other than that—nothing."

"Like I thought," I said. "Goofing off."

"If I was going to goof off, Gil, I'd do it with you."

"What would Pilgrim say?"

"He'd understand," she said, her voice whispering like silk sheets. "He's very sharing—unlike me. You stay away from those Oktoberfest barmaids."

"It isn't October," I said.

"I've seen the commercials; it's always October in Germany."

"Put the phone to Pilgrim's ear," I said.

She said, "Okay, it's there."

"You take care of her, boy."

Pilgrim gave a little *woof*.

"I'm back," she said. "Put the phone to Max's ear."

I looked over at Max, lying on my bed ... watching.

"I don't think that's a good idea," I said.

Sarah laughed. "Then *you* take care of you."

"I will."

"You better."

When we were done, I turned and looked at Max again. "She doesn't even like you."

He just stared.

There was a knock on the door. It was Billy.

"Ready?" he asked.

"For?"

He gave me exasperated. "To get to work."

"I've *been* working," I said. "Now, I'd like a shower and a bite to eat."

"Ain't nobody got time for that," he said, doing a pretty good imitation of the internet lady that had coined the phrase. "If you've been working, what did you find out?"

I gave him a quick rundown on what I'd learned from Kenny and Sarah.

"What did the universe guy mean when he said there were bad guys everywhere?"

"Well, he *could* be talking about you and your friends," I said.

"Funny."

"I don't know what he meant; I should have had him clarify," I said, now wondering myself. Billy was actually pretty sharp. I looked up at the ceiling, spread my arms out, and said, "Mr. Universe, what did you mean?" I slowly circled, my arms still out, half expecting him to answer.

"What are you doing?" asked Billy, looking like he thought I was crazy. "You look like a crazy man."

I dropped my arms. "Yeah," I said to the ether, "that's what I thought; it's all a trick." Only I wasn't sure I was convinced.

"Is this another lesson?" asked Billy. "Like that Bible thing? Or the cutting board?"

"No," I said, "it's ... it's like his shtick ... his gimmick. He's always listening, always watching, or he pretends to be ... it's ...," I saw the way Billy was looking at me and waved a hand at him. "Forget it. I'm taking a quick shower. You get some food ordered up here. After that, we'll head to the boat dock where they landed with your grandfather."

"Why there?" he asked. "We watched the videos your universe guy sent. What could we get there? They took him off their boat, stuck him in the trunk of the car, and took off. Shouldn't we start where the cameras lost them?"

I pulled off my shirt, tossed my Smith & Wesson 4506 onto the bed next to Max, stretched, and headed for the shower. "Cameras don't catch everything. People ... people catch things. I want to talk to anyone that was there." I looked over at Max; he hadn't even flinched when the gun landed by him. "You can stay here with Max if you want. Otherwise, call me when the food gets here."

Billy looked at Max. Max looked back at him. Billy left the room.

Like I said, Billy was actually pretty sharp.

16

She watched the men inside her house from the relative safety of the barn. She was cold and hungry, and she'd walked the mountain for hours before realizing she wasn't going to be able to make it to town before she froze or before the men or the wolf got her. And so, she changed course and headed back to her home. She thought she might be able to hide from the men there. She knew every hiding place, and there was food—the chickens' eggs, the goats' milk. She thought the wolf would be too afraid to come for her there. And if he did, maybe one of the men would shoot it. Like the man had shot her father.

Irmgard fought back the tears. It was hard ... even painful, but she was getting better at it.

She counted eleven men at her house and more out on the mountain. Her father's binoculars were on his workbench in the barn, and with them, she could see pretty well through the windows. Irmgard kept the windows clean; it was one of her weekly chores. There were also knotholes in the old wood walls that she could watch through when men got close. One of the men she saw was the man who killed her father, and another was the man they'd taken from the trunk of the car.

The chicken coop was a good sprint toward the house and away from the mountain. The eggs would be waiting for her, but she was afraid to collect them yet, even though it was already later in the afternoon. There wasn't much to hide behind or under. The goat pen was closer, but still, there was an open space before she could reach it.

The man from the car was tied to a chair and had a black hood over his face. He sat in the kitchen, by the table where she had refused to eat her peas.

Her father's body had been moved, and though she searched with the binoculars, she couldn't see where they had put him. She thought she might have to wait until night to go to the chickens and the goats. But she was so hungry, and the goats' udders would be swollen and painful for them.

Groups of men, three and four at a time, had come and gone all day—probably looking for her. One group had come back with an injured man. Blood soaked his clothes, and he could only stand with the other two supporting him. Both of those men kept looking about with their eyes, holding their rifles in a one-handed ready position, as though they were afraid they were about to be attacked.

Irmgard smiled. It must be the wolf.

She was afraid of the wolf, but so were the men. And that made her smile.

The workbench held an assortment of tools, and Irmgard found a rusty pocketknife in one of the cubbies. Dust, webs, and mouse droppings filled the cubby, but she ignored them and dug out the knife. If the men or the wolf tried to grab her, she would stab them or cut them. She'd sliced her thumb once on a kitchen knife, back before her mother had gotten sick, and it bled badly. Her mother had washed it and dabbed some ointment over it before tenderly wrapping her finger in white gauze. It had hurt so much. Even after the cleaning and bandaging, it throbbed like a hot ball of poison under her skin. The thought of hurting the men who'd killed her father felt good.

But the men were so big, and she was just little.

She wanted to be brave—like the princess in the movie who could make cold and snow and ice. She wished she could make a giant snowman that would fight for her, but all she had was this rusty old knife. Her mother was dead, and so was her father. The men wanted her, and so did the wolf. She didn't know what to do.

Irmgard wanted to be strong, but she was only a skinny, eight-year-old girl. She was tired and hungry and scared.

Looking around the barn, she saw her father's old truck. Irmgard didn't know where the keys were. And she didn't know how to drive.

Back at the workbench, she found other tools: a hammer, a wrench, some pliers, things she didn't know. Under the bench were old boxes. One of them had a couple of sticks of dynamite that her father had used to blow out tree trunks after he cut them down. Irmgard thought about throwing them at the house and blowing the men up, but she didn't know how the dynamite worked, and she couldn't throw very far. She was much better at running. Besides, she didn't want her house to be blown up.

She sat by the window and watched the men in the warm house that used to be hers. And though she tried not to, she cried.

ANTHONY CARLINO WAS TIED to a chair in the kitchen. His finger ached—so did his ribs and his face where the men had punched and kicked him—but his finger most of all.

He knew he was in a kitchen because he could see bits here and there from the bottom of the hood that covered his head and face. More than that, he knew because of the smells. After decades of cooking, the remnants of spices, savory meals, and the crusts on frying pans had soaked into the wood, leaving the unmistakable aroma of a well-loved kitchen.

Bella had been a wonderful cook.

The gag in his mouth—an old rag shoved in deep and tied with a bandana—made his mouth dry and threatened his gag reflex. His will alone kept him from choking. He wouldn't give them the satisfaction.

His hands and feet were zip-tied to the legs of the chair. If they had used handcuffs or zip-tied him in the front, he could have gotten free in seconds. But they knew what they were doing. Or at least their leader did. And sometimes, that was all it took—a good leader.

Anthony stretched as far as he could with his fingers, feeling for a weakness in the chair or the zip-tie itself.

There was always a way to escape.

Anthony had been in some tight scrapes, mostly in his youth, of course, before he became a *made man* and long before he was crowned as Boss. But he had always escaped, and more, he'd always gotten revenge. This would be no different. Well, that wasn't exactly true, he thought, as his hands and fingers played their searching game. What he would do to the men that had cost him his finger and his ring would be far worse than anything he had ever before done to another human being.

The darkness of the hood and the stifling gag in his mouth were hard to endure. It felt like he was simultaneously drowning and choking. A lesser man might gag and throw up, but that could mean asphyxiating on his own vomit, and again, that was a satisfaction he would not allow them.

When this was all said and done, they would be the ones choking ... on their own blood.

Anthony allowed his thoughts to go to the one man in all the world he truly admired. *Chuck Norris*. The actor was far more than an actor. He was the real deal. A true martial arts expert. Maybe the best, in his prime, the world had ever known.

The memes were no accident. They were pale reflections of the truth.

Chuck Norris hit 11 out of 10 targets with nine bullets.
Chuck Norris built the hospital he was born in.
Guns carry Chuck Norris for protection.
Chuck Norris doesn't turn on the shower; he stares at it till it cries.

When Chuck Norris left for college, he told his father, you're the man of the house now.

Chuck Norris once fought Superman; the loser had to wear his underwear on the outside.

Chuck Norris threw a hand grenade and killed fifty people, then it exploded.

Chuck Norris doesn't dial the wrong number; you answered the wrong phone.

Anthony remembered the movie where Bruce Lee and Chuck Norris fought, *The Way of the Dragon*. In that movie, Bruce Lee wins. To Anthony, that pretty much summed up Hollyweird.

Phony.

In tough times, Anthony would often ask himself, *What would Chuck Norris do?* And when he came up with it, it always worked.

Anthony asked himself the question now, and almost immediately, the answer came to him.

He would have to forgo his pride, but that was okay because it would only be a ruse, a trap.

Anthony started to cough, to choke, to shake, and to moan. He acted like he couldn't breathe. Anthony was no great actor, not like Chuck Norris, but he did pretty well. Good enough that someone yelled, in German, of course, that their captive was dying. They had to get the hood off and the gag out because they couldn't afford for him to die on them—not yet anyway.

And then hands were grabbing for him. The hood was wrenched off, the bandanna jerked away, and the gag pulled free.

He sat looking at them. Three men, tough, big, and uncaring. But then their boss entered the room. He knew he was the boss by his bearing and by his voice. He'd heard the voice and seen the man the night before, standing by the man he'd just killed. He also knew he was the boss by the way he stared down at him. This man was the only one to show any fear. Anthony knew the man felt fear because only he understood the consequences of allowing Anthony to die before he was supposed to.

Shoving the men aside, he checked to make sure Anthony was breathing, then looked back at them.

"Fools," he said. "Shoving the gag in like that could have killed him!"

One of the men shrugged and said, "You didn't say how to gag him; you just said to keep him shut up."

The leader shoved a gun into the man's mouth.

"I didn't tell you not to put a gun in his mouth to shut him up either, but you didn't think of doing that, did you? Why not?" He backed the man against the wall, the gun grinding deeper. "Well, why?"

The man tried to garble out an answer, but it was impossible to make out.

"That's right," said the leader, "because it might kill him. And what happens if he dies? Well?"

The gun dug in. The man screamed.

"We don't get paid, and we all die, that's what. Do you want to not get paid? Do you want to die?"

The leader ripped the gun free of the man's mouth, teeth chipping against the metal.

He strode over to Anthony, who did his best to look old, haggard, spent. The leader gripped his chin and forced his face up.

"Can you hear me, old man?"

Anthony acted as if he did not comprehend his words.

"No ... non comprende..." he stuttered.

The leader of the men looked down at him with contempt, turning his face this way and that. Finally, he let him go, disgusted.

Anthony Carlino noted that the man had grabbed his chin with a lopsided grip, and he remembered the missing thumb and first two fingers.

The leader spoke again, this time in Italian.

"If I leave the gag out, will you keep your mouth shut?"

"Yes, yes," said Anthony, acting exhausted and coughing weakly.

"Understand, if you start talking, to anyone, for any reason, the gag goes back in. And this time, I'll have them use your underwear.

You understand? Speak only when spoken to, like a child, and then only to answer. Nothing else. If you yell or scream or try to turn my men against me, I'll break out your teeth."

Anthony nodded, and the leader turned his back on him. He didn't catch the look in Anthony's eyes. Anthony had done well in feigning exhaustion and acting as though he'd been choking, but he was not a good enough actor to hide what was behind his eyes.

Still, he had achieved much. They left the gag out, the hood off, and he learned something that would be useful sooner or later—the deformity of the leader's left hand.

Such a man would be easy to find.

17

The port was small, with only a few docks dotting the beach and a single shack at the top of a sizable area that had been plowed flat for parking. The beach itself was littered with fist-sized rocks and shells and thick, rubbery clumps of seaweed along with the occasional crushed plastic cup and scrap of water-logged paper.

I had the Mafia boys, except for Billy, stay back at the cars while we went inside the shack. Three old men sat inside around a potbellied stove, smoking pipes and playing cards. They looked like ancient versions of Popeye the Sailor Man. They had thick forearms, but their shoulders and biceps were withered, and their backs bowed as if gravity had finally won the age-old battle.

"Hi," I said in English.

The closest gave me squint eye, pipe smoke dancing a murky waltz past his toothless gums. He turned back to his crewmates.

"American," he said. And they all chortled quietly.

I let it go.

"Do you speak English?" I tried.

Squint Eye played a card.

"Do you?" he responded, without turning back to me. The other two completely ignored my presence. "Because it doesn't sound anything like English to me." He took another card, slapped it down, and sat back. He adjusted his pipe with one hand, settling the stem against the pulp of his gums. "Not English. Maybe it's that Spanglish I heard tell of a few years back. Is that your language, Spanglish?"

"No," I said. "You were right the first time. American."

He took a couple of puffs on the pipe.

"What is it you want, American?"

I showed him the photos I'd had printed from the videos Mr. Universe sent me of the cars and the men.

"Did you deal with these men yesterday or the day before?"

Old Squint didn't even glance at the pictures.

"You some kind of cop? Landespolizei."

He puffed on the pipe. The odor was not pleasing like some pipe tobacco. This smelled old and tough and cloying ... as wrinkled as he was.

I looked back at Billy. He stood by the counter next to the door, nonchalant like, waiting to see how I played it.

"No, I'm a private investigator."

The squinted eye opened wide with the other one. His two companions gave me their attention as well.

"Private investigator?" He wagged a thick finger at me. "Like Magnum PI?" He turned to his friends and hooked a thumb at me. "Magnum PI," he said. They both stared at me. Squint Eye turned back. "You don't look like him." He gave me the once over. "*Tom Selleck.* You don't look like him." He turned to his mates. "Doesn't look like him."

"Not as tall," said one of the men.

"No mustache," said the other.

"More stocky," said Squint Eye.

"Where's your Ferrari?" asked the first man.

"And the women in bikinis," said the other.

Squint Eye head checked Billy. "He don't look like Higgins."

"Doesn't look like TC either," said the first man. "TC's black. He's not black."

"Where's his helicopter?" Asked the second man.

"I'm not Tom Selleck," I said. "But I am a private investigator." I flipped out my badge and let them all examine it. They smoked their pipes while they passed my badge and wallet, the card game momentarily set aside.

Squint Eye handed it back to me.

"Tom Selleck's better looking. Probably why he gets the girls in bikinis."

Couldn't argue with that.

I held the pictures out to him again.

"Did you see them?"

This time he took them and gave them a once over before handing them to the next man down the line.

"Ja," he said. "I seen them dock and get in their cars and drive away." He stood and went to the window. I followed.

He pointed toward the farthest dock. "One of the cars backed down close to the dock there. They waited till everyone else got off, then two men carried something off the boat and to the trunk of the car. I couldn't tell what it was because it was covered up. A blanket, maybe a big rug."

"Did they come in?" I asked. "Get directions, ask about food, gas, or lodging? Use the restroom?"

Squint Eye squinted the one eye even harder, smiling and pointing the stem of his pipe at me.

"You ask questions like Magnum," he said. "But nein, none of them came inside. They met the men in the cars, put whatever it was in the trunk, and drove off."

"Did you recognize any of the men?"

He shook his head.

"Anything stand out about any of the men?"

"Stand out?" he asked. And then his squint un-squinted again. "Oh ... you mean the hand?" He looked back at his friends. "He means the hand." Both of the old men around the stove nodded like they knew it all along.

"What about the hand?" I asked.

"The man with the fingers," he said. "*Two*, only two fingers on the one hand. Is that what you mean?"

And then it hit me like a coconut falling from a Hawaiian palm tree. The last time I had been to Germany was when I found Max. Max was being held by a criminal type that ran a dogfighting ring. He seemed like small potatoes to me back then, but maybe he'd moved up in the criminal ranks. The room almost tilted as I realized I wasn't that far from where I rescued Max from them. And the one outstanding feature of the man I had rescued Max from was that he had only two fingers on his left hand.

I learned later that Max had eaten the other three.

Wow, Magnum PI would be proud.

MAX WAITED IN THE CAR, smelling the air.

The Alpha came out of the shack and got into the car along with Billy.

Billy drove while the Alpha instructed. They took winding paths that led up and up, the woods growing thicker on either side and the air growing thin. Minutes turned into hours, but with each kilometer, Max grew more excited.

It all felt so wonderfully familiar.

The air, the scents, the taste.

Max knew where he was.

He was home.

And the Great Gray Wolf was close.

Max would have his revenge, and neither the man sitting in the car next to the Alpha nor the Alpha himself would stop him.

18

T he wolf had become the hunted. *It wasn't the first time.* Over the years, he had learned there were two ways to handle being hunted. He could run, move to another territory, stake a new claim. Or he could turn on his attackers, making the hunters the *hunted.* It would be easy to run—safer. And it was the course he usually took when humans came for him. But …

He wanted the girl.

He had claimed her.

Only once before had any creature that he had claimed escaped him. The bear and the man had interfered, robbing him of his prey. He had searched for the dog for days after—the dog and the man. But they were gone. Later, the wolf had found the bear. Its leg was broken, and it had been shot and killed by the man. But it was good food, and he ate well, staying close, hoping they would return. But they did not return.

And so, the wolf had moved on. But he didn't forget. He had their scent, and if they ever came back, he would kill them both.

He detected the girl's scent.

She was close—down where he had killed the sheep and where

the men that hunted him now denned. And so, he stayed, hunting the hunters.

They were easy prey. Slow, clumsy, *loud*. But they were pack animals. They hunted together, which was always dangerous for the solitary hunter. And they had weapons that could kill from far away.

The wolf, of course, had no concept of guns or bullets. But he understood the effect and danger of man's weapons. He did not fear them—*he feared nothing*—but he respected the danger.

The humans were easy to track. To track and to *backtrack*. He had killed some of them—*injured more*. He would lead them on for a way, then circle and come at them from the side or behind, picking off the stragglers with a quick attack before retreating. Once he blooded them, they became careful, less confident, scared.

As well they should be.

Like the party of five that hunted him now.

At first, the wolf had left an easy trail for them, using deer trails and purposefully stepping in soft dirt and leaves. But then, once they were following, he made it steadily more difficult, taking them through trees and up over rocks and foliage, winding around the mountain into the higher altitude. The men were quickly winded and fatigued, hunching over, sometimes using all fours, to continue the climb.

He had skirted to the side from up high, dropped down and around, and now lay by a large outcropping of rocks as the staggering line made its way past him, following his tracks. There were still patches of snow, as well as wet, dead leaves and spots of dirt. Leaving track was easy but it was just as easy to not leave track when he so chose.

The fifth man in the line was fat. He used his rifle as a walking stick to help make it up the mountain. He huffed and puffed, sweat shining his face.

He was not scared—no adrenal dump, just tired.

That was about to change.

The wolf walked up behind him, within an arm's reach. He stopped when the man stopped. The man leaned against his rifle—

breathing hard— his eyes closed—he stretched his head back trying to take in air. The wolf waited—eyes locked on the exposed throat. The man's head slowly turned—sensing something—*death*—he saw the wolf—stared into the monster's eyes—sucked in a breath to scream ...

And the wolf lunged, engulfing the man's face in his massive jaws.

The man tried to scream.

The wolf crushed in, imploding the bones of the man's jaws and cheeks, shattering teeth, puncturing tender meat and nerves. It dragged the flailing man away, his hands trying fruitlessly to push against the agony, his legs limp and useless, his fat weight hardly hindering the wolf as he trotted away to the trees and rocks. And once hidden, he finished the job—swiftly—but not too swiftly.

The men had now noticed their companion was missing and were looking for him. The wolf came out from the trees and went high above them before circling back. Now the first in line would be last. This would be the strongest of their pack. The wolf watched as the man pointed his gun this way and that, never coming close to his position. After a short time, the man lowered his weapon and continued his search down the mountain.

The wolf walked up behind him, waiting for him to stop.

IRMGARD HAD STOPPED CRYING. From her hiding place in the barn, she had witnessed the men running into the kitchen and pulling the hood off the man in the chair. She watched as the men argued and saw the man that had killed her father put a gun in another man's mouth. She was too far away to make out what they were saying, but she caught the yells and cries of pain. When they were done, they left the hood off of the man in the chair.

The sun was getting low in the sky, making the shadows grow and the yard and pens dull and dark. The light in the kitchen glowed, and she could still see the man in the chair sitting there.

No one had come down from the mountain in over an hour. She

wondered about the last group. If they stayed out there, in the dark of night with the wolf, she didn't think they would ever be coming back.

Good.

Irmgard decided it was time to try for the eggs. She sneaked out of the barn, careful to open the door just enough to slip through. She ducked low and ran for the coop. The chickens hardly rustled as she entered—they were used to her. She grabbed the basket she had used for years to gather eggs, scooped out five from under the hens, and placed them in the basket. She left the coop and started for the barn when two men came stumbling down the path from the mountain. They were screaming, clearly terrified. In response, two men from the house burst out the front door, and two sentries left their good hiding places.

Irmgard had not seen nor had she known the men were there until they converged on the screaming men. Her only choice was to duck, run to the side of the house, and lay in the dirt to hide.

The men pointed back up the mountain, their voices echoing, but she could not understand them. The man that had killed her father, the one with only two fingers on one hand, came out of the house and went to the group of men. The two that had made it back collapsed now that they felt safe.

The two-fingered man hauled one of the men to his feet and punched him. Everyone was quiet then, and the man talked to the two-fingered man, pointing back the way they had come. Halfway through his explanation, he started crying and blubbering. The two-fingered man hit him again to make him stop so he could finish the story.

Irmgard didn't know what he was saying, but she was pretty sure it was about the wolf. That made her happy. She hoped he would kill them all—especially the man with two fingers.

When the man finished talking, the two-fingered man gave orders and the house practically emptied. A big group of men, including the crying man, started up the mountain, wearing heavy coats, and carrying rifles and flashlights.

The man with two fingers and three men went back into the

house, and the once hidden sentries went back to being invisible. But now, Irmgard knew about them. They would never be invisible *to her* again.

She let a little time pass—let everything go quiet. Then she stood, still crouching, and stepped away from the wall. She heard a strange sound, glanced toward the kitchen and its light, and stared right into the eyes of the man tied to the chair.

Terror stopped her heart and her breathing.

She was caught.

The man looked at her, then he winked and bumped his chin toward the barn, telling her to go.

Irmgard ran, staying low, and made it to safety. She grabbed the binoculars and peered into the window. The man was looking straight at her, as though he could see into her eyes even though there was no light in the barn behind her. He winked again, smiled, and turned away.

ANTHONY CARLINO SAW the girl as she entered the chicken coop, but she didn't see him.

About a minute later, she slipped back out and started for the barn. Suddenly there was yelling, shouting, and men running about.

At first, he thought the commotion was because someone had spotted her, but then he understood that it was hunters, who had probably been looking for the girl, coming back from the mountain. He saw her change direction, come up alongside the wall directly beneath him, and then he lost sight of her. As he continued to watch for her, he saw a growing group of men gather around the hunters. After everything played out with the men, Anthony waited. And sure enough, the girl rose and started for the barn.

Anthony made the quietest of "tic-tic-tic" sounds, stopping her instantly. She looked at him, and he saw her fear. He winked at her and indicated she should continue to the barn.

She did.

And she made it safely.

He quickly realized that she must be the daughter of the man killed the night he arrived. And what little child didn't know every nook and cranny and hiding place of their home?

Anthony lost sight of the girl once she went into the barn, but he was fairly certain she could still see him.

And she would be watching.

He winked again, smiled, and turned away. It wouldn't do to draw attention to her.

The little girl might well prove to be useful.

It was like in the movie, *The Princess Bride*, when Wesley, still paralyzed from being *mostly* dead, asks for an inventory of their assets, and the wheelbarrow is momentarily left out.

Anthony Carlino never left assets out of his tabulations.

The little girl had just become an asset.

19

Two Fingers gave the men their orders then went back into the house. As he entered the kitchen he scrutinized the hostage. The man was old, but Two Fingers wasn't fooled by his act. No one remained godfather of the Mafia for decades without earning it. The man was dangerous. And so, as he walked by, he took note that Carlino's hands, legs, and feet were still tied to the chair.

Opening the refrigerator, he took out a bottle of beer, popped the cap, and took a long drink. He shook his head and blew a stream of air toward the ceiling. While taking another drink, he pulled a chair out from the table, tossed a leg over the seat so that he was sitting on it backward, and looked at the old man. Two Fingers studied him for a few seconds. The old man didn't speak, just blankly looked back. Two Fingers held up the bottle—an invitation. The old man nodded, and Two Fingers held the bottle to the old man's lips, turning it slightly upwards so he could drink.

"For now, you can talk," said Two Fingers.

"Thank you," said the old man. "For the beer too."

Two Fingers nodded, taking another drink himself.

"You know who I am?" asked the old man.

A small smile played at the corner of Two Finger's lips.

"I know," he said.

"Then you know your danger."

Two Fingers smirked, took another sip of the beer.

"*Life* is dangerous," he said. Two Fingers looked around the chair toward Anthony Carlino's hand. "Your finger, that wasn't me."

"I know," said Anthony. "And that's why I *may* let you live."

Two Finger's eyebrows rose, as did his grin.

"May? Very generous of you."

"Yes," said Anthony, "but not just you. You, your family, your extended family, their families, your friends, your acquaintances, your favorite elementary school teacher, your pets. Anyone and anything that ever meant anything to you your entire life. I *may* let you, and them, live." Anthony looked hard into Two Finger's eyes.

Two Fingers pursed his lips, took another drink.

"That may well be the scariest threat I have ever heard. I see why I was warned not to talk to you."

"But you *are* talking to me," said Anthony, "which means you must be interested. So, let me finish because there's more. Whatever they are paying you, I will triple."

Two Fingers took another drink, then rested his chin on the back of the chair, tapping the bottle against the wood.

"The men that hired me are very dangerous," he said.

"No," said Anthony. "I am very dangerous. Besides, a wise man once told me that life itself is dangerous. And triple makes the danger three times worth the risk."

An echo of gunshots far up the mountain rolled down over them. Two Fingers looked out the window and sighed, shaking his head.

"Fools," he said. "They are probably shooting at each other." He looked back at Anthony. "Good help is hard to find. Did you have the same trouble when you ran things?"

Anthony thought back to his bodyguards at the villa. They had been good men, but still, they died. Being good wasn't always enough.

"No. I've always had an eye for talent, and as the boss, I choose who I want to choose. That's why I'm talking to *you* and not the lackeys working for you."

Two Fingers took another drink, and then he held the bottle to Anthony's lips again. Anthony drank.

"I will think it over," said Two Fingers. "In the meantime, do not try to escape." He gave a brief whistle, and instantly a powerful looking dog padded into the room and sat next to him. "This is Odin, the greatest fighting dog the world has ever known. He has killed every breed of dog there is, and he would make quick work of you. So, be patient, let me consider. Do not try and turn any of my men. Do we understand one another?"

Anthony nodded. He did not like the look of the animal. Scars crossed his muzzle, chest, and shoulders, and something about the way he stared told more about him than the scars. He pulled his eyes from the creature and looked back at Two Fingers' marred hand.

"Did he do that to you?"

Two Fingers raised his hand, turned it this way and that.

"No," he said, "not Odin." He thought of the mangy monster that had ravaged his flesh, changing him forever. The dog and the American. One day he would meet them again.

Anthony saw the change in expression, cataloging it for future use. A possible weak spot. And weak spots could be leveraged.

"Thanks for the beer," he said.

Two Fingers stood, nodded, and left the room. The monster dog stayed for a second, staring at Anthony, then he too stood and followed his master.

20

I checked my cool new Swiss compass against a paper map and the car's GPS as we drove to the loose set of buildings where Max had been caged and forced to fight other dogs in the ring of death.

We were in the mountainous territory of the legendary Black Forest, backyard to the Brothers Grimm fairy tales.

I made a call to Vincenzo and another to Kenny, giving them both a detailed description of the layout, my best recollection of where the dogfighting site had been located, and what they needed to be able to find exact coordinates.

The compass beat the GPS by two-tenths of a degree.

Gotta love the Swiss.

As we pulled into the lot, I noticed Max sit up in the seat and look out the window. There had been a subtle change in his demeanor as we began the upward climb into the mountainous regions. He seemed almost ... *anxious.*

Billy stopped the car, and our pack of bodyguards pulled up behind us. I got out and opened the door for Max. He hopped down and sat, looking at the buildings as if they were an enemy.

In a way, I guess they were.

I noticed a quiver in his right hind leg ... something I'd seen in a lot of Mals before, but never in him. I gave him the stay command and walked up to the main house with Billy and the other men.

It was almost dark, and there were lights on inside.

The last time I'd seen the place, it was on fire, *a fire that I may or may not have started*, and Max and I were fighting his captors to get out alive.

The door opened before I could knock, and an old man with gray hair, glasses, and stooped shoulders smiled out at me. The smile faltered a bit when he saw the cadre of camo-suited soldier types bracing me. He said something in German that sounded like he was asking if he could help me.

Billy said, "He's asking if he can help us?"

I said, "Ask him if he owns the place."

"Ask me yourself," said the old man. "I speak English." He looked around at all of us again. "What do you gentlemen want?" I saw him look to the side of the door and thought he probably had a weapon leaning there. A weapon he probably wished he'd picked up before answering the door. I bladed my body so that I could more easily intercept if he decided to make a play.

"Do you own the place?" I asked again.

"I heard you the first time," he said. "Why are you asking?" He glanced again at the inside of the doorjamb. I was guessing a shotgun, considering the locale. You don't have to be a good shot when you have a shotgun.

Since he was getting right to the point, I decided I would too.

"I was out here a while back when the place was being used as an illegal dogfighting arena. I'm looking for the owners."

He gave us another look.

"You the police?"

"Do we look like cops?" said Billy with a bit of a sneer.

"Then I have nothing to say to you." He went to shut the door.

I stopped it with one hand.

He looked up at me, surprised, then glanced to the side of the door again, estimating his chances.

I wasn't in the mood for games, and I hate dogfighting and anything or anyone associated with it. I remembered Max's condition when I found him here. I dropped my veneer of civility and let him see my eyes ... my real eyes ... the eyes that had witnessed the murder of my wife and daughter ... my dog eyes.

The old man turned pale, and for a second, I thought he was going to go for the gun. But then, what he saw in my eyes took its full effect, and he cowered back.

"Have them check the barn," I said to Billy. "See if they're still using it for dogfighting."

Billy sent two of his men to check.

"You ... you can't just ...," started the old man, but the words choked in his throat at my expression.

"Max, *here*," I said.

Max was instantly at my side. *He wasn't—and then he was—like teleportation.* The old man took a step back, terror gripping him.

"*Odin*," he stammered. "How ... how did you get Odin?"

He looked toward his weapon again, and this time I thought he might go for it.

"If you reach for the shotgun," I said, "Max here will rip out your heart."

The old man glanced from the gun to Max then back to me.

"It'll hurt," I said. "The whole time you're dying, it'll hurt."

He looked back at Max. Max looked back, stoic.

The old man shook his head and held up his hands in surrender.

"No, no. Do what you want."

Billy's men came back and spoke with him.

"Yup," said Billy. "Still set up for dogfighting."

"They sure?" I asked.

Billy gave me exasperated.

"Two things my guys know," he said, "blood sports and gambling."

I looked at the old man.

He started to shake.

"I just take care of the place. That's all."

I pushed the door the rest of the way open and stepped in, the old man giving way. Next to the doorjamb rested an over-under shotgun. The barrel looked like it was a mile long and the gun itself a hundred years old, but it would still get the job done.

"Anyone else here?" I asked.

"No," he said. "Just me."

I said to Billy, "Search it." To the old man, I said, "Kitchen."

Billy's men searched the house while Billy, the old man, Max, and I went to the kitchen to talk about things old and things new.

MAX KNEW THIS PLACE. A strange sort of terror he had never known before swept through him. The buildings were different ... the same ... and yet different. *Newer*. But the smell was the same. Blood, sweat, fear ... *death*.

Max wanted to attack that smell ... to kill it.

The big barn was in the same place. Max had almost died here. He had fought while sick, feverish, starving, and still, he won time and again—killing his own kind for *their* pleasure.

The old man came to the door, and the Alpha soon called Max to step forward to his side.

The old man smelled the same as the barn.

Max wanted to kill him.

But it was the Alpha that had saved him from this place, and so Max would wait for his command.

Max smelled fear on the old man. That was good, *wise*. Death bubbled like hot lava in Max's veins, waiting for the chance to erupt.

The old man was thinking about attacking the Alpha. Max saw it in the change of his body posture. He smelled the rising adrenal dump through his pores, heard the racing of his heart, tasted the salt of his sweat as it misted into the night.

If he moved, Max would not wait for the command. Max would rip out his throat.

Max smelled no fear from the Alpha, but the Alpha was ready —cautious.

The Alpha wanted something from the old man, but the old man was resisting. The Alpha was considering killing the old man too. Max could feel it. Yes, the old man was *wise* to fear, but maybe not wise enough.

And then the old man surrendered.

Max smelled, heard, saw, and tasted the change instantly. The fight had gone out of him. *Wise.*

But not what Max wanted.

Max followed the Alpha through the door to the kitchen while the others searched the house. Max knew there was no one else here, but he didn't care about that. He cared only that the old man might still do something that would allow Max to kill him—*him and the smell.*

But the old man did not give Max the chance, and a few hours later they got back in their cars, Max sitting in the backseat. And soon, the bad smell was lost in the distance. But there was another smell—faint—almost not there. And then it was gone. But it had been there—a scent Max would never forget.

There was no terror associated with this scent. Instead, a strange, almost peaceful sense of impending completion filled his being. A sense of life and death coming full circle.

Max was close and getting closer.

Max would find the Great Gray Wolf.

And Max would kill him.

21

Irmgard finished the eggs, eating them raw. They were gross, but she was so hungry. She checked through the cracks and knot-holes and watched as the guards hid in their places. Some of them smoked, some of them coughed, some of them spit. Others would shuffle their feet, trying to keep warm. Irmgard had not known of their presence until the two had come out of hiding and almost found her. But now that she knew they were out there, they were easy to spot. So she decided it would be safe to try for the goats and their milk. She was even more thirsty than she had been hungry. The slimy white of the eggs had done little to help quench her thirst.

She slipped out from the barn and made her way to the pen. None of the guards saw or heard her. She found the most engorged udder and suckled away on one of the teats. She'd brought a pail with her from the barn and relieved three goats of their supply. Then she scanned the landscape, plotting her way back to safety. Again, she spotted the guards without them seeing her.

But, as before, the guards were not the only hunters out on the prowl for her this night.

∼

THE WOLF WATCHED the girl leave the barn. He'd detected her scent as it drifted on the shifting currents and had followed her essence from three miles up the mountain.

He smelled the guards as well. *Six of them.* He could have taken them, one at a time, but he didn't want them—*he wanted her.* He'd claimed the girl, and he would have her. There would be time for the rest later.

These mountains were his. He'd carefully marked his territory. These men had ignored his warnings, ignored him, hunted him. And they would pay. But first, the girl.

The Wolf's mind worked in simple terms. Simple, but *cunning.* There was room for only one alpha in this territory. Anything that opposed him would die.

He slipped past the men who were supposed to keep him out, staying to the shadows, the dips in the ground, the bushes. Sometimes crawling, sometimes sprinting, until he crossed the path she had taken to get to the goats.

The hunter knows the prey, so he understood, in his primitive way, that if this was the path she took from the barn, it would be the path she would use to return.

The wolf bedded down in the dark.

Waiting.

~

TWO FINGERS CLENCHED his two remaining fingers into a simulation of a fist. He'd just gotten off the phone with Elias, the old man who watched over his gambling property.

Very interesting.

They were obviously here for Anthony Carlino.

But that wasn't the interesting part. He'd known there was the possibility that Mafia soldiers would come for him—after all—they were the *Mafia.* But he was surprised they had found him so quickly. Germany was not their territory, especially these mountains.

This added a wrinkle, and he didn't like wrinkles.

Two Fingers reached down to pet Odin who sat silently beside him. The monster dog arched his head into him.

Shots sounded in the night, breaking his attention.

That blasted wolf.

And that reminded him of the girl.

He needed to find the girl; she was a witness.

More wrinkles.

He would have the girl already, but that wolf kept getting in the way—injuring and even killing some of his men. He'd wanted to keep the hired guns to a minimum, but because of the girl and the wolf, he'd had to call in reinforcements. And now, with this new wrinkle, he'd need even more. Maybe a lot more.

He made a call. Ten more should be enough. They were lackeys, local toughs, but they would know nothing and be allowed to know nothing. Ten extra guns, bringing his force to over thirty, should easily be enough to handle the wolf, find the girl, and take care of a handful of Mafia soldiers who were out of their element.

Wrinkles.

But, with enough heat, wrinkles could be ironed.

IRMGARD WAS close to the barn when she saw him. The wolf was low in the dead grass, lying on his belly like a snake, watching her, perfectly still. The moon had given him away, revealing his gray-black fur against the dusty brown grass, but just barely, he was so still. Another ten feet, and she might have stepped on him. But there he was, blocking her path to the safety of the barn. She looked back toward the house and the pen, but there was no way she could reach either before he would overtake her. The pail of milk in her hand started to tremble.

The wolf stood.

Irmgard's breath stopped in her lungs.

"Hey! You there, stop!" The guard broke from his position and ran toward her.

The wolf was on him before he took three steps.

Irmgard *felt* the impact. Literally felt it—like a push of air filled with pain.

The wolf's one hundred and sixty pounds caught the man full in the chest, knocking him back and down to the ground. Before he could pull up his gun, the monster savaged his throat, casting blood in arcing streams that gleamed in the moon's light. The man's finger jerked back on the trigger of the small automatic weapon, firing a long burst of nine-millimeter missiles into the ground and the night.

Voices sounded from various locations ... men running toward the commotion.

The wolf turned and stared at Irmgard. He started toward her when dust and pieces of vegetation exploded all around him. Bullets chipped the hard ground, sending shrapnel in all directions. Instantly the wolf spun and ran, the earth erupting behind him as more men took aim and fired.

Irmgard saw the men, but they didn't see her. All attention was on the wolf. She wanted to run to the barn, but men were too close. Dropping the milk pail, she ran diagonally, away from the house, the barn, and away from the direction the wolf had taken. She ran as fast as her thin, eight-year-old legs could speed her along. After a while, when her lungs ached and her side felt like fire, and the echoing shouts and gunfire seemed far enough away, she stopped and hid beneath a tree, the ground thick with pine needles.

The temperature had dropped to a freezing twenty-eight degrees, but her flesh had not registered that fact due to her fear and physical exertion. She crouched under the tree, hugging her knees and breathing hard. She wanted her daddy ... her mommy. She wanted to wake up from the bad dream and just be safe with her family in her home, with no bad men or monster wolves chasing her. She cried quietly for a time and then fell asleep.

While Irmgard slept, snow began to fall, and a half hour after that, a group of five men walked past her tree in a ragged line, their guns at the ready. The man the wolf attacked had died, choking to death on his own blood, and none of them wanted to end in such a horrible way.

Rumors were starting to circulate among them. Rumors that the wolf was no wolf at all, but a *wolfman*, like in the books and movies. Rumors that would sound foolish under the light of day, with people and civilization around them. But in the dark and the cold of the mountains, alone, with the wind freezing their noses and ears and feet and souls, those rumors didn't sound so foolish

Irmgard awoke an hour before sunrise, curled up in the fetal position, shivering. The tree limbs protected her from the snow and blunted the wind and the cold, but still, her tears had frozen on her cheeks. Her toes and fingers were numb, and she could barely stand. She carefully scooted her way out from under the tree, not realizing that snow had filled the men's tracks. They had passed by her hiding place during the night, and she had no clue that they had come so close to discovering her.

Instinctively, she started walking horizontally. Not down and not up, just straight, the powdery snow giving way before her as she broke path. No plan, no direction. Just moving her body, trying to recoup some of its lost heat before it came up empty and started shutting down. Only the eggs and the little bit of milk she'd suckled from the goat kept her going—the eggs, the milk, and one thing more. Although Irmgard didn't yet know it herself, she was a fighter.

Two Fingers was furious. He'd seen the wolf himself. The beast was huge ... enormous. He'd thought to send Odin after it as it dodged bullets, but it escaped through a loose ring of twenty men who were shooting at it. He knew if he released Odin, one of his men might just see a running animal and hit him by mistake. Besides, after seeing the beast, he wasn't sure Odin could win against it.

Two Fingers looked down at his dying man and remembered the agony he felt when Max destroyed his hand. He remembered the look in the dog's eyes and the terror he felt. The helplessness.

He'd seen enough of dying men and death to know there was nothing he could do for the man beneath him, and so he put a bullet in his forehead, ending the man's pain.

Looking after the wolf, he decided it was time to take matters into his own hands. He ordered all the men to report to the front yard and sectioned them into squads of five. Two Fingers led the last group, equipped with his best men, and they all headed out. The wolf would die, and then they would find the girl. He no longer cared about taking her alive. He didn't want her as a witness.

He'd mapped everything out for the squads, each with a man in charge of the others. They would all meet at the upper meadow at nine in the morning. The *line* would force the wolf up and in until they had him trapped. Two Fingers was an old hand at catching wild dogs, and really, that's all the wolf was, a wild dog. His mind went back to the dog who ate his fingers, a familiar phantom ache throbbing where they used to live.

But even that dog had not eluded him.

The wolf was as good as dead.

22

Anthony Carlino thought his chances of *turning* the man with two fingers was maybe one in five—not the best of odds, he chuckled to himself. Anthony believed in playing the odds, so he had been working on the zip ties all night, carefully scraping them back and forth, just a little here and there, keeping the sound to a bare minimum. After the commotion with the wolf, Two Fingers was gone, having left with most of his troops.

Why did they want this stupid wolf so badly? Did it have something to do with the little girl?

Anthony had missed her when she left the barn to go for the milk, but he caught sight of her on the return trip. He'd noted the positions of the guards and was impressed that she must have done the same. He thought she was going to make it when suddenly she stopped. Anthony thought that she must have seen a guard, but then the wolf stood.

A shudder ran down Anthony's back. He hadn't seen it, and he didn't know how she had, but there it was, giant and dark, like some monster from childhood. He knew instantly that she was dead. There was no place to run, and any idea that she could save herself from this creature was nonsense. He was about to yell to distract the animal when the guard broke position and ran toward the girl.

What happened next was a new experience for Anthony. He'd witnessed numerous executions and murders. He'd even carried out more than a few himself. This was something else. This was something primal, primitive, brutal—in a way that guns and knives and clubs could never be. The pure impact with which the animal struck was one thing, but then came the feasting. The utter savagery.

Anthony looked away for a moment, an involuntary reaction he couldn't remember ever having before. But then he forced himself to watch, to learn, and to see if the attack on the guard had saved the girl.

She was running, even before the shouts and the bullets started pelting the wolf.

Good girl.

She was smart, this one. Smart and strong.

He turned his attention back to the zip-tie. *Scrape—scrape —scrape.*

The two men in the other room were paying no attention to Anthony. They were busy on radios talking to the men hunting the wolf.

Anthony worked harder, faster, being a little less careful of the noise. This could easily be his best chance, with Two Fingers momentarily out of the picture.

Scanning the kitchen, he noted a knife lying on a cutting board on the farthest counter. If he could get a hand free, he'd try shuffling his chair to reach it. By getting the knife and cutting the ties, he would be able to kill the two men and escape. They were young, strong, and, as far as he knew had all their fingers, but he was confident he could sneak up on at least one of them. And after that, there was only one man left to stand between Anthony Carlino and possible freedom. And that man, no matter who he was—*except maybe Chuck Norris*—would die.

Watching the entryway to the kitchen, he redoubled his efforts.

Scrape—scrape—scrape.

~

THE SUN CRESTED the eastern plain, rising like hope and life, its light chasing away the shadows and the cold with its long-reaching rays of orange, red, and yellow. Irmgard shivered as she plodded along, the long jacket occasionally tripping her frozen, clumsy feet. She kept her hands pressed tightly against her bare belly under the jacket and her shirt, trying to warm her stiff fingers.

She'd given up on trying to keep her teeth from chattering. All she wanted to do was lie down and sleep, *just for a little while*, but she remembered her father telling her that was how people died in the cold winters on the mountains. He said that if she ever felt like that, she had to make herself keep going, no matter how hard it might be.

And so she kept going, pulling her left boot out of the three or so inches of new snow and thudding it down a half a length ahead of the other and then repeating the same maneuver with the right. Her toes felt frozen, but they still hurt.

Thankfully, the snow had stopped falling a half hour ago, having dusted the trees and the ground with fresh powder. But the trail was still treacherous, steep, with icy patches hidden under the new snow. She'd slipped several times, each fall making her colder and quickly depleting what energy she had left.

Her thoughts drifted to her father and mother. How nice it would be to cuddle with them in front of the fireplace, blankets piled high, eating cookies and drinking milk. But then she remembered, and the bad feelings swallowed her. She was too tired and too cold to cry aloud, so she cried on the inside. She couldn't help it. She wanted to be strong, but she didn't know how.

Irmgard didn't know where she was going anymore; she'd gotten lost, something she didn't think could happen to her. Perhaps it was that her mind wasn't working well enough to orient her correctly. Either way, she was just moving to get far away. Away from the men ... away from the wolf.

The ice patch beneath the snow caught her entirely unaware, and her foot went out from under her. She landed on one knee and then tipped over and tumbled, the snow filling her mouth, nose, and eyes. The world circled around and around as she picked up speed, her arms and legs pinwheeling. For just an instant, she focused enough to realize she was falling. In a state of panic, she started to scream, but the cold air and the snow in her mouth made it impossible. She continued her silent tumble, like an out-of-control gymnast, whirling and twirling, rolling over rocks and branches and all the time picking up speed as she spilled down and down and down.

Her last thought, before she fell from the precipice, was of the fireplace, the blankets, and her mother and father.

And then the ground and the rocks and the snow were gone, and only empty space was left.

THE WOLF HAD ELUDED the men all night long, but now he had been forced up and in toward the big meadow on the other side of the ridge. His mind understood the basic concept of a trap—*he'd set many himself*—but nothing of this complexity. And so, he continued, not knowing men would be waiting for him in the meadow.

Waiting to kill him.

Even though the sun had risen and the dark no longer protected him, he increased his speed. He stayed to the trees when he could— the trees and the boulders.

He could hear the men coming. They made no attempt to remain silent, as he would have done.

Twice he tried to circle them, but there were too many, and they were working as an organized pack, guarding their rear. On his second attempt at a sneak attack, one of them had burned the skin over his right shoulder with a bullet. It hadn't drawn blood, but it had stung. Instinctively, the wolf understood he was in real danger and so did not try a third time.

Angling up the mountain, he used every skill at his disposal to remain invisible to the enemy, trusting his strength and his endurance. He could go for days without tiring, and the hunters had always proven to be weak and to tire quickly.

He thought they would give up.

But this time, the wolf was wrong.

23

The sunrise was stunning. Brilliant colors splashed across the sky. *God was painting with real passion this morning. And I thanked Him for it.*

"You sleeping?" asked Billy.

I peeked one eye.

"Praying."

"What are you asking for?"

"I'm not asking ... I'm *thanking.*"

"Thanking? For what?"

I opened both eyes and hitched a thumb toward my side window and all the splendor.

"The beauty."

He looked where I was pointing.

"Oh, yeah, nice."

"Really? Nice?" I gave him unbelievable. "The mountains, the snow, the sky, the Sun."

He shrugged.

"Yeah ... nice."

"Do you see the colors? The way the sunlight sparkles off the ice crystals in the snow? Look at how blue that sky is. Like sapphire. It's incredible."

He ducked his head, looking across me to see out my window again.

"Okay, so? I mean, yeah, it's a nice day. A bit cold, but yeah, pretty."

"And why is it pretty?" I asked.

"Why?" He shrugged. "Like you said, the colors and sparkles and stuff ... I guess."

"Do you think a cow looks at the same scene and thinks it's pretty?"

"A cow?"

"A cow," I said, "You know, like moo-moo? A cow."

"I know what a cow is."

"So, would a cow think the mountains and snow and sky are pretty?"

"I don't get your point," said Billy, giving me exasperated again.

I get that a lot.

"The point is that a cow or a duck can't appreciate the beauty. It's just a part of their existence, their surroundings. They don't have the ability to enjoy the splendor the way we do. Now, do we need that ability to survive? The cow doesn't need it, so why would we? But the beauty *does* affect us. We see it, we like it, we admire it. We have the *ability* to admire it. God didn't put that ability in us so we could survive. He gave us that gift because He wants us to be able to *enjoy* His creation. After all, He created it *for* us." I gave him back his shrug. "That's why I thank Him."

Billy drove for a few minutes without saying anything, just watching the winding road. He glanced out the window a couple of times.

He looked at me.

"It is pretty," he said.

I looked back at Max. Max was staring at the beauty. I sat back in the seat, smiling.

"Yes," I said. "Yes, it is."

MAX HEARD the gunshots before the Alpha and the other man. The gunshots, the screaming, the voices, and the commotion. It was still far off, but they were fast approaching.

And then he caught the scent.

The Great Gray Wolf.

He sat up in the seat and scanned the surroundings.

The scent was faint—a shifting of the wind. There and gone. *But it was him.*

Max circled in the back seat, something he never did.

The Alpha sat up and looked back at him. Max stared hard out the window. The Alpha looked where he looked, scanning now too.

Good.

THE WOLF TROTTED over the ridge and down toward the meadow, falling perfectly into the trap. Five men broke from the trees. The first one fired, and a spray of white powder exploded a foot away. The wolf darted to the right as bullets punched through the snow all around him.

Almost any animal in a situation like this would try to escape. The wolf turned and charged the men as another group of five emerged from the tree line fifty yards to the right. Like the first group, they opened fire, snow spraying behind the wolf as he accelerated. The few inches of powder did not hinder his speed as he moved in a straight line for fifteen yards toward the first group—zigged—zagged —bullets flying to no effect.

The closest of the men took his time. He aimed at the big chest as it rushed toward him, slowed his breathing, took up the slack on the trigger, and pulled. The rifle bucked as the wolf canted and bolted

forward, instantly appearing ten times bigger. The scope smashed
into his eye socket, and rows of razor-sharp teeth tore into his face
and head. Suddenly, the man felt the massive impact of the giant wolf
slamming into his back.

The wolf ripped out a chunk of the soldier's skull. He dropped the
dead weight and spun about, ready to attack again. And now he was
in the middle of the remaining four. They panicked and fired toward
the center—*complete crossfire.* A bullet ripped through one man's
thigh, another through a man's chest. Both went down. The wolf took
out the other two as they stalled to reassess. The man shot in the
thigh tried to reload, blood spraying from his wound in a tight arc.
The wolf tore into his intestines and then left him helplessly trying to
shove them back inside his body, his blood spreading into the white
snow.

Two more groups were running from the trees now and Two
Fingers, commanding from the farthest, ordered the men to take
their shots regardless of their wounded comrades in the line of fire.

There was nowhere for the wolf to retreat, so again he charged.

SEEING MAX'S REACTION, I started paying attention to my surroundings instead of just admiring them and running my mouth. I rolled
the window down, the cold air rushing in. And there it was ... gunfire
... echoing off the tightly packed sides of the mountains.

We'd just come over a ridge that opened into a massive meadow
dotted with scattered copses of trees. Converging toward the center
were several groups of men hunting a dog. No ... *not a dog.* Too big ...
too powerful. A *wolf.* And something about it sparked a memory. I
grabbed my binoculars and sighted in. Yes, the unusual coloring, the
size, the way it moved. I had seen this animal once before. *The first
time I saw Max.*

"Over there," I said to Billy. "Get us there now."

Max circled in the back seat.

THE WOLF TOOK another bullet-burn along his right flank, this one bringing blood. But then he was on them—*in them*—amongst them. And they had learned nothing from the first attack. Again, they were placed in a crossfire, and again they shot into one another while the wolf attacked with reckless abandon. He severed a hamstring, crushed a knee, tore into a groin. Bullets flew, striking snow and friendly flesh, but nothing else hit him. He slashed with his fangs—moved—dodged—slashed again. Screams and blood flooded the air around them, steamy breath misting the sky as the pure white snow turned crimson with the men's blood. The wolf slipped in and out and over and under—*attacking—disappearing—attacking again.*

The other groups opened fire, but they were too far away to make a difference. They ran as fast as they could through the inhibiting snow, but they were tired and slow, just as the wolf knew they would be. And so, he finished with the last man near him and sprinted for the trees. The men were running and out of breath, and their bullets didn't come close.

He made the trees and circled up and around, playing his old game. He had confused his prey, and they were too undisciplined to recognize the ploy and defend against it.

The wolf would slaughter them.

TWO FINGERS WAS furious as the wolf disappeared into the woods. The men were fools—useless against this master of the hunt.

But Two Fingers was no fool. And he had an ace up his sleeve.

The men themselves were cheap, and he would waste their blood as needed. In the end, due to their sheer numbers, they would kill the wolf. And then he would find the girl.

He stuck the remaining two fingers of his mangled hand into his mouth and whistled.

~

BILLY HAD GOTTEN us as close as he could, and we piled out of the two cars. We were all in the provided snow gear, thick parkas, and insulated boots. The guns were the same, short-barreled, fully automatic rifles and semi-automatic pistols for the Mafia goons. I had my usual Smith & Wesson 4506 in my back waistband, a cute little revolver on my ankle, my short buckle knife, a not so short Tanto knife, an AR15 with a suppressor and scope. I also had night tactical gear—which was completely unnecessary at this time of day, but who knew about later?

It took us about five minutes to reach the gunfire. We came out of the trees just in time to see the converging groups of men shooting at the wolf who was disappearing into the trees on the opposite side of the clearing.

Two groups of men had been attacked at divergent sites and were either unmoving in the snow or crawling through it, begging for help.

We spread out in a line, and Billy, not breathing hard at all, even at this altitude, stepped up beside me.

"Looks like they're hunting a wolf," he said. "What's this got to do with finding my grandfather?"

"Way too big a party for hunting a wolf," I said. "And the guns are too sophisticated. Something else is happening here."

Billy shrugged, watching the men chasing after the escaping animal.

"If you say so."

"I say so," I said.

"Okay, what's the play?"

Max bumped against my thigh. I looked down and saw him running toward the trees we had just come through. I looked back at the men in the clearing, then back at Max ... but Max was already gone. I looked around, searching for him.

"Where'd he go? Max, where'd he go?"

Billy's head swiveled, looking.

"He was right there," he said, "just a second ago."

I searched where I'd last seen him and found his tracks moving in a diagonal into the trees at a slight angle from our path in.

"That way," I said.

"You want us to go after him?" Billy asked.

I looked back at the men across the clearing, maybe three hundred yards out.

"No, he can take care of himself. Let's see what they're up to." I turned to the men who were with us. "Be ready. I've got a bad feeling about this."

I had never been more right in my life.

MAX CAUGHT the scent and heard the scream at the same time. It was not the scent he had been searching for, but he couldn't ignore it. Fear, pain, approaching death.

Max moved faster.

And then he did catch the other scent.

The Great Gray Wolf.

They were destined to meet and meet they would, but something about the scream grabbed him and wouldn't let go.

Max angled down and around. The trees, the shadows, and the snow filled his world. He didn't track; he didn't trail. This was straight air scenting, catching wisps of odor, losing them, finding them again as they were scattered and battered and torn on the wind and the branches, bouncing off the sides of the mountains and gathering in the scrub and the grass poking up through the snow.

His paws and claws scrambled over ice-encrusted rocks, never once losing their purchase. He leapt over a crevasse and onto a fallen tree, down a ravine, and through a tangled mass of bush.

This was familiar terrain. This was home. Not this exact spot. Not this exact location. But this land—these mountains.

Home.

Where everything had been taken from him. His family. His freedom.

Max increased his pace, sensing an urgency he could not explain.

He broke through a thick section of undergrowth and stopped.

The little girl's body was lying buried in snow, only her right hand and a little bit of hair visible.

From far, far away, gunfire echoed.

But that was no longer Max's concern.

24

I rmgard once dreamed that she could fly. Her mother and father were alive then. She'd had dinner, played with her dolls, was tucked into bed, kissed by her parents, and fell fast asleep. In the dream, she was in her old home in the city. Outside their small apartment, the sun was shining, and it was warm and bright. She looked up at the sky, saw a cloud, and decided to touch it. Her body tilted, and her feet lifted off the ground. At first, she felt wobbly and thought she might fall. Her legs kept trying to float faster than the rest of her, like when she was in the swimming pool and went out too deep, but then, using her arms to balance, she righted herself and slowly, shakily, rose higher and higher into that beautiful sky.

It was nice.

This was nothing like that.

She had time for one scream, and then the ground was gone. Empty space allowed gravity to exert its full force on her tiny body. Her arms pinwheeled, her legs flailed, her breath left her, and the terror of freefall flooded her senses. Instinctively, she reached out, grasping for anything that might save her, but there was nothing there.

It started slow, but that changed just as fast, and the ground rushed at her with terrible speed. She was moving at it headfirst now. Remembering how she used to do somersaults out by the sheep pen, she tucked and rolled as best she could. But there was nothing to push off from to start a roll. No hay bales or fences. The best she could manage was to land on her shoulder blades, saving her from a broken neck. The impact blanked her consciousness so that she was unaware of her awkward path down the mountain, arms and legs flopping loosely in the snow, hair flying.

The snow, the slope, and the partial somersault saved her from serious injury, but she came to a jarring stop. Lying face down in the snow, her mouth and nose and eyes clogged with suffocating white, she felt nothing.

Sometime later, she jerked awake, coughing and shaking her head. With nearly frozen fingers, she scraped the ice from her eyes, nose, and cheeks. She tried to push herself upright, but the snow was deeper here. Her arms could find no purchase, and she sank shoulder-deep into the snow.

A chill that had nothing to do with the fierce cold tickled her neck, and a terror, as great as when she had first stepped out into the nothingness of space, enveloped her.

She turned her head—slowly—and saw the monster's eyes staring down at her.

~

TWO FINGERS SAW the men approaching. They were dressed in camouflage gray and white parkas with fleeced hoods, all sporting military-grade weapons. They were not police, and they were not his men. And they were certainly not hunters.

There was only one possible reason for them being here.

He gave the order, *"Kill them."*

Two Fingers threw his rifle to his shoulder and sighted in.

His men all did the same.

~

A MAN who appeared to be the leader shouted something and pulled up his weapon. Before I could say anything or even get my AR up, Billy fired a short burst that shredded a man's chest and face.

Nice shooting ... we were still at least seventy yards out.

In the next instant, bullets were flying everywhere.

They had us by numbers, but Billy's men were professional—way better shots. Bodies started to fall on their sides as we all ran full-on at each other.

I went for the leader.

Two more groups of men came from the trees. They were farther back, but they started running and shooting, coming closer. I took a knee in the snow and put my holographic red dot sight on the leader's chest.

But he was gone.

He'd seen me aiming at him and dropped to the snow. I changed target acquisition and squeezed off three quick shots taking the next closest man in the torso. He went down, blood decorating the white around his body. I sighted in on the next and put two into him. The first hit him low in the belly, the second in the top of his shoulder as he bent over, tearing through his back in a red mist.

And then a hail of bullets exploded the snow around me, and I heard the buzz of high-velocity projectiles as they flew way too close to my face. I was up and running, firing as I went. My shots were not nearly as accurate as usual ... but neither were theirs.

And then I saw it, breaking from the trees a hundred yards back.

The wolf.

It took the closest man from behind and destroyed him.

Sweet!

The enemy of my enemy and all that.

But then I saw something that froze my blood.

Max—coming from the trees. *How had he gotten all the way over there?* And he was running full speed straight at the wolf.

I saw another group of five men enter the battleground, and they started shooting at the wolf ... *Max in their line of fire.*

I dropped to a knee again so I could give Max cover fire. I let loose with a burst that missed but was close enough to draw their fire away from Max and toward me.

I got off three more bursts, but we were a hundred yards apart, and there was a melee going on between us. With my attention on my dog, I probably didn't hit anyone.

The wolf was still preoccupied with the man he'd attacked when Max got to him. Max didn't slow—didn't pause or hesitate. He leapt from ten feet back, moving at maybe thirty miles an hour, the wolf's back to him.

This would be over quickly.

The wolf had no chance.

I know my Max's abilities.

But at the last instant, the impossible happened. The wolf dropped the man and spun around, his giant jaws catching Max at the throat. The wolf twisted and flipped, landing on top of Max. I saw the wolf's massive head rip back, blood flying. Max was yowling and trying to make his feet as blood jetted, still trying to go after the wolf as it moved away without a second look, sprinting to the next target.

I stood ... I screamed.

"NOOOOOO!"

Max tried—but he couldn't—he couldn't. He fell over into the snow, convulsing.

Three men converged on him and pumped automatic rifle fire into his body and head.

Still screaming, I aimed, tears blurring my vision, and fired again and again. One of the men went down, his head exploding.

Bullets tugged at my parka and spewed snow in geysers all around me. I ignored them. I kept walking forward, shooting and shooting and shooting. Another man went down, and a bullet hit my AR, *spanging* off its rails and nearly ripping it out of my grip. But I held on and kept firing.

Three more groups of men poured from the trees, and suddenly Billy was at my side, dragging me back, his men coalescing around us, providing cover. They dragged and pulled while I continued to scream and fire.

We made it back to our side of the tree line, and I was out of bullets. There were too many of them. Billy was shouting into my face that we had to go, and it finally got through to me that Max was dead and there was nothing I could do for him.

Sanity returned, and we vanished into the trees and the shadows until we found the cars and sped away, leaving blood and death and Max behind us.

25

Max went to the body. The girl was still alive, but she wouldn't be for long. She was unconscious, suffocating, the snow and the cold killing her. Max nuzzled into the snow, grabbing the back of her hood with his front teeth. He dragged her from the snowpack and shook her small body with a few thrashings of his head. Thick snow covered her face, so he knocked some off with his nose, then licked at her face until most of it was gone.

The gunfight echoed to him, growing in intensity. He started to move toward it; the *Alpha might be in danger*. He made it to the trees— stopped—turned back to the girl. *She would die without him.* He looked back to where the battle raged, then back to the girl.

She moved.

She coughed and brushed at her eyes, nose, and mouth. She tried to get up, but the snowdrift was too deep. She was stuck.

The girl's head turned, and she looked straight into his eyes.

Up the mountain, the battle turned into a war. Max had to leave the girl; he had to go to the Alpha.

Instead, he padded slowly to her, gripped her coat at the hood as he had before, and pulled her out of the snow. He then dragged her up to the trees, where the snow was only a few inches deep.

He dropped her.

IRMGARD SAW the monster staring at her from the shadow of the trees. The wolf had her; there was nothing she could do. But then it stepped into the light, and it wasn't the wolf at all.

It was just a doggy.

It grabbed her coat and dragged her out of the snow and back up into the trees.

She was so cold.

The scattered streaks of sunlight shining through the skeletal tree limbs and bushy pine trees did little to warm her. Her shoulders and arms and legs shivered uncontrollably, and her teeth wouldn't stop chattering.

The doggy let her go, and she curled into a ball, trying to blow on her frozen fingers. She saw the doggy looking down at her, so she reached a shaking hand and petted his nose.

MAX KNEW he had to leave the girl. *Pack* demanded it, and the girl was nothing to him. The Alpha could be in danger.

He looked back at her.

She reached up a hand and touched his nose, his muzzle, his throat.

He left her and trotted back to the deep snow where she had been buried. He dug through the icy crust and down to the dirt, then widened the area, scooping the snow out with his forelegs and shoveling it out of the opening between his hind legs.

It didn't take long.

Max went back to the girl and dragged her to their newly made den. Once inside, he curled around her, shifting his body until he had her covered, top to bottom. He angled his legs, getting her tiny hands into the warm pits of his forelegs. She wiggled her fingers, tickling him, and hugged him tightly.

Even three feet under the snow, Max could hear the shots and the screaming and the death. He lay his head over the girl's tiny face and gave her all the warmth he could.

26

Anthony Carlino had worked at weakening the zip-ties all night. The rubbing had done more damage to the chair arms than it had to the plastic. He was tired, hungry, thirsty, and cranky. The stump of his missing finger ached horribly.

Outside, the sun was bright in a cloudless sky. According to the old clock on the wall, it was ten-thirty. Two Fingers had left only one man to work the radio and watch over Anthony, but if he couldn't get free, the point was moot.

The radio squawked in the other room, and the man gave instructions into the microphone. Anthony used the opportune noise to jerk back and forth against the ties. The right one snapped cleanly. Scooting the chair to the counter, Anthony gripped the knife. He sliced the other tie and then the ones around his ankles.

The kitchen wall shielded him from the view of the man at the radio. He stood and stretched, feeling every bit of his age. He didn't think he had ever felt so stiff. After taking a couple of deep breaths, he stretched a final time, then walked into the other room and came up behind the man on the radio. With his left hand, the one that ached so badly, he grabbed the man roughly by the hair and jerked his head back. At the same time, his right hand thrust the knife into the base of his skull—all the way to the hilt. The man's body locked tight in spasm for a second. Anthony Carlino twisted the blade back and forth twice in a move that, back in the day, they called scrambling the eggs. The man went limp, and he let the body slip from the chair to the floor.

On the desk, next to the radio, was Anthony's golden lighter. The one Bella had given him. Anthony put it in his pocket and gave the corpse a good kick in the ribs.

Searching the body, he found a SIG forty caliber. He also located a four-inch folding knife and some cash. No car keys. He checked the rooms, but there were no more guns, no cell phones. And no keys.

No matter.

Anthony boosted his first steal when he was seven. He'd do the same now.

Time to leave.

Opening the front door, he stepped out just as a car loaded with men slid to a stop in the snow in front of the fence. They jumped out, and Anthony opened fire. He put three rounds into the windshield and one into the thigh of the closest man. And then bullets exploded against the side of the house and around his feet. Anthony kept firing as he tried to get back inside, but the splintering wood, rock, and lead blinded him. He floundered to the side of the building, blasting in their direction. The shooting stopped as Anthony squeezed the trigger a final time, but there was no resistance, and he saw the slide locked back.

Empty.

Looking over the sights, he saw two more cars had pulled up. He also saw bodies lying all around the first car.

"Grandpa!"

Suddenly, Billy Carlino, his grandson, dressed in a parka, was running to him. The boy grabbed him in a giant bear hug, lifting him off the ground and spinning him around like he was weightless.

"How?" Anthony could hardly speak.

"Uncle Nick sent us to rescue you," Billy said through tears and laughter. "Leave it to you to rescue yourself before we could get here."

Billy set the big man down and pointed to Gil.

"This is Gil Mason; Uncle Nick hired him to find you. And—well —here we are."

"We've got to go," said Gil. "Get him in the car."

Gil, Billy, and Anthony got in the first car, with Billy driving, as the other five loaded into the second. As they pulled away from the house, they saw two trucks speeding up the mountain, loaded with armed men in the open beds. Bullets pelted and thunked against the metal of their vehicles.

"You call this a rescue?" said Anthony Carlino. "Somebody give me a gun with some bullets."

WE'D GOTTEN AWAY from the men in the meadow and headed for a farmhouse the old man at the dogfighting ring had mentioned. I forced myself to stay focused. It wasn't easy, but I've been to war—I know the drill. I'd seen friends blown to pieces right next to me and had to ignore it while I handled the situation at hand.

But Max!

I couldn't believe it. Fury rose inside me like a blazing flame, and again, I pushed it down. This wasn't the time.

The road twisted and curved down the mountain. No one followed ... *yet.* The farmhouse shouldn't be far, but it was possible that we would be too late, and Anthony Carlino was already dead. But if so, why the heavily armed presence? No, my money was on him still being alive and at the house. When I first saw the men shooting in the meadow, I thought maybe another group of Nick's men had already made it to the area and that they were fighting over the prize. But there was no indication that any of the men were guarding anyone. We would just have to keep on to the farmhouse, and if he wasn't there, we'd deal with it then. I wasn't going to allow Max's death to be for nothing. If Anthony Carlino could be saved, we were going to save him.

The road took a final turn past some trees, and there it was. The farmhouse. As a man stepped out onto the porch, a group of men got out of a car, and a battle erupted in front of us.

"That's my grandpa," shouted Billy.

I was out of the car and aiming before it even stopped. A man wearing a green army coat was shooting at Anthony Carlino, so I put four rounds into him—all four, center mass. It was overkill, but I couldn't get Max out of my mind. The man dropped, and I shifted to the next closest. He saw me and stopped shooting at the old man to train his weapon in my direction.

Too late.

He took three to the chest and one to the face.

Before the others could even react, Billy and our carload of body-guards obliterated them.

Billy ran to the old man and picked him up.

I saw that his left hand sported a bloody wrapping around the ring finger and palm.

Anthony Carlino, all right.

He looked pretty much like what one would expect of a Mafia godfather. Tall, big-boned, a slight paunch, mostly gray hair but sprinkled here and there with jet black strands, the standard Italian nose and jawline.

He looked nothing like Nick Carlino.

But this was no time for a reunion.

I put in a new magazine and got everyone into the cars. As we began to head out, we saw two trucks filled with men coming up at us. Everyone I could see was armed, so it was an easy bet they were bad guys. I leaned out the window and emptied a magazine into the windshield of the closest truck. I couldn't tell if I hit anyone or not, but the truck swerved, clipped a tree, and turned onto its side, spilling the men to the ground at about thirty miles an hour. The second truck turned to miss the men on the ground, giving me time to toss in another magazine and repeat the *shoot-into-the-windshield* trick, only now the men in the bed of the truck were shooting back. A series of holes raced the fender in front of me, and I ducked back inside as hot lead sizzled past my face like angry hornets.

Billy jerked the wheel hard, and the Mercedes' tires fishtailed as we spun. As the tires caught traction, we completed the spin, then headed back up the mountain. Behind us, our bodyguards were destroying the truck and its inhabitants, but a few hundred yards farther down the road, we saw more trucks coming our way. Billy continued the drive up.

"The guys from the meadow will be heading down," I said. "We're going to need to go off-road."

"These cars aren't made for that," said Billy.

"They're rentals, right?"

Billy grinned and turned off into the trees. It didn't take long for our bodyguards to catch up.

~

TWO FINGERS WAS NOT a happy man.

Odin was dead.

He'd put a bullet into his head himself. The wolf had taken him out in an instant. The greatest fighting dog he had ever seen, and the wolf had treated him like he was nothing more than a barely weaned pup.

Impossible.

He would never have believed it if he hadn't seen it himself.

But he had.

And now the men they'd been fighting had escaped him—for the time being. He knew where they were headed, and he'd already called in reinforcements. There was only one way off this mountain, and it would be secured within a half hour.

They would not escape.

He'd tried to get hold of his man guarding Anthony Carlino at the farmhouse, but there was no answer, not on the radio and not on his cell. Two Fingers assumed they had already gotten there and had taken him.

That he could not allow. The people who had contracted him for this job would not accept failure. They would kill him ... and not quickly. Not to mention Carlino himself. Two Fingers had no illu-sions about what his people would have done to him if he were able to tell them who he was.

No. They could not be allowed to escape.

As Two Fingers and his men neared the farmhouse, the sound of gunfire reached him. Two Fingers yelled for the driver to speed up, even though they were already moving too fast for the terrain and snow. As they rounded the last bend, Two Fingers saw a Mercedes follow another Mercedes off the road and into the trees.

Two Fingers smiled.

"Get them."

~

ANTHONY CARLINO CHECKED the magazine of the Beretta Billy had given him. It was full, and he slid it back into the gun, racking the slide.

He sat in the backseat, his finger throbbing. The man in the front passenger seat—*what had Billy said his name was?* Gil something or other. Seemed pretty capable. His *shooting-out the-window* bit had worked well, but something about the man bothered him. He didn't know what it was exactly. The guy reminded him of something. Something that hit on Anthony's radar. *A Cop.* That was it. The guy gave him the cop vibe. Anthony didn't like it. Anthony didn't trust him. He might be Fed or maybe Narc, but definitely a cop of some sort. He wondered how Billy had missed it. Hadn't he'd taught him better? He considered putting one behind the cop's ear. It would be easy. Just reach forward and ...

The man turned and looked at him.

"Whatever you might be thinking," said the man, "don't. I'd kill you before you got halfway there."

That took Anthony aback. It was as though the guy was reading his thoughts.

"You got the cop stink all over you," said Anthony.

"Used to," said the man. "Not anymore."

"Bull," said Anthony.

"It's true, Grandpa," said Billy. "Gil used to be a cop; now he's a private dick. And he owes Uncle Nick. That's why he's here. You can trust him."

Anthony didn't like it. The guy just didn't fit. And what kind of a name was 'Gil' anyway? What was he, a fish?

Stupid.

Anthony didn't trust this stupid fish cop. He didn't trust him at all.

I HEARD the mobster in the backseat take out the magazine and put it back in. What was it that Nick had told me?

That his father was the most dangerous, ruthless man I would ever meet in my life?

He didn't seem like that much to me. In his seventies, a little taller than average. But just then, a feeling swept over me, and I knew he was thinking about taking me out. I looked back at him, my hand pulling on my gun and resting it in my lap.

"Whatever you might be thinking," I said, "don't. I'd kill you before you got halfway there."

He just looked at me, his expression neutral. And just like that, my opinion of Anthony Carlino did a complete 180. Without him knowing, I pointed the gun under the armrest at his chest.

"You got the cop stink all over you," he said.

"Used to. Not anymore."

"Bull."

Billy took my side, and I knew the danger was over ... for now anyway. I let the gun rest back in my lap and looked out the window, no longer thinking of Anthony Carlino.

I thought of Max.

I'd had to deal with a lot of loss lately. An old friend turned enemy, and an enemy turned friend. Pilgrim ... *almost.*

Gail.

I shoved all thoughts of her out.

And now Max.

"We got company," said Billy.

I looked in the side rearview mirror just as it shattered. *A bullet.* Streaming behind the bodyguard car were at least three vehicles. And they were raining lead at us. Luckily, shooting from moving vehicles is not nearly as easy as they make it look in the movies. Still, put enough missiles in the air, and something is bound to get hit.

Billy stepped on the gas, but like he said, these cars weren't made for *off-road*—and especially not off-road *in the mountains*—and even more especially, not off-road in *heavily wooded* mountains—*with snow*.

Our car of Mafia bodyguards shielded us from most of the gunfire, and they were returning fire at a far more accurate rate. But then their front windshield was washed in red, and a hole punched through the glass from the inside. I knew that the driver, Leonardo Esposito, had taken one through the head. The car skewed to the side, smashing into a tree.

I expected Billy to stop—to help his buddies—but instead, he gunned it. He turned up, then over a hill and around trees, then down sharply out of sight of our pursuers. The last I saw of them, our bodyguards had taken cover behind the car and in the trees and were laying down an impressive display of cover fire, allowing us to make our escape.

Billy looked at me.

"The job is to save my grandpa," he said. "Everyone else is expendable..." his eyebrows drew down. "*Everyone* else. You understand? Even me."

I didn't like it. I already thought that Billy had the makings of ten Anthony Carlinos, but he was right. It *was* the job. The mission ... just like in the Marines.

I clenched my teeth and gave him a single nod.

He smiled and went back to driving. We went over a snowdrift, the front tire hitting something unseen, and the Mercedes started its roll. As the car tipped, I saw what I couldn't a second before. We were on a cliff. I couldn't tell how far of a drop it was ... but it was far enough.

For just an instant, I considered going for Billy. But just like in *Guardians of the Galaxy,* when Quill pulls the trigger to kill Gamora rather than letting her fall into the hands of Thanos as he promised, I'd promised Billy I would put the job first.

I dove into the backseat and grabbed the door handle with one hand, pulling it as I wrapped my other arm around Anthony Carlino's neck, allowing my momentum to push us both out of the car an instant before it disappeared into space. We hit the snow and rolled several times, the white powder acting like a gymnastic mat and protecting us from serious injury.

I heard the crash. It took a few seconds and sounded like way too far a drop for much chance of survival. I stood up and made my way to the edge. I couldn't see the wreckage—the slope of the mountain blocking it. I yelled for Billy, but all I got in return was the drifting sounds of growing flames followed by an explosion that told me the gas tank had blown.

Anthony Carlino walked up beside me.

"You saved me instead of my grandson?"

"It was the job," I said. "I made a promise."

His old eyes filled with tears, and he pursed his lips.

I didn't know how much time the bodyguards could buy us, but if we left now, Billy's death might buy us some more. They'd have to check the wreckage.

"Let's get out of here," I said.

To his credit, Anthony Carlino paused for a moment.

"I love you, Billy," he said. When he turned to me, his eyes were no longer wet. And for the first time, I saw up close and personal what Nick Carlino had meant.

They were the eyes of a very dangerous man.

27

Billy jumped, but he was too late. He reached for the ledge, his strong fingers brushing snow-covered rocks and sliding free. Blindly, he reached out again, gravity sucking him down at impossible speed. He gripped a branch, the bark ripping through his grip, burning his fingers and palm like a red-hot rope. The move shifted his arc back toward the rocks. His right hip smacked something, and instinctively he grasped for any purchase with both his hands and his feet. He'd done his fair share of rock climbing, and his muscle memory was excellent. One foot smacked against a ledge of rock but broke through it, slowing him just enough that his left hand could snag a purchase. He almost lost his grip, the momentum dragging at him like an anchor, but his fingers held, and he dangled by one hand.

Reaching with his other hand, the tips of his fingers found a narrow ridge. He pulled himself up to eye level when the rest of the ledge gave way. Sliding down the side of the unforgiving mountain, he grasped for anything—found nothing—falling—but close to the wall now. He grabbed for another branch or root—snagged it—lost it —fell—hit the wall—saw sparks and flashes behind his eyes— grabbed again—caught something—hit the wall hard—bounced off

—blood flowing into his eyes—spinning him around so that he saw the earth rushing up at him—

And then, just like in a dream, everything went black, and he saw no more.

⁓

TWO FINGERS KNELT by the side of the cliff. He looked over the edge but couldn't see the car. What he did see was black smoke billowing up from the ground below. That meant the car was still burning. He turned his head, staring at the two sets of tracks in the snow heading to the west.

Two of them made it.

But which two?

The hired help didn't count; only Anthony Carlino mattered. If he didn't get him back, he was dead. Two Fingers held no illusions about that.

If he'd had Odin, he would have sent him after the walkers. But Odin was dead. The thought of it infuriated him.

The wolf!

He shook his head, fighting for control. What was done was done. There was nothing to do about that. Later, after he had Carlino, he'd deal with the wolf.

For now, he would do what he had to do.

Two Fingers was an excellent tracker. He walked over to where the tracks were fresh, away from the skids and tire treads in the snow. He knelt and examined them. One set of boots, the other some type of walking shoe, maybe a gardening sole? And big, like what Anthony Carlino had been wearing.

It seemed unlikely that the old man could have made it out of the car alive, but the shoe pattern was the shoe pattern.

He picked ten men, the best of the lot, and slinging his rifle over his shoulder, started off with them, after the walkers. The path they'd taken was impossible for their truck. He sent others back and around in the vehicles to get to the bottom where the car was burning.

The tracks weren't old; they had maybe an hour start on him. He thought if he pushed it, they could catch them before dark.

If only he had Odin. He'd miss that dog.

~

IRMGARD WOKE. Yawning, she stretched, her hands and feet pushing against fur-encased muscle. Her eyes shot open, and she saw Max staring at her, his head on her tummy, just inches from her face. Then she remembered him. He had pulled her out of the cold and dragged her into the little snow house he had dug. He had covered her like a warm blanket.

She smiled big and grabbed his head, pulling him close. She rubbed her nose against his, her hands so warm now. She kissed him a dozen times, all over his muzzle and head. The big dog's expression never changed. He just looked at her. He didn't growl. He didn't pant or try to get away. He didn't lick her.

He just laid there, limp, still giving her his heat.

"What's your name, boy?" She asked, scrunching his jowls between her fingers. She checked for a collar, but there wasn't one. She thought about what name would be good for him. Looking into his deep brown eyes, she squinted, thinking even harder. He looked back, not saying anything.

She poked at his shoulder. Her finger parted the short fur but went no further.

Solid as a rock.

"Petra," she said with confidence. "My rock." Like Peter in the Bible, she thought. She liked it. She hugged him again.

~

MAX LET her hug him and scrunch him and kiss his face. She had been very close to death. She was still weaker than she knew—*but he knew.* He smelled it on her. The weakness, the hunger, the cold. But she was strong, too. He could sense an inner strength in her—a refusal to quit. Strange in a human so young.

He respected it.

The gun battle had stopped hours ago. Max knew he should leave, but the girl would die without him. He could take care of the hunger—there were rabbits and squirrels and birds. He could keep her warm here in the den. And for water, there was snow.

But the Alpha.

The Alpha could take care of himself.

The Alpha would have to wait.

The girl needed him, and he would not let her die.

Max endured another series of kisses and hugs, but then he heard the men. Heard them ... smelled them.

They were close.

28

We were well into the woods before the trucks made it to where Billy and the car had gone over the cliff. The wind was drifting down toward us, so I heard them before I saw them. The bodyguards had bought us a reasonable amount of time. I had to assume they were all dead. I hoped I was wrong; they had proven to be capable men.

The real danger for us now was the snow. The bad guys could simply follow our tracks. In the movies, we could just grab a branch and sweep off our path, but in real life, a swept path through virgin snow would be a lot easier to follow than footprints. I had Anthony Carlino spread out about thirty yards from me right at the start. One set is harder to follow and find than two. Plus it would split their forces—at least a little. We stayed in visual contact, and I hit every rock, outcropping, and dirt patch I could to try and throw them off. But if they had anyone worth their beans in tracking, it wouldn't be enough.

I looked through the branches at the sun; maybe an hour of daylight left. Once it was dark, we would be safer. Tracking footprints in the snow, over mountainous terrain in the dark, would be slow going for them and allow us to move along a lot faster.

We made our way in silence for another thirty minutes. Anthony Carlino kept up pretty well for an older guy who'd been injured and badly treated for several days. It was rough, cold going, and he didn't even have boots, but he never complained once and never asked for a break. He drifted closer to me until we were side by side.

"Should be dark soon," he said.

"Yeah," I said.

He stopped, and I stopped with him. He was breathing hard, but so was I.

"Just so ya know," he said. "If you'd saved Billy instead of me, that would have been okay in my book."

I breathed in and out, steam billowing between us. I nodded

"I understand," I said. "He was a good kid."

"Yes," he said.

Reaching into my pocket, I pulled out one of the transponders and handed it to Anthony Carlino.

"What's this?"

"It's a transponder. Billy had one, I have one, and that one's yours." I clicked it on, hoping that if Billy had somehow survived, he might have turned his on.

Nothing.

"If we get separated," I said, "for any reason, turn yours on. I'll find you."

"Why'd you turn that one on?"

I shrugged. "Hoping Billy might have made it after all."

He nodded and put his in his pocket.

I started walking again, the snow crunching under my feet. Anthony Carlino followed.

"So," he said, "since we probably ain't gonna make it out of this alive anyway, what are you? Fed? DEA? What?"

"I'm exactly what your grandson said I was. Former cop, private detective that owes your son, Nick, a favor."

"What kind of a favor? You don't strike me as being the *on-the-take* type?"

"He helped me save a little girl who had been kidnapped. An old enemy of Nick's framed him to look like he was good for it. I went after Nick, and he caught me. He could have killed me; instead, he helped. So, saving you is repayment."

He nodded, breathing hard again.

"Okay," he said. "That sounds legit. That fits."

We circumnavigated an outcropping of rocks, and he almost slipped as we hit the snow again, but he caught himself. He was good on his feet for a big, older gentleman

"So, what's with the name, Gil? What's it, some kind of fish thing or something?"

"One L," I said. "Not two."

"Oh, like *Gilligan?* From *Gilligan's Island?*"

"That would still be two L's," I said.

"No, no, no, that fits. Sure it does. You're Gilligan." He laughed. "That makes me the Skipper." He laughed again. "Yeah, the Skipper and Gilligan. Too bad I ain't got a hat to hit you with, *Li'l Buddy.* That's what the Skipper always called him, Li'l Buddy."

I gave him the look, but he ignored it.

"*Hey Gilligan, you can't fly! It's impossible!* Ha! You remember that one? Gilligan built these wings, and he was flying—flapping those big feathers—and he was flying fine. But then the Skipper—*that's me* —tells him, 'Gilligan,'—*that's you*— 'you can't fly! Its ...'"

"Yeah," I interrupted, "I saw it, I remember it. It was funny."

He laughed so hard he almost fell, but again, he caught himself. He laughed some more, and this time I kind of wished he would fall.

But he didn't.

MAX WAS UP and out of the den before the girl could react. He moved fast, making the trees before the men came into view. The men might not see the den, but he and the girl would be trapped inside if they did. Max watched from the shadows.

Watched and waited.

He saw them take a few steps from the trees and stop, scanning the open area. Max would have gone back into the woods to come from behind them and attack from the rear, but the mountain was in the way.

There was too much distance for a direct attack. He would have to wait.

There were three of them.

All armed with rifles.

They started forward, stretched out in a ragged line.

Max's eyes searched for other targets. The landscape filtered into his apex predator brain, his genetic instinct cataloging assets and dangers.

Snow drifts.

Rocks.

Trees.

Shadows.

Depressions.

Slopes.

Angles.

The speed and direction of the wind.

If they passed the den, he would let them live. If not...

Max would protect the girl.

They continued forward, wary, careful. These men were better than the ones he faced earlier.

They were a danger.

To the girl.

Max felt the battle lust rise.

They were moving downward. If the men continued on the same path, they would miss the den and not cross his tracks.

Their scent reached him—*tobacco, gunpowder, sweat*—a thousand others.

They passed below the den and continued toward the opposite tree line.

The girl crawled out of the den.

Her eyes followed Max's tracks in the snow until she saw him in the trees.

Her face broke into a smile, and she raised a hand and stood.

She did not see the men.

They had not yet seen her.

But they would as soon as she spoke.

Max's mind calculated the variables without knowing it was doing so.

As she opened her mouth to call out to him, *he charged*.

The snow didn't slow him at all, and the downhill slope helped. Reaching her in seconds, he vaulted high, his outstretched limbs sailing over her head.

Max landed running, straight at his targets.

The closest man took the impact at about thirty miles an hour.

Max's teeth caught him in the side of the neck just as he was turning and whipped him around.

The sheer violence of the attack broke the man's neck, and the two of them landed in a cloud of white that obscured what was happening from the other soldiers.

Before they could adjust, Max was up and attacking the second man.

The lack of distance didn't allow Max to reach top speed, but the crushing power of his jaws, combined with the scimitar sharpness of his teeth, ripped into the man's thigh, forcing a scream of pain and fear.

Max had him by the right leg, and he thrashed massively, bringing the man down. The two of them tumbled in a chaos of limbs.

The third soldier aimed at them, trying for a shot, but he was too slow.

Rolling close, Max released his hold on the second man's thigh and exploded into the third man. The rifle went off, but the bullet hit the second man in the same leg that Max had been biting.

Max missed his first lunge, his teeth slicing through cloth and sliding free, allowing the man to swing up with the rifle, catching Max across the muzzle. Max flopped into the snow but was back up before the man could take advantage of the strike. He seized him just below the chin, tearing an enormous chunk of meat and flesh out of the man's throat and jaw. The dying man dropped his rifle and grabbed at the wound, trying instinctively to hold in his blood. The effort was useless. The carotid and jugular had both been severed. He would be unconscious in seconds and dead in minutes.

The man shot and bitten in the leg scrabbled through the snow on his belly, trying for the rifle. Max dove onto his back, gripping him around the neck. He crushed in, but the thickness of the coat stopped his spine from snapping. Max thrashed, gripping harder. The man fought, but in the end, his arms fell limply to his sides, and he was still. Max held him there until the last of his life drained away. Then he dropped him and went to the first man he'd attacked.

This man was also dead.

Max looked up toward the den. The little girl was still standing where he had leapt over her.

Watching.

THE DOGGY JUMPED up and ran out of the den, but it was cold out there, and she didn't know why he had left. She decided to wait for him and curled back into a ball. But then she heard footsteps crunching in the snow, and it didn't sound like Petra.

It sounded like people.

Irmgard waited a little longer, and when she couldn't hear the footsteps anymore, she cautiously crawled out of the small hole. At first, she couldn't see because the sun on the snow was so bright, but then she saw the tracks in the snow—the doggy's tracks—*Petra's* tracks.

She loved him.

She followed the tracks with her eyes, even though the brightness of the white hurt. He was standing by a tree, the shadow almost hiding him.

She smiled and waved and was about to call to him, forgetting about the people whose footsteps she had heard. Suddenly, Petra was running straight at her.

And he was running so fast.

Petra had seemed far away when she saw him, but he reached her before she could move. He jumped right before crashing into her and sailed over her head, raining snow down on her shoulders and face. He landed on the other side, and when she turned to follow him, she saw him smash into a man so hard they fell into the snow and tumbled, like a snowball rolling down a hill in a cartoon.

And then she just stood there.

She couldn't move.

Her eyes frozen.

She watched everything that happened.

Part of her was scared—*so scared*—but another part wasn't scared at all. That part, the part that wasn't scared, was glad.

These men had murdered her father. They had chased her—hunted her. They wanted to do things to her. She didn't fully understand what they wanted to do, but she knew it was *bad.*

And so, she watched.

She heard.

She saw their blood.

She felt their screams.

And after a little while she wasn't scared anymore. Not *any* part of her.

When Petra was done, he walked up to her. She rubbed his head, her hand coming back wet with red.

Irmgard looked at the blood on her hand and then back at Petra. She thought of her daddy—thought of the cold and the snow and how the men had tried to catch her. She thought about the cliff and the fall and how frightened she had been.

She smiled at Petra.

"Thank you," she said.

29

Billy pushed up from the snow and turned over. He sat up, then rubbed his forehead with his hands. He felt a cut and a knot on his temple, just a little higher than where Gil Mason had smacked him with the cutting board.

It hurt.

The bleeding had stopped and crusted the side of his face and along his cheek and nose. He looked over at the burned-out car fifteen yards away. Smoke drifted from the inside, but it was lazy and slow and easily broken apart by the breeze flowing down from the mountain.

Tilting his head, a movement that caused a sharp twinge of pain in his neck and shoulder, he saw how far he had fallen. How he was still alive, he could barely guess.

He felt for his pistol and found it snugged securely in the holster strapped to his leg. He scanned for a rifle but didn't see one.

His head hurt.

His neck hurt.

Actually, just about everything hurt.

But nothing seemed broken.

He felt a nasty lump on his hip that had already started bruising, but again, it didn't feel broken.

Billy decided he had to get on his feet. He didn't want to, but it had to be done. Planting his right palm behind him, he pushed his right leg under his bottom and back and stood straight up, his left hand and leg *at the ready,* in case an attack came for him. It was the traditional Jiu-Jitsu 'protect while standing from a sit' move that had saved him in numerous matches.

Once up, he gave his head time to catch up with his body.

The world tilted just a little.

After that, he walked back to the car and searched all around it for weapons. After a few seconds, he came up with a fully loaded shotgun with five extra rounds in a sleeve strap along the barrel, an AR with a scope, night vision, and a thirty-round magazine taped together to its upside-down twin with thirty-rounds of its own.

Billy was hoping for a few grenades or some of the C4 they brought along, but the good stuff had been in the second car.

He figured someone would be coming down to check the car to find out if his grandfather was in it or not, so he needed to get out of the area. He did a quick, last search around for weapons and ammo, but, after finding nothing more, he set out towards the trees and safety.

"WHERE WE HEADING?" asked Anthony Carlino. He'd decided that Gil was who he said he was—the whole thing about his son Nickolas catching Gil and then helping him save a kidnapped little girl had brought him around. Up until then, he'd planned on getting him to admit he was undercover; then he'd kill him. Turned out he probably wouldn't have to. Anthony thought that was good because he was starting to like the guy—a little. The way he got them out of the car by jumping from the front seat to the backseat and snagging him while opening the car door at the same time was quite impressive.

Almost a Chuck Norris move.

"The farmhouse," said Gil.

Anthony Carlino stopped.

"What? Why would we go to the farmhouse? I just escaped from there."

"Cars, weapons, radios, and or phones," said Gil. "We need them. They have them. Also, it's the last place they'd expect us to go."

Anthony Carlino gave it some thought. He nodded his head.

"Okay, makes sense. I guess the Skipper's gonna follow Gilligan."

Gil shook his head and kept moving.

"You got some good moves," Anthony said. "I mean, you ain't no Chuck Norris, but you're quick."

"Chuck Norris?" said Gil without turning or stopping.

"What? You don't know who Chuck Norris is?"

"Yes," said Gil, "of course I know who Chuck Norris is."

"He's the greatest fighter of all time, that's who he is," said Anthony. "He's practically a superhero, is what he is."

Gil didn't say anything, just kept moving.

"What? You don't *like* Chuck Norris?"

"No," said Gil. "Of course I like him. Who doesn't like Chuck Norris?"

"Exactly," said Anthony Carlino. "Chuck Norris is the greatest. You know who Simon is? The Simon says, Simon?"

"What?" That made Gil stop and look at him.

"You know, Simon says put your hand on your head?"

"Okay ...?"

"Well, Chuck Norris tells *Simon* what to do."

Gil just looked at him for a few seconds. Then he chuckled. Then he laughed.

"That's pretty good," said Gil. He laughed again.

Anthony kept going.

"Chuck Norris can kill your *imaginary* friends."

Gil laughed harder.

"He can hear sign language—make an onion cry—he lost his virginity before his dad did—he knows Victoria's secret—he can *speak* Braille—when he does pushups, he's pushing the Earth down —the flu has to get Chuck Norris shots once a year."

~

I COULDN'T STOP LAUGHING. It was crazy. We were being chased by an army, stranded on a mountain, snow everywhere, Max was dead, Billy was dead, the bodyguards were dead, and I was stuck with a retired Mafia godfather who thought I was Gilligan from *Gilligan's Island* telling me Chuck Norris jokes. And I could not stop laughing.

"Chuck Norris sleeps with a pillow *under* his gun—he's the reason *that* Waldo guy is hiding—a bulletproof vest wears Chuck Norris for protection ...."

"Stop," I cried through actual tears. "Just—just stop. Let me catch my breath."

He went on as if I hadn't spoken.

"He narrates Morgan Freeman's life—he can make a Slinky go *up* the stairs—Chuck Norris beats rock, paper, scissors—missiles, jets, nukes—I could go on."

I went down to one knee. No sound was coming out; it was all stuck somewhere deep in my diaphragm. I held up a hand to stop him.

A bullet chipped a tree a foot from my face, spitting splinters into my cheek.

That sobered me.

It stopped Anthony Carlino too.

I saw a guy about fifty yards up the mountain with a rifle, adjusting his sight picture. I hit the ground, pulling out my pistol. It was a long shot, what with the trees in the way and shooting uphill, but I fired three rounds in his direction, and the guy ducked behind a tree of his own.

Anthony Carlino shook his head. "Chuck Norris wouldn't have missed."

I gave him incredulous and got back to my feet.

He shrugged and said, "Well, he wouldn't have."

I grabbed him by the bicep, and we took off and down, gunshots racing after us. I got us a safe distance away, then angled slightly up and around. *I could really use one of those rifles.* I stashed Anthony behind a tree.

"You stay here," I said.

"Where you going?"

"Scouting. I need to see how many there are. And I want to get one of those rifles."

"Get two," said Anthony Carlino. "All I got is this pea-shooter." He held up the gun from the car.

"If you had that, why didn't *you* shoot the guy?"

"I never claimed to be Chuck Norris," he said. "I couldn't make that shot in my best days."

I shook my head, maybe rolled my eyes a little.

Anthony Carlino said, "What?"

I pointed at the tree. "Just stay here. And stand *behind* the tree."

"Like I don't know that."

I moved through the trees as quickly and quietly as I could, listening for movement. The gunman had stopped shooting and was now in stealth mode. Forget the rifle; what I needed right now was Max. Thinking about him made me rage again, but I suppressed it ... *mostly*.

And then I saw him, maybe twenty yards up, peeking around a tree he was using for cover. But he was looking in the wrong direction. At this angle, I had a good view of his head and a portion of his back. He was carrying a nice-looking hunting rifle with a scope. I sighted in.

A sound came from behind me. It was light—just a shifting of snow—and close. *But not close enough.*

I slowly turned my head and saw a guy, about ten feet away, aiming right at my face. He was already pulling back on the trigger.

Max hit him so fast, all I saw was a blur in the fading shadows as they rolled away down the hill.

I turned back to the man behind the tree. He spun around fast, but he hadn't thought the move through. The barrel of his rifle smacked against the tree trunk, knocking it from his hands and into the snow. I pumped two rounds into his chest and one into the spot between his upper lip and nose. While scanning for other possible combatants, I ran over and grabbed the rifle. Upon frisking the corpse for ammo and weapons, I came up with a pistol and magazines for both. I shoved them into the pockets of my parka and turned back to help Max.

Only Max didn't need help.

Max was dead.

Standing a few yards away, I saw the thing that had killed the man who was about to kill me. The thing with fangs bared and eyes glowing in the dimming light—was not Max.

30

T he rabbit was hard to eat. It was raw, cold, and all the bones were in it. Its head was still on, and the little black eyes stared at her. She hadn't been a farm girl long enough to think of eating something like this as normal; they'd only moved from the city a few years ago. She could milk the goats, fetch the eggs ... feed *all* the animals. But killing chickens, sheep, pigs, or anything else had been her mother's job until she died, and then her father had taken on those chores.

Petra had skinned the rabbit after hunting it down and killing it. She didn't see or hear him do it. He had trotted off into the woods, and when he came back a few minutes later, he had the furless rabbit in his jaws. And even though she hadn't been a farm girl for long, she knew rabbits didn't come to you dead and skinned and ready to eat.

She tugged at the tough, pink meat with her teeth, gagging with every bite, but she was so hungry that she finally managed to get a portion of it down without throwing up.

Irmgard sat cross-legged inside the den, Petra lying beside her. He wouldn't eat any of the bunn—*rabbit*. She had to tell herself not to think of it as a *bunny*. Rabbit was easier for some reason. He'd just plopped it down in front of her and watched until she started picking at it.

Forcing another bite, she remembered her father telling her to eat her vegetables the night—well—*that night.*

I would eat the peas now, she thought, and not just because she was hungry.

She missed them so much. *Both of them.*

Wiping at her eyes, she forced herself not to think about them.

Petra stared at her.

Petra made her happy.

Smiling at him, she made herself eat a little more. It was his gift to her.

After Petra killed the men, Irmgard traded the jacket for the shortest man's coat. Like the jacket, it was much too big for her, but it was thicker and warmer. She rolled the sleeves up as best she could. It hung on her like a dress, but this one didn't get in the way of her feet. There was some blood on it, not a lot, but a little. She thought about wiping it off on the snow, but her father's face flashed across her mind, and she decided to leave it.

Light still glimmered through the hole at the front of the snow cave, but she didn't think it would last for long. The temperature was dropping, and she was starting to get cold. She hugged the new coat, blood and all, tight around her shoulders.

Now that it was getting colder, she wished she'd kept the jacket and taken the other men's coats as well, to use as blankets and maybe a door for the cave. She considered going for them now, but the wind was picking up, and she was very tired.

Lying down, she curled into a ball and tucked her chin into the dead man's coat.

She wished she knew how to start a fire.

As though he had read her mind, Petra pushed in and around her, blanketing her with his fur and heat.

She stroked his head and face, feeling a welt she hadn't noticed before. It ran from his ear to his nose. It hadn't broken the skin, but it was swollen and hot.

Remembering the horrible battle, she smiled. *They deserved what happened to them, and they couldn't ever hurt her now.* But they'd hurt her poor Petra. She kissed him on his *owie*, just like her mother used to do for her. She held his jowls in both hands and rubbed noses with him.

Her Petra.

~

MAX LET her rub noses with him. She was getting stronger. The rabbit had helped, but on a primitive level, he understood that she could not survive for long out here. He had to get her to the Alpha. He had cleared a wide search pattern while hunting the rabbit and but still caught no scent of him.

It was not yet dark, but the girl was tired. Although she had eaten very little, it wasn't long before she fell asleep. He waited until she was warm and in a deep slumber before quietly rising to leave the small den.

He had to find the Alpha.

As the cold evening air surrounded him, another scent wafted past him. It was slight, almost nonexistent, but it was there, and it was a scent he would never forget.

The Great Gray Wolf.

He cast about, his nose lifting high in the air, scenting. Making wide circles—north, south, east, west. *And then he caught it again*—light—a wisp—but stronger than before.

The little girl was forgotten.

The Alpha was forgotten.

Max followed his nose.

~

THEY WERE STILL SEARCHING for him. These men were quieter than the others had been—better at hunting. Still, the wolf understood, on a basic level, that they were nothing compared to him. He was the apex predator of these mountains.

He would kill the ones that presented themselves. And then he would find the girl.

She had ignored his markings, just as the men had.

But she had escaped him twice.

That could not be allowed.

The men were just ahead. There were two of them. He smelled them—the ones he had been hunting. But then his keen senses caught the *other* two. Through centuries of genetic imprinting essential for survival, he understood that larger numbers meant a more significant threat. Tactics required that he retreat until the numbers were more in his favor, but the wolf's perception of his abilities had been heightened over the years. His confidence had been fueled by a constant stream of victories so that he feared nothing.

He would not retreat.

One of the men stepped from behind a tree and walked out into the open, pointing a rifle at another man whose back was to him.

The wolf attacked, moving downhill, his footing sure. At forty miles an hour, he leapt, striking the exposed man full-on with his one hundred sixty pounds of muscle, bone, and teeth. His aim was flawless. His fangs sank into the soft flesh of the man's throat with such impact the man was dead before he hit the snow.

They rolled down the hill, ice and dirt flying, until they came to a stop on a stretch of level ground, the wolf on top. The dead man was limp and gave no resistance as his throat was savaged.

Disengaging, the wolf padded back to the other two men. One was down and, as the wolf stopped, the standing man turned toward him.

The wolf would kill him before he could escape.

wo Fingers was cold, frustrated, and irate. How had they lost them? He knew the answer—too much area, not enough men. But what choice had he had? If he hadn't split his forces to search out the car and the old man was there, then what? No, he'd done what he had to do. He was fairly confident he was on the right path, but it was close to dark, and the two they were tracking were very good at sticking to rocks and fallen trees and whatever they could find to erase their prints. He'd sent several parties in different directions to scout for tracks, but so far, they had found nothing.

And then he heard the shots—about half a mile away. He radioed, asking who had fired and where they were. Simultaneously, he motioned for his men to follow him in the approximate direction he'd heard the gunfire. There was no response from whoever had fired, but his other squads were radioing where they thought the shots had originated. Two Fingers ran full out, his ten-man force following in a strung-out line.

Five minutes later, they came to a series of tracks that led down a steep hill and disappeared into the trees. Making their way down, they followed a twisting path that wove in and out of trees and around formations of jagged rock.

From somewhere down below, they heard another series of quick shots.

Leading the way, Two Fingers tried to go faster, but he slipped and fell, rolling twenty feet before colliding with a tree. He made it to his feet, retrieved his rifle, and continued at a slower pace, the world spinning as if he were still tumbling.

Considering the distance, the treacherous terrain, the downward slope, and the growing darkness, they managed to make good time.

But by the time they got there, it was all over.

It was a wolf. And not just any wolf. It was *the* wolf. The wolf that had killed Max.

It leapt.

Over a hundred and sixty pounds of primeval fury moving faster than any creature I had ever seen strike ... right at me.

Good.

There was no time to aim. I jammed the mid-portion of the rifle into the giant maw, widening as it came for me. I punched the carbon fiber weapon in as hard as I could, rocking its head back, but the rest of him slammed into me, knocking me off my feet and onto my back as if I were a child. I maintained my double-handed grip on the rifle and continued to press into the wolf, making it impossible for him to spit it out or rip it from my hands.

The monster on top of me wrenched back and forth with incredible force and fury. I could hear its teeth grinding against the metal and crushing the composite.

I was skilled at pugil sticks in the Marines and had had to kill more than one enemy combatant with the butt of my rifle during the war, so I was well versed in how to fight with blunt force instruments. But this was a bit different.

Usually, the opponent isn't gripping your rifle with its teeth.

I struck up into its belly with a knee, a good hard blow that would take out most fighting men. The wolf didn't seem to feel it, but I thought I could see something in its eyes—a fire that suddenly raged hotter. I brought up the other knee and then wrapped the giant animal with my legs as if I were grappling with a man.

When I told Billy there were other ways to fight than MMA, I hadn't meant I'd never studied MMA. I took my first lessons in Jiu-Jitsu from a skinny old Brazilian on a crabber boat when I was barely a teen.

Those lessons saved my life.

And I had another advantage. I knew canine physiology like the back of my hand—all the physical weak points. Where to punch, gouge, and grab. But knowing how versus delivering the proper blow to the exact spot it needs to land without getting mauled or killed in the process are two different things.

Two very different things.

Over the years, I've run into a lot of guys, some tough, most *pretend* tough, who would brag they could take out a trained K9 with one blow.

Kind of like Napoleon Dynamite's secret Ninja skills.

In the K9 world, we have a name for guys who actually try it.

Stub.

Because that's what they pull back after giving it their best shot.

Of course, most guys, *the vast majority of guys*, lose all their courage as soon as they come face to face with the real deal, instantly giving up any notion of fighting the snarling beast that wants, and actually has, the ability to eat them.

Still, there *are* vulnerable spots in a canine's mechanical structure that allow some possibility of survival, depending on the given animal's acquired skills and natural genetic abilities.

I'd seen how the wolf handled Max—something I would never have believed if I hadn't been there myself, so I figured my odds of succeeding against this monster were somewhere between slim and none. But since this *thing* had killed my Max, forget the odds—I was going to get my revenge. I let loose of the stock of the rifle with my right hand while shifting my hips at the same time, punching as hard as I could from my weak position into the wolf's chest. Canine chest plate bones are relatively weak, somewhat similar to the human collar bone. I thought the blow would stagger the wolf, giving me a chance to maybe grab at its jowls and perform an alpha roll, but it didn't even register the punch. It just took the opportunity to jerk the rifle out of my grip and throw it aside.

I was reaching for its jowls when it snapped back, laying hold of my left forearm. Even through the thick parka, I felt its fangs puncture into me, nearly crushing my bones. Attempting a simulation of a brachial stun, I punched into the wolf's neck with my free hand, hitting the thick muscles protecting its brachial artery with repeated snapping jabs. I shifted back and forth on my hips as I punched, pulling the powerful animal close with my tightly gripped legs. The move caused me a lot of pain, allowing the wolf to maul my arm while I struck, but it gave me leverage so that the punches were hard and fast. After the fifth one, the wolf released and tried for my fist.

But I was ready for it and bucked up with my hips, throwing it over my shoulder. I rolled with it and came out on top. One of its paws hit my forehead, the jagged, sharp claw lacerating me. I punched down into its chest, trying to crack the bone while keeping my hand as far from those massive fangs and powerful jaws as possible. As I swung down again, the wolf flawlessly performed what we in the Jiu-Jitsu community call a shrimping maneuver, and it shot out the side and away from me.

Before I could recover, it hit me with its shoulder and bowled me over onto my back. My left arm was numb and useless now, leaving me completely open. The wolf struck for my throat. I skittered to the side just in time so that its teeth took me in the left trapezius, saving my life but making the pain in my forearm seem like a scratch. I wrapped my right arm around the back of its neck, feeling the sheer strength and power corded in that column of muscle, and pulled it in as tight as I could, stopping it from going into a thrashing frenzy that would rip me to shreds. I tried to cradle its belly with my legs again, but it had learned that trick and twisted to the side, dragging me with it.

Its teeth slid grooves through the meat of my trap, partway to my upper pec.

This was going from bad to worse.

I had knives on me, a pistol too, but my left arm was dead. If I let go of its neck with my right, it would kill me instantly. So, I did all I could do. I moved with it, like turning into a skid when you hydroplane, using as little muscle as possible, making it drag dead weight, and using up its energy stores while resting mine, waiting for an opportunity.

I didn't scream ... I didn't yell. I concentrated on my breathing. Slow and even ... keeping every aspect of the fight I could under my control.

We danced that slow dance of death for twenty or thirty seconds, the wolf on top, me on the bottom, shuffling through the snow and into bushes and over rocks. The only sound in the otherwise quiet mountain air was our movement.

The wolf didn't growl or snarl or whine, confident in its power, endurance, and the final outcome.

I could feel blood flowing and soaking my clothing, but the thickness of my parka helped protect me, and I didn't think I was in any real danger of bleeding out. I tried to shift my arm and legs to maneuver for a sleeper hold, but the wolf was still too strong and wouldn't let me off my back. If I could get my legs around its belly, putting it in *the cradle*, I still might be able to secure the hold by inching my legs up and use its shoulders to push into its throat, cutting off the blood supply to its brain. But it would be hard without my left hand to secure at least one front leg. I tried to flex my fingers, but I still couldn't feel anything.

The wolf attempted to pull back and up, but I dragged it tight into the bite, hugging it so close we were stuck like glue. It was painful, and it bit down harder, but I took it, knowing that even this brute could maintain that kind of bite pressure for only so long. Dragging my dead weight around had to be taking a toll.

And so, I rested, as best I could, with my flesh in his teeth and my blood leaking out, hugging the monster closer and tighter than any lover's embrace.

I rested ... and waited for my chance.

BILLY HID behind a tree as the men passed. The closest was twenty feet away, and Billy could have put a bullet in his eye, but the other three would probably take him out before he could get them all. And so, he stayed still, lying on his belly under a pine tree, his camo parka and matching snow pants blending perfectly with the terrain. There were four of them, and they were hunting. And, if they were still hunting, his grandfather must still be free.

That gave him hope that Gil had gotten him away after jumping out of the car. It also meant he should try and cut their numbers at every chance. But how to do that without getting himself killed in the process? He had the shotgun, the AR, and the pistol, but shooting would be noisy and might attract others. He pulled up his right pant leg and slid out a long-bladed dagger from its sheath. It was black and double-edged with a tip as sharp as a sewing needle. The knife was made for one thing and one thing only—*killing*. And that's exactly what he meant to do.

Leaving the rifles in the snow, he crawled out from under the pine tree and rose up. The last man in the staggered line was moving down the mountain, about thirty or so feet back from the next man. Billy ran up behind him, covered his mouth, and shoved the dagger into the side of his neck, savagely slicing it back and forth in a brutal line. He let the body puddle silently to the snow and moved forward to the next man. He was almost to him when he heard gunfire from below and to the south.

Everyone stopped, Billy included. The men strained their ears, searching for the location of the gunfire.

Billy realized they were about to discover his presence, so he sprinted to the next man just as he was turning toward him. The man tried to raise his rifle, but Billy stabbed the dagger into his heart. He pulled it out and stuck it in again. The other two men saw him and started shooting. Billy grabbed the man, who had dropped his rifle and was clutching his chest, and dragged him around, using him as a *meat shield*. Both men missed their first shots but zeroed in quickly, punching holes in their comrade's back and legs. One bullet grazed Billy's inner thigh. Billy drew his pistol and returned fire, hitting one man in the hand, sending fingers flying. The man Billy had stabbed and used as a shield finally realized he was dead, and his legs sagged. Billy held him up with the strength of one arm while sending rounds at the unhurt soldier. But the burden of holding the weight spoiled his aim, and the enemy was able to put three more .556 slugs into the shield's back, one of which went all the way through him, hitting Billy in the ribs. The bullet tore through the parka, his shirt, and his flesh, striking bone and sliding around his ribcage before punching out his back.

The pain brought clarity to Billy's aim, and he pumped five bullets into the man, knocking him onto his back, still holding his rifle.

The man Billy had hit in the hand was on his knees, searching the snow for his fingers. He found one and was trying to stick it back in place. Billy shot him in the head as he walked past him on his way to the man on his back. Standing over him, Billy looked down into his eyes. The man was coughing up blood.

Billy touched the wound on his ribs where the bullet had bit.

"You shot me," he said to the man.

The man said nothing, just continued to choke and cough on his own blood.

Billy put two bullets into his chest, then went and found his dagger. He retrieved his weapons from under the tree, scavenged a few AR magazines, and headed toward where he thought he'd heard the original shooting.

The entry and exit wounds hurt, and to stop the bleeding, he had to apply direct pressure to both his front and back at the same time as he walked. His grandfather was out there, and Billy was going to find him.

32

Anthony stayed behind the tree, just as *Gilligan* told him to—for about a minute. Then he snuck up after him, traveling from tree to tree. He lost sight of him pretty quickly, but he could see his footprints.

It was harder going up the mountain than it had been going down, what with the snow and his gardening shoes. He slipped several times, falling to his knees, but used the tree limbs to make it back to his feet. He reached for a branch, missed, tried to get it again, but his foot went out from under, and he fell, rolling down the slope, hitting tree trunks, and bouncing over submerged rocks. He tried to grab for branches, exposed roots, or anything that protruded out of the snow, but instead of slowing him down, his efforts and the gradient just sped up his tumbling descent until he gave up and rode it out. He finally crashed full body into a thick tree trunk, stopping him cold.

He didn't lose consciousness, but he lost his air. The sky swirled and whirled over his head, the way it had when his papa would swing him in giant circles by his arms when he was a little boy back in their tiny Italian village.

Anthony tried to stand but instead threw up and fell over onto his back, the sky still spinning. He heard gunshots and screams from up where Gilligan was and knew he had to go and help him, but his ribs hurt and his legs hurt. He was dizzy and nauseated and exhausted and *old*.

But he was also something else.

He was Anthony Carlino.

And men—virtual armies, entire organizations, politicians, even the *law*—once trembled at the sound of his name.

And so, he stood, looked up the mountain, gritted his teeth, and started the climb.

I WAS BEGINNING to get some feeling back in my left arm and hand, which was good because my right was getting tired. Even though I was mostly just holding the giant wolf's head in tight to its bite, it was an awkward angle, and fatigue was starting to set in. I'd gambled that by resting and letting the wolf do most of the work—dragging, biting, and attacking—I could outlast it.

It was starting to look like I might lose that bet.

The wolf showed no sign of tiring.

I decided to change tactics and again shifted my hips, thrusting up with a knee and making contact with the wolf's testicles. Canines are not nearly as sensitive in that area as human men; still, no male likes to get attacked there. He shifted, and as he did, I flipped my hips the other way, whipping my legs under and around its belly.

Finally, I had him back in my cradle.

I twitched the fingers of my left hand, and all I felt was pain from the bite. But pain, in this case, was better than nothing. I locked my ankles together and started working my legs up around its chest. I moved my fingers, shook my wrist, and managed to bend my left arm at the elbow. The nerve shock was dissipating, but my arm still felt clunky and numb.

Too bad.

It was now or never.

Slipping my legs up, I pinched them tight against the wolf's front armpits and locked its right leg in with my left hand. Pulling down on its giant head while at the same time stomach scrunching, I cut off the blood supply to its doggy brain from the carotids.

The wolf tried to bite harder, but I was shoving its mouth tighter into my chest and trapezius muscle. I felt the weakness in his back legs first—an unsteadiness—*then a wobble.*

It let go of the bite and tried to back out, but I held firm, jerking its snout in even closer.

Panic.

It was trapped, and as the realization dawned, he went into a frenzy, jerking and trying to claw and bite, his jaws snapping and turning, but he was in too tight, too close. His teeth ripped at my parka but made it no deeper. I pulled his head lower, jamming his shoulders into the sides of his neck, further restricting blood flow.

I had him.

There was no escape.

And once he went out, I was going to put a bullet into that brain of his.

He had killed my Max.

His back legs collapsed.

Suddenly, with the sheer strength of his neck, he lifted me off the ground—a move I would have thought impossible. He slammed me down so hard that the weight of my body compacted the five inches of snow under me into the ground, almost breaking my spine. I held on as he lifted me again, slamming me even harder. Again, and again, and again, faster and harder each time. How he was still conscious, I couldn't fathom. But I wasn't about to let go ... if I did, I was as good as dead. And then my head smacked against a rock under the snow, and everything blanked out for just a second. When I opened my eyes, I was flat on my back, and the wolf was lying on its side a few inches away.

He saw me.

I saw him.

He tried to get to his feet.

I tried to reach the gun in my back holster.

He staggered and fell.

I couldn't get my hand up under my parka.

It was a race, and everything was getting dark, my vision restricting, the world spinning. I felt the butt of my Smith & Wesson 4506 and released the thumb snap as the wolf finally made it up.

Dragging the heavy gun as if in slow motion, I managed to pull it halfway out of the holster, shifting to my side from my back before feeling it snag in the folds of my parka.

The wolf was up, standing over me, and there was no parka to snag him.

I'd lost the race.

THE SCENT WAS unmistakable and unforgettable to Max. The Great Gray Wolf had murdered his family—his *pack*. And he was here —*somewhere*. Not close—*but not far*. Max would find him. Kill him. Nothing would stop him.

But the little girl.

Her voice broke through the fading light of the early evening.

She was calling him. Not *Max,* but the new name she had given him—*Petra*.

The words she called meant little to him. It was the way she said them—the tones and inflections.

She was scared.

Cold.

Max had traveled a fair distance in a short amount of time. The scent was difficult to detect as it fragmented on the shifting winds, scattering through trees and the changing elevation. But he was motivated and highly skilled. He followed the tattered remnants of scent like a shark homing in on a drop of blood through the currents of the ocean. He kept his nose high, air-scenting back and forth, dodging trees and branches, moving ever upward as he followed the fraction of a percent of particles that floated out and about in the open air, forming the weakest of scent cones. And as he climbed, the scent grew ever stronger.

"Petra! Please!"

He stopped, looking back at the way he had come.

To go to her would mean letting the Great Gray Wolf escape.

"Petra, where are you?"

Max would not go back.

"Please! I need you."

He would not let the Great Gray Wolf go.

"Petra!"

Max could hear the fear, the tears in her voice. He looked up to where the scent beckoned him.

"Please..."

Max would not go to her—not this time. He would kill the Great Gray Wolf, and then he would find her. Protect her.

But not now.

Not yet.

"Here, boy—*please*—*Petra!*"

Max looked back, a final time, toward the echoing pleas, then turned and followed his nose.

IRMGARD'S EYES OPENED. Petra was gone, and she was alone. She'd been dreaming—*a bad dream*. In the dream, her father was calling for her. But he was dead, a hole in his forehead, with blood running down his face as he walked in wobbly circles, calling her name, saying he was cold and he needed her, his eyes cloudy and dull and not really him. No not him, but something else—something *bad*.

But still, he walked about in those strange, meandering circles, calling her name and telling her he was cold.

And then she woke up, and Petra was gone. She was all alone, and it was getting dark, and she was afraid.

She crawled her way outside, looking all around. She saw the humps down by the trees where the snow-covered dead men lay.

They hadn't scared her before, but now, with Petra gone and her by herself and the wind...

Trembling, she looked away, but she found that looking away was just as terrifying. What if they were shaking the snow from their frozen bodies and ...

She called for Petra and listened.

He is out getting her another rabbit, she told herself.

She waited, watching the light bleed out of the sky.

She called again, this time louder.

The wind whistled its hollow song through the trees.

Irmgard looked over at the dead men again. She didn't want to— told herself not to—but she couldn't help it.

The breeze picked up, blowing snow into little flurries. She saw movement from the shapes in the snow.

What if the man wanted his coat back?

She shook her head, mentally and physically. They were all dead and dead people don't feel the cold. But then she remembered the dream and her father and how he said he was cold and needed her.

One of the shapes moved. *The one with no coat,* she thought.

It's only the wind ... only the wind ... only ...

It moved again.

Irmgard looked away.

"PETRA!" she screamed.

She remembered a story a friend from school had told her about a little boy who was poor and hungry. He'd found a big toe, tossed it into his mother's meager stew, and made sure he scooped it up and ate it that night for dinner. When it was dark, and the boy was in bed, the man had come looking for his big toe.

She looked back at the shapes.

Just the wind.

She looked away.

I want my big toe.

She peeked.

Something moved.

I want my ...

Only the man didn't want his big toe—*he wanted his coat.*

"Petra, PLEASE!"

Irmgard tried to look anywhere but at the men. She thought about going back into the snow cave but remembered the boy in the story—hiding in his room and under his covers as the man came calling, saying, *"I want my big toe!"*

She screamed for Petra.

She was so scared now.

She didn't want to be, knew she shouldn't be. Her father would not be proud of her. *But her father was dead, just like her mother, and she was all alone. Alone and wearing a dead man's coat. A dead man who was just down the hill and moving. And where was Petra?*

She started crying. Again, she didn't want to, but she couldn't help it. She dropped to her knees in the snow, not caring about the cold or the wet. She didn't call for her father or her mother. She called for Petra, over and over again, calling, then yelling, then screaming, and finally just mumbling as she covered her face in her hands, the tears flowing.

And then she felt a presence, and a terrible fear swept over her.

"I WANT MY..."

She moved her hands to look, and there was her Petra, sitting before her. She wrapped her arms around his thick neck and wept.

Irmgard wasn't afraid anymore.

～

ANTHONY CARLINO SAW Gilligan wrestling with a wolf. And then he saw what was left of a man by a tree. His throat had been torn out, along with most of his lower jaw. Blood soaked the snow. It was as grisly a scene as Anthony had ever witnessed—and he'd witnessed a lot.

Gilligan was beneath the wolf, gripping its chest with his legs and pulling down on its head like he was hugging it. Suddenly the wolf picked him up off his back and slammed him into the snow. The impact was so hard Anthony thought it should have knocked Gilligan out cold, but it didn't. The wolf slammed him repeatedly, and Gilligan finally did go out. But the wolf did too. He fell flat on his side and lay there—panting hard.

To see if he could get a better shot, Anthony moved around the trunk of a tree, grabbing the bark to keep from slipping. As he gained his footing, he saw the wolf was on its feet.

But then he saw Gilligan was awake too, reaching for something.

The wolf fell—got up—started for Gilligan.

Anthony was on an uneven, slippery slope, but he aimed and fired as fast as he could. The first shot ripped a line of fur and blood across the top of the wolf's neck. The animal instantly sprang away into trees, evading Anthony's second and third shots.

And then it was gone.

One moment he had it in his sights, and the next, he didn't—as if it vanished.

Gilligan had a big pistol in his hand now and was scanning the woods, but he couldn't spot the wolf either. Anthony went to him and helped him to his feet.

"You okay, Li'l Buddy?"

Gilligan just looked at him, his eyes wide and glassy. He shook his head.

Anthony wished he had a boat captain's hat.

It would have been hilarious.

33

I pushed Anthony hard, and we made good time—after I checked the dead men's boots and found a pair that would work for the ex-godfather, that is. They were a bit snug but still better than running through the drifts in gardening shoes. I had him snag a parka too. It was starting to get cold.

I did a quick check of my wounds. The wolf had torn some nasty grooves from my trapezius muscle down to the upper portion of my chest. It hurt like blazes but wasn't bleeding badly.

I'd live.

We'd made some noise, with the fight and the shooting and all, and I was pretty sure it wouldn't go unnoticed.

So down we went. About ten minutes in, I went back to finding whatever bare patches of leaves, dirt, and rocks I could to camouflage our trail. It slowed us down, but it would be harder to follow, especially after dark, which was fast approaching.

I hoped to lose them then in the dark, giving us a chance to rest and recuperate.

We both needed it.

We went until we could hardly see where we were going, then I switched back to moving faster straight downhill. I set us on a relatively even line in the direction of the farmhouse until it got too dark for us to continue with any margin of safety. We didn't have flashlights and wouldn't have used them even if we did.

A broken leg or even a sprained ankle could spell death for us, so we stopped and rested for about an hour. We didn't have food, drink, or fire, and it was getting cold, even with the parkas, so we got moving again, slow and easy now ... careful not to fall or get off course.

I kept a little distance between us, mainly to keep Anthony Carlino from talking. I was getting tired of all the Gilligan stuff.

Li'l Buddy.

Not to mention Chuck Norris.

Sheesh!

I shook my head and instantly regretted it. My neck, shoulder, and trapezius were painfully bruised around the punctures. My left side was no longer numb ... but now I kind of wished it was.

On a good note, we had rifles. I hadn't heard any sign of pursuit yet, but I was sure it was coming. The best solution might well be to set up an ambush in the morning. Try and *thin the herd*. And put a little fear into them to slow them down.

The rifles made that a possibility.

I stopped at a tree, checking my Swiss compass to see if we needed directional correction. Anthony Carlino stopped behind me.

"Getting tired, Li'l Buddy?"

I closed my eyes, took a deep breath of the crisp mountain air, counted to ten. Shook my head.

Lil' Buddy.

THEY'D LOST the tracks several times, which was very perplexing to Two Fingers because he was an exceptional tracker. Whoever was leading the old man must be highly skilled in evasion tactics. And now that it was dark, the situation was proving to be too much for his men.

Two Fingers had surveyed the battle scene. The slaughtered man with the mutilated throat and face had to be the work of animals after the fact. He and his men had probably scared away whatever was eating on him when they approached. But the other man had been shot three times—excellent shot placement. And their rifles *taken*.

He didn't like that. They'd have to be more careful, and careful meant slower. He would have called for more men, but it was going to be hard enough managing what he already had, not to mention keeping things quiet once they retrieved Carlino.

At least he knew the old man was still alive. One of his men had found the gardening shoes, and since the man who'd been shot was missing his boots—well—pretty obvious.

Two Fingers had sent five men ahead to follow the tracks leading down while he checked in with his other search parties and had them start converging on this area. He and the rest of his group had caught up with the party of five about a half hour ago.

They'd completely lost the tracks, and it took Two Fingers nearly an hour to backtrack and reacquire them. The path was easier now, and they were making better time.

He wanted them captured before morning.

BILLY CUT a diagonal path toward the gun battle he'd heard earlier. It called for him to go around and back up, almost to the area where he'd landed after jumping out of the car and falling, but, as his grandfather used to say to him, *"Such is life."* He was young, in great shape, *except for the injuries,* and was well equipped.

The uphill hike hardly fazed him. Now that the bleeding had stopped, the bullet wounds seemed mostly trivial. He ignored them and kept moving, but not for long. When he heard men's voices, he hid under a thick pine tree and watched from under its plump, green needles.

A party of heavily armed men passed his position, twenty or so yards out. He caught glimpses of them through the trees.

He followed.

Eventually, they came to an area where there had clearly been a fight. Two men were dead. One of them had been torn apart, the other shot.

Billy thought of Gil and Max—but Max was dead.

Still, his money was on this being the work of either his grandfather and Gil or Marco and his group. When they discovered the gardening shoes, he knew for sure.

His grandfather and Gil.

Keeping a safe distance, he moved down with the men. Billy had the advantage; he knew where Gil was headed. As soon as they lost the track, he silently left the soldiers and continued on his own, quickly outpacing the strung-out line of men. He'd counted thirteen in all. Tough odds.

Billy didn't worry about finding tracks in the snow. Instead, once he was confident the hunters wouldn't come across his tracks, he cut straight toward the farmhouse, gambling on meeting up with Gil and his grandfather.

He kept his senses alert for any possible scouts. If he got the chance to take any out, he was ready.

He had his dagger.

34

Max smelled the storm long before it arrived. His primal senses told him it was going to be powerful, dangerous.

Protecting the sleeping girl and keeping her alive might prove difficult.

But he would do it.

He wrapped himself tightly around her. In response, she rubbed at his fur and hugged him close.

Still, the danger was real. And far more deadly than man.

The storm hit within the hour, the wind wailing like a lost soul. Snow slashed down with brutal force, startling the girl awake. She lifted her head, trying to see through the darkness, but she couldn't see Max. Sensing her terror, he rubbed his chin on her face and pushed her head back under his fur, protecting her from the wind that funneled through the small entrance to their cave. Max knew he should go out and dig snow and dirt to cover the hole, but he didn't want to leave her just now.

She needed him.

Her thin arms and chest shuddered and quaked, and her breathing came quick and short. Instead of closing the hole, he stayed where he was, sharing his heat and his strength. After a while, she calmed, and her breathing slowed. Her arms and chest relaxed into an easy natural rhythm.

Eventually, she slept while Max patiently watched over her.

Irmgard dreamed of the man who had killed her father and of the monster wolf that had chased her. In the dream, she climbed a tree and watched as the man and the wolf paced about looking for her. Then the wind came, blowing the tree and pushing at her with invisible fingers, shoving her out of the tree. She landed in front of the man and the wolf. They both grinned and jumped for her.

She jerked awake, her heart racing. Still shaking and afraid, she began to realize there was no man with two fingers, no wolf, and she wasn't under the tree. She was in the snow cave with Petra, *safe*. She hugged him and listened to the wind and snow as it howled and raged and beat at their tiny shelter. But that was out there, and she was in here. Petra wouldn't let anything bad happen to her. Closing her eyes, she drifted back into a peaceful slumber. Now she was sitting at the table in the kitchen of their farmhouse, her mother and father alive and happy and smiling at her as she scooped up peas in her spoon and gladly ate them.

They tasted so good.

They were the best thing she had ever eaten, and all she wanted to do was sit there with her parents and see them smiling at her as she ate the peas with the warm summer sunshine glowing through the windows.

As she slept, she hugged Petra closer and smiled into his fur.

The wolf dug a den and lay inside as the snow and wind attacked. The bullet had torn the skin along the top of his neck. It stung, but pain meant little to him. He didn't care about the snow either. What he did care about was his prey.

The man.

The girl.

They were out there, both of them, *somewhere.*

And now there were others, defying his markings, his boundaries, his warnings.

He would kill them too.

But they would all have to wait. This storm was not one to contend with. It started strong and was steadily getting worse.

Standing, the wolf turned and used his front paws to shovel snow and dirt between his back legs until he'd almost completely covered the opening, slowing the heat loss and preventing the wind and the wet from entering. He trampled the remaining snow and dirt at the center of the den by circling a dozen times until it was packed tight. He then curled into a tight ball, his eyes staring at the entrance as the skies spent their fury on the earth below.

His prey would not escape.

If *he* couldn't hunt, *they* couldn't run. They would be there for him when the storm stopped. The primitive operation of his mind understood these truths in a way that no human could. And so, he was patient, calm, and sure in the certainty of his eventual success.

The storm would stop.

And he would hunt.

But then the scent reached him through the tiny hole in his cave. It was strong and close. Sleep and rest would have to wait.

THEY FOUGHT the snow and the wind for as long as they could, but eventually, Two Fingers had to admit to himself that he was being foolish. If they didn't make shelter, he would start losing men. Besides, the snow instantly covered any tracks, so going on was useless anyway.

The men gathered together, pitched tents, and started fires. They ate, drank, and hunkered down. Most had served in the military, so they were familiar with the harsh snows that the German mountains could deliver. They were hard men, none of them above breaking the law or doing blood work when required. And today, their training in warfare had been brought home in a very real way.

Two Fingers reasoned to himself that the old man and his rescuer would have to hold up just as well.

Unless they died.

At this point, their death would be an acceptable outcome. Far better than them escaping. If they died, any information about himself or the men who'd kidnapped the old man would remain hidden.

The one drawback would be that *proof of life* would no longer be possible, which could prove problematic. But still, better than the alternative.

Two Fingers ate a forkful of rehydrated chicken and listened to the wind as it beat against the side of the tent.

Where were they headed?

Most likely, they were wandering about, lost, hoping that going down the mountain to look for a road was their best option.

There was no cell reception in these mountains—the closest cell tower was over fifty miles away—but the possibility that they might have access to a satellite phone was a real danger.

Nothing he could do about that.

Two Fingers had learned a lot since losing his fingers to the mangy fighting dog that had eaten them. The injury had almost destroyed him. Alcohol and drugs called to him, but instead, he found a strength he didn't know he possessed. Instead of succumbing, he grew. Ironically his injury became a badge of honor among his peers. It started with the nickname, transforming his image into something akin to a superhero. He was easily recognized, easily remembered. His reputation grew, and soon, things he had nothing to do with were attributed to him. Stories circulated about his cruelty, courage, and cunning. The organization began trusting him with bigger jobs, and to his credit, everything he touched turned to gold.

Until now.

The loss of the old man, if he didn't make it right, would be the death of him.

He forked another chunk of chicken and held it before his eyes. It steamed as he twisted the utensil slowly.

He had come too far to lose now.

And so, he would not let the old man escape.

35

I found a shallow cave with a nice overhang in the side of the mountain and decided to use it as a base. Luckily, the snow was heavy, wet, and easy to pack and shape, so I built a wall around the opening of the cave. We wouldn't be able to stand upright, but we did have some arm room. It was no igloo, but it would do for now.

By the time I finished, I could tell Anthony Carlino was spent. Gathering some twigs and branches, I started a small fire inside the cave and told him to sack out while I took the first watch. He was asleep almost instantly.

As I sat, listening to the wind, I thought of Max. My physical wounds hurt, but they were nothing compared to my heart. I kept seeing him leaping at the wolf and the horrible aftermath ... the snapping of his neck ... the ripping of his throat ... the men shooting into him. I tried not to think about it.

Didn't work.

Couldn't do it.

Couldn't *not* think about it.

I snugged the parka close, tightening the fur-lined hood around my face, and crawled out of the cave.

The wind and sleet-like snow hit me instantly. I squinted against the storm and stood up. I'd made a small hole in the top of the cave wall so the smoke from the fire could escape. It looked fine for now, but I'd have to be careful it didn't clog up. I could have done a better job with a shovel, but at least I had gloves. Growing up in Colorado had its advantages. I'd been building igloos since I could toddle. Just rough snow caves at first, but as I got older, they got better. And when I ran away to Alaska, I mastered the skill.

Hunting in this weather would be nearly impossible, but I could set a couple of traps. Nothing fancy like lines or snares, just a few deadfalls, hoping for mice or squirrels once the snow stopped.

Marching into the trees, I set a few rocks and sticks into position to catch some food, but the snow was falling so fast and hard, I had misgivings about any success.

When I finished setting the deadfalls, I was getting cold and considered heading back in, but Max flashed across the inside of my eyes again ... *the wolf ... the blood ... the men standing over him ... shooting into him.*

I decided to check the perimeter and circled the camp. I found a little trail that led me up and over our cave. From above, I could see the fire flickering through the hole, but nothing else. The smell of smoke was tattered to pieces before it could rise to my level, making it undetectable.

Good.

I didn't think the army searching for us was tough enough to keep on through this, but you never know, and I didn't want to get trapped.

After finishing the circuit, I went back inside. Anthony Carlino was awake.

"Nature call you, Li'l Buddy?"

Li'l Buddy.

I shook my head, sending snow flying.

"Security sweep."

He gave me surprised.

"In this? You really think they're out walking around looking for us in this?"

"Probably not," I said. "Best to be sure, though. I think they want you pretty bad."

He grinned, nodding and holding his hands toward the fire. He looked at the bloody bandage covering the stump of his missing ring finger.

The grin disappeared.

"Hurting?" I asked.

His eyes met mine, and I could see it wasn't so much physical pain he was feeling. I saw in his eyes what *I* was feeling about Max.

"We've got the ring," I said. "Your son, Nick, is taking good care of it."

I saw him sigh, and the look in his eyes softened a little.

"Thanks for that," he said. "I never once, since the day she put it on me, took that ring off my finger."

I removed my gloves and warmed my hands opposite his.

"You're married," he said, noticing my ring.

"Widower," I said. "Like you."

He pursed his lips and canted his head.

"You seem young for that," he said, the question implied.

I nodded, staring into the fire, Max momentarily forgotten.

"I have a habit of working dangerous professions. Danger followed me home one day."

He nodded, sighing again.

"I'm sorry to hear that," he said, and I could tell he meant it.

There was a lot of nodding and sighing going on.

I pointed at his bandage.

"Infection?"

"Nah. They shot me up with antibiotics and gave me pills. Real sweethearts they were."

We both grinned at that.

"That wolf get you pretty good?"

I touched lightly at the wound.

"Nasty animal," I said. "I'm going to kill it."

"For biting you?"

"It killed my dog ... my best friend in the world."

"Wow," he said. "Again, sorry to hear that. If it makes you feel any better, I managed to hit it in the neck. Don't know how bad, but I saw blood fly."

"Thanks," I said. "And yes... it does make me feel a little better."

We both grinned again.

"What was his name?"

"Max. Most perfect dog I've ever seen, and I've seen a lot."

"More to it than him being the perfect dog, though, right?"

I stared back into the fire, remembering the way he lay in my bed when I thought Pilgrim was going to die. The way he let me pet him.

"Yeah," I said, my voice a raspy whisper. "Yeah, a lot more than just that."

"Then you do it," he said. "You kill that wolf. Do it for Max—and do it for you. Sounds like Max was *worth* killing for."

I didn't exactly know what to say to that, and I didn't have to because the transponder in my pocket started beeping.

"What's that?" asked Anthony Carlino.

"It's the transponder," I said, digging it out. The red 360 indicator arrows were pointing to the northwest.

"What does it mean?"

"Like I said before, only three of us have them, Me, you, and ..."

"Billy," he finished.

"Yeah, Billy."

~

BILLY WAS FREEZING TO DEATH—AND not figuratively.

He was dying.

Searching his pockets, he found a lighter and dragged it out with numb fingers. He found something else in his pockets too.

The transponder.

He slid the casing back, pushed the button to indicate his position, and saw the red lights circle and blink.

Maybe they would find him.

But who, and how long would it take?

He knew there was a way for him to track the others with the device, but his numb mind couldn't put all the pieces together to remember how.

He put the transponder back in his pocket, gathered some twigs and pine needles, and piled them into a small teepee, the way he'd learned in Boy Scouts. Then he tried to start a fire with the lighter, but the needles and twigs wouldn't light. And when he tried to warm his hands with the lighter, he found the wind too much to battle, and the flame kept blowing out.

After finally giving up, he pulled his gloves back over fingers that felt as frozen as icicles. He forced himself to stand, clenched his teeth and started walking.

He stayed on his feet and kept moving for as long as he could, but eventually, he fell to his knees. Lacking the strength or the will to get back up, he told himself he would just rest for few minutes. But a few minutes stretched to fifteen, and he found himself curled up in a fetal ball.

He didn't even remember lying down.

Closing his eyes, he felt the snow cover his face, the cold rushing through him.

The wind howled, and the ice felt like tiny bullets smacking any exposed skin they could find.

He thought of trying his cell again, but it had proved useless the dozen or so times he'd tried before. And besides, he admitted to himself; he just didn't have the energy. Not yet. He needed to rest.

He was so cold that he was starting to feel warm, and that scared him. He'd heard how people going into hyperthermia sometimes took off their clothes because they felt hot. But that wasn't going to happen to him. He'd just rest for a couple of minutes and then get going.

Billy thought of his grandfather, father, and uncle, and a strange sensation of guilt invaded his mind. He felt like he was somehow letting them down.

But he wasn't—*he wouldn't.*

He just needed a few minutes. He promised himself and his family that he would get up after that—like hitting the snooze on his alarm clock when he was back in school. Just five more minutes, Mom, I promise. *And how did that work out?* How many times had he been late? How many times had his mother had to drive him because he missed the bus? But not this time, he promised—just a little longe—

And then he saw Gil Mason looking down on him with contempt.

Only he wasn't really there; Billy knew that much.

He could see the snow slicing through him—*and the trees.* He could see the trees as though Gil were a ghost. He closed his eyes and tried to blink him away. He'd heard somewhere that was what you did to get rid of a mirage—*mirage? was that right? or was that only for deserts—illusion?* Maybe illusion, he thought.

But Gil was still there, and now he was talking.

"I knew you were a loser," he said. "First, my dog beat you, then I beat you, and now you're going to let a little snow beat you."

"It's not going to beat me," Billy said. "I just need to rest."

"That's a lie, and you know it. You've given up. It's easier that way. Just go to sleep and never wake up. No one to judge your failure."

"I'm not giving up," Billy said. "I never give up. I'm a cage fighter. I just need ..."

"Yeah-yeah-yeah. *Just a few minutes.* I heard you already. Is that what you say when you're getting pummeled in the cage? *Time out, I need a few minutes.* Is that the way it works in there? Because that's not the way it works in the real world. In the real world, it's like in the kitchen with the cutting board. No rules. No time-outs. No, *just a few minutes.* In the real world, you either get up and fight, or you die. And that's just what you're going to do, Billy. You are going to die. Because you're a quitter, a loser."

Billy tried to grab him, to put him in an ankle lock or maybe take out his knee, but his hand passed through empty air, and Gil was gone.

"I'm not a quitter ..." he said, "... not a loser."

He pushed himself up to his knees. The warm feeling was instantly gone, and he felt the horror of the cold. It was almost enough to make him lie back down and close his eyes. Instead, he pushed his foot back, raising one arm to block any attack, just as he had thousands of times in MMA practice, and executed a wobbly stand.

Billy pushed on, the wind and snow battering him like a human foe. He couldn't see. The sleet and the dark blinded him as he stumbled. Using trees to keep himself upright, he kept on.

Up ahead, he saw something. It was just an irregularity in the drifts of snow, but it was enough for him to know that it was out of place.

His feet were ice, his gait a zombie stagger but refusing to give up, he shuffled forward. He tried to yell, but he was too weak, too cold. He made his throat work and croaked out a whispered cry for help, but the wind whipped the words out behind him. He tried again, this time a little louder, but it was like yelling into a jet engine.

His knees buckled, and he dropped. But he wouldn't quit—he couldn't. Not when he was so close—fifty yards at the most. He had to stand. He reached out for a tree, his hand slipping off the icy surface, and he fell face-first into the snow.

It was starting to feel warm again ... nice ... good ...

He gritted his teeth, telling himself to get up, to fight. But then he sensed something—something that made the hairs on the back of his neck stand up straight. Something deadly—deep and dark. He remembered the wolf and opened his eyes, and when he saw what he saw, he wished he'd kept them shut and just let himself die in the warmth of the snow.

But the snow was not to be his fate.

Billy screamed.

$\backsim$

GILLIGAN TRIED to get Anthony to stay in the snow cave, but Billy was his grandson. There was no way he was staying behind. Anthony felt the wind-swept snow slap him in the face as soon as he stepped outside. He had to squint his eyes nearly closed and hold up a hand to deflect some of its fury to be able to move ahead. Almost immediately, he was lost in the storm, with no sense of direction. There was only the dark and the cold and the wind and the snow. It took his breath away, and the drop in temperature from just a few hours ago was unimaginable.

He felt a hand on his shoulder and heard Gilligan yelling in his ear; he could still barely make out what he was saying.

"Stay close. If you lose me, you'll die. Sure you don't want to stay?"

Anthony shook his head and motioned with a hand for him to get going.

Gilligan was right, though; he needed to stay right on his heels to keep from losing him. If Billy was out in this, he wouldn't last long. And Anthony, still amazed that Billy might have survived the car going over the mountain and the explosion, wasn't going to lose the chance of saving him.

Gilligan had told him not to get his hopes up. He said this could be a trap. The bad guys might have found the transponder on Billy's body and decided to try and lure them by turning it on. Or an animal scavenging his body might have dragged it off and accidentally activated it. But Anthony knew how tough the Carlino clan was and banked his money on his grandson.

They moved west, parallel to the mountain, the going difficult, *exhausting*, the snow already past their knees, with patches of ice beneath, making the footing treacherous. How Gilligan was able to follow the signal was a mystery to Anthony, but follow it he did. After what seemed like a mile, they turned down, making the trek even more difficult because of the increased risk of slippage. They used trees and branches when they could, but Anthony's bad hand hampered him. Gilligan's wounds didn't seem to be bothering him at all.

Kids, he thought.

Then a thought struck him. How would they find their way back? Glancing up the mountain, he saw the storm was instantly obliterating their tracks. And then he realized that no matter what, this was going to be a two-way trip. That meant they were going to have to go back *up* the mountain, already tired, *in this*.

Maybe I should have stayed in the cave.

Too late now.

What had he said about the Carlinos being a tough clan?

Time to prove it.

After all, he was the patriarch. He would have to act the part. He'd hoped to be done with all this *adventure* after turning the organization over to his son, Nick, after Bella died. He shook his head at his foolishness. He should have known better. No one ever got out, not alive. The sins of the past find you—*sooner or later*— they find you.

His foot slipped, and he almost fell, but he grabbed a branch and stayed up. The depth of the snow was helping now by bracing their knees and legs.

After Bella died, it was as though he had fallen asleep. The zest for life that he had always felt just wasn't there anymore. It wasn't that he wanted to die, not exactly. It was more like life itself had become different.

Dull.

Unimportant.

Gray.

So hard to put into words, not that he would even try. He wasn't that kind of guy. He was no poet. He didn't snitch, and he didn't whine. But here and now, to himself, in the cold, looking for his grandson who was probably already dead, he could admit it. He'd hoped and planned to be working on his vineyard until he died and that would have been that. He could accept it. Maybe even try and do a little penance, give to charities, light some candles, be nicer to people, love his grandkids.

Not kill anyone.

But *they* had to go and wake him up.

Fools.

Anthony Carlino looked back up the way they had come and then to Gilligan in the lead. The snow and the wind had gotten worse, but suddenly they felt good against his flesh. They felt real and powerful and—*alive.*

He felt alive.

They should have let him sleep.

36

The wolf heard the man before he smelled him. Maneuvering carefully, he could see brief snatches of him through the dark and the storm. He changed direction, remaining hidden by the trees, and moved downwind of his prey. The man was scared, cold, angry, tired. In small tatters, a collage of scents reached the wolf—adrenaline, cortisol, norepinephrine, and a host of others telling him what he needed to know about this target.

But his last meeting with a human left him cautious. Until that encounter, he considered humans weak and relatively easy prey. But that man had been different.

Dangerous.

The wolf slowed his pace and let the snow and the cold do their work on the man. Soften him. Instead of attacking straight on, he waited. He watched.

The man walked. The snow fell. The wind was as strong as the wind ever was.

And still, the wolf waited.

Until it was time. And then he attacked.

~

I GLANCED BACK JUST as the old man slipped and nearly fell, but he grabbed a leafless branch, slick with snow and ice, and somehow managed to stay upright.

Color me impressed.

I'd set a hard pace and only had to slow up a few times to keep from losing the once *mob boss*.

Anthony Carlino was still pretty tough.

Even with the missing finger.

Plus, he'd saved my bacon with that wolf.

The transponder indicated we were getting close, which was good because the storm was only getting worse, and the footing was scary bad. Not to mention the cold. The scene from *Dumb and Dumber*, where Harry and Lloyd are riding up the mountains of Colorado on a scooter with frozen snot and spit and ice clinging to their nostrils and mouths, kept flashing through my mind.

Self-consciously, I swiped at my nose with a gloved hand.

Nothing.

Yet.

I held up the snotless hand, signaling Anthony Carlino to stop.

I thought I heard something up ahead.

Anthony Carlino must not have been familiar with the correct usage of hand signals because he didn't stop, then slipped as he bumped into my back, almost knocking us both down the slope.

I gave him the look, but I don't think he even noticed.

Too tired.

He was breathing hard now, his breath coming out in clouds that were there and gone in the wind. Ice crusted his eyebrows, but thankfully I saw no evidence of frozen snot.

So there, Lloyd and Harry.

Giving him a few seconds to rest, I tried to scan the area, but the screaming snow, wind, and the dark made it nearly impossible to see anything more than a few yards ahead.

Rechecking the transponder, I touched Anthony Carlino on the shoulder and motioned in the direction I wanted him to follow.

As we started down, I thought I saw movement down and to the right, but I couldn't be sure. It might be a tree.

Might be a bad guy with a gun too.

Or a wolf.

I hoped it was the wolf.

We had unfinished business, he and I.

There it was again. I checked the transponder ... same direction.

I transitioned the AR I'd taken off the bad guy from my back to the front using its sling. With no night vision, no thermal vision, just a scope ... it was useless in this storm. Still, the gun could throw sharp metal objects at speeds that break the sound barrier ... *better than nothing.*

I directed us to the right, skirting a small outcropping of what I thought were slippery rocks hidden by snow and ducking under skeletal branches, then headed down for about forty yards—and there we were.

The point where the transponder said Billy should be.

Only he wasn't.

I scanned and rescanned.

It was about where I thought I'd seen the movement. No tracks. Clean snow.

It had taken us fifteen, maybe twenty minutes, to get here from where we'd been when I thought I saw something move.

Enough time for this snow to cover stuff up.

I started digging. Maybe Billy was lying under the snow right here. I'd seen it in avalanches. Freezing ... suffocating.

Anthony Carlino caught on and started digging with me.

My glove caught something about a foot and a half down. I grabbed hold and pulled it up.

The red lights flashed up from my hand.

It was Billy's snow-encrusted transponder.

TWO FINGERS HEARD the scream and immediately awoke. It was a terrible sound, filled with fear and pain. The other three in the tent with him had grabbed their guns and were staring, wide-eyed, toward the tent flap, as though they expected a monster to come in any second. Two Fingers motioned at them to go outside and see what was happening.

The king sending pawns into danger ahead of him.

He checked his pistol and got out of his sleeping bag.

The storm was torturous—the wind nearly knocking him over as he ducked out of the tent. Men were scrambling about, shining flashlights that were useless in the slashing snow.

Two Fingers contacted the perimeter guards using the radio until he got to the third out of five, who didn't answer. He grabbed two men and proceeded to the guard's location.

The guard wasn't there.

They searched for him together, the flashlights almost as useless as they had been in camp. There were no footprints or disturbances in the snow, the storm filling any depressions almost instantly.

Working in a spiraling circle, Two Fingers had his men search outward from where the guard was supposed to be. Fifteen meters to the northeast, one of the men saw a glove with just a patch of color showing through the snow. When they pulled it out, Two Fingers saw fresh blood on it. He checked it carefully but found no evidence of tears or holes—just blood.

They continued the circular search pattern, and at about twenty-five meters, they found a fur-lined boot, the heel barely exposed. There were no tracks leading up to it.

The wind howled.

There was no blood on the boot. They surveyed the area, Two Fingers meticulously directing the search, flashlight beams reflecting off the savage snow and blinding them. Wisdom dictated they go without the lights, but the dark was too oppressive to consider it.

The glove, the boot, the dark, and the absence of tracks were affecting the men.

The radio crackled, and another perimeter guard's voice came across.

"*Boss—boss! There's something out there. I can't see it but ...*"

Two Fingers waited for him to finish the transmission, but he never did.

After a full minute, Two Fingers looked at his men.

"That was Hans. East perimeter."

He headed out at a fast pace, the other two following, and they were able to make it to the guard's location before the snow could finish covering the scene. They didn't find Hans, or his glove or his boot. But they did find something.

They found tracks.

They found blood.

A lot of blood.

IRMGARD FELT Petra curl around her, sharing his warmth. It was nice. She had gotten cold when he left. When she'd awoken to find him gone, she had been scared, but then she told herself Petra must have gone outside to go pee or maybe to find her another rabbit. She'd closed her eyes and gone back to sleep until she felt him bump gently against her. He'd brought something in with him. Something big. Bigger than a rabbit. Maybe a deer. Irmgard loved deer. Her father was a good hunter and often brought home game. Deer was her favorite, but she was much too sleepy to eat just now. She rubbed Petra's head and snout, her small fingers slipping under his lip and running along his teeth and gums. She didn't mind the slick wetness. His teeth were so hard and sharp and perfectly formed. They filled her with a sense of peace and ease. She saw in her mind what he did to the men. Nothing could hurt her as long as Petra was with her.

The tip of Petra's tongue stuck out from his lips. Irmgard couldn't see it in the blackness of the den, but she felt it and rubbed it lightly between her thumb and index finger. It was dry and nubbly and

adorable. He was so sweet. She was so glad that he had found her and
stayed with her.

She loved him.

Putting her face against his muzzle, she rubbed noses with him
and smiled into his lips. Then she kissed him, closed her eyes, and
fell asleep again, her face pressed tight, her hands resting in his fur.

In her dreams, bad men were everywhere, but Petra was at her
side, and no one dared come close.

37

By the time we made it back to our shelter, Anthony Carlino was pretty done in. Still, the fact that he made it at all was testimony to his willpower and fortitude. How many guys in their seventies could have made it at all after what he'd been through —in this kind of storm, on this kind of mountain, in this terrain, and in pain from his finger and other injuries?

Chuck Norris?

Maybe Marine Corps Legend Chesty Puller—or Jack LaLanne—a couple more maybe—but not many.

Except for the transponder, I couldn't find any sign of Billy Carlino. I tried brushing the snow away from the area where I dug it out, looking for tracks. Sometimes, if the snow is powdery and light, you can sweep it away and find tracks beneath where the snow has blown over them. But the snow from this storm was too wet, too heavy. It filled everything in and smooshed it all together.

I warmed my hands over the fire. Anthony Carlino did the same, but I was afraid he might fall asleep and land face-first in the flames.

"He might still be alive," I said. "The fact that his body isn't there is a good sign. He survived the car falling off the mountain. He's a tough kid."

"How do we know it was him who dropped the gadget? Maybe they found it at the car and were trying to set us up."

I shrugged. "Yeah, that's possible. But if that were the case, seems like they would have staked it out so they could pick us off when we came to check it."

"Pick *you* off," he said. "Me they want alive." He gave a half-grin. "Besides, it might have fallen out of the guy's pocket without him even knowing. These guys ain't exactly Chuck Norris."

I nodded, turning my hands to warm the other side. "Yeah, maybe." I was tired, fatigue setting in now that we were out of the wind and the cold and the danger.

"You ain't exactly Chuck Norris, neither," he said.

I gave him the look. "I rescued you ... got you this far ...."

"You call this a rescue?" he interrupted. "Messed up rescue, Li'l Buddy."

I saw Max ... *leaping* ... the wolf turning ... the blood ... the bullets.

"Well," I sighed, "I can't argue with that."

"Hey," he said, "you did okay. I'm still alive. No Chuck, like I said. If Chuck was here, I'd already be at home sipping a nice Chianti, with my finger sewn back on and all these Krauts dead. So, no Chuck, but maybe a—a Schwarzenegger—maybe better—maybe a Stallone. Depends on how this turns out. We'll see."

My lips twitched at the corners. I gave him my best Lloyd Christmas from *Dumb and Dumber*. "So, you're telling me there's a chance."

"Who the heck are you trying to sound like?"

I shook my head. "Lloyd ... you know, from *Dumb and...*"

He shrugged me off and lay down, closing his eyes.

"You're back to Gilligan," he said.

I gave my hands another turn.

Everyone's a critic.

At least I didn't have frozen snot sticking out of my nose.

                                     ~

TWO FINGERS never found his sentries—not exactly. He did find pieces of the second one. Not big pieces, but pieces. Enough to let him know that it wasn't a human he was dealing with.

It was that wolf!

He brought the perimeter in closer and doubled the manpower, two men at each post. It would cost them sleep, but that was better than being slaughtered one by one.

The storm showed no sign of letting up, but in a way, that was good. Even with his satellite phone connection, Two Fingers couldn't get more help up here—the roads were impassable. But if the old man's rescuers had a satellite phone, and he had to assume they did, then they wouldn't be able to get help or an escape vehicle either.

It bought Two Fingers what he needed most.

Time.

He wanted to utilize as much of it as possible but sending men out in this would be foolish. They'd get lost, or worse, *eaten*. No, he'd have to wait at least until morning.

Looking at his watch, he realized he might be able to get a few hours of sleep—provided he could conk out. He needed rest. He closed his eyes and tried, but it wasn't easy. He had worked so hard to get where he was, and if he didn't find Anthony Carlino, it would all be ruined. *They* wouldn't let him live.

Either side.

Carlino's side would probably make it take a long time. A long, painful time.

There had been so many obstacles. How had it gotten so out of control? The escape, the wolf, the farmer hearing Carlino in the trunk and needing to be killed, the little girl escaping, Carlino's men coming to get him, the storm. He shook his head, trying to clear it so he could sleep.

Fat chance of that.

After another few minutes, he gave up and started planning how to tackle the search in the morning.

Out in the night, a lone howl pierced the savage storm's wind.

Two Fingers looked at the tent wall as it shook and shuddered beneath the onslaught. A supernatural fear he was wholly unfamiliar with flooded over him.

In the dark, his mind saw the pieces of the man in the snow.

He saw the boot.

He saw the glove.

That wolf.

ANTHONY CARLINO TURNED AWAY from Gilligan and closed his eyes. He didn't sleep. He thought about his grandson Billy.

Billy was dead.

Anthony knew this, no matter what Gilligan said. He couldn't possibly have survived the fall from the cliff. No one could. Not to mention the fact the car exploded on impact and burned up. He didn't know why his grandson's body wasn't in the car when they found it, but he figured the Germans had gotten there first and taken him. That's how they got hold of the transponder. That's how they set the trap for them. Why they didn't wait to spring the trap, he didn't know. *Maybe they got cold or tired or scared.* But that scenario was a lot more plausible than believing what Gilligan wanted him to believe.

Another crime to avenge. He mentally flipped through several members of the Cosa Nostra, their faces flashing in his mind's eye like a deck of cards. Which family, or families, were responsible?

So many possibilities. Was it one working alone? Or a group of them? Either way, he would make them pay. He had caught glimpses of faces and heard bits of conversations before being thrown on the boat for Germany. He didn't know who had orchestrated the kidnapping, but with what little he did know, his connections would be able to figure it out.

And what he would do to them when he did find out.

He was as old-school as old-school got. And he would pay them in old-school style. They had cut off his finger, murdered his men, killed his grandson. But they could not hope to comprehend what he would do to them. They would die slowly—but that would only come after. First, he would capture them as they had captured him. Only he wouldn't just keep them. Each and every day, they would be shown pictures, video—with sound, articles of clothing—maybe by themselves—maybe attached to something—like his finger with the ring. *They had given him the idea—set the example.* Doing it his way, they would do more than see. More than hear. His way, they would smell, touch, *taste.* His way, they would truly experience what everyone they had feelings for would have to go through before death finally set them free.

He would start with the outliers, their associates, acquaintances, favorite teachers maybe, school friends. And then he would move inward, coming closer and closer to those they loved the most. Siblings, parents, spouses, children.

A lesson would be taught.

In the old days, there were rules.

Respect.

They had thrown all that away. They had dishonored the code.

They needed to be shown why the rules were set in the first place.

And he would show them.

38

Billy awoke with ice crystals pelting him in the face. Spits and spats of snow were blowing in through a partial opening directly in front of him. He was curled in a ball and had been dreaming that a giant wolf was dragging him down a dark hole where he intended to eat him. In the dream, he was powerless to stop the monster. His arms and legs wouldn't work, and there was no one around for him to yell to for help. It was like when he had gone to try and scare Gil Mason before he knew who Gil Mason was—and Mason's dog, Max, had attacked him. It felt just like that in the dream —helplessness, despair, regret, terror.

Through the opening, Billy could see dark gray clouds blocking the morning sun. Snow, driven by a slashing wind, streaked past in an icy blur. The tiny slivers of ice that swirled through the opening stung his cheeks and forehead, forcing him to close his eyes.

As he tried to turn away, he felt pain and a cracking sensation where he had been shot. The blood had dried and clotted. His ribs ached like a sore tooth, only a sore tooth didn't usually hamper your breathing. Pushing up on one arm, he noticed a little girl was sleeping next to him.

On turning his head a little further, he came face to face with Max.

Billy jerked back, almost collapsing, but gathered himself, his pain wholly forgotten.

Max moved like drifting fog, seating himself between Billy and the girl. His eyes never left Billy's. He didn't growl. He didn't snarl or curl back his lip, but Billy had the distinct impression the dog wanted to tear his throat out—to complete the job he'd started that night at Gil's.

Billy didn't understand how this was possible. Gil told him that Max had been killed in the skirmish on the meadow.

But it was Max.

Billy would never forget him.

He considered trying for the hole, but remembering how fast Max was, he knew he wouldn't have a chance. And then he thought about how he ended up here. He remembered the eyes, the teeth, and being dragged. He'd been on the verge of death.

It hadn't all been a dream.

Somehow Max had found him and brought him here. Only ... where was here? And who was the girl?

Two things were for sure: Max had saved him, and Max was protecting the girl.

Billy cleared his throat; it was dry and scratchy and sore. "Okay, boy. I get it. Thank you for saving me." He reached up to pet his head. Max didn't move, didn't flinch, but something in the atmosphere of the small cave changed. Billy's hand stopped in mid-motion, inches from Max's head.

Billy backed off, returning his hand to his side.

"Sorry," he whispered.

Looking at the girl, Billy asked, "Who's this?" He pointed at her, keeping his hand close to his chest. "Can I—can I see her? Would that be okay?" Carefully, slowly, he reached out a hand.

Max watched him, then moved aside, allowing Billy access to the girl.

Billy first checked for a pulse at her neck. She was warm, and her heartbeat strong and fast beneath his fingers. He could see some scratches and bumps on her forehead and face, but she seemed okay. He brushed back a wisp of blondish brown hair from her cheek and tucked it behind her ear.

Irmgard roused and opened her eyes. On seeing him, she smiled.

"You're not a deer," she said in German.

"A deer?" Billy responded, also in German.

"Petra dragged you in last night. I thought you were a deer, and we'd eat you for breakfast."

"I'm sorry to disappoint you."

She shook her head.

"I'm not disappointed," she said, yawning and stretching. "But I am hungry."

"You're not scared of me?" asked Billy.

She grinned, her teeth white and even. She shook her head to the negative. "If you were a bad man, Petra would have killed you."

Billy looked at Max, still watching him silently.

He nodded.

"Yes. You seem to have a guardian angel."

Irmgard reached up and petted his muzzle.

Billy almost jumped forward to try and save her, but the monster dog did nothing. Just let her play with him as she wished. Billy didn't see a muscle move on the dog. He was like a scary bronze statue.

"I'm Billy," he said. "Who are you?"

"Irmgard." They shook hands.

"How did you get here?" asked Billy.

"Like you," she said. "Petra saved me. Bad men killed my father. They shot him in the head and tried to catch me. But I ran away and fell off a mountain, and Petra saved me."

That shook Billy.

"I fell off a mountain too," he said.

Irmgard nodded. "The bad men chased me here, but Petra killed them." She pointed a finger toward a wall of the cave. "They're out there in the snow."

Billy looked at the cave wall, following her pointing finger, as though he could see the dead men's bodies. In his mind, he almost could.

Irmgard rubbed the fabric of her coat. "This was one of the men's coats. It has his blood on it. It's mine now, and none of them will ever hurt me again."

A chill ran down Billy's neck and shoulders.

Max moved gracefully around them and disappeared out of the den and into the storm.

"Where's he going?" asked Billy, surprised that the dog would leave him alone with the girl.

"Well," said Irmgard, "since you're not a deer and I'm still hungry, he's probably getting us some breakfast." She smiled at him.

Billy smiled back, his stomach rumbling.

"Good."

MAX CHECKED THE PERIMETER, searching for signs of a possible threat. He found none but remained cautious—the strong wind made it unlikely he could detect scents swirling from anywhere downwind, and that was dangerous. While hunting for food, he'd picked up the man's scent as well as fragments of the Alpha's. He was disappointed when he found that the Alpha was not with the man. For several minutes, Max watched the man, evaluating what he should do next. The man was close to death, so Max's first inclination was to leave him and go back to the hunt. But the Alpha had accepted the man into the pack, and so, the dilemma.

When the man collapsed, Max made his decision. He grabbed the man's hood and dragged him to the den where he and the girl were taking shelter. It was a long, bumpy way through the snow and wind and storm. The man passed out along the way, which made him easier to drag. If he had tried to fight or hurt Max in any way, Max would have killed him. The Alpha may have allowed him into the pack, but Max didn't like him and thought he should have killed him when he had the chance. But the Alpha had ordered him to stop

—to not finish the job, and so now Max had another person to watch over.

Getting the man into the den hadn't been easy. Max had had to widen the opening and then drag him down and in. The man took up too much room for Max to be able to close off the entrance properly, his face reaching almost out of the cave, even though he was bent into a ball. More heat was escaping into the night than Max would have usually allowed.

That eliminated Max's ability to finish his hunt. He needed to stay with the girl to keep her warm.

But now that the man was awake, Max was free to find them some food while at the same time giving him the chance to mark his territory and check for possible intruders.

The badger stuck its head out of its burrow at precisely the wrong time. Max snatched the fourteen-pound animal out with a lightning-fast clamp of his jaws and a powerful snapping motion that broke its neck. Taking hold of the carcass with his front paws, he shoved it against the side of its sett, or den, for support while simultaneously pulling back with his powerful neck muscles, shredding the fur and skin from the badger. It took him about a minute and a half to fully skin the creature and start back to his own den—almost the same amount of time Max thought it would have taken to kill the man.

Instead, he was going to have to feed him.

THE WOLF SNIFFED the spot where Billy had fallen and lost the transponder. Layers of wet snow covered the scent, but the individual odors were still there, separating and diffusing through the two hundred eighty million or so olfactory receptors, sprinkled like stars across the galaxy throughout the ethmoturbinates of his nasal cavity and the vomeronasal organ —deciphering and analyzing the separate chemical and molecular agents creating the smells.

Finely honed cell receptors, passed down through thousands of generations, were able to identify the differences in the scent signatures of Billy, Gil, Anthony Carlino, their clothes, their injuries, their weapons, the metal and plastic and glass of the transponder itself. Even the tiny traces of ozone produced by the electrical current passing through the circuitry of the transponder was trapped by the snow.

But there was also another odor—more powerful than the others. It was a smell he remembered from his past.

He smelled Max.

The tactical part of his brain cataloged and remembered every enemy he had ever faced. He remembered killing Max's mother, father, and siblings. A primal concept and understanding of *pack* were at the core of his very being, the scents instinctually painting a picture of their lineage and bloodlines, linking the members together as clearly as a physical chain.

He remembered almost killing the dog—*twice*. He remembered the bear and the man.

Sniffing the area, he picked up two separate paths veering in different directions.

Gil and Anthony Carlino going one way—Max and Billy going the other.

The wolf wanted to kill the dog, to finish what he had started. To protect his territory. But he also had a score to settle with the men—both of them. They had hurt him.

And then there were the other men, and the little girl. He had killed two of the men from the camp.

Easy prey.

The wolf did not think Max or Gil would be so easy.

The men from the camp were the logical choice to go after. In the storm, they were helpless against him. Survival instinct dictated he take that path and leave the others for later.

But ...

The wolf was more than just a creature of instinct—he was the alpha predator of these mountains.

They were his.

He stood where the two paths divided, looking from one to the other while glancing back toward the camp of hunters higher on the mountain.

The storm beat at him unnoticed.

The wolf was more powerful than the storm.

It took less than a minute for him to reach a decision, nearly an eternity for the complex, tactical computer his mind was, but once decided, he put his nose to the snow and started tracking.

There was killing to do.

39

S arah scraped the food from her plate into Pilgrim's bowl and then walked to the kitchen and washed it off before placing it into the dishwasher. Pilgrim looked at her with warm, loving eyes and commenced eating. She was so happy and relieved that Pilgrim was better—and he *was* better—so much better. She could hardly believe it. When she thought about how close he had come to dying, it brought tears to her eyes.

She would have to talk with Gil about taking him out on jobs and into danger. He was too old for that kind of silliness. He'd done enough, and now it was time to let him rest easy. Easy and safe. Yes, she would definitely talk with Gil. Besides, he had Max now, and Max was more than enough.

As much as she loved and admired Pilgrim, and as good as he was in his prime, Max was just on a different level. So, let the old boy stay home, or better, give him to her, and she would love him and cuddle him and watch movies and eat popcorn with him, snuggled under a blanket on her couch with flames crackling in the fireplace. That's how and where a warrior deserved to finish his years.

And thinking of warriors, Gil could just come with Pilgrim and stay with her too. She remembered the time when Gil had stayed

with her, years ago, after what had *happened.* She had been so afraid
the monster would come back to finish what he started.

And he did come back.

She didn't like to think about what had happened, not the first
time and not the second either.

But she did like remembering how it had been with her and Gil.
How he protected her and made her feel safe. He and Pilgrim.

She knew she would be good for Gil. She knew he needed her.
She could help him with his pain, just as he had helped her with
hers. But how to get through to him? How to break the hold of
—*ghosts*? Sarah thought she might have a chance against a woman of
flesh and blood.

Like Gail.

If that horrible liar hadn't turned out to be what she was, Sarah
was confident that Gil would have come to his senses and chosen her
over Gail.

Sarah closed the dishwasher and went back to the living room,
smiling as Pilgrim hopped up next to her and plopped his big head in
her lap. She rubbed his snout and ears lightly while he panted and
tried to lick her arms and hands.

"You are such a goof," she said and rubbed him some more,
loving his massive structure and gentle heart.

Her cell phone sounded on the little end table by the couch.

"Hello?" She wasn't expecting a call. She hoped it was Gil.

"Hi, Sarah, this is Kenny."

She thought for a minute.

"Oh, Gil's friend. Have you heard from him?"

"No. I tried to get him on the satellite phone, but it's dead."

"Is he still in Germany?"

"I think so," said Kenny.

"Think? I thought Gil said you always know everything."

"Yeah," said Kenny. "I usually do. But not this time. He doesn't
have reception on his phone, and a big storm moved in over the area
where he probably is."

"A storm? Is he in a hotel?"

"I don't think so. I got some photos before the storm began. I think they are on foot in the mountains—with a bunch of bad guys possibly chasing them. Once the storm started, I lost them, but there are still a lot of thermal signatures in the mountains."

"How could you possibly get photos?" This wasn't making sense to Sarah. Who was this guy?

"I hacked some military stuff. It's what I do. The important thing is that I think Gil could be in a tight spot.

"Nick Carlino will be coming by Gil's place in the morning," he continued. "I don't want to talk with him. I don't want him even to know that I exist—too much chance of him tracking me down. He has a lot of resources. So, I'm calling you to let him know that Mal —Gil—has his dad, but he might need some help making it out of there. I'm sending you some data, GPS coordinates. Let Mr. Carlino know he needs to get men there fast, or it might be too late. I don't know how his guys will get through the storm, but they need to. Tell him that."

"Okay," she said, her heart quickening with fear, "I will. But how do you know he's coming over tomorrow?"

"The Wave, it sees everything, nothing can hide from it. Well— almost nothing. Mother Nature's pretty tough. Oh, and Gil is right."

"Right? About what?" She asked.

"You really are the most beautiful woman in the world."

Kenny clicked off before she could respond.

KENNY WENT BACK to his screens, running through algorithms and vid feeds, trying for any scrap of data that might help save Gil. He owed the man more than he could ever repay. What Gil had done for him was on a scale too large for Kenny ever to pay back. And he would not let him die out there. He hacked into a Russian satellite flying over the Black Forest. Their operators would start screaming as soon as he took over their main surveillance cameras and activated every thermal imaging system the expensive and highly sensitive piece of equipment had built into it. Their computers would start their tracing algorithms almost instantly, which Kenny's advanced rerouting sequences could detour for about ninety seconds before they broke through and had him. This meant he had to be done and out at seventy.

Fingers flying across three different keyboards, he played the Wave like a master pianist. Bach, Chopin, Mozart, performing their finest.

Sweat broke out on his forehead, and his forearms ached, his eyes racing back and forth, up and down, scanning the screens and the feeds and the wavelengths.

The storm must be crazy out there. That alone would be hard to survive in those mountains, but if Kenny were right about the small army of men hunting him, it would be impossible.

He'd tapped into Nick Carlino's phones and dropped a sneaky little algorithm into his matrix that listened for specific words that instantly shuffled the conversations into tight little packets of data streams that interacted with other algorithms, sorting and sending and storing and alerting Kenny to their importance and meaning.

Kenny knew that Nick had men stationed around the area, but they weren't as close as Kenny thought they needed to be.

The Russian asset splashed a brilliant image across his primary monitor showing a green background with brighter slashes of green intermixed like noise— but *there*—right there— as a whitish splotch showing through the green, with even lighter splotches scattered about.

An encampment with thirteen tents, fires lit inside.

Checking his timer, he saw he had forty seconds. He zoomed out and back in on a different area. *Nothing.* Another— *nothing.* Six more —*nothing.* He was running out of time. *Wait, there was a splotch.* Lower than the encampment, and then, farther, he spotted the farmhouse. He knew it was a farmhouse because he'd located it earlier and made a note as a possible rest spot for Nick's men if needed. He had the blueprints and title papers stored.

Time ran out. He disconnected from the flying machine that

soared high and fast in geosynchronous orbit above the atmosphere of the Earth.

Breathing hard, he checked the data he had acquired. His shirt was dark with perspiration, and his hands and arms ached.

But he had them.

It had to be them. Who else would be on those mountains in the middle of the storm of the century?

Gil and Max and an army of bad guys. That was them all over.

Tossing up several maps, Kenny ran them through simulations to find the best way up there, from where Nick's men were. It would take hours—maybe days, depending on the storm.

Kenny compiled the data, translated it into simple enough terms for laymen—*gangsters*—and sent it off to Sarah's phone.

He hoped it was enough.

SARAH WAS JUST ABOUT to call Nick Carlino when her phone vibrated. The name showed it was Tina DeWitt, a K9 handler for the Colorado State Patrol. Sarah had testified in several of her arrest cases, and they'd gone on girls' nights out, more than once.

"Hi, Sarah, this is Tina. I'm sorry to bother you this late, but I've been trying to get hold of Gil Mason, and I know you two are friends. Do you think you could ask him to call me when he gets a chance?"

"He's out of the country right now, working a case, Tina. But I'll certainly let him know you called when he gets back."

"Where's he at, Mars? I mean cells today reach everywhere."

"Germany, on a mountain, in a bad storm. At least that's the last I heard."

"Sounds about right, from what I've heard about him. Hey, he's single, right?"

That caught Sarah off guard. It took her a second to recover.

"Widower," Sarah said.

"Yeah, I remember all that. But he hasn't remarried or anything?"

"No."

"Is he seeing anyone—I mean serious like?"

Another pause.

"Not ... not that I know of."

"His wife was killed years ago if I remember right," said Tina. "Seems like it would be good for him to get back into life. And hey, he and I have a lot in common, right? I mean, he was a cop; I'm a cop. He's a dog handler; I'm a dog handler. We both have Mals. Not to mention, we're both hot, right?"

Sarah felt her teeth clench together.

"Anyway, you and I should get together for another girls' night. I can pump you for information about him. And since I'm spying, I'm buying."

Sarah's jaw worked back and forth.

"Yes," she said finally. "Yes, we should do that."

40

K enny worked the Wave like never before in his life. Well— there was that one other time. The time the Wave failed him, and it took Gil to save his sister. But it had now been two days since Kenny had talked with Sarah, and the storm continued to rage on the Black Forest in Germany. He'd hardly slept. *Did Gil have the supplies he would need to stay alive in that blizzard?* From monitored conversations he'd intercepted, he knew that Gil and Billy had a band of five adept soldiers with them, but those were slim numbers compared to the army of men arrayed against them. He couldn't know if any of them were even alive, except that the army was still out there, which hinted they probably were too. Otherwise, why brave the storm?

The time he'd spent gathering data had not been wasted. He had satellite photos and video of the battle in the meadow, thermal feeds of campfires at three different campsites, and scattered heat signatures, several of which might be human.

Kenny plotted out what he thought might be the *bad guy* army camp, as well as a smaller camp that he thought might belong to Gil, Anthony Carlino, and whoever might still be with them. He'd compared several thermal shots and could only detect two signatures at this camp—two men. He knew they were men because he caught their signatures when they came out of a structure to answer nature's call. The structure, possibly a cave, blocked most of their heat, but once they came out, the image was very clear—*streams and all*—before they disappeared back inside.

A third heat signature showed up on a couple of shots not far from the first two. But there was a lot of tree cover, and he didn't have enough data to be sure.

Kenny was about to call it a night when he caught a glimpse of a transcript from a tapped conversation between Billy Carlino and the head of his group of bodyguards, Marco Brambilla. There was a brief mention of *transponders*.

Kenny couldn't believe he'd missed it.

Transponders could be tracked and tapped. All he needed was frequencies. And any frequency that rode the Wave through the Verse could be found.

Sleep would have to wait.

~

MARCO BRAMBILLA SAT around the fire with his two men in the snow cave they had constructed. The storm raged like an angry woman outside—a woman whose lover had cheated on her. Marco loved women, loved them with a passion most men could never know. And he had made more than a few angry with him.

So he knew.

The snow cave they had built was well constructed. Marco and his men had found an actual cavern that went into the mountain about seven feet. But they were big men, so they had to build it out until they had plenty of sleeping room. The fire was warm, but errant gusts made their way in now and then, trying to put it out.

They had all done time in the service; they'd all seen war, a lot of war.

Marco took the loss of Leonardo, who'd been shot while driving, personally. He would have his revenge. Of course, they had all acquitted themselves proudly, killing many of the enemy. He knew they would—he had trained them himself.

When Marco had been very young, Anthony Carlino was like a father to him. He had personally brought Marco into the *family*, vouched for him as a made man, paid his way through college, helped him get to America, join the military, learn what he had learned, and then brought him home to use his skills and teach them to others.

Marco knew that if he had been in charge of guarding Mr. Carlino, he would never have been kidnapped. The vineyard would have run red like wine with the blood of his attackers.

The night the storm struck, Marco had scouted the area and located the enemy camp. He had planned on attacking later, but the storm made that impossible.

But a storm could only last so long, and Marco was patient. Marco had been a patient boy; it was his nature. Mr. Carlino had remarked about it often. The military taught Marco to be even more patient. Patience had saved him and his men on many occasions.

One of his men, Piero Romano, had taken a bullet to the right side of his chest. It had gone straight through, which was lucky. They'd gotten the bleeding stopped, but it had begun to show signs of infection, which was not so lucky since they lacked medical supplies.

Marco considered heating a knife and running it through the wound as he'd seen in the field during a very desperate situation. The infection had seemed to be getting better, but the man died before they could be sure. The consensus, at the time, was that the wounded soldier died of internal bleeding, nothing to do with the heated knife. But who could be sure? Marco decided he would wait before trying the knife. And then a third choice presented itself to him.

The enemy camp.

If Marco could sneak into the camp and kill the men inside a single tent while they slept, he could steal a medical kit, which he felt certain they would have, and bring it back for Piero.

It would entail going back into the storm, but that meant little to a man like Marco Brambilla. Marco had been through many storms, both natural and man made. He'd once been shot five times while killing pirates off the Gulf of Aden during a typhoon. Two of the bullets had been stopped by the Dragon Skin body armor he'd worn, and the three others hadn't even slowed him. He'd killed seven pirates that day, rescuing thirty tanker crew members. The private company he worked for gave him a sizable bonus, comparable to the amount of blood and flesh he'd lost. The money was unimportant —*mostly*. What was important to Marco was the excitement, the victory.

The fire had dried his socks and boots, and they felt good as he slipped them back on.

Enzo Bianchi looked at him from across the flames.

"Going somewhere, boss?"

Marco nodded, zipping the second boot.

"Recon."

Enzo raised his eyebrows. "In this?"

Marco nodded toward the wounded Piero.

"Thought maybe I might find something for his infection."

Enzo gave it some thought before speaking.

"He'll live another day without it. You might not—not in this."

Marco grinned. "Afraid I'll get lost?"

"Yes," said Enzo.

Marco took up his weapons and said, "I'll tell you a secret," he pulled on his backpack as he looked back at his man, "I don't get lost."

And with that, he went out into the storm and the dark.

He'd never felt more alive.

But there were other things on the mountain that he should have considered. Things more dangerous than the dark or the cold, or even the blizzard.

～

MAX SILENTLY DROPPED the food inside the den while both Irmgard and Billy still slept. He turned in a tight circle and went back out into the blasting wind and snow. He moved fast, breaking a path through the crusted snow at a pace that no man could hope to match.

Once in the trees, he quartered, trying to locate the scent—his nose going high then low, then back to high.

Traces—but so minuscule—billionths of a part. He would latch onto them only to have the wind tear them away.

There and gone.

His head whipped back and forth, his body along for the ride as he concentrated, focusing every iota of his will into locking them down. The splintered traces led him up the mountain in a vague, twisted, winding path.

The scent was not the Alpha's—*but it was familiar.* It wasn't Billy's. He was back in the den with the girl. It was someone who had been in their party—their pack.

The short one, he thought, but he couldn't be sure—not yet. When the men had first joined their pack, back at the airport, Max had evaluated each of them, deciding which he would kill and in what order, if it came to it. The short one had been first on the list. He was a dangerous predator—capable—efficient. The man's muscle and sheer mass would be an obstacle, but his lack of height would help compensate, eliminating the need for vertical jumps or leaps. *His throat was in easy reach.*

A gust of wayward wind hit him, bringing an encyclopedia of information. He followed it upwind as best he could, and *yes*—it was the short man. But there was something else. Something far more important—something that almost made him forget about the short man, about Billy or the Alpha or even Irmgard.

It was *the* smell he would never forget—*could* never forget. The scent that haunted his dreams and his every waking moment.

The Great Gray Wolf.

And he was close.

∾

THE WOLF WATCHED as the man approached the tent. He had caught his scent as he was leaving a snow cave. He would have ignored it, but the man's odor was intense and close, and he was heading toward the human's camp up the mountain.

He would be an easy target.

Easier than attacking the cave.

The cave had one entrance.

One entrance was dangerous.

The wolf detected two humans inside. The space would be tight.

Also dangerous.

And he would be fighting two instead of one.

And there was fire, another danger.

The wolf did not quite understand what fire was any more than he knew guns, cars, or optical sights. He had never lived in a house, nor had he been burned, but he knew its danger on a primitive level.

His experiences had prepared him well for his war on these trespassers to his territory.

And so, he had left the cave with the men and started tracking the *lone* man. He'd caught up with him quickly and could easily have attacked. He had the advantage of surprise, but the man's scent alerted him that the man was hunting. The wolf waited to see *what* the man was hunting. As the man made his way through the storm, working his winding path through the deep snow, he was noisy, clumsy. The wolf could have killed him at will, but he was in no hurry. The storm could not hurt the wolf, nor could the man, and so he would give him time, let the human show him what it was that he was hunting.

Then he would kill him.

The man stopped thirty kilometers from an outlying tent and knelt behind a tree. The wolf smelled the guard a hundred kilometers to the east and another two hundred to the west. The wolf didn't know if the man knew of their presence, but neither was a danger, so he ignored them for now.

He would kill *them* later.

For now, he wanted to see what the human was going to do.

The human sprinted from the tree until he was close to the tent, then he stopped and slowly made his way to the side, where he knelt and waited. The wind beat at the tent and the man, making it hard even for the wolf to hear. Carefully, the man unzipped a flap and entered quickly. The bright scent of fresh blood brushed past the wolf in a flood, almost driving him to attack, but he controlled himself and stayed where he was, understanding the man had killed or been killed.

Blood scent was different than flesh scent and, until the two could be linked, were ineffectual for target acquisition.

The man came back out and started toward the trees, moving in an almost straight line toward the wolf.

He would kill him now.

The man had attacked the other humans, which, in other circumstances, might make him an ally. *But the wolf needed no allies.* The wolf *wanted* no allies.

He crouched in the dark beside a tree as the man ran closer.

A tent flap opened, and two soldiers holding rifles came out. They shot at the man, their bullets missing but punching holes in the snow and trees around the wolf.

Killing the man would have to wait.

41

I heard the echo of the shots as they rolled down the mountain and wondered what they were hunting. It wouldn't be food, not in this storm, so ... what?

Billy?

I rubbed my thumb over the face of the transponder.

Not likely. How could he have survived the car crashing off the mountain? And if he had, why wait till now to activate the transponder? And why leave it in the snow?

Unless the bad guys caught him and he dropped the transponder as a sign, not wanting us to fall into a trap looking for him.

It seemed far-fetched to me. Most likely, the bad guys found his body at the crash site and maybe found the transponder and later lost it while hiking back to their camp.

But then again, maybe he had been there, and maybe he'd gotten away.

Even less likely ... but ... *still*. What if he had and they were hunting him out there?

I tried to push the thought out of my head. My job was here, protecting the old man. But truth be told, what Anthony Carlino said earlier ... about how he wouldn't have minded if I'd grabbed Billy and saved him from the car going off the mountain instead of him ...

worked on my mind, and I had to admit ... I wished I *had* grabbed Billy.

The old man was snoring, he hadn't heard the shooting.

As quietly as I could, I suited up. Outside I listened, and soon I heard a series of shots, rolling through the storm and bouncing off the hills of rock. I couldn't be sure, but I thought they were coming from the west and up. I started after them. A hundred steps. A hundred, hard-fought, digging-through-thick-wet-snow steps, and I looked back. My tracks were filling in fast. I had my compass, but it would be hard. Chances were I would get lost in the blizzard. I should stay. It was the job, the mission.

But if Billy was out there ... *being hunted* ...

I kept going. I'd already lost Max. If there were any chance of saving Billy ... I was taking it.

The snow lashed like a whip at my exposed skin, feeling like it was leaving welts. I ducked my head and pushed along. Sporadic gunfire kept me directionally oriented. *I hoped.* The echo effect could easily be throwing me off. But I did have a lot of experience with gunfire and how the sound signature worked in real-life situations. The thickness and depth of the snow kept me from slipping, so there was that, but the cold and the gale strength of the wind were monstrous. Not to mention the energy it took to break path through the heavy white. Snowshoes would have been great, but nobody anticipated us getting caught in a blizzard.

I stopped, looking up the mountain, the ten or so yards I could see, breathing heavily.

Another shot ... *that way* ... I started moving again.

The wind whipped the words right out of my mouth, but I said them anyway.

"I'm coming, Billy. You are not alone."

~

MARCO DIDN'T HEAR the men, but he heard the rifle fire. Something hot and deadly punched through the hoodie of his coat, just missing his cheek. He ducked reflexively, hearing his old drill instructor from the shooting range laughing at him and saying, "Too late to duck, maggot, once you hear it or feel it you're either dead or okay. So either lay down or get back to work."

Marco got back to work.

He zigged and zagged, as best he could in the near waist-deep snow. Going downhill helped, but only so much.

Chancing a quick glance behind him, he saw the two men, spread out and shooting as they ran. Marco spun, knelt, almost disappearing in the snow, snapped up his rifle and sighted in, waiting for the snow to let up just a bit.

The first man was thirty yards out, shooting wildly, pushing his way through the snow.

Marco took in a deep breath, let out two-thirds, pulled back on the trigger, feeling the slight kick to his shoulder, repeated the action twice more so quickly it sounded like automatic fire.

The man stopped shooting. He stopped running.

Marco watched as the man crumpled to the snow in a loose heap.

The second man saw what happened and stopped and dropped to the snow.

A small geyser erupted about a body's length from Marco's left elbow. He tried to sight in on the last man, now lying prone, but the blizzard and the dark made it hard to spot him. A second geyser, this one closer, but on his right. Only this time Marco saw the flash from the rifle's muzzle as it spit death towards him. Marco remembered an old story his great grandfather used to tell about how in the war, in the dark, snipers used to be able to kill the third man lighting his cigarette on one match. *That's how quickly they could sight in.* Marco didn't need three. He put a single round downrange, and even against the wind he heard the meaty smack of bullet striking flesh.

But more men were coming.

Marco slung his rifle, stood, and ran for the trees.

~

TWO FINGERS GRABBED up five men and ran toward the gunshots. He'd radioed three other men to come down from the north so they could flank whoever was attacking. By the time they arrived they found the tent with the dead men inside as well as the two outside, their blood still seeping from the holes in their corpses.

The storm had not yet covered their killer's tracks.

Two Fingers set his jaw, fighting mad that his men had again been attacked and killed. But he had their tracks, still in the snow, which meant he had them.

Gathering his soldiers, he started the hunt.

∼

THE WOLF HEARD the ricochets as they chipped bark from trees and bounced off rocks. None of the bullets came close to him. He moved down and around and then burrowed under the ice until he was completely hidden.

Waiting.

∼

MAX HEARD THE SHOOTING.

It meant nothing to him.

He smelled the Great Gray Wolf.

He moved faster.

The scent was still sketchy, mixing and twisting and breaking, this way and that.

But it was there. And it was *him*.

And sooner or later Max would lock in on it.

The blizzard was growing stronger, the wind an unstoppable force, the snow stinging like hornets. The upward trek was hard, the snow so deep now, that Max had to leap up and forward to make progress.

All of this also meant nothing to Max.

He would find the Great Gray Wolf.

Find him and kill him.

~

THE SHOOTING WAS CLOSE NOW, still up and to the right of me, but close. I slowed my pace, not wanting to take an errant bullet. I rested, catching my breath, feeling the tightness in my chest. The altitude was higher even than my Colorado heritage had prepared me for, and the physical exertion was taking its toll. Under my coat and hood I was sweating, which wasn't good. If the sweat froze I could be in trouble. But I'd have to worry about that later. I had enough to worry about ... like automatic gunfire and killer wolves.

I wondered what Chuck Norris would do.

Not that it would matter. I was feeling more like Gilligan than Chuck just now. Visibility was nil, I had no idea what I was walking into, and it was just me going against, *what sounded from the gunfire to be an army.*

But then again, if I'd wanted a desk job I could have taken one a long time ago.

The wind hit me hard, the ice crystals stabbing at my face and eyes. I was pretty sure that at least some of the men I was going to fight had been the ones who shot Max after he'd been attacked by the wolf.

Feeling my lips twitch at the corners, I went toward the sound of the fighting.

~

MARCO'S FOOT took a turn and he fell to his side. He tried to reach out, grabbing at snow, but the wet whiteness gave him no purchase and he tumbled and rolled down the slope, the stock and barrel of his rifle smacking his shins and head and knees and elbows. It was like he was in a fight with himself—and losing.

He hit up against a tree and managed to grab hold and hang on. His face and hoodie were packed with snow and it took him a few seconds to dig it out. When he opened his eyes, he saw his path through the snow. He had to admit, he'd rolled a lot faster than he'd been running, putting some distance between him and his pursuers.

Marco did a quick inventory. He still had the medical kit, and his weapons seemed intact. He checked his downward trajectory, considering if he should just roll the rest of the way down. It would be faster, but there were lots of trees and rocks and who knew what else. Besides, his body felt like he'd gone through a gauntlet of fighters, and that was with the soft snow under him.

No. He'd just have to try to be careful, while being fast too.

The hairs on the back of his neck stood to attention.

He'd had the experience before, too many times, in war and working for *the family*.

But never before in his life, this strong.

Something was watching him.

Something dangerous.

Something deadly.

Marco curled his finger around the trigger as he slowly turned, a sixth sense telling him he was already too late and that he was a dead man.

But what else was there to do?

THE WOLF WATCHED as the man crashed and rolled down the slope and ended up stopping right in front of him.

His saliva glands pumped full force and he had to exert all his will not to attack instantly. But he didn't know how close the others were. So he held his attack in check. Knowing that his time would come.

And soon.

HEARING THE COMMOTION, I moved forward as fast as I could, working against the elements and my body's own limitations. I crossed a small clearing and pressed my back against a thick trunk, aiming up and around, seeing nothing but sweeping snow and dark shapes. I thought maybe I heard grunting, but it was hard to tell with the wind.

Shoving my thighs through the snow I pressed on, moving from tree to tree, hoping whoever was coming toward me was at least as blind as I was. Holding the rifle by its pistol grip, I used tree limbs to help pull myself up and through. It was hard and way slower than I liked, leaving me open to attack from numerous angles. SWAT commanders and good NCOs would tell me I was being a fool, that I should dig in and wait for the enemy to come to me. *The ambusher always has tactical advantage over the ambushee.* But if it was Billy being attacked, I couldn't leave him alone, so safety and time were luxuries I couldn't afford just now.

The shooting had stopped. So had the commotion, whatever it had been. I tried to slow things down, commanding my breathing back under control, while still pressing forward. Leaning into the thick snow, I let go of the limbs and held my rifle in the ready position, expecting to be in a gun battle at any second.

I made it to another tree, swiveling around, and there he was. He had a rifle at the ready, just like me, only he wasn't looking at me. He was looking at something else.

I almost shot him. It was very close. I had him dead center, his back to me. But I saw something in my peripheral vision ... something in the snow ... something in the dark.

And in that instant, I thought we *both* might be dead.

42

Anthony Carlino awoke suddenly. He'd been dreaming of his wife. It was a nice dream. They sat together on their balcony in the old country, drinking expensive wine and watching the boats slipping through white-capped waves. But something had disturbed his sleep, a sound maybe, or a gust of wind. He looked over and saw that Gilligan was not in the cave.

Carlino wiped at his eyes. He wanted to go back to sleep—back to the balcony and the boats and his wife. Instead, he ducked low and braved the night and the cold and the wind.

He thought maybe Gilligan had gone out to relieve himself, but he was nowhere to be seen. He went back in and stoked the fire, warming his hands. Gilligan must have gone out to search around. He was like that. Trying to be something he never could, trying to be Chuck Norris. Anthony laughed a little at that. Not that Gilligan wasn't good. Anthony had come to respect the man's skills. The way he braved the cold to search for Billy and the fight with the wolf—but he was no Chuck Norris.

Billy had died under Gilligan's watch.

Chuck Norris would never have let that happen.

All the bodyguards had died.

Some of them he could understand—it was a war after all—but *all* of them?

Bad form.

Not to mention they were probably not going to make it off the mountain alive. The odds were stacked against them, and having been a casino owner, he understood stacked odds.

The storm, the kidnappers.

No, the odds were not good. And that was all right, he thought. Anthony Carlino was almost at peace with it.

Almost he could accept it.

Almost.

But not quite.

He had scores to settle. There was the loss of his finger, and more importantly, the loss of his ring, no matter that Gilligan said his Nicky had it. It still had been taken from him, like his Bella had been taken from him. The ring was the one part of her that nothing had been able to steal from him.

But they had.

They had!

And so—no—no, he was not all right with dying.

Not yet.

So, even though Gilligan would never be Chuck Norris, he would have to do. Because Anthony Carlino was going to make it off the mountain, and he would have his revenge, no matter the odds.

But for now, he would wait for Gilligan; resting was necessary if he was to make it off the mountain alive.

He closed his eyes, trying for sleep and hoping for balconies and sailboats.

And Bella.

~

KENNY WORKED the computer keyboard like a master pianist. His fingers flew over the keys, palms working separate mouse devices, clicking and rolling, dragging and pausing, cutting and pasting, blending readouts into heat maps and 3D renderings, and then mixing the whole of it into algorithms that shifted, searched, and extrapolated data into tight, concise bitmaps that spit out their contents into carefully deciphered information.

But ...

... it paid off.

He had it.

The frequency for the transponder, as well as the encryption code that would allow him to access its latitude and longitude. Wiping his forehead, his hand came away wet. He was drenched in sweat, and he couldn't remember ever being so tired. He was even breathing hard as though he'd just completed a workout. But it was worth it.

Gently he entered the frequency, pausing as the numbers displayed themselves on the screen. Green against black, streaming numbers flowing down like trickles of water. It reminded him of the movie *The Matrix* when Cypher tells Neo he doesn't even see the Matrix anymore; he just sees the images.

It was exactly like that for Kenny. His mind no longer consciously recognized the numbers themselves, but rather what they produced in the reality of the digital world. Pictures, words, songs, coordinates.

With near reverence, Kenny touched the return button. The main screen switched from the eerie green and black to a thermal black and white, so bright that Kenny sat back in his chair, the columns of numbers replaced with real-time video. The scene was of the Black Forest region. The cold snow appeared as black, blanketing or erasing heat signatures and interfering with imagery.

The computer screen on his left blinked to a grid displaying an overlay of the main screen's topography, listing elevation and coordinates. The screen on his right flashed to a perfectly clear video of the same satellite course from five months prior, during the heart of summer when there was no snow. It incorporated the data from both screens, with an addition—a bright flashing dot that began to blink on and off. And then a second dot. Kenny waited; there should be three.

After five minutes, Kenny concluded the third was not active. He wasn't sure what to think about that. Probably the third transponder had been damaged or destroyed. He wondered whose transponder was missing and if the person that had it had been damaged or destroyed as well.

He hoped it wasn't Gil's.

Either way, he had two of them, and they seemed to be very close to where the thermal signatures from the earlier Soviet satellite pass over had burned through the cold of the storm.

Again, Kenny considered sending the information straight to Nickolas Carlino, and once again, he decided against it. He didn't think Carlino's men could make it up the mountain until the snow stopped anyway. And, even with all of Kenny's elaborate systems to keep himself hidden, there was just no sense in letting a man as powerful as Nickolas Carlino know that both he and his organization were able to be penetrated. Carlino would see it as a danger. And worse, he might see it as a *weapon* to be used against his enemies.

Kenny sent the data to Sarah's phone.

SARAH WAS UP EARLY. She made a quick breakfast, scrambling some eggs and cooking bacon for Pilgrim and herself. She knelt next to him as he ate, stroking his big head and smiling at him. He was so wonderful.

A string of cars pulling up outside distracted her. She stood and went to the front door.

Nicholas Carlino was already coming towards the front door, his cadre of bodyguards, with guns at the ready, encircling him.

Sarah walked through the circle, the bodyguards parting for her and instantly filling back in.

Nickolas took her hand, bowing his head.

"You are even more beautiful than your pictures," he said.

Sarah was taken aback by how handsome a man this mobster, *this Godfather*, was. She hadn't expected this; she didn't know what exactly she had expected, but certainly not this.

"You have pictures of me?"

Nick smiled, revealing dazzling teeth.

"For security purposes only, I assure you," he said.

She handed him the thumb drive containing the data she'd transferred from her phone and computer.

"I'm supposed to give this to you," she said.

Nick took the small device and handed it to Sal, who was standing next to him. Sal went back to one of the limos and ducked inside.

"Thank you. What exactly is on it?"

"I don't know what all of it is, but there are coordinates of where Gil and your father are. The person who sent the data said they are in danger and that you need to get your people to them as quickly as possible."

Nick nodded. "Sal will take care of that, thank you. Who sent you this information?"

"I don't know," said Sarah. "A friend of Gil's."

Nick nodded again. "Gil Mason has many friends."

"Yes," she said. "He's a good man."

Nick looked back at the limo. Sal was still inside. He turned back to Sarah. "I could find out who sent you this information."

Sarah stared into Nick's eyes and felt a chill run through her body. It was not a nice chill. Suddenly, Nick didn't look so handsome to her anymore.

"I believe you," she said, "but Gil wouldn't like that."

"No," said Nick. "I don't suppose he would."

Sal stepped out of the limo and came back to Nick.

"Holy crap, boss, they got a whole army chasing them. They're stuck up on a mountain in the middle of a blizzard. It looks like everybody's stuck in place because of the storm, but according to whoever put it all together, the storm's supposed to end in a few hours. He says if we don't get troops up there, they probably won't make it out. I called Vincenzo in Germany, but he says it'll take time to get things in place, and even then, he doesn't know how they'll get up the mountain. The roads are all closed with like ten-foot drifts."

Nick turned from Sal to Sarah. He sighed.

"Thank you for your assistance," he said. "I need to leave to make arrangements."

"Do you think you can help them?" She asked. "I mean the snow, if the roads are closed ...."

"It is a small thing," said Nick.

The smile had returned, but it was tighter, with no teeth showing. And something about it was very different, no longer flirtatious or charming, but instead—*knowing*. As if she had revealed something to him without her even realizing it.

He continued, "They have bulldozers in Germany, just as we do here. When price is not a consideration, and true authority takes control, mountains can be moved. Snow is nothing compared to a mountain, and I promise you, Miss Gallagher, where my father is concerned, I would move heaven and earth to save him."

The look that came over his face as he said it was one of the scariest looks Sarah had ever seen on a human—except maybe the look on Gil's face after—well—*after*.

Nick Carlino and his army left as unobtrusively as they arrived. Sarah stood, watching as they drove down the twisting road until she heard the doggy door flap. Pilgrim's head nudged under her hand. She petted him, still watching the cars until they were out of sight.

Sarah was worried about Gil making it back, but suddenly she was even more concerned for him over this man. Nick Carlino might be handsome, charming, and alluring, but underneath—*underneath*—there was something else. And Sarah didn't like it. She didn't like it at all. But worse, whatever it was, she was afraid of it.

VINCENZO CONSIDERED himself the best in the world at what he did.

And what he did was arrange things.

Aquire things.

Men, machines, vehicles, weapons—*whatever*.

Vincenzo was the ultimate facilitator of plans that others put into motion.

And as such, he had set up men, weapons, vehicles, false IDs, medical personnel, and, of course, safe passage out of Germany, all for the American's team, once they located and extracted Anthony Carlino.

Now that he had met him, Vincenzo did not doubt that the American would succeed. This Gil Mason was a leader. A winner. Vincenzo was an excellent judge of men. In his line of work, he had to be.

Vincenzo had taken Gil Mason's advice, securing extra men from two different US military bases in Germany. Three more Carlino conscripts had been contacted and called into service, and a handful more were available if needed.

He had everything in place—covered all the possibilities.

Until the storm hit.

Once again, the weathermen were less than accurate in their predictions.

And now the entire region was snowed in.

He was in his hotel, still impeccably dressed and sipping a glass of fine wine, when he received the call from Sal.

Bulldozers.

Looking out the window, he had to admit that nothing less than dozers could hope to prevail against the storm, which was why he had thought of it hours before Sal's call.

Vincenzo knew people.

Vincenzo had made his calls.

But someone had beat him to it.

Nearly all local heavy equipment had been put into use by the city, and the few machines that hadn't had been bought outright by an unknown third party.

This, of course, raised red flags for Vincenzo. The local area in question, just now, held importance to only two opposing factions. The Carlinos, and whoever had kidnapped Anthony Carlino.

But Gil Mason had given Vincenzo the answer already.

Vincenzo punched numbers into his cell phone. It was late, but the man, as important as he was, would answer Vincenzo's call.

Gil Mason had alluded that Vincenzo was akin to Harvey Keitel's character, Winston Wolfe, in *Pulp Fiction*. Vincenzo had seen the film and thought it quite excellent. Very fun.

But Winston Wolfe was a rank amateur compared to Vincenzo.

Vincenzo was the ultimate fixer.

And he did it for real.

43

M

ax lost the scent but continued searching.

Nose high, he sniffed for any possible trace.

With brutal force, the wind slammed into him—
usually a good thing for scent molecules, but not at this speed. It was
like a shark trying to scent a drop of blood in whitewater rapids, the
currents spinning and mixing and bouncing before being blasted
away into trillions of particles, making it impossible to home in on
them.

Sticking close to the side of the mountain, Max scented for
lingering odor, an old trick he'd learned while hunting the region as a
pup. This same trick had been reinforced through *trailing training*
with the Alpha. Following the lay of the land, he curled up and
around, weaving through trees and scrambling over snow-covered
boulders, but the wind obliterated any trace of scent.

He continued to work forward until he was deep into the trees
and high up from where he had started.

Still no scent.

But Max had other senses.

His ears perked at the sound.

Gunfire.

But far away ... very far away.

And much lower.

It wasn't The Great Gray Wolf—it was man. But if man were near, The Great Gray Wolf wouldn't be far.

Turning, Max started down.

~

THE WOLF WAS ABOUT to attack. The man's back was to him, and the others were too far away to matter.

Massive muscles coiled into steel springs, their kinetic energy held tight, waiting for the command to explode.

All of the wolf's senses were locked in on its target, so that he almost missed the *other* man. But a shift of movement from his peripheral vision alerted him just in time. He saw the man. And not just any man—the man he had fought before. The man that had been there with the dog and the bear. He was coming from below, *almost on him.*

The wolf held himself in check.

Once again, patience was required.

The wolf blended back into the snow.

~

THE WOLF WAS MAYBE ten feet away from me—about the same as the man, but to the left.

A deadly triangle.

Who to shoot first?

If I took out the wolf, the man would have a chance to turn, his rifle already up. I might be able to hit him before he got a shot off. *I know my skills.* The problem was, I didn't know *his.* Plus, I knew how dangerous the wolf was. I wouldn't feel comfortable without putting at least two rounds into him ... and I'd prefer three ... maybe four ... maybe a lot more. Every shot would take time, giving the man more chances to put sharp, pointed pieces of copper-jacketed lead into me.

The other side of the coin was just as dangerous. If I took out the man, it would give the wolf its opportunity to attack. As fast as I knew I was, I doubted I was quick enough to shoot the man *and* get a bullet into the wolf before he got to me. I'd already gone a round with him, and frankly, I didn't want another *hand-to-fang* rematch.

I'd rather just shoot him.

A decision was required. But truth be told, it really wasn't that hard. The wolf had killed Max, so no matter what, he had to die.

I moved the sights to the wolf and pulled the trigger.

But the wolf was already attacking, and I hadn't even seen him move.

MARCO TURNED SLOWLY, first his head and then his body, his rifle pointing, ready to fire. But he was too late. The wolf hit him full force in the chest, knocking the rifle from his hands. The strap kept it close to him, but the creature's fangs ripping into his jaw and throat made him completely forget he had it.

Somewhere in the melee, his ears registered a gunshot, but it seemed to be coming from another world.

Pain was an old companion. He'd been shot three times, suffered shrapnel wounds from a grenade, taken a machete strike to the ribs and a host of minor punctures and slashes and strikes and punches and kicks and tumbles.

But this pain was different. He couldn't say exactly why; maybe it was the eyes staring into his as the terrible teeth sank into his flesh. Or perhaps it was the hot breath pushing against his face as the intense pressure closed in on him. Maybe it was the combined jolt of the impact to his core, like getting hit by a speeding car—*an unimaginable shock to his system*—along with the horror of a living animal trying to eat him alive. Whatever it was, it was different—worse than the bullets or the shrapnel or even the machete.

As an adult man, Marco had never screamed due to pain or fear.

But this time, he did.

He screamed.

Fear overrode his training.

It overrode his courage.

It overrode his entire thought process.

On his person was a knife, a pistol, a rifle.

He had mastered them all.

He thought of none of them.

He was no longer *thinking* at all.

He was operating on primal instinct alone. *Flight or fight* had kicked on in full force, and even though in the past, *fight* had always taken over, it wasn't to be this time. Because this truly was different. His brain had shunted from the frontal lobe, back to survival, and survival demanded that he flee, forgoing all defense, knowing only that he was being devoured and that he had to get away.

He tried to run, but the waist-high snow held him in place as the wolf crushed down.

Marco screamed a second time, his hands flailing helplessly, grabbing at handfuls of fur.

His knees unhinged, and he flopped onto his back, the wolf on top. The wolf's mouth came away. Blood—*Marco's blood*—rained from its teeth and lips, falling into Marco's eyes.

Blinking it away, he saw the giant head striking down.

Death.

Coming for him at last.

It happened so fast I didn't even see it. The wolf was there ... and then he wasn't. My bullet struck the snow where he had been. I heard a scream and swiveled back to the man. He was on his back in the snow, the wolf on top of him.

Impossible.

Too fast to be believed.

I heard the man scream again and put my rifle on them.

I would just shoot them both.

THE WOLF WATCHED BOTH MEN, and then the one he had fought before turned ever so slightly toward him, triggering his survival instincts. Before the turn was complete, he exploded into the other man, hitting him full in the chest and biting him in the face. They fell back into the snow, and the man tried to put his hands up in defense, but the wolf was not to be stopped. He ducked under and ripped into the man's chest, tasting the blood and the fear.

The man screamed.

The wolf released and launched at the man he had fought before. *Aiming at his throat.*

∽

I TOOK AIM, my finger pulling back on the trigger. But then something about the scream registered.

Marco?

That moment of hesitation both saved Marco's life and almost ended mine. As my rifle lowered, the wolf launched into me. I tried to get the muzzle into his chest, but he was too fast. His teeth rushed for my throat as I continued the upward swing of the rifle, thrusting the metal flash suppressor up into his lower jaw, effectively jamming his mouth shut. I heard his teeth snap like a bear trap, slicing right through my rifle sling, and felt the impact as his snout and chest crashed into me. The AR went spinning out of my hands, disappearing somewhere in the night. I grabbed the wolf by the jowls on both sides of his neck and head and let the momentum of the impact carry us over and to the side, throwing in a little hip and performing a near-perfect Judo throw.

It was what we in the K9 community call an *alpha roll*. We use it when a canine attacks the handler for whatever reason. It's tricky, dangerous, and often painful. But when it works ... *it works.*

However, I'd never tried it on a giant feral wolf before.

I landed on top of him, his neck twisting and his teeth snapping. He writhed and tried to flip while at the same time trying to catch my wrist, forearms, and fingers. His legs flailed, his claws—*I don't say nails because they were literally the claws of a werewolf*—raked at me, shredding my coat and pants and bringing blood to my thighs and arms.

But I held on, thanking the good Lord that I'd kept up with my physical fitness. It took every bit of my strength to hold him down. The snow, slowly compacting beneath his head, shoulders, and back, helped by hindering his thrashing.

The usual steps in an alpha roll are the grab, the toss, and the mount, followed by screaming into the dog's face, "*NO*" or "*NEIN*" (German for no) or "*PHOOY*." We shake the animal's head up and down until it tucks its tail between its legs and it rolls its eyes away, showing subservience.

I was at the shaking and screaming stage of the movement but somehow didn't think that part was going to work.

Not with this creature.

No. This animal was the apex predator of these woods, and only in death would he relinquish his alpha position.

So, in effect, I wasn't actually performing an alpha roll—it was more of a *survival* roll. And the finishing point would be to put a bullet through its giant skull.

I couldn't afford to release a hand and go for a gun, so I did the next best thing.

I screamed for help.

"*Marco!*"

～

Two Fingers and his men had been blundering through the blizzard blindly. They hadn't heard or seen the man they were chasing for nearly ten minutes, and he was afraid they'd lost him, but then a rifle shot sounded from below, making him grin. He sent three soldiers on up ahead, the rest of his men and himself following.

It was time to finish this.

～

THE SNOW and the wind disturbed sounds just as they did scents. Max was moving as fast as he dared. He didn't want to overshoot them again. But the gunfire had stopped, and the wind was so powerful he hadn't been able to pick up any odor.

Genetic instinct and survival hunting had taught him that quartering in circles was the best bet in these situations. But the pitch of the slope, combined with chest-deep snow, made that technique extremely difficult and used up an incredible amount of energy.

The cold was becoming a real danger. He should seek shelter, but of course, that was not going to happen.

As he turned, a gust of wind pushed him nearly off his feet so that he had to stagger against the side of the mountain to keep from losing his footing. A slight hollow had been carved in the cliffside, not enough to be called a cave, but enough to catch and hold odor. Max breathed deep and caught the familiar scent again.

Not the Great Gray Wolf this time.

And not the army of enemies either.

It was the Alpha.

Max moved carefully along the wall, sucking in the scents, trailing their movements until they broke from cover and pointed in a direction before scattering in the wind.

He was just about to start when the gunshot broke through the banshee wail of the storm.

And it came from the direction the scent had led.

Max bolted, racing through the snow.

arco turned to his belly and pushed up. Black streams poured from his face to the snow, and after a few seconds, he realized what the black streams were.

Blood.

His blood.

Why was he still alive?

He remembered the men chasing him, the wolf hitting him, *the gunshot,* pain, and fear.

I should be dead, he thought, but then he heard someone screaming his name, and he saw someone kneeling in the snow. He scrambled for his pistol.

"Marco!" he heard through the storm. It was the American. "Get over here and kill this thing!"

Marco stood. It took great effort, and the world tilted, but he made it. He took a step, then another, and now he could see that the American was on top of something—*something fighting*—something that wasn't a man.

The wolf.

He ran the rest of the way, pointing the gun.

As he made it to Gil's side, he saw the thrashing monster pinned under him, nearly buried in the snow.

Extending his arms, he took careful aim.

"Don't miss! Don't hit me," said the American.

"No," said Marco, thinking of what might happen to him if the monster got away again. "I won't miss."

MY FOREARMS, wrists, and fingers were burning. The wolf's strength and ferocity were unmatchable. Of course, I'd once thought that of Max. But Max was gone now, and this creature was responsible.

Marco made it to my side. I almost didn't want him to shoot it. I wanted to choke the life out of it. I wanted to feel it die beneath my fingers.

But that was stupid.

I was almost done ... nearly spent.

If the wolf got out of my grip, it would be bad—*messy*. I'd still kill it. Nothing was going to stop me from avenging Max, but I'd probably have to go for my buckle knife instead of my Smith & Wesson due to distance and the wolf's speed, and the buckle knife was short. The wolf would hurt me, maybe kill me, *but it would die too. I'd make sure of that.*

And that was all that mattered.

So, instead of telling Marco to let me finish it, I told him not to miss.

He pointed the gun at the wolf's face.

I tried to hold it as still as possible, but it was a brute, and the wind and the snow were blinding. Marco was pretty messed up, but I'd seen Marco in action, so I trusted him.

I gripped with all my strength ... and hoped he wouldn't take off a finger.

Two Fingers had his men spread out through the trees, holding at about five meters apart to avoid losing contact in the storm. He tried to keep them in ranks, staying as even as possible, but they were not real soldiers in a real army, practicing drill movements every day. And those that had been in the military at one time had forgotten what little drill they'd learned. Added to that were the depth of the snow and the bashing of the elements.

They could barely hear Two Fingers' orders, even with the radios. So, they wavered, and they moved, and their line curved and swayed across the slope and between the trees.

Later, Two Fingers would think that they could have taken them alive if only he had kept the line even. They would have captured both men and obliterated the wolf. Instead, Two Fingers' first man to see them was nearly fifteen meters from the next.

Two Fingers had ordered his men not to shoot until contacting him, but a break in the snow gave the man a shot.

And he took it.

~

Marco felt the bullet take him in the upper right thigh just one instant before he could pull the trigger. The impact threw him off balance preventing him from taking the shot—*the American was too close.*

Not only did the bullet throw him off balance—*it hurt—a lot.*

Jerking back in the direction of the sound of the shot, he sprayed the trees until he saw a muzzle flash and felt something wicked move past his face. Sighting in, he cranked off five quick shots. A man screamed and, through the slashing snow, Marco thought he saw something fall by a tree. He put three more bullets into what he hoped was the shooter and turned back to Gil and the wolf.

But he was too late.

~

THE WOLF REACTED IN FEAR—SOMETHING he had never done before—but he found himself pinned to the ground on his back, his jaws and teeth powerless, kept in check by mere hands that were capable of holding him in place.

He scrambled with his paws, scratching, clawing, and tearing, but the man would not release him. Another human came running up, pointing a rifle at his face, but then, a shot sounded, and the man stumbled back and out of the wolf's line of sight.

The man holding him was weakening.

The wolf could feel it in the trembling hands and forearms.

This was his chance.

The wolf jerked, first to one side, then to the other, and the man's grip lessened.

He twisted again, this time to the opposite side, and one hand slid off.

The wolf went for the wrist of the hand that still held him and clamped down, just as something sharp ripped into his ribs. He crushed down with his teeth, felt a knife pull free from his body, and then stab back into his shoulder.

Letting go of the wrist, he spun and bolted, surging out of the snow hole. Pivoting, he faced the man.

Rage flooded the wolf. He wanted to attack, to kill, to utterly destroy the human who had dared to trap him—to *hurt* him. But then he heard the soldiers approaching, and there was still the other man.

The human with the knife advanced.

Instinct demanded he run now and return later to attack from cover when the odds were in his favor. His entire life experience told him this was the thing to do.

But the man raised the stubby knife, and the wolf saw his own blood on the blade.

Instinct and experience gave place to *rage*.

~

MY HAND SLIPPED, and suddenly the monster had my wrist in his mouth. My coat helped—saved me, really—but the pain was mind-numbing. I've been dog-bit before in my career, *and not just a few times,* but the pressure the wolf inflicted was something else. I felt my bones compress, threatening to snap.

The buckle knife slid free, and I thrust it into his ribs. It was only a couple of inches long—*too short to reach his heart or organs*—but it had width. Surely it would hurt almost as bad as he was hurting me.

In my mind's eye, I saw Max leap into the air as the wolf seized him and then ripped out his throat.

I pulled out the knife and shoved it at the wolf's chest, but he moved, and I missed, stabbing him in the shoulder instead.

And suddenly he was gone.

I don't know how it happened.

I was on him, my wrist in his mouth and my knife in his shoulder, and then he just wasn't.

The hole in the snow was empty.

Spooky.

Reminded me of Max.

That made me mad.

And there was the wolf, standing in front of me.

I had time. I could reach back and pull out my Smith & Wesson 4506, *shoot him dead*. I could do it. I *should* do it.

But, like I said, I was mad. I kept seeing Max. I kept seeing him lying there. Dead.

So, instead of doing what I should have done, I took a step and raised the knife so the wolf would see it.

He saw it.

Only it didn't end the way I'd planned.

MAX IGNORED THE SNOW NOW. He ignored the heaving in his chest as his lungs combated both exhaustion and the cold. He ignored the metallic taste of blood in his mouth and the wind and the ice in his face.

A massive flurry of gunfire ahead spurred him to ignore all but finding the Alpha. And as he raced through the wind, moving ever closer, another scent registered. A scent that intermixed with the Alpha's—the Great Gray Wolf.

Max ran faster.

~

TWO FINGERS SMASHED HARD against a tree. He'd slipped and almost gone down, but with the help of the tree, he maintained his balance. The storm was extraordinarily intense, even for these mountains and this time of year. He pulled his goggles up, hoping it would help, but it only made things worse. His ski goggles were the blue-blocking type that helped with both the dark and the snow. Sliding them back in place, he caught movement down below. An instant later, gunfire ratcheted the woods, and splinters of bark pelted him. At first, he thought he'd been hit, but it was just the wood. He heard a man scream five trees away, almost parallel to him. The man dropped to the ground, and two more shots rang out.

"I'm throwing a flare," he said into the radio. "As soon as it lands, concentrate your fire on anything that moves down there."

He popped a flare and threw it fast toward where he'd heard the shots.

Blazing red light cut through the raging snow and landed next to a man, outlining him in the scarlet glow.

"FIRE!" yelled Two Fingers.

Four rifles roared in unison.

~

THE LANDSCAPE LIT UP, bloody red, and I saw the wolf's eyes glowing back at me like a demon from the pit. I saw his muscles bunching, his shoulders and haunches knotting and writhing, preparing to launch toward me. I'd witnessed his speed and strength and knew I was about to be hurt, maybe killed, but I was good with it ...

So long as I killed him first.

My knuckles snapped and popped around the small blade as I readied myself.

Gunfire blasted the night, and through the red glow of the flare, I saw a tuft of hair puff out on the wolf's haunch. Something clipped past my neck and then through my side, bringing blood.

I almost charged the wolf—*and he almost charged me*—I could see it in those hollow holes of fire.

But we were both too smart to do it.

The move I was about to make would allow the wolf to kill me if he decided to take it, but I had no choice.

I dropped, giving the wolf his chance, but he was already gone.

Looking back, I saw Marco, buried in the snow as though it were a foxhole, shooting away.

The foxhole idea was a good one, so I dug myself down. The problem with snow foxholes is that snow doesn't stop bullets nearly as effectively as dirt, but at least we were somewhat hidden.

Pulling out my 4506, I put two big .45 rounds down their way. The sweeping snow made it impossible to see a target, but one had to hope.

The flare was working against us, illuminating our position while blinding us to theirs.

Sighting in, I split it in two with one shot. It didn't put it out, but it would shorten the burn time by more than half.

The snow erupted as the enemy rained lead at me.

The shift in targets gave Marco a chance to take aim. He was in a better position than I was, and he took his time placing his shots. After the fifth one, someone started screaming that he was hit, that he knew he was going to die, and he wanted his mother. He begged for them to *please not let him die* and that *it hurt* and that *he wanted his mother.*

Marco could have put him out, but he let him go on.

A good tactic—harsh, but smart. He would distract them. Demoralize them. Fear is incredibly infectious, and once it takes hold, it can decimate an entire army. I've seen it, *experienced* it ...

... like the story in the Bible where a man dreams about a loaf of bread rolling through the enemy camp, terrorizing them, and causing them to flee even though they outnumbered the Israelites a hundred to one.

So, Marco let the man live, his screams, cries, and pleas for help causing the others to think—to realize that this could happen to *them*. That it could be any one of them lying and dying in the snow and the cold—*alone*—bleeding out while crying for the comfort of a mother who would never come.

Fear! It might not save us—probably wouldn't—but then again, maybe it would.

The shooting stopped while the man blubbered. Maybe they were going to him. Maybe they were staying in place, *contemplating*. Either way, it was quiet, except for the wind ... *and the man*.

Minutes passed.

Finally, someone yelled out.

"Let us get to him! Don't shoot."

"Okay," said Marco. "Go ahead; we won't shoot." I saw him dig the butt of the rifle into his shoulder and aim toward the sound of the screaming.

Marco was going to shoot.

Again, harsh. But this wasn't a game. It was life and death and *they* started it—like the cutting board with Billy.

We didn't know how many were out there, and we had to take every opportunity to reduce the odds.

"Help me! Please help me!" screamed the wounded man. *"Don't let me die! Oh, oh, oh, there's so much blood. Is this my blood? Oh, mama, help me."*

"Okay," said the other man, "I'm coming out to go to him. Don't shoot!"

There was movement behind the trees.

Marco fired three times.

The man went down.

He didn't scream at all.

And with that, they started shooting at us again.

45

The sound of thunder rumbling through the mountains awoke Anthony Carlino. He looked over and saw that Gilligan had not yet returned. He sat up, stretching.

His finger—rather his *not* finger—hurt. He unwrapped the bandage and held the stump closer to the fire. It didn't look infected.

It didn't look pretty either.

His lips twitched at the corners. He'd never been considered a handsome man, but he also wasn't hideous like his old friend William—Bill the Kill, they used to call him. He had killed over twenty men and was a made man before Anthony. His ugliness was legendary, but he was funny and fun to be with, and he took right to Anthony from the start. The feeling had been mutual, and of course, Anthony admired the man's courage.

Bill the Kill.

Anthony Carlino hadn't thought of him in years. Someone had gone at Bill's face with a knife when he was just a boy. It was rumored that the attack had been at the hands of his own father and that Bill had killed him in his sleep—*his first kill*—but Billy never talked about it. The only time Anthony had seen someone, *a drunk*, mention Bill the Kill's face, Bill had instantly lived up to his name.

Bill was long dead now, shot to death in the turf war with the Palladino family back in the seventies. Anthony Carlino had been there with him, back in the old country, shooting from behind some trash dumpsters in an alley. He'd ducked behind the metal boxes to reload his AK-47—*even back then, Anthony had hated the Russians, but he loved their rifles*—when Bill the Kill broke out from behind his dumpster and charged the four Palladino men, shooting at them.

Anthony Carlino had snapped the new magazine in as fast as he could and let the bolt fly home, following Bill the Kill into the open. The move was insane, but he would not let his friend and mentor go it alone, even if it meant his death.

Bill the Kill was a big man, and his body absorbed the bullets that hit him in the chest and belly like a meat sponge.

And he kept going.

He ran right into them, shooting with a rifle in one hand and a pistol in the other. He took out three of the four before falling to his knees.

As the fourth man stepped up with a pistol and placed it next to Bill the Kill's temple, Anthony Carlino put a string of 7.62s from the man's hip to his ear. Not one round missed.

When he got to his old friend to help him to his feet, he saw at least twenty holes punched through the front of his shirt. It looked like someone had splashed a bucket of fresh red paint into him, but there was not so much as a scratch on that face.

"Did we get 'em?" asked Bill the Kill.

"Yeah," said Anthony Carlino, tears dripping from his eyes because he knew his friend was a dead man. "Yeah, *you* got 'em. You got 'em all."

"Good," he said, smiling as if he was in perfect health, "good. That should end the war. Four of their top shooters taken out with no losses on our side. The Palladinos will have to call it quits with losses like that. Right?" He smiled up at Anthony Carlino.

"Yeah, right. They will have to."

Bill the Kill fell forward, dead. Anthony Carlino caught him in his arms and cried for him.

But the Palladino's did not call it quits after all. And Anthony Carlino was glad for that because it allowed him to extract a heavy toll for the death of his friend.

It hardened him, sharpened him. Like fire and the hammering of steel forges a sword. His reputation grew, and soon, his number of kills far exceeded Bill the Kill's.

Thunder rumbled again, but this time Anthony Carlino was fully awake, and he knew it for what it was.

Gunfire.

And a lot of it.

Throwing on his boots and coat, he took up the rifle and the handgun and walked out into the storm. The blizzard hit him instantly, tearing at his eyes and clothes, stinging and freezing all at once. He looked for footprints in the snow, but there was nothing. He had no idea how long Gilligan had been gone, but knowing what he knew of the man, he was sure the shooting had to involve him.

Looking up the mountain where the sounds of gunfire echoed, he wondered if he would be able to find Gilligan or make it back to the cave.

Probably not.

Didn't matter, really. He could no more leave Gilligan to fight alone than he could leave Bill the Kill in that alley all those years ago.

Pulling the magazine from the rifle, Anthony Carlino snapped back the bolt, extracting the round. He caught it expertly in his right palm, just as Bill the Kill had taught him all those years ago. Then he let the bolt go home and reinserted the magazine after replacing the cartridge. Holding onto the barrel, he used the rifle as a walking stick, climbing up toward the sound of war.

TWO FINGERS THREW the flare and saw the men. He fired, fast as he could, as did the others. Both men fell, and for an instant, Two Fingers thought they were dead. But then bullets started chipping the bark near him again. None came as close as before, but they were close enough for him to know the men weren't dead.

Squinting to see through the diagonal slant of the incessant snow, he used the tree he was hiding behind as a base and took careful aim. He fired at the closest man lying in the snow. When he looked up to see if he'd scored, the man was gone. Only he wasn't. He'd dug in. Two Fingers saw his head pop up and then a muzzle flash. He heard the whistle of hot metal as it soared somewhere to his right. He jerked his head and body back behind the tree, trying to squeeze as much of himself as he could behind the wooden barrier.

These men were good.

Two Fingers was angry that he hadn't grabbed a couple of grenades. He could have taken care of them nicely if he had.

Putting the radio close to his mouth, he keyed the mic.

"Do any of you have grenades or any type of explosive?"

Static ... silence.

Two Fingers gave them time to check while the shooting continued from both sides.

"I have three grenades," said a voice from the radio.

"Who is this?" Two Fingers closed his eyes. Was he working with idiots?

"Hans, it's Hans, sir, from the village."

"Have you ever thrown a grenade, Hans?" Two Fingers didn't want to get blown up from a dropped explosive. He'd seen it happen once.

A brief pause.

"Yes, but it's been a while."

"Do you think you can toss it down there? Can you get it to where it will take them out?"

"Not from here," said Hans. "But I see a spot where I could throw it from and maybe get them both."

"Get ready," said Two Fingers. "Everyone else, when Hans says *now*, give him cover." Two Fingers slipped around the tree, keeping as much of himself hidden as he could, and aimed at the man that had dug in. "On you, Hans."

"*Now*," said Hans. He broke from cover and started through the trees, everyone else shooting.

Two Fingers heard Hans scream and when he looked, saw him fall by a tree.

Hans started screaming and begging almost immediately.

Everyone stopped shooting.

Two Fingers thought the men from below would finish him off. It would be an easy shot. They could have done it by sound alone because of all the noise Hans was making.

But the men didn't.

They let Hans scream.

Two Fingers felt a chill go down his spine that had nothing to do with the storm.

It was fear.

Someone yelled out that he was going to help Hans and for the men not to shoot him. From below, Two Fingers heard the go-ahead from the men and the promise not to fire.

As soon as the man broke cover, he was shot and then shot again.

Two Fingers and the others returned fire.

Yes, these men were good, *as ruthless and accurate as Two Fingers himself*, but it would do them no good.

Two Fingers felt the shoulder tap, signaling an ally was now with him, and grinned as more men took their positions and began shooting downrange.

His reinforcements had just arrived.

MAX SLOWED up and then lay still as the men charged past him down the mountain. There were a lot of them, and they were in a hurry.

The Alpha was not with them, nor did Max smell the Great Gray Wolf.

He recognized the scent of some of the men from the earlier battle.

They were the enemy.

Max would wait for the last man to pass before he attacked.

And then the shooting started back up down below.

Perfect.

No one would hear his attack.

Max hit the man from behind, knocking him face-first into a tree, and then whipped him around and down into the snow. The man coughed and tried to grab for something, anything, but Max had him by the back of the neck. Max spun him again, letting the land's pitch and gravity do most of the work. At the same time, he crushed down, feeling bones snap and crackle and crunch between his teeth.

But the man was tough. He tried to stab Max with a knife that he had somehow pulled out without Max realizing it.

They were tumbling now, and the man rolled right over him as they continued their spinning descent. Max held his grip, the vertebra in the man's neck grinding and splintering as they tumbled along in a shower of snow.

The snow stopped them after twenty or so yards, and Max let go, standing over his prey. The man had died sometime during the fall.

Max shook the snow from his fur and started toward the next target.

BULLETS WHIZZED past Marco like crazed wasps. One of them ricocheted off the barrel of his rifle as he was taking aim, and he quickly ducked back into his hole. Rounds punched through the snow above him, disappearing into the wall near his booted feet, leaving perfect little holes of their own.

Using his body, hands, and feet, he dug deeper. The angle was not in his favor, and sooner or later, the lead missiles were sure to find him.

And then the flare died.

"Marco?" It was the American. "Can you dig out?"

The enemy's accuracy had decreased with the absence of the flare's light.

Marco took a chance, rose out of the foxhole, and ran toward the sound of the American's voice. He could see almost nothing in the dark and the snow and almost punched out as a hand gripped his left bicep.

"This way," said the American, who then pulled him down the slope of the mountain and away from the sound of gunfire and whistling death.

As they stumble-ran through trees and snow, Marco's eyes searched frantically through the impossible elements, straining to see any trace of the thing he feared most. Marco's rational mind knew that if it were out there, he would not see it until it was too late, but he couldn't keep himself from looking. Fear, an alien emotion to him before tonight, would not let him stop, even though he tried—even though he told himself he had to stop. He knew he should simply run and let whatever happened *happen*, as he had had to do a thousand times before in dangerous situations, relying on his own prowess and reflexes to come out alive. But this time, it did not work. This time fear had him, and it would not let go. The tactic he had implemented on the enemy with the crying, wounded man was now affecting him.

It wasn't a fear of death or dying or bullets that had hold of him.

It was the wolf.

It could be behind any tree, around any corner, or even lying directly in their path. And they would never see it. Not until it was too late. Not until that giant head was rushing toward them.

That head ...

... and those teeth.

～

I GRABBED Marco by the arm and ran down the mountain with him, bullets chasing us as we fled. I'd lost the rifle back in the fight with the wolf, but my faithful 4506 was still with me, even though my wrist felt like the bones were severely compromised. Thinking of the wolf made me realize he might still be nearby. No time to worry about that, though. If he showed up, I'd shoot him ... a lot ... and with painful bullets. In fact, I hoped he would show up.

And then I heard the explosions behind us.

46

M ax took out two more men before getting to the main party. The first was easiest, going down and out with little fight, but the second had been tough. He was a big man with hard punches, and he managed to hit Max several times. Max finally had to resort to hamstringing him and then gripping his throat and strangling him while absorbing blows until the man passed out. The saving factor had been that Max was on top, preventing the man from bringing his hips, shoulders, or bodyweight into play. The man had to swing from an awkward angle while on his back, partially trapped in the snow. But just before he went out, he managed to jab a long-bladed knife into Max's left shoulder near his neck. Max wrenched to the side the instant the steel punctured his flesh, sending the knife spinning away, but the tip had passed through muscle and touched bone, and he was still bleeding from the wound.

Lying beneath a tree, Max watched the long line of men, as best he could, through the still falling snow. The rifle fire was deafening.

He tried to catch the Alpha's scent, and just as he thought he might have it, the mountain suddenly shook as explosions detonated in rapid succession from where the remnants of odor had been.

Max dug into the snow until he found dirt and pine needles, and then he dug deeper. From beneath the tree, he watched as the men threw grenades, the fiery explosions blasting dirt and snow into the night. The sound was deafening compared to that of the rifles.

Max could barely stand it.

He decided to put a stop to it.

Sighting in on the last man along the line, Max rose to a low crouch, stalking forward.

Max would kill this man and then move down the line until they were all dead.

And then he would find the Alpha.

Just as Max was about to sprint for the attack, the wind shifted, bringing the scent to him.

At that moment, something suddenly jerked the man off his feet. He screamed once and then disappeared beneath a black shape that covered his entire body.

The scent was unmistakable—the only other animal on this mountain capable of sneaking through an army and devouring one man amongst the rest.

It was the Great Gray Wolf.

And he was right in front of Max.

At last.

TWO FINGERS CRANKED off the last round in the magazine and popped in another, but he held off from returning fire. Instead, he went for his radio and ordered those with grenades to let loose.

It was time to end this.

Explosions rocked the mountain, lighting the landscape in flashes that even the blizzard could not obscure. Shockwaves blasted out through the trees, shaking them more powerfully than the wind.

Two Fingers felt their nausea-inducing power roll through him. Gripping the tree for support, he ordered the bombing to stop.

Shrapnel continued to patter down on him for nearly a minute, falling through branches and blowing about on the wind.

Throwing a flare, he peered through the driving snow, straining to see if anything moved below. But the storm had grown more intense, and he could see nothing.

"Anybody see anything?" He asked into the radio.

The radio crackled back with negative responses from several men.

Two Fingers held off for another minute and then ordered his men to move in. He seated the stock of his rifle firmly into his shoulder, took a careful step down through the snow, and then stopped almost instantly. Down below, in the trees to his left, he saw something his brain couldn't accept.

Odin.

Rising like a ghostly apparition from beneath the ice, he was crouched low and stalking forward slowly, his attention fully intent on something ahead.

Following Odin's line of attack, Two Fingers saw the wolf devouring one of his men. His mind blanked, and he froze. He remembered Odin charging the wolf and how easily it had snatched him from the air, killing him instantly.

But how was it possible that he was here ... now?

Two Fingers did not believe in haunts or spooks or anything supernatural. *But what else?* How could Odin be here?

Two Fingers put the metal gun sights on what he thought was the center of the wolf—*moved them to the ghost of Odin*—back to the wolf —sweat started on his forehead, despite the freezing wind.

He knew he had to decide. The muzzle went back to Odin—but what to do? The man he had been before losing his fingers would not have been able to make the decision.

But he was no longer that man.

He had grown since that day. He'd learned and matured.

Deciding, he moved the barrel and pulled the trigger.

∿

ANTHONY CARLINO THOUGHT his lungs might explode. His thigh muscles were burning, and he couldn't get enough air. His body was sweating while his hands, feet, and face were freezing. The snow beat at him with fists of unrelenting fury. He wanted to stop, to rest, or better yet, *to go back.*

But he would not.

Besides, he'd never find his way back, not on his own.

The shooting had stopped briefly but then continued stronger than before.

And then came the explosions.

Didn't matter.

He kept going toward the sounds.

Trying to see through the blizzard was impossible. His goggles slushed over almost instantly, but without them, the snow whipped into his eyes with such brutal force he couldn't keep them open even as slits.

But he could hear, and he was close enough now that the echoes no longer confused him. He thought he should probably chamber a round in his rifle.

No telling how soon he might run into punks that needed shooting.

Although it made good sense, a part of him thought he might be using this as a good excuse to stop and rest for a moment. He stopped and brought the rifle up. The barrel was clogged with snow, but he figured a bullet going through it would melt it fast enough. He pulled back on the bolt and then let it go, hearing a round seat.

On wiping his goggles, he saw two men running at him from above. Muscle memory took over, and he adopted a hip stance, switching the weapon to full auto.

It was like the old days, only then it had been a good old American-made Thompson submachine gun instead of a Russian AK, but what did it matter? They both put out a lot of bullets—really, really fast.

∼

"Don't shoot, Skipper," I said as Anthony Carlino turned the AK on us.

"Gilligan," he said, "what are you …"

"No time," I said, pulling Marco along. "There's an army after us. Head for those trees." I pointed to a thicket spreading down the slope to the south.

We all moved out as fast as we could and didn't stop until we reached them. My thigh, side, and wrist were hurting—probably from the bullets and wolf bite.

Marco didn't look much better.

"I'm glad to see you're alive," Marco said to Anthony Carlino.

Anthony Carlino grinned and patted the younger man's cheek. "It is *I* that am glad to see *you* are alive."

Marco's head nodded toward me. "Thanks to him," he said. He looked at me. "You are a warrior among warriors, my friend." He looked back at Anthony Carlino. "Billy?"

Anthony Carlino shook his head. "No," he said.

"We don't know that for sure," I said, checking our *six* to make sure no one was coming up behind us. The back trail looked clear for now, and the snow was filling in our tracks quickly.

I prayed it would be quickly enough.

"Gilligan is an optimist, "said Anthony Carlino. "Did any of the others survive?"

"Piero and Enzo," said Marco. "We're in a cave about a kilometer up that way. Enzo's okay, but Piero has a chest wound. I think it's infected." He reached into his coat and pulled out the first-aid kit. "I stole this from one of their tents. The occupants won't miss it." He grinned slyly. "They won't miss anything ever again."

Anthony Carlino smiled and nodded.

"I took a couple of them out," said Marco. "And then the American and I took out a few more."

"Good," said Anthony Carlino, "good, you both did good."

I heard sounds. It was tough with the wind, but I heard them. I checked my ammo, not good. It was time to either run or dig in and make a stand. We had the trees, the snow, the dark, and the advantage of ambush. They had numbers, flares, bullets, and grenades.

I didn't like the odds in a fight.

"What do you think, Marco," I asked, "can you run?"

He looked up the hill on hearing them.

"If it's that or take on the army, I can run."

I looked at Anthony Carlino.

"You up for it?" I asked.

"I don't want to fight an army either," he said, grinning.

"Ok, stay to the trees for as long as we can. If I break into the open, move fast."

I didn't like the odds on our running much more than I did on fighting. With their numbers, the enemy could spread out and move fast. And even though the blizzard covered our tracks in a matter of minutes, it might not be fast enough. That meant I couldn't take us straight to our cave. We had to hope for things that would slow the enemy down—some bare rocks or a creek. Things that would hide our tracks long enough to make them search them out. And then we had to hope that, in the time it took them to search, the blizzard would obscure them once we went back to fresh snow.

It was a long shot, but better than *getting* shot.

Leading the way, I moved them out.

Two Fingers fired three quick shots into the darkness that had been the wolf, but it was gone. Instead of hitting the monster, his bullets jerked the body of the man the wolf had been eviscerating.

Instantly, Two Fingers jerked the muzzle back to where he had seen Odin's ghost.

But that too was gone.

Scanning the surrounding area as best he could through the storm and the dark, he saw nothing of either the wolf or Odin.

Desperate, he yelled through the night.

"Odin! Come! Odin!"

He saw some of his men turn and look up at him. He motioned for them to continue forward.

It had to be Odin—*it had to!*

He must have just been injured—stunned. Two Fingers remembered how his men had shot into the body and the carnage they had made of him. But it had been in the middle of a gun battle, with chaos and confusion everywhere. It must have looked worse than it was. Odin was the toughest dog he had ever seen.

Except maybe one.

The thought made his missing fingers ache.

Shaking his head, Two Fingers gave up on it. He still needed to kill the men and find Carlino. He scanned again with his scope, then continued down the mountain after his men.

～

THE WOLF WAS fifteen feet away, downwind from both the man and the dog. He could see them both, smell them, hear them. But they were triple-blind to the wolf.

The human wanted him, so did the dog. If he attacked one, it would give the other its chance. He wanted both of them, and he would have them.

One at a time.

～

MAX HAD STARTED his move when the Great Gray Wolf simply disappeared. Three shots sounded through the storm just to the side of Max. He sprang for the trees, diving fast, then turned and came back around from lower before staring out from under a thick pine. He saw the dead man and the moving man with the rifle. But he did not see the Great Gray Wolf.

Scenting, he searched for any trace of the Alpha or the Great Gray Wolf, but all he could smell were men and gunpowder and ground disturbance.

Something felt wrong.

Max could not see the Great Gray Wolf. He could not hear him or smell him. But somehow, he knew he was here ... close ... very close.

And suddenly, Max realized that he was no longer the hunter—Max was now the hunted.

He lay in the snow and waited for the Great Gray Wolf to make its move.

47

A hundred yards down and around, I stopped to let everyone catch their breath. I rested with my hands on my knees. So did the others. I'd taken the lead so I could break path through the snow to make it easier for them, but still, I was again impressed that Anthony Carlino hadn't slowed us down.

We'd heard some shooting about ten minutes earlier, but nothing since then. It had sounded farther away than I would have expected.

Perhaps we'd caught a break.

"Marco," I said, "how far is your cave now?"

He sucked in some air before answering. Maybe he was hurt worse than I thought.

He pointed. "That way, and up. Twenty—thirty minutes, at this pace. Maybe more."

I nodded, feeling the fatigue myself. "My place is closer and downhill. We'll head there."

I saw him look up the way he'd pointed.

"You think they'll stay put?" I asked, knowing that he was thinking of Enzo and Piero.

"I hope so," he said. "I wouldn't want them to come looking for me and run into the bad guys."

I almost laughed at that one, a *Mafia elite soldier* calling other guys *bad*. Still, I agreed with him just now.

"Also," he added, taking in more air, "Piero needs the antibiotics in the kit I took."

"We could split," I said. "Your call, but it's risky. You might run into them yourself, not to mention the wolf, and there's the danger of getting lost." I pointed in the general direction of our cave. "We're down that way—half a mile, I'd guess. Maybe a little farther. If you feel you have to go, I'll take the Skipper with me, and we can try to meet up in the morning."

I looked at Marco and saw him staring at me.

"Mr. Carlino goes with me," he said. "He's my responsibility."

I could see there was no changing his mind. I looked at Anthony Carlino. He was about used up. I doubted he could make another trek *up* the mountain. To tell the truth, I wasn't so sure about Marco either.

"No," I said. "He's *our* responsibility. And I'm not letting him out of my sight. There's no way he can make it up to your cave without a long rest—*a long rest we don't have time for.* I think he can make it to my cave—down's easier. And if not, it'll be easier carrying him down than up. So, we'll just have to take the chance on Enzo and Piero. I don't know how bad Piero is, but I doubt *you'd* go out solo in *this*," I held my hand up to the blizzard, "like you did if he wasn't bad. So, you good with this?"

Marco was a soldier, and so he understood exactly what I was saying without actually saying it. Piero, maybe Enzo too, might well die if we didn't go to them.

He was going to have to make a choice.

"No," he said. "I'm not *good* with it. But they would do the same."

"Okay," I said. "We've gained a little time. Our tracks are almost gone." I pointed to another big group of trees. "We'll head there, around the bend, then cut straight down and hope the snow does the rest." I stood up straight. Anthony Carlino and Marco followed suit.

"Let's go."

~

MAX SAW nothing but snow and waving trees. The men had moved down the mountain until his senses were no longer able to detect them.

Still, he waited.

If the Great Gray Wolf was out there, Max would not let him escape. Nor would Max make himself an easy target.

Twice before, Max had fought the Great Gray Wolf. Once as a pup and once when the bear had interjected.

The bear and the Alpha.

Both times the Great Gray Wolf had won. The first time he had knocked Max unconscious. The Great Gray Wolf had won the second time by being smart enough to put Max closer to the bear and leaving before he could be injured.

This time would be different.

Max was no longer a pup.

This time no bear, no sickness, no human, would come between them.

Max waited a little longer, stood up, noisily shook the snow from his coat, and walked out from the trees into a small open clearing.

The Great Gray Wolf thought himself the hunter rather than the hunted.

Time for him to understand the truth.

~

THE WOLF WATCHED as Max stood, shook, and walked out into the open.

The wolf almost exploded out of his hiding place.

Instead, he stayed where he was, silent and hidden.

His golden eyes stared through the blizzard, watching Max's every move, his tactical brain calculating faster than a supercomputer.

Max's act was not an accident.

Not foolishness.

It was a trap.

The wolf wanted to kill this creature.

And he would.

Just as he had killed Odin. But the wolf would not fall for the trap, whatever it was.

He would kill Max, but he would do it at the time of *his* choosing. In the place of *his* choosing.

The wolf would not fall into Max's trap.

Max would fall into his.

MAX SCENTED high but caught no trace of the Great Gray Wolf. His ears took in only the wailing wind. Finally, he thought the Great Gray Wolf must be gone.

Turning, he sprinted, chest-deep in the snow, and began following the men who were chasing the Alpha.

He stopped briefly at the site where the grenades had exploded. Here the scent of the Alpha hugged close to the snow. Max followed it until he realized the men he'd been following were headed in the same direction. Their scent was everywhere and much easier to follow.

Faster.

Making excellent time, he came up behind a straggler and took out his hamstring. The man screamed, but due to the storm, it didn't carry far. Lying on his back, the man continued to scream. Max left him and quickly caught up to the main group. But this time, someone saw him and started shooting in his direction.

The deep snow hampered Max's movements, and he barely made it to the trees before bullets whizzed all around him.

Moving from tree to tree, he tried to burrow beneath the snow, but the bullets splintered the trunks and burned holes into the ice and snow too close for him to stay in place. Max kept moving, but the men and their bullets were closing in. Something hot and fast scorched through his coat along his back.

Slowed by the snow, attacking the men straight on or trying to turn and make it up the mountain would be suicide.

But these were his only choices.

Max had nowhere to go.

Ducking low behind a tree, his shoulder and haunch muscles tensing, he prepared to attack.

∽

TWO FINGERS SAW Odin running from tree to tree before crouching down and aiming straight at his men. In turn, his men aimed their rifles.

"Stop!" he screamed. "Stop, don't shoot him." He ran between Odin and his men, the dog fifteen meters back, the men closer. The snow gusted and blew as if the storm god himself were raging.

"Odin," he said, facing him and holding his hand out to him. "Odin, here!"

The dog stared at him through the dark and the snow. The lights on his men's rifles did little to help, their beams bouncing off the slashing snow and reflecting the light.

But Two Fingers had no fear of Odin.

Odin was his body and soul.

Two Fingers had *beaten* it into him. The dog was subservient to no one but him and would never again consider challenging his absolute mastery. The consequences were too horrible for even *his* dog brain to contemplate.

Of this, Two Fingers was supremely confident.

Two Fingers squinted through the storm, his headlamp illuminating the creature in front of him. It was shivering and cowering now that it realized who he was. Laughing at his complete mastery over the animal, he ordered him again.

"Odin, here!"

The dog obeyed instantly, just as Two Fingers knew he would.

∽

MAX WAS ABOUT to attack when the man ran between him and the others and faced him.

The wind swirled, and Max caught his scent. He knew Two Fingers well. The man had tortured him, and Max had, in turn, given Two Fingers the reason for his name.

Two Fingers ordered him to come.

Max was only too happy to oblige.

WE MADE the cave a half-hour later. We could have done it in fifteen minutes, but I took us on a few detours just in case they were closer than we thought.

Once inside, Anthony Carlino collapsed by the smoldering embers of the fire. I threw a few bark chips on top to get it going again and then small twigs until it was ready for dead, wrist-thick chunks of branches.

Marco's face shone, bone white, in the rising flames. His wounds were telling on him. He sat, breathing hard.

"You okay?" I asked.

His eyes swiveled to me, and he nodded slightly. I could see that even that tiny motion cost him in energy.

"Think you can stay awake for a while?" I asked, stripping off my gloves and warming my fingers over the fire.

With his teeth, he pulled off first one glove and then the other. His hands were wrinkled and whiter than his face and shook as he held them close to the heat.

"Yes," he said. "You want me to take first watch?"

"You're taking the only watch for now," I said. "I've been giving it some thought. We need Enzo, maybe Piero too. There's no telling how many might be at the farmhouse, and another gun or two could make the difference."

"I should go," he said.

"No. You watch him. That's your main responsibility, right?"

Marco looked over at the bulk of Anthony Carlino, sleeping quietly, pushed up against the back of the cave.

He nodded again. "Sure you can find it?"

"You give good directions. I remember, from the airport to the dock." I gave him a grin I couldn't feel. Truth was, I was talking a lot more confidently than I felt. I was near frozen, more tired than I cared to admit, and the last thing I wanted was to go out into the blizzard, climb a mountain again, and then repeat the journey dragging an injured man—all while dodging an army and a deranged werewolf. Still, it had to be done. And not just for the reasons I'd given to Marco. I'd ridden with those men, fought with them. They deserved better than to be left behind. It's something Marines just don't do.

I pulled down my pants and examined the wound to my thigh. The bullet had dug a groove through the muscle. Looked nasty, but it didn't hurt that bad ... *yet*. I had a feeling it would hurt plenty by morning. The bullet's heat had mostly cauterized the wound, so the bleeding was minimal.

Marco tossed me the first-aid kit. I cleaned it out and bandaged it up. Messing with it caused a little more bleeding and had upped the pain a bit, but what's a Marine to do? Besides, I had to get going. Sunrise wasn't that far off.

I popped five aspirin from the kit, gave my hands another few minutes, re-gloved, picked up Anthony Carlino's rifle, checked its ammo, its bolt and strap, and the first-aid kit, and headed out of the cave, meeting the elements head-on.

My body swayed with the wind's force.

Behind me, I heard Marco say, "Be careful, my friend. Mother Nature is very dangerous tonight."

I turned halfway, looking in on him. "Yeah, well, my Father God can take your Mother Nature any day of the week."

He grinned and gave a weary nod.

Turning, I looked toward the sky, insane snow smacking me in the face and making my teeth ache.

Saying a small prayer, I started up the mountain.

MAX LAUNCHED straight into Two Fingers, twitching his massive neck muscles and snapping his jaws as his head passed the outstretched mangled hand before him. His razor-sharp teeth sliced through the glove and the remaining fingers as though they weren't even there, and, after that instant—they no longer were.

Turning his shoulder in, he struck Two Fingers solidly in the chest with his follow-through, smashing him into the snow. Max landed beyond him in front of one of the soldiers and ripped out the man's left knee before streaking between his legs and striking the man next to him on the inner thigh. The man screamed and shot at where Max had been, sending a high-velocity bullet through his own leg, shattering the femur and narrowly missing the femoral artery. He screamed even louder and fell to the snow as his companions opened up, shooting into their mates while trying to hit Max.

But the dark, the snow, the blood, the confusion, and terror had done their job, and Max was already gone, hidden in the trees and moving back up the mountain, the dark shadowing him like a long-lost friend.

TWO FINGERS SCRABBLED to his knees, his headlamp activated and glowing at the severed fingers, blood spurting from what had been his namesake like macabre little fountains.

In that instant, he knew the truth.

It wasn't Odin.

Odin really was dead.

It was the *other* dog.

The dog that had taken his fingers on their first meeting.

The dog he had tortured and tried to kill.

The dog he had burned with the stick.

He didn't know how it was possible.

But it was true.

He knew it was true.

Capping the squirting stumps with his good hand, he made it to his feet, shouting for his men to cease fire.

The pain was beginning to register, watering his eyes and making him cringe. He held the hand to his chest—cupping it—protecting it. But in a strange way, it cleared his mind, the pain and shock focusing his thoughts.

The dog was gone.

The men were gone.

But he knew where they would have to go.

Down.

To the farmhouse.

It was the only possible way off the mountain in this blizzard.

One of his men came to take a look at his hand. Alexi Stepanovich, a man with a dubious past and a penchant for surviving difficult situations, had been a medic in the Russian army a lifetime ago. He pulled the blood-soaked glove free, popped a flare, and cauterized the stumps with typical Russian speed, efficiency, and mercilessness.

Alexi examined his doctoring.

"You'll live," he said in German, with a heavy Russian accent. "But you'll need a new nickname." Canting his head and pursing his lips, he said, "*No Fingers*." He gave a single curt nod of his head as if the matter were settled. "Back to camp?"

"Yes," said No Fingers through gritted teeth. He hadn't screamed. He'd watched while the fire closed his flesh.

He wanted the pain. Wanted to see it, hear it, feel it.

The dog would experience far worse.

48

I saw the slight glow of the cave's fire and angled toward it. Marco's directions had been good, but even so, I'd almost missed the mark. The snow had slowed, and the wind had dropped, but that meant my tracks wouldn't be hidden. Thankfully, I hadn't seen or heard anything from either the army or the wolf.

Pulling my goggles up on my hoodie, I stood next to the entrance and called inside.

"Enzo, it's me, Gil Mason. Marco sent me. I'm coming in. Don't shoot me."

"The American," said Enzo from inside. "Come in."

The cave was bigger than mine, so was the fire. I stripped my gloves and waggled my frozen fingers over the flames, trying to bring them back to life. Pins and needles prickled my skin, and I knew they'd be alright.

I tossed the first-aid kit to Enzo.

"Medicine for Piero."

Enzo took the kit and opened it up.

"Nice kit," he said. "Lots of meds and lots of tools." He held up a needle with a flattened end that was as long as my forearm.

"You going to stick that into him?" I asked. I mean, I'm not squeamish, but it seemed like overkill for a shot of antibiotics.

He grinned, putting it back into the bag and rummaging.

"No," he said. "That's for a collapsed lung. I could practically operate with this kit." He grinned and pulled out an ampule and a regular-sized syringe. Setting them aside, he rolled up Piero's sleeve and cleaned it off with an alcohol swab.

Piero roused, but he looked feverish. It was obvious he wouldn't be able to walk on his own.

"What do you think?" I asked Enzo.

He filled a syringe and injected it into Piero. Shrugging, he recapped the needle and put everything back in the bag.

"Penicillin," he said. "Good. I'm a little worried at how fast the infection took hold. Could be the bullet broke apart, and a piece of it might still be inside. But I'm no real doctor."

"We have to get back," I said.

"Marco's okay?" He asked.

I nodded. "I left him with your boss. He's a little shot up, but who isn't?" I smiled.

"Billy?"

I shook my head to the negative.

He closed his eyes. "I'll make them pay for that," he said. When he opened his eyes, I saw the crackling fire reflected in them.

I knew exactly how he felt.

Enzo looked over at Piero, who had drifted back to sleep.

"I don't think we can move him," he said. "Might kill him."

"No choice. We have to beat the bad guys to the farmhouse, and it looks like the storm might be slowing. If we don't get some vehicles and get off this mountain, we're dead."

I could see he didn't like it. I didn't like it either. But *not liking* it didn't change a thing.

"He can't walk," said Enzo. "How far?"

"Too far to carry him. Plus, Marco and I already stirred the hornet's nest. Could be bad guys are still out there looking for us."

"How many?"

"You know how in movies guys shoot guns and never run out of bullets? It's like that. They never seem to run out of people. Oh, one more thing. There's a monster wolf hunting me."

"A what?"

I shrugged. "Just thought you should know."

I looked around the cave.

"We can hook the rifle straps to make a harness for Piero, and then we'll drag him down the mountain. With the grade and the snow, it should be fairly easy. Bumpy, maybe painful for him if he wakes up, but easy—fast."

Enzo nodded then looked me in the eye.

"A monster wolf. That I would like to see."

"No, my friend," I said, standing and pulling the three-point-strap from my rifle, "you really don't."

~

MAX ENTERED HIS DEN QUIETLY. He'd searched for any sign of the Alpha or the Great Gray Wolf but hadn't caught any scent after fleeing the men shooting at him. Their gunfire had forced him up and in the wrong direction of either of them.

Eventually, Max had been able to circle around and make his way back to the den. But it was rough going and had taken time.

Billy was awake, holding a pistol and pointing it at him.

Max ignored the man and went to Irmgard. She slept fitfully, her arms wrapped tightly around her tiny body as she softly snored.

Billy lowered the gun.

"Glad you made it back," he said. "I heard shooting. Figured you were killing people."

Max continued ignoring him and wrapped his body around the girl, sharing his warmth. He closed his eyes.

"Did you find anyone? Gil? My grandfather?"

Max opened his eyes and stared at the young man.

"Give it up," said Billy. "The whole intimidation thing kind of went out the window, seeing you acting like a plush toy for the girl.

Big bad killer dog. You'd probably let her dress you up and put make-up on you. You don't scare me. Not anymore. So don't even try."

Max just stared.

~

BILLY STARTED to say something else, but the shadows inside the den shifted a little—maybe the clouds breaking to let the moon splash through or maybe just movement—but it was enough for the dog's eyes to become momentarily visible in the pale light.

Billy stopped himself before whatever he was going to say could break past his lips. A ripple quivered through him, and he suddenly had nothing more to say. He closed his eyes and tried to fall back to sleep.

It didn't work, and after a few minutes he opened them and saw Max was still staring at him. Billy looked away, wishing Gil Mason were here.

~

MAX DETECTED the change in the human's tone and the inflection in his words. His dog brain couldn't understand the words themselves, but the *meaning* of the words didn't matter. He understood the emotions and intentions behind the words, telling him far more than human speech ever could.

He considered killing the man.

Not because Billy was a real danger, but because Billy *thought* he could be a danger to Max.

But Max was tired and hurting, and he didn't want to disturb Irmgard.

So, Max let Billy live.

Maybe he'd kill him in the morning.

~

BY THE TIME we made it to my cave, the sun was only an hour or so from rising, and I was dead tired. We'd taken a chance and moved straight down the mountain, no diversions or detours. We saw zero sign of the bad guys or the wolf.

It was a pretty rough trip for Piero, and he cried out more than once, but he made it. Marco and Enzo both fell to checking his wounds and administering some pain killers included in the kit.

The storm had stopped, and the sky was clear, except for a few puffy clouds way up high.

I wanted to sleep ... *I needed to sleep.* But there was no time for that. I envied Anthony Carlino, snoring at the back of the cave.

Marco had kept the fire going strong, and I warmed my fingers and toes.

Thirst was no problem; we all just popped snow into our mouths as we went, but none of us had eaten in a while, and we were all hungry.

"I should have stolen some food from the tent when I got the med-kit," said Marco.

"Doesn't matter," I said. "This is the end game now. Either we're on a plane heading home by dark, eating the best, or we're most likely dead, our bodies freezing in the snow."

"At least where I'm going, it will be warm," grinned Marco.

I was too tired to respond, but I made a mental note to talk with him later. The Holy Spirit moves in mysterious ways.

"Twenty minutes," I said. "Then we move out."

I shook Anthony Carlino. He yawned and stretched and looked at me.

"Gilligan?"

"Time to get up, Skipper," I said. "We've got a big day ahead of us."

I had no idea what an understatement that was.

49

N o *Fingers*, as the men were already calling him, got no sleep. The pain was excruciating. He'd taken medication but wouldn't let them put him out. He had to be aware, *awake*, thinking.

The break in the storm gave both him and *them* a chance to get the upper hand. He was sure they were heading for the farmhouse. There were vehicles there, the radio, but most importantly, the road down to the town ran right past it.

He'd already radioed for reinforcements, but seven-to twelve-foot snowdrifts were making that impossible. In the interim, he had men stationed at the farthest point he could on the road leading to them.

At least Anthony Carlino and his men would be closed off from their escape until the roads were cleared.

The weather reports showed another storm moving in by three. No Fingers vowed to have them captured or killed before then.

By sunrise, they struck camp and were ready to move.

And move they did.

∼

THE WOLF WATCHED the men as they traveled down his mountains. Their numbers had thinned, but there were still enough of them that they could spread out in a line. They were staying in sight of one another and making it unsafe for him to take out the ends on either side without being detected.

Instead, he followed them, confident they would lead him to at least one of his targets. And sooner or later, as with any herd or pack, someone would become lax and stray or linger, *the weakest of the group.* And he would take them—kill them—*practice* for his intended prey.

He remembered the fight with Gil, how the man had hurt him, almost killed him.

Rage burned within.

This was not the human's territory, not his mountain. The wolf had been master here for longer than he could remember. No one would take it from him or make him cower. Both the man and Max had to die. And the wolf would do the killing.

Holding his rage in check by an iron will, the wolf continued to follow.

As silent and invisible as death itself.

BILLY CRAWLED OUTSIDE and saw the sun in the eastern sky. Every part of his body ached. The snow around the den was undisturbed except for Max's tracks. Billy looked towards the area he thought the firing had come from last night. Although the shooting had been far off, it was still too close for comfort. And if any of the bad guys made it this way, they'd see paw prints ... leading straight to the snow den.

It was time to leave.

But where would they go?

Irmgard crawled out of the dark and stood up, blinking and rubbing her eyes.

Max was at her side.

Billy had been looking right at her as she emerged from the den, and he was sure Max hadn't been there, but suddenly—he was.

Billy remembered those eyes staring at him the night before.

He brushed off the shiver as best he could and spoke to Irmgard. "Did you sleep well?"

"Yes," she said, "thank you. Petra kept me warm." She rubbed her face against the top of Petra's head. "And you?"

He and Max watched each other's eyes as though sharing a secret, the little girl oblivious that each was considering killing the other.

"As well as can be expected," he said. "All things considered." He curled a lip at the dog.

Max started licking himself.

"Anyway, we need to start down the mountain."

"Leave the cave?" she said. "But I like it here."

"The bad men might be coming," he said. "There was shooting last night."

Irmgard scrunched the skin on Max's head, making the folds nearly close his eyes. "Petra will protect us."

"Not against guns," said Billy. "They'd shoot him. You don't want that. Besides, we need food."

"Petra feeds me."

"Raw badger? We can't live on that. And his name isn't Petra. It's Max."

Irmgard stood straight.

"No, it's not," she said. "He's my dog, and his name is Petra."

"He belongs to a man named Gil Mason. The dog's name is Max, and all three of us are from America. I'm sorry."

"Gil ... that's a stupid name," she said, crossing her arms.

Billy didn't say anything to that.

"This American, he is a good man? Not one of the men chasing me?"

"No, he's good. He's with me. We came to rescue my grandfather from the bad men."

"The old man from the trunk of the car? The night that man killed my—killed my father?"

Billy nodded. "Probably."

"Then this man named Gil owes me Petra. If he is good, he will give him to me."

"I don't know that I can argue that," said Billy. "We did sort of bring this trouble on you. But that dog isn't what you think it is. It's not a pet. It's dangerous."

Irmgard wrapped her arm around Petra's neck.

"Only to bad people," she said.

Billy almost told her what Max had done to him, but then remembered he had been in the act of breaking into Gil Mason's home at the time, planning to scare him, maybe do more, maybe hurt or kill him, and realized he couldn't argue this point either.

"Anyway, we've got to go. Get whatever you've got to bring."

"Where?" she asked.

Billy shook his head, scanning the landscape. "I don't know. Down, I guess."

~

MAX IGNORED the conversation between Billy and Irmgard. He wanted to scout the area, mark his territory, hunt some food, kill the Great Gray Wolf, but Irmgard was hugging him, and Billy kept giving him looks and sending off little spikes of adrenal scent.

The Alpha had accepted Billy into their pack, at least for now, but Max would brook no challenge from him. If he sensed any aggression, Max would attack. And this time, the Alpha was not here to stop him. Max would finish what he had started on the night Billy trespassed.

Irmgard stopped talking and went back into the den, leaving Billy and Max alone—*watching each other.*

Max smelled the sweat breaking on the man. The adrenalin spikes evened out into a heightened wave, his heartbeat thudding faster and faster, his pupils dilating.

The man's hand moved to the pistol in its holster at his side.

Max's chance.

The Alpha was not here.

Irmgard was inside.

But the fear smell was so strong and obvious that Max snorted once and trotted off, giving his back to him.

Making a wide circle, he passed the dead men he had killed. The snow had completely buried their bodies, but he could smell them. Max marked where he needed to while searching the immediate area. He did not smell the bad men, the Great Gray Wolf, or the Alpha.

The wind was doing strange things. A new storm was moving in. Max checked the boundaries of the hills. He circled about where eddies rushed and mixed, scenting high and low, following the path of every current he could cross. But nature was too busy, the streams too strong and erratic.

Spying a tall tree with no leaves, he broke a chest-deep path through to it. Jumping vertically, his rear claws tore into the bark of the tree, four feet off the ground. He scrambled up and around, faster than a squirrel until he perched thirty feet high.

Scenting long and deep, he still did not locate his targets, but he did catch the scents of Billy and Irmgard. He saw them, walking away from the den toward the trees.

Down the mountain.

~

BILLY LIFTED her onto his shoulders, the way her father used to do before her mother died. Irmgard hadn't wanted to leave without Petra, but Billy had said, "He'll find us," and held out his hand to her.

She knew it was true. Petra would find her no matter where she went.

Plus, Billy had smiled at her.

He reminded Irmgard of the actor that played Thor in the Marvel movies, Chris Hemsworth. His hair wasn't as long, and it was darker, but he was tall, he had really big muscles, and his eyes crinkled when he smiled. Just like Thor's.

And he was a *good* guy.

He was helping to save her.

Still, she missed Petra. She felt safest when he was near—*although she felt pretty safe with Thor too.*

Neither of them knew where they were going except for down. Billy said they should head for the nearest town, but Irmgard had never been this far into the mountains. She had gotten so turned around that she didn't even know where her house was from here.

Irmgard wondered about the stupid man named Gil and what she would do if he tried to take Petra from her.

She wouldn't let him. No matter what. Petra was hers. And she was his.

If stupid Gil tried to take Petra, she would have Petra bite him. She would have Petra bite stupid Gil so hard that he would run away and never come back.

The image in her mind made her smile.

Billy looked up at her as they walked along.

"What are you smiling about?" he asked.

He smiled, too, as he asked the question. Irmgard felt her cheeks grow warm and rosy. Still smiling, she quickly looked away at the snow-covered trees surrounding them. His smile was so nice, so friendly, so ... *handsome.*

"Nothing," she said.

Irmgard peeked shyly at Billy and thought to herself, *Well, maybe nothing at all.*

I MOVED us as fast as I could, nearly straight down. It was dangerous.

Using branches and coats, we rigged up a travois to haul Piero. He didn't look good. He was pale, drifting in and out of consciousness ... delirious. But we didn't have a choice, and as I said before, he knew the risks before he signed on for the job. I'd expect them to do the same with me if it came down to it.

Still, it itched at my conscience a little.

Marco and Enzo took turns dragging the rig carrying Piero while Anthony Carlino and I broke trail in the front. While Marco pulled, Enzo covered our *six* and vice versa.

It wasn't exactly full coverage, but it was the best we could do under the circumstances.

Down was brutal, but it was easier and faster than up. The sun shone brightly—no snow or torturous wind. Ice crystals glistened, the trees swayed lightly, and the fresh, unpolluted air filtered through the sunbeams like golden energy. My leg wound hurt when I first stood up, but the ache had worn off with the exercise, and I felt really good. I could use some sleep, but that would have to wait.

"You shouldn't have left to find them without me, Li'l Buddy," said Anthony Carlino. He grinned and clapped me on the shoulder. "But I'm glad you did. It's the kind of thing Chuck Norris would do."

"*If* Chuck Norris could do it," I said.

The smile disappeared.

"If? If? Let me tell you something, Gilligan. When Chuck Norris gives you the finger ... he's telling you how many seconds you have to live."

It took me a second to get it, maybe because of the lack of sleep. Or perhaps because I was distracted by keeping a lookout for a murdering army. But once I got it, I couldn't help but crack a smile. And then I laughed—hard. It felt good. Here, in the pristine mountain air, with solid comrades next to me and an almost impossible task before me, it felt *really good*.

I kept walking, pushing forward and breaking through the crust of the snow so the dragging of Piero would go smoother, but now I was also laughing, just like that first time Anthony Carlino had hit me with the Chuck Norris legend bit. That recollection made it worse somehow, and I laughed harder, tears breaking through and running down my cheeks. I wondered what Max would think if he could see me now. He'd probably attack, and that made me laugh and cry even worse. I tried to hold it in; this wasn't the time or the place, and it certainly wasn't the situation, but I couldn't stop ... until I saw the look on Anthony Carlino's face.

He was worried.

And that stopped me.

I knew that this *general of decades* had seen men break before, and I realized that this was what it looked like. I'd seen it myself, but it had never happened to me ... well ... *once*. But never in combat. Never quite like this. But his look said it all.

And he was right. I was close. The loss of Max, the lack of sleep, the injuries and tiredness and hopelessness of the situation.

Close.

Maybe closer than close.

Somehow, I was on my knees in the snow, and everyone had stopped.

I looked up at Anthony Carlino and held out a hand. He took it and helped pull me to my feet.

I wiped my face. I was okay. The moment had passed.

"No more jokes," I said. "Not till this is over. Okay?"

Anthony Carlino looked deep into me—so deep I felt a little naked.

I looked right back at him.

He nodded his head. He had seen what he needed to see.

"Okay," he said.

We started walking again.

"Only, I wasn't joking," he said.

Luckily the moment truly had passed, and all I did was smile and shake my head.

50

Kenny had showered, then brewed up a pot of coffee, its deep, rich aroma filling his space in his mother's basement. He toweled his hair dry as he sat at his computer, a second towel around his waist. While punching up the latest feeds, he scrubbed at his hair, giving them time to load.

He had grown up here in this very basement—his room down the hall and beyond the bathroom. There was an empty bedroom upstairs, but he was more comfortable down here. And, as much as he loved his mother, she could be a chore at times. He liked the distance the basement provided. Ever since his father died two years ago, his mother steadily became more dependent on him, which was okay because he loved her. But she could be—*naggy*.

Kenny called it his mother's house, but technically it was his. He'd paid off the mortgages. His parents had taken a second and a third just to make ends meet when the bank was about to foreclose. Kenny wasn't about to let that happen. He paid off all the debt and put five hundred thousand dollars into their account.

More than a decade earlier, Bitcoin made Kenny a multi-millionaire. He didn't *buy* into it like most. Kenny mined it himself. He started with one dedicated, low-end gaming computer that he retrofitted and geared up for mining. It digitally dug away twenty-four/seven producing the e-commerce and storing it in its hacker-proof digital vault. Six months later, the basement was outfitted with ten high-end dedicated computers.

The timing couldn't have been better. The Russian oligarchs did their thing with the economy, and the value of his coins skyrocketed. Kenny made his first million within a year. He hit over ten million the next. As a brilliantly weird agoraphobic with no girlfriend, he had very little to spend his money on except for computers and their accessories.

Other than his parents, his little sister was the love of his life. From the moment of her birth, she had been his exact opposite. Bubbly, adventurous, outgoing, beautiful, and petite.

Loved by everyone.

But loved by Kenny most of all.

He remembered the first time he saw her; he was four, and he'd gone with his aunt to the hospital to see her. She'd just finished breastfeeding and was still resting in her mother's arms. She looked at him, straining to open her eyes, and when she did, she smiled the biggest smile.

And that had been it.

From that day forward, there was nothing he would not do for her.

At seventeen, Kenny had warned her about her boyfriend. He already knew how to find things out through the internet, but she wouldn't listen. And then what happened—*happened.*

Kenny didn't like to think about that.

Kenny found Gil Mason, and Gil Mason had done what *he* did.

What *only* he could do.

What only he *would* do.

And so, Kenny would now do *anything* for Gil.

No matter how dangerous.

Kenny's computer beeped, signaling he had a phone call, which was very strange because Kenny never had phone calls.

He stopped wiping his hair and looked at the caller identification.

Nick Carlino. How could Nick Carlino have gotten his number? How could he even know who he was?

What to do?

Answer it?

Not answer it?

Kenny was a genius when it came to computers, equations, and algorithms, but not when it came to gangsters, kidnappers, and killers.

Another beep signaled an incoming text message from the same number.

"Answer your phone," it read. *"Now."*

Putting in his earbuds, he touched the *answer* button.

"Hello, Kenny, this is Nick Carlino, but you already know that don't you?"

Kenny didn't say anything. He was too scared.

"You and I have much to discuss. Very much indeed."

SARAH GALLAGHER FINISHED at the lab and drove back up Gil's mountain. Pilgrim met her as she got out of the car. He wasn't quite up to jumping and wrestling like he used to, but he wiggled and waggled and licked at her hands, demanding attention. She rubbed him and scrunched him and kissed him until he was, at least for the moment, appeased. The two of them went inside, and she gave him a cup of dog food and made sure his water was okay. After that, she took out a frozen dinner, nuked it in the microwave, and took it to the kitchen table. She set up her laptop, slipped in the thumb drive she'd brought back from the lab, and called up the information.

The meal was okay, but she was already too deep into the data to pay much attention. Food was just for sustenance, something to fill the hole while she searched and tabulated. She'd found some things she hadn't expected. *Her kind of things.* The kind of things that told her other things. DNA things.

Touch DNA had been around for many years now, but develop-

ments in the sensitivity of these tests had increased exponentially—
to the point of being almost scary. So much so that if you looked
closely enough, you could almost always find *something.*

And found something was.

Sarah had lifted trace amounts of DNA from the severed finger
and packaging. She had grown it and segmented it, something maybe
only three people in the world could have pulled off.

Sarah was one of them.

She started the trial of referencing and cross-referencing the DNA
matches.

Surprisingly, there was no match in any of the criminal databases.

Sarah smiled.

Of course not, that would be too easy. No challenge at all. And
Sarah lived for the challenge.

Moving to the genealogy trees, she branched out, sending algorithms, searching matches, close matches, and far matches, looking
for relatives and relatives of relatives: siblings, cousins, second and
third cousins, then moving out from there. Her fingers danced across
the keyboard, and if Kenny was a *maestro,* she was a *magician*, weaving
her spells and incantations like a lost language.

She tapped every genealogy site, government records outside of
law enforcement, military, medical, religious institutions.

The data flowed back to her, rippling through cords and airwaves,
flooding her computer, and flashing before her eyes.

Sarah took it all in, her intuitive mind absorbing, recording, and
deleting. A hint here, a trail there, she crossmatched and reconfig-
ured and blended, until she sat back, nearly exhausted, the food
forgotten.

Filling the hole no longer mattered.

She'd filled another, far more important hole.

Sarah knew which criminal family was responsible for Anthony
Carlino's kidnapping.

The Scavos.

∾

VINCENZO WAS VERY TIRED, but that sometimes went with the job. He had been up all night, rousing people from their beds and making them work.

It had taken hours, and it had required the calling in of many debts as well as the promise of not a few favors.

Vincenzo always calculated jobs into a dollar figure, and this one-night venture cost the family over three million dollars.

And that was if everything went off smoothly. If not, it could run into the tens of millions.

The one asset alone was worth more than six million dollars.

Still, he had succeeded.

He would be ready.

All that was left was for the American, Gil Mason, to succeed.

51

Still riding tall on Thor's shoulders, Irmgard thought his muscles felt like boulders under his thick coat. She rested her chin on top of his head; her arms wrapped tightly around his neck. His dark hair was curly and soft, his jaw strong. He made her feel safe ... protected.

About an hour after they started down the mountain, Petra magically appeared in front of them. Like the rock she had named him after, he was sitting tall and strong. Irmgard dropped down and ran to him. Flinging her arms around his neck, she kissed his face and squeezed him as tight as her thin arms could.

Billy stayed back, watching. When she saw him, she laughed.

"He won't hurt you, silly."

Billy said, "I told you he'd find us."

"That's because he loves us," she said. "Don't you, Petra?" She looked between the two of them.

They stared at each other.

Finally, Billy turned away and started walking.

"We'd better get going," he said.

She gave Petra a last kiss on the head and then ran to catch up with Billy, slushing along through the path he made in the snow. She took his hand in hers and looked up into his wonderful blue eyes. He looked down at her and smiled.

Glancing back, she saw that Petra hadn't moved. She stopped, forcing Billy to stop with her.

"What is it?" he asked.

Irmgard pointed to Petra.

"Petra's still sitting there."

Billy shrugged.

"He'll catch up like last time. Let's go."

He started to walk again, but Irmgard held fast.

"No. He didn't bring any food, and he's not moving. I think we might be going the wrong way."

Billy shook his head.

"We aren't going *any* way," he said. "Just down."

"I mean, I think he wants us to follow him."

"And what makes you think that?"

It was her turn to shrug.

"I know him," she said.

"Look," said Billy, "I'm telling you, this dog isn't what you think he is. He's not that dog on TV, *Lassie*. He's nothing like that. He's a killer, plain and simple. He's not going to tell you that Timmy fell in the well or how to get down this mountain. He's more likely to *snap* and take a chunk out of you."

"You don't know him at all," she said, dropping his hand and running back to Petra. "Go ahead, Petra, show him. Where do you want us to go?"

Billy stayed where he was, hands on his hips.

Petra turned and angled down in the opposite direction.

Irmgard grinned at Billy and held out her hand.

Shaking his head, Billy walked over to her and took her hand. Together they followed the dog.

"I guess one way down is as good as any other," he said.

Irmgard just smiled and squeezed in closer to him as they walked on.

~

MAX LED them into the trees and to the south, away from the army of bad men up ahead. Earlier, he had picked up the Alpha's scent, and although it had been weak when he first detected it, it had grown stronger as his course veered toward other smells.

Sheep, chickens.

Max had broken off then and went to find Irmgard and Billy. That hadn't taken long, but it had been close. Another five hundred yards, and Irmgard and Billy would have run straight into the enemy.

Max reacquired the Alpha's scent and was taking them to him, skirting No Fingers' army.

The Alpha was not alone.

Max's keen canine brain had imprinted and cataloged Marco's, Enzo's, and Piero's scents when he first met them at the airport. Those scents were now locked in and would never be forgotten.

The path down was fairly easy for Max but grueling for Irmgard. Max could have made the journey in less than an hour, but the humans moved at a lumbering pace.

Billy picked Irmgard up and placed her on his shoulders again. It helped a little, but he was still slow. He stumbled numerous times and had to brace himself with tree limbs. Twice went down to one knee.

But he didn't completely fall, and he never dropped Irmgard.

Max gave him credit for that.

Overhead, the sun beat down through the high mountain air. The sea of blue remained nearly cloudless, but Max could smell the storm coming.

Max had not caught a trace of the Great Gray Wolf, but he was wary. If he missed him, Irmgard might pay the price. Max was not going to allow that to happen.

Stray tendrils of scent, tossed about on the light breeze, told Max that the army was paralleling them and converging.

They would meet at the Alpha.

Max planned on beating them there.

No Fingers pushed his men hard, but no more than he pushed himself. The pain in his hand was agonizing. He'd taken aspirin, four of them, chewing them to get them into his system faster. He didn't think they helped. Still, he refused to take anything stronger, feeling confident the farmhouse would be the final battle. He had to get there first. His mind had to be clear.

He had plans for the men that had rescued Anthony Carlino.

Plans for the dog, too.

The pain he was suffering would be nothing compared to what they would experience.

Fire.

Once he had the dog captured, he'd light him on fire. It seemed only fitting. After all, the dog had taken his first fingers after getting burned. And No Fingers had had to suffer the pain of the flare's cauterization because of the dog's second attack.

So, he would start with fire.

And then he would maybe cut off his paws with bolt cutters.

Irony.

He liked that.

After that, he would get creative.

No Fingers would have his revenge.

The dog would suffer more than any animal had ever suffered.

Grinning at the thought, he pushed his men faster.

We left Anthony Carlino way up behind us in the trees to guard Piero while we continued down. When we were fifty yards from the farmhouse, we stayed hidden behind a five-foot snowdrift about thirty feet long. I'd borrowed Anthony Carlino's rifle and used it to check the grounds. Through its high-powered scope, I saw the sheep moving around behind the house in their pens and a big old rooster strutting on top of the snow, the ice still crusty enough to support his weight, even with the sun's rays making it almost warm out.

I saw three trucks and four men. The trucks were snowed in up to their beds. There were probably more men inside the house. I figured Marco, Enzo, and I could take them. The trick would be to get from here to there without being detected.

"How do you plan to get to the house without being seen?" asked Marco.

"Yeah," I said. "Good question." I scoped it some more. "We've got three rifles. You, me, and Enzo can take one man each from here, then the last one together."

"It will alert the men in the house," said Marco, who was also scoping the grounds. "They will call for help."

"Maybe there's no one in the house," I said.

"Maybe," said Marco.

"And really, who're they going to call?" I asked. "They probably have everyone but these saps out looking for us up higher on the mountain. What really worries me ... is *that*." I head-jabbed toward where the road was supposed to be. "There's no road. I doubt any of those trucks can make it through four feet of snow, let alone the drifts."

Marco nodded.

"We could use the house as a fort against the rest when they show up," said Marco. "We'd have cover at least. And we could act like the guards so that we could ambush the first to arrive."

I gave it some thought.

"Yeah, maybe, if we have to. But they have grenades. And even if they don't have any, they could always burn us out."

"Not if they want the boss alive," said Marco.

"I think we're beyond that. They used grenades against *us*, remember? And they had no way of knowing he wasn't with us then."

"What's the alternative?" asked Marco.

"How long do you think it would take Vincenzo to mobilize troops to help us out, if we can call him from inside?"

It was Marco's turn to calculate.

"Too long," he said.

I took in a deep breath, let it out slowly. It felt good. I scanned the area again.

"We could go around and try to make it on our own ... parallel the road and far enough back to stay out of sight. Try for the town?"

Marco gave a grunting laugh.

"Peiro would slow us down too much," he said. "Besides, they're bound to have men waiting for us at the bottom."

I looked at both of them.

"That's it for me," I said. "Either of you have anything?"

Enzo pointed to a high snowdrift and some trees to the east of us.

"Once we take the house, I can dig in over there, create an ambush. I'll hold back till they pass me and shoot them from behind. It'll buy you a little time and take out at least a couple of them before they figure it out."

"They'd flank you once they did and swarm you pretty quick," I said. "Not much we could do to help."

He gave me a slight grin.

"They might," he said. "Or maybe it won't go their way. I could move—hit and run. Either way, it's the job, right?"

"Okay," I said. "The house it is." I pointed at the guards, counting out a number for each man as I did. "One, two, three, four. Name your target out loud, sight in, and say when you're ready. I'll give the signal."

The three of us used the snowdrift as a berm to rest and aim our rifles.

Marco said, "One, ready."

Enzo was next. "Two, ready."

That left number three for me.

"Three, ready," I said, but before I could give the signal, everything changed.

52

Kenny's belly did a flip-flop under his skin. Another text message appeared on his computer screen.

It was his address.

And his mother's full name and her date of birth.

"You can't hide from *me*," said Nick Carlino in his ear. "Do you understand, or do I need to prove it to you?"

"I—I understand," stammered Kenny. His entire world had suddenly changed. He was no longer an anonymous spy gathering and disseminating information and then disappearing into the ether, leaving no trace except the ripple-like consequences of his actions. In an instant, he had been outed. And the cost could be devastating to him.

"You work for me now," said Nick Carlino.

"I don't work for anyone," said Kenny.

"You know things," said Nick Carlino, "things about me. Things about my—*operations*—that no one who doesn't work for me can be allowed to know and live."

"You can't save your father without my help."

"So, you see," said Nick Carlino, "you are already working for me."

"No—not you. Gil."

"Yes, and Gil Mason works for me. You are like a *subcontractor*. But ultimately, you are all in my employ. And that is a good thing. A very good thing. It's better for all of you. Safer."

"I don't need your money," said Kenny, feeling lost and afraid.

"No. You are a rich man. But there is *something* that you need from me. Something that only I can supply. A favor."

"I think you already owe me one," said Kenny, "for how I've helped you with your father."

"That is between you and Gil Mason. I contracted him to pay off a debt already owed to me. He contracted you, paying off a debt you owed. So that is between you and him." Nick Carlino paused. "However, it is exactly that situation I was referring to in that you already require my help."

"What are you talking about?"

"I'm talking about your sister."

Kenny's mouth went chalk dry.

"My sister."

"I know what Gil Mason did for the both of you," said Nick Carlino. "But he did not complete the job. He saved her ... killed some very bad men, but others were involved. Others that are still—*upset*—over the proceedings. *Others* that Gil Mason knows nothing about. These men have long memories, and they are patient. They never forget, and they never forgive. Left unchecked, they will one day make an example of everyone involved."

"Are you ... are you threatening to tell them who we are?"

"No. No, you misunderstand me, my new friend," said Nick Carlino. I'm offering to *kill* them for you. I'll kill them all. Every last one. And I promise you they will die in agony. *They deserve to die in agony.* And most importantly, they will die knowing *why* they are dying."

Kenny tried to swallow, found that he could not.

"I'm not ... I'm not a murderer."

"I'm not judging," said Nick Carlino. "I applaud your courage. You did what needed to be done, as did your agent, Gil Mason. Men that caused harm to you and your family were—in turn—*harmed*. As was only fair and right. But some of them were out of reach at the time. And they remain out of *your* reach. Gil Mason cannot help you with this, but I can. No one is out of my reach. I will make them pay, and they will never pose a threat to you or your sister again.

"Your family matters to you, just as my family matters to me. When you work for me, you *become* family. You become part of *my* family. *Your* enemies become my enemies."

"And, if I say no?" asked Kenny.

"If you say no, then you are not part of my family, and you pose a threat to me and mine," said Nick Carlino. "But ..."

Kenny's computer lit up with a list of names, locations, images, and streaming video. He saw his sister, his precious baby sister, and even though it was years ago, he saw what they were doing to her.

"... you won't say no."

And Nick was right.

Kenny watched, horrified, and he didn't say no.

SARAH GALLAGHER TOOK a bite of her piece of pizza. It was cold, dry, and delicious, and it brought back fond memories of studying during her college days. Unlike most, Sarah loved studying.

Something nudged her knee, and she saw Pilgrim's big face and overlarge brown eyes staring up at her.

She took another bite and gave him the rest. He swallowed it without chewing. One chomp, and it was gone, crust and all.

Smiling, Sarah kissed him on his big, wet nose. He licked her hand and then her chin.

She sat back in her chair and continued to pet him absently with one hand. The action was supremely calming.

"I'm making you my official fidget-spinner dog," she said.

Pilgrim closed his eyes, loving the contact, and pushed his head further into her palm.

Her phone, set to silent, vibrated on the desk.

At the same time, her laptop's computer screen blanked. Almost instantly, it was filled with three words.

Answer your phone.

Sarah expected Kenny and was surprised when Nick Carlino's finely tempered voice touched her ear.

"You have news for me," he said. It was not a question.

"How did you hack my computer?" she asked.

"Mr. Universe—*Kenny*—is not the only genius with computer skills. Many people with various talents are in my employ. You, being far from the least."

"I don't work for you," she said.

"Semantics," he said evenly. "Let's not mince words. You are certain the Scavo Family is responsible for my father's abduction?"

Sarah wasn't surprised. If he could hack her computer, he could probably intercept her messages to Kenny.

"I could send you the DNA mapping—the intersections—the genetic markers. But I think you already have everything. I also think you have *qualified* people checking my work as we speak. So, really, what's the point of this call?"

"I wanted you to know that I appreciate your work and what you have done for me."

"Not for *you*," she said, "for Gil."

"I had a similar conversation with your Mr. Universe just moments ago. And, although I don't want to appear rude or forceful, it is imperative that you realize—you, Kenny, and Gil Mason—you all work for me now. And you will continue in my employ until I deem it otherwise."

"I never agreed to that," she said, but inside she was beginning to feel queasy. "I'm not like you. I'm not a criminal."

"No?" said Nick Carlino. "You are a law enforcement officer who has used her position, state's equipment, computer resources, privileged access, all to assist a known Mafia Godfather without permission and without informing your superiors. You know full well just how illegal all that is. So, when you say that you are not a criminal like me, it's just a matter of degree. Maybe you don't murder people

..." he paused, changed his tone "... *or maybe you do*. After all, there was the matter of the man who raped you. You had him murdered."

Sarah thought she might throw up.

"I ... I didn't ... I ..."

"You knew he was coming back; that was his, what do you types call it? MO? Method of Operation? And you had Gil Mason set a trap, and he fell into it. And when he did, you had your man murder him. Exactly what you wanted all along."

"No, no, that's not ... it's not ..."

"It is exactly what you did," said Nick Carlino, in a very gentle voice. "And I admire you for it. I only wish I could have killed him for you myself. I would have made it last."

Sarah felt hot tears run down her cheeks.

"Stop, please. Just ... just stop."

All the memories of the rape flooded back to her, the terror, the disgust, his hands, his lips, his breath.

Sensing her distress, Pilgrim growled and began looking about for whoever was bothering her.

"Why, why are you doing this?" she choked out.

"Because," said Nick Carlino, "you need to understand that we are *not* so very different. You have done what needed to be done. A lesser person would not have been able to survive and do what you did. In that, you are like me, like Gil Mason. You are capable of making the difficult decisions that need to be made when they *need* to be made. You are not cruel. Not evil. Not capricious. Neither is Gil Mason, neither am I. We are not monsters. We *stop* the monsters."

Sarah sobbed into the phone, helpless to stop the memories so long suppressed, pounding at her like fists—*like his fists*—as he ripped at her—as he *destroyed* her.

"Stop, please, just stop."

"I will have need of you," said Nick Carlino. "Not now, not today; you have done enough. But sometime ... in the future. It might be a small thing. It might be a big thing. But what it will be doesn't matter. What matters is that you know that whatever it is, it will be to fight monsters. And because you know what it is to have fought a monster, you will be able to live with it. In time, you will even become thankful that I have chosen you to be part of it. From this moment on, you are family. I will protect you. No monster will ever again hurt you."

"Please, please ... *stop!*" she cried, just as she had on *that* night. But on that night, *he* did not stop. *He wouldn't*. It went on and on.

"You are thinking of that night," said Nick Carlino. "For that, I am truly sorry. But now it is time to forget what he did to you and instead think of what you did to *him*. You are alive. You survived. He is dead. He will never hurt you or *anyone* again. Ever. And you did that. You killed the monster. What you did was good. Think on that. Think on those you saved *from* him."

And she did. She remembered his face as life fled, the bullets tearing through him. She remembered, and it gave her strength.

He had no power over her. Not her or anyone else. Not ever again.

The tears stopped.

"Rest," said Nick. "You are safe. And you always will be."

Nick Carlino clicked off, and her computer returned to what it was before.

But Pilgrim still growled, searching out the evil that had invaded the room.

53

No Fingers continued to push his men hard, trusting their superior weapons and numbers to save them from a possible ambush. The rugged terrain and deep snow helped take his mind off the pain. That, and the fantasies he conjured up about what he would do to both the man and especially the dog once he had them.

The sun made his thick coat nearly hot, but the storm would be moving in soon, and they had to be ready for it.

His ankle twisted beneath the crust, slipping off a hidden something. He stopped himself just before any damage could be done. He was taking a big chance here, and he knew it, but it had to be. If Anthony Carlino were allowed to escape, his *own* life would be forfeit. And his passing would not be easy. The Scavo family was famous for their ability to keep people alive while torturing them.

No Fingers was not about to let that happen. He would retrieve the old man, kill the others, and take his time with the dog.

They were getting close; the farm was less than a mile ahead.

No Fingers checked the line, making sure his men were all accounted for. A few fell, but they got up and kept going. Like him, they sensed the end of the chase was near. Everyone was eager for this to be over and to get off the mountain. No one wanted to be caught in the next storm.

And they wouldn't. No Fingers was confident. Victory was near.

The old man would be his.

The old man and the dog.

And even through the pain that was his barren hand, he felt his lips curve into a grin.

FOLLOWING the Alpha's scattered scent, Max continued to lead them. The farm smells were strong now—sheep, chickens, tobacco smoke.

Men.

Max saw the barn and the house. He stopped.

Billy, with Irmgard on his shoulders, came to a halt behind him. Max had brought them up behind the barn, in line with the house.

Irmgard climbed down and hugged Max's neck.

"Good boy," she said. "Isn't he the best, Billy?"

Billy looked down at Max.

Max looked up at Billy.

"Yeah," he said. "I guess he is."

"You say there's a truck in the barn?" asked Billy.

"Yes," said Irmgard.

"There are men at the house," said Billy. "Guards."

"Petra can take them," said Irmgard. "Can't you, Petra?"

Billy looked at Max again.

Max looked back.

"Well," asked Billy, sarcastically, "can you?"

Scenting the air, Max ignored him and walked slowly ahead.

"There's something else in the barn," said Irmgard.

"What's that?" asked Billy.

"Dynamite," she said. "Daddy used it to blow out tree stumps. There's a box inside the barn. Maybe you could use it to blow up the bad men."

Billy's eyebrows raised.

"Maybe I could," he said. "The barn it is."

Max hit a current of freshly blown air that brought familiar scents to him.

Spying the heads of figures behind a snow berm, he went past the barn.

The Alpha.

But there was another scent.

He searched—*and there*—he saw it—crouched low, crawling on its belly from the dark shadows of the trees behind the men, heading straight for the Alpha.

The Great Gray Wolf.

Max broke from a slow walk into a sprint.

"Where's he going?" asked Billy.

Irmgard shook her head. "Maybe to kill the men at the house?"

"He's going the wrong way," said Billy.

But Max was not going the wrong way.

Billy saw the wolf. He saw something else too. He saw Gil Mason and Enzo and Marco.

Billy ran after the dog.

Leaving Irmgard.

Alone.

～

THE WOLF HAD FINALLY TRACKED the men. He'd caught their trail a mile or more away and wound his way down until their odor was strong enough to air scent.

And now he had them.

He moved forward slowly, hidden in the shadows. He would kill the man he had fought earlier first, then take out the short man, and finally the weakest.

His highly sensitive ears suddenly caught the sound of the army coming down the mountain toward them.

But they were too far to make a difference. He could kill these three, then go back into hiding and pick them off, one by one.

Before him, the three men pointed their rifles toward the farm-house, their backs completely open and their attention focused on their targets.

The wolf leapt, his jaws clamping on the back of the big man's neck, slamming his body into the drift, his rifle lost in the snow as the two of them fell to the side.

The thick parka and hood blunted the attack, but not enough; the wolf ended up on top. One whip-snap of his head and the man's spine would splinter, ending his life.

The other two men were turning toward him, but they were too slow to save the man.

Nothing could save him.

The wolf crushed down and snapped back and forth.

SOMETHING SLAMMED into me from behind, pushing me hard into the snow and making me drop my rifle. Teeth tore through my coat and sank into the flesh of my neck, crushing in with horrible, mind-numbing force. My body was flung to the side as though I were weightless, and I landed on my face in the snow, unable to get a breath. I tried to turn my head, to steal a gulp of oxygen, but the monster on my back wasn't having it.

Instantly, I knew it was the wolf, and I had to fight the panic that tried to overwhelm me. Being intimately familiar with canine attack behavior, I knew what was coming next, and if I didn't counter it, I was dead. I tightened my neck muscles, anticipating the whip-snap that was coming, while simultaneously pulling my shoulders up as far as I could. I tried to shove my arms up over my head, to lock my neck even straighter, but they only made it partway before the wolf snapped.

The pain was excruciating, and I almost blacked out. But no bones cracked, and I was able to complete forcing my arms up, turtling my neck and head as deep into my shoulders as possible.

I tried to turn, but the wolf and the snow made it impossible. I had to buy time so that my partners could see what was happening and take action. But the wolf was too savvy an adversary. He attempted the snapping motion once more, and when that failed, he began to twist to the side, his teeth ripping through my flesh as he did, trying for the carotid and jugular.

Recognizing the maneuver, I knew I was helpless to stop him, but again, I was trying to buy time so the others could blast him out of existence. Spreading out my legs and digging my toes into the snow slowed his movement. He jerked my neck, an action that pulled my face from the snow, and I saw my companions staring at us, shock on their faces.

I had run out of time.

As good as they were, they were just too slow for the wolf, and he had maneuvered me just enough, despite my attempts to slow him, to break my neck.

As he jerked my neck out of the protection of my *shoulder shell*, I tried for my buckle knife but realized I was too late.

Max hit the Great Gray Wolf with a burst of speed, flying over the snow and into the creature's massive frame. The angle prevented Max from the kill shot at the neck, but he didn't have time to correct *and* save the Alpha at the same time. Instead, he bit down on the heavy muscle of the right shoulder and allowed his momentum to bowl him straight into the giant beast. Max shoved through, but his legs got tripped up going over the Alpha's body. He landed on his side in the snow, the violence of the action ripping his teeth free and shoving all one hundred and sixty pounds of the Great Gray Wolf's body into Marco and Enzo, who stood there, fumbling for their weapons. Both men were smashed into the snowdrift, and the Great Gray Wolf instantly attacked Enzo, who was closest, tearing into his thigh and then releasing to face Max.

Max sprang to his feet and charged, but a bullet whistled past his ears, kicking up snow beside the Great Gray Wolf.

Max dodged to the right as another bullet sped past him on its way toward his adversary. Again, it missed them both, but not by much.

Max dove into the snow, spinning to meet this new threat, and saw Billy, sixty yards away, firing at them, but the Great Gray Wolf was already back in the safety of the trees. Max stood, preparing to give chase, when the Alpha grabbed him, hugging him to his chest.

"You're alive!"

And then the men from the house started shooting at them.

SCRAPING the snow from my eyes, I saw the wolf attack Enzo. And then I saw Max sprinting toward the wolf, making giant leaps in the snow.

Max?

It wasn't possible.

Max was dead. I saw him die. I saw it.

But here he was, saving my life, *again.*

And then Billy was shooting at the wolf, with Max in the line of fire.

Billy?

My mind sort of freaked.

Billy was dead too.

Was *I* dead?

Were we *all* dead?

I knew better than that. This was *not* Heaven.

It was too cold to be Heaven.

But this wasn't the time to contemplate.

This was war.

I grabbed my rifle from the snow and turned to shoot the wolf.

But the wolf was gone, his tracks disappearing into the trees.

Max was about to go after him.

I came up behind him and hugged him tightly. Tears rushed, hot and fast, and I let them fall. Max was alive ... *alive and in my arms.*

Suddenly I didn't care about the stupid wolf or the army of bad guys or even Anthony Carlino.

All I cared about was Max.

54

The wolf found the safety of the trees, then turned sharply and ran hard for a short span before turning again, making a "U" that aimed him back to his prey.

He heard the shooting and would wait till it was safe to attack.

But attack he would.

He would kill the man.

Kill the dog.

But he'd also detected another scent.

The girl.

He would kill her first.

And the path he was taking would lead him straight to her.

THE SHOOTING SOUNDED CLOSE. No Fingers knew they were almost on them now. The men he'd left at the house must have engaged them. If he could get his soldiers in place fast enough, they'd have Anthony Carlino's men flanked and take them out quickly.

Charging in front of the line, he led his men straight down. His soldiers followed, hurrying to catch up. A couple of them fell, but sensing the urgency, they got up fast. And soon, the line was coming apart, no longer even. If the wolf had been waiting in hiding, he could have taken several men.

But the wolf was not there.

～

IRMGARD STARTED to run toward Billy but stopped at the movement breaking from the trees. It was far away, but she saw him just the same.

The wolf.

He was moving fast and right at her.

Irmgard screamed Billy's name, but the shooting was so loud he couldn't hear her.

Turning, she ran for the barn. The snow made it hard—so hard. Like running away from a monster in a dream when her legs would move so slowly while the monster was free to come for her at full speed.

Irmgard forged ahead, afraid to look behind her, afraid the wolf would be right there.

Sheer terror clutched at her, locking her breath in her chest and making her heart race. Little sounds broke past her lips, and she started to cry. The barn seemed so far and the wolf so fast.

There was no way she could make it.

In her fear, she thought she could feel the wolf's breath hot on her neck.

She was so scared.

But then she thought of Billy and Petra—how they were always so brave—and that helped a little.

She forced her legs to obey. She ran, lifting her knees high and stretching out her gait as far as she could, the dream-feeling fading and the barn coming closer and closer.

Chancing a glance over her shoulder, she saw Billy running toward her. He was so handsome, but he was too far away. He would never get to her before she reached the barn because the barn was just there.

So close now that she was reaching out her arms, thinking that she might make it.

But she was wrong.

Her little legs really weren't moving very fast through the thick snow.

And the monster really was right behind her.

BILLY CRANKED off another round at the wolf. He almost shot Max, but he considered the dog's death as an acceptable loss, so long as he got the wolf.

Max broke right, leaving Billy a clear field of fire, and he blasted away. The wolf turned and moved faster than Billy thought possible, especially in this snow. Billy tried leading him, but the animal was too fast. And then he was gone. Swallowed by the trees and shadows.

Gunshots sounded, and Billy saw men shooting at him from the house.

Running toward the snow berm, he changed targets and shot back.

Enzo, Marco, and Gil followed suit.

Out of his peripheral vision, Billy saw Max running right at him. For a second, he thought of trying for a shot but realized Max would have him before he could hope to sight in. He breathed a sigh of relief as the dog sped past him.

Following Max's movement, he saw Irmgard running for the barn. *And then he saw why.*

Billy suddenly felt a new kind of fear. A fear he had never known.

While he was distracted, the wolf had curved through the trees and come out at an angle closer to Irmgard. And was moving at her with the speed of a missile.

Billy stopped running, aimed at the wolf, fired twice, missing both times, and then he was out of bullets, and he had no more magazines.

Dropping the rifle, he started running again, but this time for Irmgard. He knew it was useless but was unable to stop himself. He cried out her name, a gesture as futile as running to her, but again he couldn't stop himself.

He should never have left her.

Billy watched as Irmgard looked at him over her shoulder, her hands reaching for the barn, still ten yards away.

The wolf leapt, his huge frame flying through the air. His giant jaws stretched wide as they turned sideways and then clamped down on the girl's tiny body, encircling her chest, flinging her up and around and then under, crumpling her into the snow and covering her in his deadly embrace.

~

LAUNCHING FROM TWENTY FEET OUT, Max reached them a moment too late. The wolf caught sight of the motion, so he let Irmgard go and spun away from her. Max's jaws clapped empty air, his lithe body bouncing off the wood of the barn. Max landed on all fours and saw the monster, its head lowered, its movements sleek and fluid as he circled, trying for an angle on the girl.

Irmgard lay on her stomach. She coughed up a gout of blood, her small fingers clutching at the snow as her lungs gulped for breath.

She tried to speak through the blood and the pain, but she could only manage a faint whisper.

No human could have hoped to hear what she said.

But Max heard.

"*Petra,*" she said.

Max had the tactical advantage with the barn guarding his back, but he gave it up, moving between Irmgard and the Great Gray Wolf.

~

MAX BROKE free from my arms and ran towards Billy. I watched him until a chorus of gunfire broke my attention, and I had to dive for the cover of the snow berm. A bullet punched through the snow an inch from my face.

Change *cover* to *concealment*. Concealment hides you; cover protects you. The snowdrift was no protection.

Marco, Enzo, and I opened up, each taking our original targets. All three men went down. The fourth man took three hits, dancing a little jig before falling. But bullets kept flying our way, and it didn't take long to realize they were shooting at us through the windows of the house.

Scoping the left window, I saw the outline of a head and put a round through it.

No more shooting from that window.

Marco and Enzo peppered the house and windows, shattering glass and plunking holes. I used the opportunity to skirt to the far left of the snowdrift and made a run for it. Knowing I'd taken out the shooter guarding that side gave me a chance.

Making it to the side of the house, I moved to the back and saw the unguarded door.

They might be waiting right inside for me.

But then again ... they might not.

I asked God to help me do my best as I moved through the door, my rifle at the ready.

I came up behind the two men who were still alive. They were shooting at Marco and Enzo through the front windows. I killed them both from behind. Not a brave move, but like I said before, this was war, and they started it.

I yelled out to Marco and Enzo that I was inside so they wouldn't accidentally shoot me and did a quick clearance of the house. It didn't take long. I found the man I'd shot through the head in the main bedroom. There was another body in what looked like a little girl's room. Other than that, the house was clear.

Marco and Enzo were just coming up to the door when I finished.

I opened it, smiling, but then I saw the army sweeping down the mountain straight toward us.

The first bullets hit the doorframe, splintering wood.

Marco and Enzo smashed through me to get inside.

Couldn't blame them.

∾

NO FINGERS SAW the men as they made it to the farmhouse porch. He stopped and took aim, ignoring the pain, and fired. The men all fell inside. He thought he might have hit at least one of them.

Before he could order his men to fire, they were already shooting. The house looked like it was being bombarded by a hailstorm. Holes punched through the walls, what was left of the windows, even the roof, sending puffs of dust and chips of wood exploding into the air. The snow around the house was dusted with tiny craters, making it look like the landscape of the moon.

His men made it to the far side of where the road would be when the first of them went down, clutching at his chest. The man closest to him took a neck shot, and the crimson stream that jutted between his grasping fingers gave the others pause so that they stopped their rush and sought cover.

No matter.

No Fingers knew that he had the men trapped.

∾

STILL STASHED up in the trees guarding the unconscious Piero, Anthony Carlino heard the initial spat of gunfire. It sounded bad, but nothing compared to what came a few minutes later.

Making up his mind, he picked up the two pistols and made his way through the snow down to where the action was taking place.

It's what Chuck Norris would have done.

From the direction he was coming, he saw the barn first, and then the little girl running toward it.

He saw the wolf flying from the trees, moving with the speed and gracefulness of an arrow, straight for her.

He also saw the dog and the man.

Anthony Carlino considered trying to shoot—but at what? The wolf? The man?

The wolf was too fast and too far; he would never hit it with a pistol. The man was so far away that he couldn't determine who he was. He could just as soon be shooting a friend as a foe.

He recognized the little girl. She was the girl he'd seen at the farm. And the wolf was going for her.

He started running, as best he could, for her.

The wolf would beat him; there was no doubt about that. Anthony Carlino was not Chuck Norris. But if he could get close enough to shoot the beast, maybe he could save the girl.

But before he could make a dozen steps, the wolf had her. The sheer brutality of the attack made him sick, and he was a man who was used to brutality.

The girl was dead. Anthony Carlino had no doubt of that. But then miraculously, the dog, Gilligan's dog, was there. How he could have gotten there so fast seemed impossible to Anthony Carlino. He had been way farther than the wolf.

And then the animals met, and the fight was on.

Anthony Carlino was still running so that he could get there after the wolf killed Gilligan's dog. He would try and avenge him for Gilligan. Him and the girl.

The dog went for the wolf, and the wolf moved with perfect precision. Gilligan's dog smashed into the barn, knocking the door partially open.

The two animals squared off, like gunfighters in a western.

Anthony Carlino tried to run faster, but he was too old, too slow. There was no hope for the dog. The wolf was easily twice his size, and he was a ... well ... he was a *wolf*. But still, Anthony Carlino ran. He had to be there, at least close enough to try a shot.

Vengeance demanded it.

And Anthony Carlino was all about vengeance.

55

Billy saw Max miss. He saw the wolf circle as Max moved between him and Irmgard's body.

She was dead. He knew that. He'd seen the loose way her body had been tossed around by the monster. Billy had seen that same looseness in too many dead men to not understand what it meant.

The fear he had felt was gone now, replaced with a rage that made him want to fight the wolf with his bare hands.

He ran full out, not even trying to jump up out of the thigh-deep snow. He just pushed straight through, his leg muscles breaking path before him.

The wounds meant nothing. The cold, the snow, the altitude meant even less. He would kill the wolf, even if it cost him his life.

He saw a man running from the other direction, also heading for the wolf. It was his grandfather. But Billy would beat him there; he *had to*. Not in time to save the dog—no one could do that now—but he would save his grandfather.

Screaming, he pushed himself past the limit, running faster.

∼

THE BAD GUYS were destroying the inside of the house. The rain of bullets ripped through the walls and windows, making it hard to take any shots of our own.

But we did it anyway.

In short order, after taking a couple of them out, they sought what cover they could, and the shooting slowed.

We had cover, of sorts, which gave us a tactical advantage.

But they had us on another front.

Ammo.

I was down to three thirty-round magazines—Marco less, Enzo a little more.

Ninety rounds might sound like a lot.

But bullets go fast in a firefight.

The enemy seemed to have an endless supply.

Very bad for us.

And of course, they probably still had the grenades ... and fire ... there was always fire.

If they lit the house, assuming they hadn't already blown us up, we'd have to make a run, either out the front or the back. The wise course would be to take off out the back—now—before they had time to set up an ambush. I was about to tell Marco and Enzo when Marco took a round through the chest and fell back against the wall. He had a stunned look on his face that lasted about a second. Then he got mad and tried to get back to the window, but another bullet hit him in the stomach, and he fell against the wall again.

This time he stayed there.

Ducking low, I made it to him and dragged him around the corner into the kitchen.

I put his rifle into his bloodied hands and pointed it at the back door.

"Marco, you with me?"

Glazed eyes looked up at me, and he nodded.

"Anyone comes through that door, shoot them."

He nodded again and looked lazily toward the door.

I went back to the obliterated living room, still in a crouch, bullets whizzing overhead, glass and wood spraying over me.

Enzo was taking careful aim, firing with scary precision.

Taking a deep breath, in through the nose, out through the mouth, I rose, aiming. I saw a man and fired, but a bright yellow behemoth filled my scope as the shot went on its way, *spanging* off thick steel. I looked over the riflescope and saw a full-sized bulldozer between them and us.

This had Vincenzo Mancini written all over it.

I started a fist bump when the bulldozer turned and faced the house ... facing *us*. The giant blade rose, protecting the driver. Bad guys jumped up on the back of the machine, pointing guns at me and letting loose. The bulldozer's engine gunned, and then it was moving fast. It busted through the fence like it wasn't there and continued straight at us.

A cheer went up from the men firing at us.

Living in Colorado, not far from Granby, I knew just how much destruction a bulldozer could do.

I looked at Enzo.

He looked at me.

We both started shooting.

There was nothing else to do.

NO FINGERS CHEERED with his men as they climbed aboard the bulldozer. He stayed on the ground, not wanting to bang up his mangled hand any more than necessary.

Finally, his reinforcements from the town had arrived. He knew that trucks filled with men would be coming up the now plowed road within minutes.

The men left in the house were almost done now. His soldiers and the bulldozer would serve to distract them, allowing him to sneak in from the back and take them by surprise.

No Fingers ducked behind the protection of the snowdrift and ran full out.

He would take Anthony Carlino alive, capture the dog, kill the wolf, and all would be right in his world.

IRMGARD TRIED to open her eyes, but she was lying face first in the snow. She couldn't breathe right, and there was a strange clicking sound in her chest.

At first there was no pain, but that was starting to change. Her arm was bent at a wrong angle beneath her, and every time her chest made that clicking sound, something twisted inside her body. What had been an ache was turning into something else—something that promised to be very bad.

Forcing her eyes open, she saw the snow. It was pink in some places, but mostly it was red.

That didn't seem right.

Sounds were coming back—muffled—far away—but slowly becoming clearer.

Sticky wetness soaked her clothes. She managed to pull her right hand, the one not trapped under her, up to where she could see it.

It was as red as the snow.

That didn't seem right either.

Irmgard tried to push herself up to get her trapped arm free, but it was really hurting now. The best she could do was to turn her neck a little.

That hurt too.

She coughed, and blood splashed out of her mouth and nose. She hadn't realized what the red was before, but now she understood. Her head had cleared that much, at least.

The growl was familiar—and it was close.

Irmgard suddenly remembered the wolf.

And it was still here.

A small whimper made it past her lips.

And that made her mad.

Petra wouldn't be afraid. Neither would Billy.

With the strength she didn't have but the will that she did, she pushed against the snow again, raising up out of the hole her body had made in the snow.

She looked up and saw the wolf moving in a slow circle—stalking her. It had never looked more monstrous or evil or huge. Fear tried to have its way with her again.

But then something moved, and she saw Petra standing between her and the wolf.

And she wasn't scared anymore.

Irmgard tried to reach out to him, to speak his name again, but something racked in her chest, and she coughed up a gout of blood. Everything went dim and the world spun dully... the dim went to dark and darker. The snow felt cold on her cheek, even with the red —*the blood*—and she knew she was no longer pushing herself up. She tried to take a breath, but it wouldn't come.

And then even the dark went blank.

THE WOLF easily eluded the dog's clumsy attack. Twice before, the wolf had defeated this dog. Once when it was just a puppy and no contest at all. The second time they met, he would have killed it, but the bear had intervened.

There would not be a fourth meeting.

This time he would put an end to it.

Circling slowly, the wolf looked for the dog's weak spot.

Every animal had one.

Every animal but the wolf.

It didn't take long.

The girl.

The wolf made a slight feint toward her. Just a movement of the body and a shifting of his head, but it was enough. The dog gave up the advantage of the barn covering its back to move in between them, protecting her.

The wolf smiled inwardly.

He shot toward the girl and saw the dog swoop down to block the attack—*just as he knew it would.* He snapped to the side—*in and out*—tasting blood.

The dog's shoulder streamed.

Time for the kill.

56

V incenzo Mancini sat back as the machine cut through the snow with ease.

He was surprised by the speed.

By the sheer power.

The giant tracks crushed everything in their path as the enormous mountain of metal charged toward the farmhouse.

Vincenzo did not often accompany men into action.

His was the brain, not the brawn.

But he decided he needed to this time. The expenditure, for one thing; the risk, another. Not to mention the importance of the goal—Anthony Carlino himself.

And so, he decided he would go. He considered himself safe, all things considered.

Nickolas Carlino's suggestion to obtain a bulldozer had been wise, but Vincenzo couldn't get one. So, he had instead taken the American, Gil Mason's, advice.

No bulldozer, but this, he thought, was better.

∽

ENZO and I both dove for the kitchen as the bulldozer punched through the porch and front room. Glass and wood and shingles rained down on us. A thick block of splintered wood smashed down on Enzo's shoulder, and he fell hard.

The bulldozer got stuck with just its blade inside the house. I started for it, thinking that I might take out the driver if I could climb over. But the cadre of men that had hopped on opened up with their rifles. I had to lay flat, near the wall, as bullets vaporized plaster and two-by-fours a few inches above me.

The bulldozer backed out, realigning its attack. I saw Marco slumped low a few feet away, still trying to guard the backdoor with his glazed eyes and gun. I didn't think he had any idea what was happening.

Maybe that was for the best.

We'd just have to try and make a run out the back. I knew it was suicide. They were bound to have an ambush set up, waiting to shoot us to pieces.

But what choice did we have? What could stop a bulldozer?

The giant metal monster backed further down the porch, shifting its massive blade. The driver maneuvered the gears, making a grinding sound, and revved the engine.

I chanced a glance. The entire front of the house was gone, and the dozer was aimed right at us; billowing clouds of black smoke poured from its exhaust like some ancient dragon readying for the kill.

I'd never make it out the back. There was just no way to grab Enzo and Marco and drag them out in time.

Leaving them was not an option.

Aiming, I took a shot that ricocheted harmlessly off the top of the blade.

I fired twice more, the slide locking back, empty. Shoving my 4506 into my front waistband, I grabbed up a pistol lying by one of the dead soldiers.

I spit five rounds at the cab.

Useless.

But bullets were all I had.

I tried once more as the metal mountain charged forward.

The explosion was as incredible as it was shocking.

The back of the bulldozer disintegrated, sending jagged pieces of steel shrapnel whistling through the air and the house.

The shockwave rippled through my body, making me nauseous, as it shoved me roughly into and under scattered debris.

Blood leaked from my nose and ears and countless abrasions as I dug myself out.

How did I do that? What did I hit? A grenade? The gas tank?

And then I saw it coming across the field from behind the farm-house, not even bothering with the plowed road.

It wasn't me.

It was *that*.

What could stop a bulldozer?

I had my answer.

A tank.

It fired again, vaporizing what was left of the yellow juggernaut and blasting me into unconsciousness.

BILLY WAS ALMOST USED UP, the exertion and the wounds all catching up with him. But he pushed harder on seeing his grandfather stumble and right himself.

Billy saw the wolf strike for Irmgard, fast as a cobra, the fastest attack Billy had ever seen. But Max moved faster, blocking the attack and taking the hit himself, saving the girl.

Billy couldn't possibly make it in time to save Max, but now he doubted he would even beat his grandfather. He gauged the distance.

Stopping, he dropped to one knee and sighted in on the wolf. It was chancy. He was breathing hard, had only his knee for a brace, and his stance on the shifting, settling snow was less than ideal. He might hit the dog or Irmgard. He thought she was already dead anyway, but if she wasn't and he shot her, he would never forgive himself. If only they weren't lined up like that. Max was in the way, shielding the wolf.

And then it hit him.

Billy *could* take the shot.

Lining up the crosshairs on the back of Max's skull, he pulled back the slack on the trigger. The dog had no chance against the wolf anyway. It would be a faster death. Merciful. The bullet would travel straight through his brain and into the head of the wolf, killing them both.

Billy didn't like it.

Max had saved him.

Of course, he'd almost killed him too.

But if Irmgard or his grandfather were to have any chance, this was it.

Steadying himself, he took in a deep breath, let a portion out, held it.

"Sorry, dog," he said in a whisper.

ANTHONY CARLINO SAW the man take a knee and aim at the wolf. Something about the man's posture, the way he carried himself, spoke to him.

It was Billy.

Anthony Carlino was about to yell out to him when he saw a giant yellow bulldozer come over the hill and turn toward the farmhouse. A second bulldozer followed right behind, passing the house and barreling along the road, its massive V-plow blade, carving snow from the road and shooting it to both sides, leaving a clear channel and making the road passable.

Anthony Carlino saw the dozer and he saw Billy—kneeling right in its path.

He screamed at him, but with the bulldozer's engine roaring, guns blasting, and the distance, there was no way Billy could hear him.

Anthony Carlino raised both pistols and started shooting at the driver. From this angle, he could see him sitting there, high in the cab. Chuck Norris could have hit him. But Anthony Carlino's shots didn't even strike the cab or blade.

The slide locked back on one of the guns.

Empty.

Tossing it aside, he took the other in both hands, changed his target to Billy, or rather the snow in front of him.

He had to get his attention.

The giant blade was coming straight at him.

He fired, expecting the snow to geyser in front of him.

But, just as with the bulldozer, the bullet didn't even come close. And now the metal monster was on top of Billy.

MAX HAD to take the hit to save the girl. The Great Gray Wolf swooped in, aiming for her body. Max knew she wasn't the real target —he was. But if he didn't absorb the blow, allowing the Great Gray Wolf his victory, the old veteran would change his attack and go ahead and kill the girl instead.

Max had no choice.

He would not allow the Great Gray Wolf to kill Irmgard.

Max let the feint work, shifting his body at the last second to lessen the damage. Instead of teeth sinking into his throat, they grazed his shoulder, just below where the man had stabbed him earlier, tearing deep groves and slipping away.

Max could have spun with the blow and taken a superficial bite at the Great Gray Wolf's rear flank. But that, also, would have left Irmgard vulnerable.

He stood his ground and allowed the Great Gray Wolf to circle back.

Max was in a dangerous tactical position. To protect Irmgard, he had decided against drawing blood, and he'd given up the protection of the barn.

Twice before, when Max was little more than a pup, they had met in battle.

Both times the Great Gray Wolf had bested him.

But Max was no longer a pup.

This would be their final meeting.

Max felt no fear. He'd known the outcome of this battle the first time he scented the Great Gray Wolf after arriving in these mountains.

The fact that he had the added burden of protecting Irmgard meant nothing.

The drawing of first blood by The Great Gray Wolf meant nothing.

Nothing meant anything now.

The Great Gray Wolf had slaughtered his pack, *his mother, father, and siblings.*

Max was going to kill the Great Gray Wolf.

Here.

Now.

And nothing on earth would stop him.

Max sensed the Great Gray Wolf readying another attack.

It would be his last.

Max was unaware of the scope sighted in on the back of his head —or of Billy's finger as it pulled back on the trigger.

57

The wolf tasted Max's blood. He tasted victory. He had discovered the dog's weakness—*the girl.* And on this attack, he would use the knowledge to full advantage, feinting in just as he had on the first run. But this time, when the dog went to block his strike, the wolf would be in perfect line to change his target, for the throat.

The dog had evaded his first attempt, but just barely, and now the wolf knew precisely how he would react and would himself counter.

Max would not survive this attack.

And then, as he lay bleeding, the wolf would slowly finish the girl. Right before his dying eyes.

The wolf waited, shifted to one side, saw the dog shift with him, just as he knew it would.

Aiming at the girl—he struck.

❧

BILLY PULLED the trigger just as the wall of snow hit him, sending the bullet straight at the back of Max's head.

Billy was so focused on the shot he never saw or heard the bulldozer coming. The snow picked him up and threw him aside, swirling him inside an avalanche of snow and ice.

He couldn't breathe, couldn't see. The world was spinning white and frozen.

Slamming down on his shoulder and neck, he rolled through snow and came to a stop on his side, half-buried. Shaking his head, he pushed himself up as quickly as he could, ice and snow falling from his hood and face. Then he saw the bulldozer make a turn, going off-road and then turning again.

Aiming straight at him.

58

Max saw the Great Gray Wolf move, once again going for Irmgard. And just as before, Max had no choice but to move to protect.

Ducking his injured shoulder, he shifted, so imperceptibly and perfectly that the Great Gray Wolf couldn't react.

The Great Gray Wolf was fast.

Incredibly fast.

But Max was faster.

So much faster.

Billy's bullet scorched past Max's left ear, burning him and narrowly missing the Great Gray Wolf.

Max ignored it.

The Great Gray Wolf twisted his neck, angling his massive jaws to the side and up, going for Max's throat instead of Irmgard.

But Max was already in motion, dropping to the ground, landing on his side, and sliding into and through the snow, under the Great Gray Wolf's open jaws. He struck up, dodging the bite, and clamped his teeth into the throat of the Great Gray Wolf.

The Great Gray Wolf instantly twisted in the opposite direction to escape. Max went limp, allowing the beast's own weight, strength, and momentum, to flip him up and over.

Max didn't let go or loosen his grip.

He held on, crushing in as his body flew.

The Great Gray Wolf's neck, rigid with knotted muscles as hard and strong as oak, twisted and wrenched and then *snapped*.

Max released, mid-flip, and landed ten feet away.

On his feet.

Casually, Max looked back.

The *wolf* stood where he was, his neck cranked at an impossible angle, eyes fixed in an eternal stare.

Its lifeless body fell silently to the snow.

Max walked over to the once apex predator of the Black Forest.

Lifting his leg, he marked his territory.

59

Billy's rifle was gone, lost somewhere beneath the snow. He reached back for his pistol and found that it was also gone.

Frustration turned to rage.

He had to get to Irmgard.

Without thought or plan, he charged the bulldozer, screaming.

The metal mountain charged right back at him, snow parting like water before its massive 'V' shaped blade.

Billy would not be able to jump to the side, not in this deep snow, but he kept on.

And then, a scant twenty feet between them, the dozer slowed and stopped. The blade dropped lower so that Billy could see into the open cab.

His grandfather, Anthony Carlino, sat in the driver's seat, smiling.

"I made up the distance while he was turning," said his grandfather. "Finally got close enough to shoot him. The hard part was climbing up into this thing. I'm getting too old for this stuff."

Billy climbed up beside him.

"No, grandfather," said Billy, "I don't think I believe that."

Anthony Carlino put the rig into gear and started moving.

"I was boosting these things for joy rides before your father was born," he said. "Let's check on the girl."

They drove across the road to the barn.

Billy saw Max nuzzling Irmgard's body. Jumping down, he went to her.

Max let him, his nose suddenly scenting high. Turning, he sprinted away.

Billy felt for a pulse and found one—*but it was so weak*. He picked her up in his arms, carried her into the barn, and laid her on the dry, straw-strewn floor.

He saw the old truck Irmgard had said was there, but it would no longer be needed now that they had the bulldozer.

His grandfather entered the barn and stood next to him.

"She still alive?" he asked.

"Yeah," said Billy. "But not by much. She can barely breathe."

Billy caught movement outside the door and dove into his grandfather as bullets punched through the wooden walls.

Staying low, Billy peered out and saw a group of four men coming toward them from behind the bulldozer.

Billy didn't have a gun.

His grandfather was checking his magazine.

"Two bullets left," he said, smoothly sliding the magazine back in place. "One in the mag and one in the pipe. They've got us trapped."

Billy looked around, again seeing the truck.

Irmgard had said something else was in the barn.

Staying low, he edged his way to the workbench and saw ancient wooden boxes beneath. He quickly rummaged inside and came out with two sticks of dynamite.

Shoving one stick in his waistband, he held the other out to his grandfather.

"Nobody traps the Carlino's grandfather. Got a light?"

"It just so happens, I do," said Anthony Carlino. He thumbed the golden lighter his Bella had given him so many years ago and lit the fuse.

Billy underhand-tossed the stick right in the middle of the advancing group, just as they reformed in front of the bulldozer.

The explosion was impressive.

Snow, dirt, rocks, and body parts erupted into the air before raining back in a grisly downpour.

Two men were gone—just gone.

The other two were lying on their backs, rolling about in shock and pain.

Anthony Carlino walked up to the closest and calmly shot him in the face. He walked to the second man and pointed it at his chest.

"Don't shoot! Please don't shoot ...," he cried in a heavy Russian accent, holding his arms out in front of his blackened face and burnt eyebrows. "I'm a doctor. A medic. I saw the girl. I can help. Please don't kill me ... please."

Anthony Carlino kept the gun pointed at him while looking back at Billy.

"What do you think?"

"Yes," said Billy, "yes, bring him."

Billy ran out and helped drag the man inside the barn.

"You won't kill me?" asked Alexi Stepanovich, still holding his hands out as they dragged him.

They dropped him next to Irmgard.

"Shut up," said Anthony Carlino. "Save her, and you live. But she dies—so do you."

The Russian scrabbled over to her and sat up. He checked her pulse, stripped her coat, and ripped open her shirt, then examined the puncture wounds and listened to her chest.

"She has broken ribs, a punctured lung. Her chest is filling with blood, constricting her heart and lungs. I ... I could save her if I had tools. But ...," he looked at Anthony Carlino helplessly.

Anthony Carlino pointed the gun at his face.

"It was worth a shot," he said.

"Wait," said Billy. He reached inside his coat, pulling out the medical kit. "Will this work?"

Nodding vigorously at Anthony Carlino and the gun pointed at his face, the Russian said, "I'll make it work."

He unzipped the medical bag, taking out instruments.

Billy nodded, sending up a prayer, something he couldn't remember ever doing before, outside of church.

Billy walked into the sunlight looking for threats and saw the bulldozer revving to plow through the farmhouse. Suddenly it disintegrated in an earth-shaking explosion that made the dynamite seem like a firecracker.

Before he could gather himself, the barrel of a tank came around the corner of the house, followed by the rest of the thundering machine.

Billy looked at his grandfather inside the doorway. Anthony Carlino gave him a head bob, telling him to go.

Climbing into the cab of the bulldozer, he started it moving toward the house, wondering how in the world the bad guys could have gotten hold of a tank.

60

Vincenzo gave his two-man crew a thumbs-up as the bulldozer erupted in front of them. He clapped the driver on the shoulder and pointed up the road where the second dozer sat idly by a barn.

"That one next," he said. "And run over anyone who gets in the way."

The American-made Abrams M1A1 spun about on its tracks, the deep snow giving way and posing no obstacle to the 67-plus tons of steel, firepower, and technology that made it the greatest tank in the world.

Rumbling across the yard, it crushed a section of fence, then turned onto the plowed road and started ramping up speed. It could travel at over forty miles an hour once it got going.

And it took no time at all *to get going.*

Both crew members were part of the Carlino family. Not by blood, but by loyalty. The driver was American-born and bred; the gunner was German, recruited years before by one of the family's scouts. The *family* had inserted them into the military to learn skills and bring them back to teach to other Carlino hitters. Vincenzo contacted both *tankers* and had them flown in from their respective bases in

Germany. Once landed, they helped him *"borrow"* the modern-day version of a T-Rex from yet a third U.S. military base. Although not part of the Carlino family, the Full Bird Colonel in charge of that command owed them a gambling debt. A *large* gambling debt. The tank was loaded on a C130 and flown just outside the town to a private airstrip with the three already on board, preparing the modern weapon of destruction.

They were running a man short. The American driver sat in a reclining seat that resembled a dentist chair and maneuvered the motorcycle-like steering device. The German took on the dual roles of gunner and loader. Much slower than in actual combat but sufficient for the mission.

Vincenzo acted as the commander, surveying the battlefield and giving orders.

It had been a logistical nightmare that only Vincenzo could have pulled off. But pull it off, he had.

All that was left was to find Don Carlino and bring him home safely.

If he was still alive.

Thinking back on his meeting with Gil Mason, Marco, and Billy Carlino, he believed the Don might just have made it. The men were exceptional. Vincenzo was never wrong about people.

As the tank picked up speed, bullets struck its nearly impenetrable skin, ricocheting harmlessly away. He considered letting his gunner go *guns free* with the smaller weapons, the .50 cals and such, to take out the insects. But he didn't know where the Don might be, so the fewer stray munitions flying about, the better.

Up ahead, the second bulldozer spun around and started driving toward them.

Vincenzo smiled.

"Take it out," he said to his crew.

~

HOLDING the last stick of dynamite in his hand, Billy saw the tank's turret swivel about five degrees and level its giant bore at him. As he looked down the monster barrel of the tank, his plan of blowing it up with the TNT and then ramming it full-on seemed as stupid as it was.

Billy looked from the barrel to the stick in his hand with its fuse, looked back at the tank, and then jumped off the bulldozer, hitting the snow, rolling, and getting to his feet.

Billy ran as fast as he could.

The bulldozer continued straight ahead toward the target for another two seconds before an M829A2 armor-piercing round hit the left side of the 'V' blade.

A giant clap of thunder swept down from heaven, slapping Billy from behind, preventing him from seeing what happened next. His legs and feet lifted out of the snow, and he was thrown thirty feet. He opened his eyes a few seconds later in the hole he'd made on impact, his clothing smoldering. Sick to his stomach, he forced himself to a kneeling position.

Except for a portion of the treads, the bulldozer was gone. The tank had turned and was moving back toward the farmhouse.

Billy saw two men converging from the outer yard and the pens toward the backdoor.

Gil was inside that house.

Billy stood.

He looked about for the stick of dynamite, but it was lost.

His grandfather was the priority. His grandfather and Irmgard. He looked at the barn, then back at the house, just as he had with the tank and the lost dynamite.

Shaking his head, he abandoned the barn and ran toward the back of the farmhouse and the men.

NO FINGERS ROUNDED the corner of the house and saw one of his soldiers stretched flat against the wall. As he ran for the back door, he spotted another of his men, ducking low as he made it to him. The last man would be there in a few seconds. No Fingers motioned for him to hurry, then hugged the wall of the house as he saw half of the running man's face turn into a red, raw mess as a big bore bullet impacted. The man fell to his side, his legs still pedaling as if he were riding an invisible bicycle.

No Fingers clenched his jaw, his nostrils flaring. There should be at least four or five more men here. He'd planned it all out before they started down the mountain. The back was supposed to be covered before the charge on the front to prevent escape.

Where were they?

MAX SMELLED THE ALPHA. The scent floated to him on the breeze as he stood over Irmgard after killing the wolf. It carried with it the odors of dirt, gunpowder, and motor oil.

And something else.

Blood, sweat, adrenaline, lactic acid.

The Alpha was hurt, maybe dying.

Max sprinted away, leaving Irmgard and Billy. He followed the wispy tendrils as they danced and were tossed about by all the activity of the men and machines fighting.

The snow slowed him—but not by much.

The first of the men Max encountered was lying prone on his stomach beside a tree, his rifle locked in on the back of the house.

Max took him at a full run, leaping up out of the snow and diving straight into him. The man had no time to scream or fight.

The second man was kneeling behind a fence post. Max came at him from the rear, the melting snow crust and gunfire masking his approach. The coat blunted his attack, the hoodie lending protection to the man's throat and almost saving him—*almost.*

But Max was still angry.

He bit harder, wrenching back and forth with savage fury, much as the wolf had done to Gil.

But this man wasn't Gil.

And Max was not the wolf.

The snow beneath them turned red.

The Alpha was in the house. Max could smell him. But he couldn't tell if he was still alive.

There were other men already at the house. Max would kill them, but first, he had to deal with the men in hiding.

No Fingers pointed at the soldier closest to him and motioned for him to boot the door. The man nodded and kicked it hard, stopping as the door crashed aside. He was standing in the fatal funnel of the doorway, an action that had cost many a law enforcement officer and military man their lives. Upon seeing Marco staring at him with vacant eyes, holding a fully automatic rifle, his mind blanked, stopping him cold. Both No Fingers and the man across from him saw the situation and flattened back against the wall as Marco emptied a full magazine of thirty rounds into the man frozen in the doorway. Most of the bullets went straight through him, whizzing bloody spray out the back door.

When the shooting stopped, No Fingers went into action, jumping over the dead man's corpse and aiming at Marco, who was clumsily trying to insert a new magazine into his rifle.

No Fingers screamed and pulled the trigger on full auto.

The gun jammed.

Tossing the useless weapon aside, he kicked Marco in the face, knocking him over and out.

No Fingers picked up his rifle from where he had thrown it and saw Enzo lying not far from Marco.

The last soldier came in from the backdoor.

No Fingers motioned to the two unconscious men.

"Kill them," he said, working the action on the bolt of his rifle to clear the jam.

The man raised his gun, pointing it at Marco's head.

⁓

I DON'T KNOW how long I was out, but it couldn't have been long. Nobody had come in and finished me off.

I was covered in dirt, plaster, and rubble. My face and eyes felt gritty and sore.

Dragging myself out of the debris, I rested for a second, trying to get my bearings. My head swam, and I could only hear muffled, warbling sounds. Nausea racked my system, and I couldn't stop blinking.

I've experienced concussive explosions before, but this one was a doozy.

I was surprised I was alive.

Gunfire exploded from the kitchen,

Marco and Enzo were both in there

I made it to my feet and staggered over. I didn't have a gun—I'd lost it somewhere in the rubble. But there was no time to look.

Rounding the corner, I saw a man with a rifle pointed at Marco. I tried to move on him, but my balance was gone and my legs jello.

Before I could take a step, a guy with a bandaged hand slammed the butt of a rifle into my jaw. My head snapped to the side and then right back at him. I punched him in the throat, not nearly as hard as intended, and then tried to sweep his legs. But, like I said, my balance was gone. So instead, I fell into him, grabbing his bandaged hand and pulling him in tight.

The man with the gun changed his point of aim from Marco to me. I jerked the guy with the bandage in front and hid my head behind his, not giving the man a clear shot.

Of course, he could just shoot through the guy to get to me.

I maybe should have thought of that—not that I had much choice.

And then there was Billy.

⁓

COMING in the back door at a full run, Billy hit the man who had been pointing the gun at Marco in the side so hard it should have put him out all on its own. But the guy was big and strong. The impact lifted him up and smashed him into the table, scattering cups, plates, a cutting board, a pistol, and then they hit the floor.

Before the man could think or react, Billy maneuvered so that he knelt on the man's stomach, his knees straddling the man's belly. As smooth as silk, Billy slid his hands into the soldier's hoodie on opposite sides of his neck, grabbing fabric in his fists. Billy leaned down close, expanding his chest, closing the 'X' that his forearms and wrists made, using the man's own clothing to cut off the blood supply to his brain and rendering him unconscious in just a few seconds.

Billy dropped the man's weight as an enormous crash sounded from the front room. A loudspeaker boomed, demanding Anthony Carlino be released and brought to them immediately, or they would destroy the house.

It was the tank.

Billy recognized Vincenzo's voice.

He turned, grinning, just in time to see No Fingers pull a knife from his front waistband and thrust it backwards into Gil Mason's stomach.

I SAW BILLY TAKE down the bad guy like a pro. As nice a choke-out as ever I've seen. But instead of watching the Jiu-jitsu demonstration, I *should* have been paying attention to the guy with the bandaged hand in my arms.

Something hit me in the stomach.

Something sharp.

Something that made me lose my grip.

Something that made me bleed.

The guy pivoted and shoved me up and into the wall, and then I felt the business end of the knife sliding across my throat.

BILLY REACHED for the first thing he could find. It was the cutting board that had fallen with them from the table when they smashed into it.

He threw it as hard and fast as he could.

Hours of playing Frisbee Golf as a kid finally paid off; his aim was right on target.

The thick cutting board crushed into the back of No Fingers' head, knocking him to the side and to his knees, the knife falling free.

NO FINGERS DIDN'T KNOW how he'd gotten to where he was—or even *where* he was. He reached to the back of his head with his hand and felt hot blood and sharp pieces of something.

Bringing his hand around to see what he was feeling, he stared at the blood and splintered pieces of skull decorating his hand.

But it wasn't the blood or bone that caught his attention.

It was his fingers.

His fingers.

They were back.

Healed.

He had his fingers back.

He held his hand up to show Gil and Billy, not realizing this was his good hand.

He was so happy.

So very happy.

He never realized how *much* he'd missed his fingers.

But that didn't matter now because he had them back.

He was *whole*.

He smiled at the men, tears leaking down his face. He wanted to thank them.

He tried. But the words didn't make it past his lips. It wasn't that he couldn't *think* the words ... they were there ... in his thoughts, but somehow, they seemed to get lost between there and his lips. He tried again, tears running down from his eyes, but only a mishmash of jumbled sounds bubbled past his lips.

Seeing his wiggling fingers and being so happy again, he forgot about the men.

MAX WALKED in through the back door, blood glistening on his shoulder and staining the fur on his chest and jowls. He saw No Fingers kneeling on the floor, red streaming from his head while holding a hand in front of his face and trying to speak. A lunatic's smile twitched the corners of his bloody lips.

No Fingers turned to Max and showed him his healed hand, grinning wildly.

The man wasn't much of a threat.

He was already dead ... *mostly.*

Before No Fingers or Gil or even Billy could react, Max darted in and ripped out his throat.

Now the man was no threat at all.

Now the man was *completely* dead.

Max turned and walked to the Alpha, smelling blood.

The Alpha staggered back against the wall.

"Not very sporting," Gil said to Max before slumping to the floor.

61

I saw Max tear out the guy's Adam's Apple.

Pretty gross. But then again, he did stab me.

Max doesn't like guys stabbing me.

Pack mentality stuff.

I mumbled something to Max, but I passed out before the words made it to my ears.

Big tough Marine.

As they loaded me into the tank, I woke up for a second and saw Billy, Anthony Carlino, and the first snowflakes of the new storm beginning to fall.

"Hang in there, Li'l Buddy," he said, clapping me gently on the shoulder.

"I'm fine, Skipper," I said as I passed out again.

I woke up sometime later to a Russian guy stitching my side wound —*make that wounds*—and using his teeth to cut the thread.

He grinned at me and said, "You'll live."

Anthony Carlino cramped in close next to him and said, "He'd better." He had a gun on the guy.

I went out again.

I dreamed of my wife and daughter.

Not bad dreams. Good dreams.

Feeding my daughter.

Lying next to my wife in bed.

Good times.

I dreamed of Max and Pilgrim.

Wrestling with Pilgrim.

Max letting me pet him after burying Jerome and Ziggy on my mountain.

All good.

I opened my eyes sometime during the flight. Anthony Carlino and Billy were huddled around a little girl on a gurney with an IV in her arm. The Russian guy was working on her. They didn't notice I was awake.

Max sat on my right, watching me.

My lips twitched, and I went to pet him, but everything went black.

A day and a half later, I woke up in a hospital in Italy. The knife and bullet wounds, as well as the sundry array of abrasions, were already healing nicely, but the wolf bites had gotten infected. They'd had to clean them out and hit me up with heavy doses of antibiotics.

The knife wound had been blunted by my Smith & Wesson 4506, which I'd stuck in my waistband earlier. It had caused the blade to slide off, basically leaving me with a deep scratch. The concussion was the worst. I had gone in and out of consciousness, time passing at very weird intervals.

Not surprising since I'd gotten blasted twice by a tank.

Max wouldn't leave my side, and none of the medical staff wanted to challenge him.

Smart.

Billy and Anthony Carlino filled me in on everything I'd missed. They told me about Billy surviving after the car went over the mountain, Max dragging him to the den, and the little girl, Irmgard (she was in a coma and still touch and go). They told me about Max killing the wolf and the men waiting to ambush us at the back of the farmhouse (they'd found their bodies). About Vincenzo getting the tank and routing what was left of the bad-guy army, bulldozers and all.

Marco survived—*one tough dude*—as did Enzo and Piero. They were all recovering in a German hospital because they wouldn't have survived the trip to Italy just yet.

Most of what they said stayed with me, but some of it drifted off into concussion land, and they had to tell me those parts again every time I woke up.

They were very patient for Mafia killers.

They kept me company for three days until the doctor said I was *out of danger*, and then they left for the States.

I remained in the Italian hospital, convalescing, another two weeks.

When I got home to my mountain, Sarah told me everything that had transpired on her end, including what happened with Kenny. She also told me how Nick Carlino had conscripted them into his service.

I arranged an in-person meeting with Nick, Anthony Carlino, and Billy.

Anthony Carlino and Billy showed up first.

Billy had a little girl with him.

Irmgard.

She was giving me hard.

Not just her eyes—her whole face.

I asked Billy if I could talk with her for a second. He agreed and whispered something into her ear. She looked up at him, then at me, still hard. But she shrugged her shoulders and followed me toward the garage.

I stopped out of earshot.

"Where's my dog?" she asked. "My Petra?

"He's around here somewhere," I said. "We need to come to an understanding, you and I."

"He's mine," she said. "He loves me."

I nodded slowly.

"I believe you," I said. "But I need him. My other dog needs him. And other little boys and girls like you need him."

"Petra is mine."

I saw tears starting to well in her eyes.

"I know," I said. "But he's not just yours. You see, Max isn't like other dogs. Max is ... well ... Max is a kind of ... superhero dog. And because of that, he sort of belongs to everyone who needs him. So, when you need him, he's yours. When I need him, he's mine."

She was quiet for a second, thinking, but at least the tears were held at bay.

"So, Petra is like ... Bolt? The dog in the animation movie?"

Yes, I thought. Max is kind of like that. A big, much more dangerous, entirely without remorse, killing machine version of Bolt.

But what I said to this little girl was, "Yes, that's it. He's just like Bolt."

"So why do you get to keep him with you? Why can't Petra stay with me?"

"Because ... I'm ... well ... I'm sort of his sidekick. He's not allowed to drive a car ... being a dog and all ... so he needs me to get him around ... to save people."

She gave that some thought, looking dubious.

"Are you trying to trick me?"

"No," I said. "I wouldn't even try. Not with you."

"Can he visit me?" she asked.

"I'll make that happen," I said. "And you can visit him here anytime you want."

"We'd have to be careful," she said.

"Careful?"

"Billy's kind of my driver, now—like you are for Petra. Petra doesn't like Billy. Petra might hurt him."

Couldn't argue with that.

"Another reason for him to stay with me," I said. "At least for now. But you are right. We'll be careful."

Pursing her lips, she looked down.

"Do we have a deal?" I asked.

Irmgard nodded slowly and looked back up at me. She was holding back tears again, but she held out her hand.

What a brave little girl.

My eyes started to sting as I thought of my own version of Irmgard, waiting for me in Heaven.

I took her hand, gently pulling her to me as I knelt.

I hugged her to my chest.

She gripped me hard, squeezing her face into me.

She cried quietly, softly, her shoulders shaking.

I cried with her, patting her back and whispering it would be okay.

Sometimes adults have to lie.

Sometimes it's all we can do.

It didn't last long. She was too strong for that. And when she finished, she let go of my hand and stood back. The two of us walked back to the others.

I invited them in, and we sat around the same kitchen table where it had all started. I scrambled some eggs, fried up some bacon and sausage, baked some biscuits, and topped it all off with country gravy. Without asking, I set plates in front of each of them, and we all ate while drinking orange juice and steaming hot coffee.

Max was watching invisibly from somewhere. I couldn't see him, but I could *feel* him. I figured he'd make an appearance sooner rather than later since Irmgard was here. Pilgrim snored from his bed.

I noticed Anthony Carlino wore his wedding ring on his right ring finger. They couldn't reattach the other one—too much time and deterioration.

I finished my food and sipped at my coffee, hot and black.

"Thanks for the breakfast, Gilligan," said Anthony Carlino.

"Sure thing, Skipper," I said, resigned to the nickname. "I hear the Carlinos have been busy since getting back to America." The retaliation against the Scavo family had been international in scope. They were able to keep it out of the headlines for now, but I had sources.

"A message had to be sent," said Anthony Carlino.

"What's the body toll?" I asked, preparing for guilt.

He looked at me over the rim of his coffee cup, his eyes mostly hidden by his thick brows and rising steam.

"Not bad," he said. "Less than what you and your dog did back on the mountain."

"Really?"

"Sure," he said.

I looked over at Billy. He closed his eyes and shook his head to the negative.

Anthony Carlino caught the gesture.

"Don't believe *him*," he said. "He's gone stupid in the head."

"Stupid?"

"Yes," said Anthony Carlino, "and from what he tells me, it's your fault."

"My fault, how's that?"

"Something you told him from the Bible, about the sins of the father and how he doesn't need to stay in the family business."

"Oh, that," I said.

"Yeah, that," said Anthony Carlino. "You're a troublemaker."

I took a sip of coffee and saw Billy smile from the other side of the table.

"I've been told that before," I said.

"No doubt," said Anthony Carlino. "Doesn't matter. He'll come to his senses. It's in his blood."

"Would you mind if I talked to Billy for a second before Nick gets here?" I asked.

"Anything for you, Li'l Buddy." He set his coffee down, gripped my hand, and looked me hard in the eyes. "I mean it, Gil Mason. If you ever need anything ... *anything* ... and I don't mean once ... I mean for the rest of your life ... no paybacks ... no return favors ... no nothing... *anything* you ever need or want... you just ask. It's yours. You understand?" His eyes teared.

Big tough gangster.

Mine did too.

"Yes," I said. "Yes, sir. I do. Thank you."

"No, thank you. Not even Chuck Norris could have gotten me off that mountain. And not just me, all of us. But you did ... *you* did."

Anthony Carlino let go of my hand and went back to his coffee. Irmgard stayed inside, finishing her breakfast. Billy and I went outside.

Max followed us—from where I have no idea.

The sun was at the nine o'clock position, shining brightly. A hawk flew over, probably hunting a rabbit or prairie dog. It smelled like Colorado, warm, dry, nice.

"About time you got back here," said Billy. "Thought you were gonna vacation the rest of the year over there."

"I was a little banged up," I said. "I didn't goof off back there, taking it easy on the mountain like you did. I worked."

"Took it easy?" he said. "*I* took it easy? "I'm the one who went off a cliff in a car."

"A cliff in a car," I scoffed. "I shot like a thousand guys."

"So did I," he said. "I fought a wolf."

"So did I," I said, pulling up my sleeve and showing him the healing punctures.

"I got shot by a tank," he bragged.

"Me too, *twice*."

"I took bullets," he said, pulling up his pants leg to show me.

I jerked up my shirt, exposing my side, like Chief Brody in Jaws during the scar scene.

"What do you think this is?" I asked.

"Which one? The hole or the stab?"

"Exactly," I said, feeling I had won the battle with the double sacrifice.

"I choked the guy out that was going to shoot you," he said.

I gave that some thought.

"Yeah, that was pretty sweet."

"And I clocked the guy in the head with the cutting board after he stabbed you."

"I taught you that move," I said.

"You taught me the *swinging* cutting board move," he said. "I came up with the *throwing* cutting board move."

"That was just a combination of the knife I threw at you first, mixed with the swinging of the cutting board. Nothing original about that."

"Besides," I said, "Max beat both of us with that whole ripping out the throat thing." I shivered at the memory.

I saw Billy shiver too.

"Yeah," he said, raising his eyebrows, "yeah ... that was ... that was *nasty.*"

"Yes. Yes, it was," I said, purposely not looking at Max.

"So, okay," said Billy, "the cutting board throw may have been yours," he grinned at me, "but I did it good, didn't I?"

I grinned right back at him.

"Yeah, you did it good, Billy. Best cutting board throw of all time."

We both laughed.

"What about the girl?" I asked. "Is she the reason you're leaving the family business?"

Billy took a step back, looking at me.

"You really are a detective." He shook his head. "Yes, she's the reason. I don't want her to grow up in this like I did."

It was my turn to shake my head. "About that. I hate to say it, but you know you can't keep her."

"You're a good detective," he said, "but you're wrong about that. She has no family—I checked. And I'm adopting her. It's all legal."

"Legal," I said, "maybe. But is it right?"

"It's right," he said. "It was because of my family she lost her father. It might not have been our fault directly, but it was because of us. This is the least I can do. And I already love her like a daughter. Now I just need to marry a good mother for her."

I thought back to Clair and Jerome.

Irmgard could do worse.

"Okay," I said, "but I'll be watching. You go back into the family, or you treat her badly, and we won't have a friendship anymore. You understand what I'm saying?"

He started to grin, but I let the facade I keep in place drop so that he could see the darkness that still lurked in my soul, and he stopped.

He took a step back, his fists balling reflexively.

Nodding, he said, "Yeah ... yes, sir ... I understand."

Just then, Nick Carlino's limo drove around the corner and over the hill. Not the caravan he arrived with last time—just the one car.

Billy stuck out his hand.

"Thanks, Gil," he said. "Thanks for getting my grandfather back. And thanks for getting me with Irmgard keeping me accountable to be a good dad to her. I'll do my best. And if that's not good enough ... I'll do better. You have my word."

Believing him, I shook his hand. He'd grown a lot in a very short period of time.

When the car stopped, Nick Carlino and Big Sal got out and came over to us.

Billy hugged his uncle.

Big Sal and I exchanged head bobs and quirky grins.

Billy went inside with Big Sal, leaving me, Nick, and Max alone.

Nick spoke first.

"Thank you, Gil Mason, for bringing my father and my nephew back alive. You are true to your word." He reached into his pocket and pulled out one of my coins. "I took this off you when you were a guest in my hotel. I kept it as a *marker* of sorts."

That was back before I knew them, when he'd caught me rifling through Big Sal's room because I thought they were involved in the kidnapping of a little girl. When I came to, I found myself tied to a chair in a basement about to be tortured. After Nick heard my story, he decided to help instead. That's why I owed him.

Nick flipped the coin to me. I caught it without looking.

"Consider all scores settled," he said. "We are even."

I tossed the coin back to him. He caught it, also without looking.

"I need another favor," I said.

His eyebrows raised in question. I was beginning to think it was a Carlino trait.

"Leave Sarah and Kenny alone."

His eyebrows lowered.

He looked down at my coin, rubbing it in his fingers.

His voice was measured when he spoke.

"Are you asking or telling?"

"Asking," I answered. "Like I said—a favor."

He thought, still rubbing the coin.

"And if I refuse?" That same even, monotone.

"Don't," I said. "They only became involved because of me."

He thought some more, still looking at the coin.

Finally, he sighed and put my coin ... *my marker* ... back in his pocket. He looked up at me.

"The beautiful and gracious Miss Sarah Gallagher is released from my service," he said. "Mr. Universe, however, is another matter. He and I have already entered into a contract."

I started to object, but he stopped me with an upraised hand.

"A voluntary contract on his part. There is something he wants. Something he needs—part of which I have already granted. The rest is in motion. That was *his* choice, separate from any business between you and me."

"I'll talk to him," I said.

"You do that. In the meantime, let's go see my father."

I nodded.

Gangsters are a strange lot. You must tread carefully. Otherwise ... you might have to kill them.

"I've got coffee on," I said, smiling.

62

M ax roved the hills, Pilgrim beside him. He had to move slowly so that the older dog didn't fall behind.

But something was different.

Something with Max.

He found that he didn't mind waiting on the older dog.

Pilgrim's weakness no longer offended Max the way it had before.

Pilgrim was showing progress and had even taught Max a few tricks he'd never considered.

Experience counted, it seemed.

Max had let Irmgard pet him and scrunch his ears and face that morning. She tossed one of Pilgrim's balls, telling 'Petra' to fetch.

Max didn't fetch.

Pilgrim did, limping a little but wanting to play, nonetheless.

She tried twice more, both times, Max ignored her. She was no longer in danger. She would always be part of his pack, but she was not the alpha.

And Max didn't play. Not in the morning, and not at night. Max was a hunter.

But tonight, he wasn't even hunting—he was guarding.

Pilgrim wasn't guarding. Pilgrim was just roaming, mostly oblivious to his surroundings.

They stopped at a stream and lapped up the cold freshwater. Overhead the full moon blazed.

Both dogs marked their territory every so often, not that they needed to.

There were no coyotes around. There hadn't been since before Max left for Germany.

He had hunted and killed so many of them for trespassing into his territory that the message had finally taken hold.

Before Germany, Max would have left the pack's mountain to find them, widening his claimed territory. But since coming home, he no longer felt the urge to hunt them down—to slaughter them.

Killing the wolf had changed something inside him.

The lust to avenge the blood of his pack, the pack that had cried out to him for vengeance, had been satisfied.

The coyotes had been a shadow—a substitute to placate his rage and pain.

He no longer needed them.

The price had been paid in full.

That part of his journey was over.

Justice was served.

Max and Pilgrim ran the hills for hours until Pilgrim grew tired. Max walked him back to the house. There had been no signs of predators, so he could have let him go alone, but it was still a dangerous world, and monsters could spring up at any time.

So Max saw his pack member and brother back to the safety of their home.

Max then went to the Alpha's room and jumped lightly up onto the bed. The Alpha did not wake—he was sleeping peacefully.

And for Max, that was enough.

He lay down next to him, his senses alert.

The Alpha was still injured. And so, Max would watch. Max would stand guard.

No one would hurt *his* pack.

The End

ACKNOWLEDGMENTS

Hello dear reader! Thank you so much for buying and reading Sleeping Dogs. This book was just plain fun to write. I knew from the beginning that Max would finally kick the Great Gray Wolf's butt ... because ... well ... because ... he's *Max*. In this book, I didn't have to worry about Pilgrim dying, and I'm excited about the prospects that Gil has grown enough to get back into life. The only real concern was how to save Irmgard. She almost didn't make it. But I think she and Billy will make a good team in the future. Also, I'm glad Max was able to put some of his ghosts to rest.

I retired from the Sheriff's Office in September of 2020, after working law enforcement for over thirty-five years—all front line (no desk work for me, says the now glued to a desk, full-time writer). So hopefully, I will be able to get books out faster. That is if I can quit goofing off with my fifteen grandkids (so far) and actually sit my buttocks down and write.

I'm about eight chapters into the sixth book in the series, *A Dog Returns*, and I'm really enjoying it. Many of my readers tell me that my books are like seeing a movie in their heads, and that's how it is for me while I'm writing them. I *see* the story unfolding in my mind like a movie. It's just as fun for me to write as, hopefully, it is for you to read.

I'll also be coming out with a book right before Halloween. It's a horror novel (so not for all my readers). It's pretty scary, so please, only get it if you are prepared to go to bed with the lights on ... for the rest of your life. It's called Bone Hill, and it's *not* a slasher-type novel (although there may or may not be some slashing). It's ... well ... *unique*, I think. It's character-driven but with lots of action and personal interaction. So, if you like horror at all and are brave, and maybe in the mood for a little *Stephen Kingish* type read (without all the profanity and sex in his books), then please give it a try.

And now, on to the rest of the acknowledgments:

As with all of my books, I had a lot of help writing and finishing this one. I didn't find and catch bad guys by myself, and I don't publish books by myself either. It's a team effort. This book entailed efforts from my wife (editor), my oldest daughter, Athena (she does all my covers), and my dear friend Barbara Wright, who gave it a final edit (she and her daughter have helped me find K9s for the Sheriff's Office).

I thank God (not an expression of speech) for allowing me the enjoyment of writing, the encouragement of my fans, and for being able to introduce small pieces of His Word to reach and encourage others (Iron sharpens Iron).

Any incorrect, outdated, or misapplied information is wholly on me, either because it worked for the story or because I messed it up. Also, my editors give me constant grief for my use of ..., —, and *italics*. I break some grammatical rules while writing, but that's because I write to tell the story and make it flow as smoothly as possible. I apologize to those who find my use of these tools a distraction, but I feel they add an effect for the average reader (me) that mere commas don't. And for me, it's all about the story experience.

I don't claim to be a great writer, but I hope I'm at least good at spinning an entertaining yarn.

And finally, it comes to you, dear reader. Thank you so much for buying and reading Sleeping Dogs. I hope to see you soon as the adventure continues in *A Dog Returns*. Thanks for being a part of The Dog Pack, and please join me in our next hunt.

Until then ...

ABOUT THE AUTHOR

About Gordon D. Carroll

Gordon Carroll is the author of GUNWOOD USA and The Gil Mason Sheepdog series. Gordon grew up at the foot of the great Rocky Mountains in Colorado. Joining the United States Marine Corps at eighteen, he served for seven years, achieving the rank of sergeant (selected for staff sergeant). After that, he became a police officer in a small (wild) city nestled snugly in the middle of Denver, Colorado, before moving on to become a sheriff's deputy.

Gordon became a K9 handler, trainer, and instructor, training and working four separate dogs for over three decades (a hundred-twenty-pound German Shepherd named JR, a ninety-pound Belgian Malinois named Max, a fifty-six-pound Belgian Malinois named Thor, and a sixty-pound fur-missile named Arrow). Gordon retired from police work in 2020 to focus on writing and spending time with his grandchildren. K9 Arrow retired with him.

Over the years, Gordon and his K9 companions assisted the DEA, FBI, and numerous other local, state, and federal law enforcement agencies in the detection and apprehension of criminals and narcotics. Together, Gordon and his K9 partners are responsible for over two million dollars in narcotics seizures, three thousand felony apprehensions and were first responders to both the 2012 Aurora Mall shooting and the 2013 Arapahoe High School shooting.

He has been married to the same wonderful woman (his high school sweetheart, Becky) for over forty years. Together they have four adult children and a whole *pack* of grandchildren.

Gordon's love of books began while he was in sixth grade when he became captivated by Jack London's *White Fang* and *Call of the Wild*. From there, he branched out, gobbling up everything from Robert E. Howard to Steinbeck to Brand, King, Wambaugh, Irving, Craise, Hunter, Rothfuss, Lowry, Card, Emmerich, and on and on.

After years of telling stories to his children and friends, his wife insisted he write some of them down. After that, he just couldn't stop. Sending short stories out, he was quickly published in several magazines in genres ranging from Si-Fi, horror, mainstream, mystery, and Christian. He then wrote GUNWOOD USA, followed by Sheepdogs (Book 1 of the Gil Mason and Max series), fictionalized compilations of real-life scenarios that he has seen, heard of, or been involved in over his years with law enforcement and military service.

The Sheepdog series, as well as GUNWOOD USA, became instant bestsellers.

Gordon is a member of Rocky Mountain Fiction Writers (RMFW) and served on speaking panels for years, as well as performing K9 demos at the annual conferences.

ALSO BY GORDON CARROLL

Made in the USA
Middletown, DE
02 January 2025

68634263R00205